On the shores of desire . . .

Maryssa's breath caught in her throat. What in God's name had possessed her? The man was stark naked . . . Irish . . . Catholic . . .

"Let . . . let go of me—" There was the tiniest pause as she groped for his name, then an answering flicker in his eyes.

"Tade. My name is Tade Kilcannon." An inscrutable expression darted across his features as he searched her face. "Look at me like that again, my water sprite, and I may never let you go." The hand binding her waist eased up, his thumb brushing the undercurve of her breast as the deep voice thickened to an almost physical caress. "And I swear by all the saints I'll make you wish I never would."

NIGHTWYLDE

Praise for Kimberleigh Caitlin's
SKY OF ASHES, SEA OF FLAMES:

Jove Books by Kimberleigh Caitlin

SKY OF ASHES, SEA OF FLAMES
NIGHTWYLDE

NIGHTWYLDE

KIMBERLEIGH CAITLIN

JOVE BOOKS, NEW YORK

NIGHTWYLDE

A Jove Book / published by arrangement with the author

PRINTING HISTORY
Jove edition / December 1988

IBSN: 0-515-09801-9

Jove Books are published by The Berkley Publishing Group,
200 Madison Avenue, New York, New York 10016.
The name ''JOVE'' and the ''J'' logo
are trademarks belonging to Jove Publications, Inc.

PRINTED IN THE UNITED STATES OF AMERICA

10 9 8 7 6 5 4 3 2 1

To Maureen Dittmar, my "Bridge Over Troubled Waters"

And to Linda Hender Wallerich
For opening the doors to my dreams

NIGHTWYLDE

Ireland 1718

One

THE DONEGAL HILLS lay rife with dark secrets, the mists drifting toward the full moon whispering of rebellion, torment, and warrings centuries old. The screams of the innocents felled by Cromwell's fiery sword seventy years past blended upon the wind with the long-stilled clash of Irish blades crushed under the heel of Protestant William of Orange forty years after. The same winds carried with them the keenings of a nation whose faith even now lay bleeding beneath laws designed to cut from Ireland's heart the Catholic religion, which the beleaguered isle had cherished over a thousand years.

Yet despite the agonies of souls long dead, despite the shattered lives of those who still struggled to wrest a livelihood from beneath the British stranglehold, the spirits of the mountains seemed to accept naught but courage. The very peaks demanded that all who dwelt on the stark lands defy their conquerers until even the night sounds bore hints of menace, and warning, and the sky itself seemed an embattled warrior, poised to drive its death-blow between its enemy's ribs.

But to Maryssa Wylder, huddled on the seat of the coach winding along the treacherous Donegal road, it was as though a steely Irish blade lay tight against her own slender throat, cutting there with another blade, far more terrifying to the young Englishwoman than even the mountains that crowded in all around her. For in but an hour's time she would be at the mercy of her father . . .

Her fingers dug deep into the squabs of the jouncing coach seat as it lurched over another rut, the jarring spilling a wealth of mahogany curls over delicate features and eyes a stunning blend of countless hues of blue, green, and gold. Dashing the tumbled tresses away from her pale cheeks, she fought the urge to stuff her peacock-feather muff into her maid's prattling mouth. For five months she had been subjected to the woman's viperish tongue as though Maryssa were the drab and Celeste Ladonne a chatelaine. And for Maryssa the past weeks, closed in a ship's belly or in the dim interior of a coach with the woman, had proved a torture worthy of Spain's Inquisition.

"A devil's moon," Celeste whispered, her stubby fingers fluttering toward the Irish night sky, "a moon for raiding, plotting, brigands at prey. Rogues who would cut out your heart and serve it at feasting."

Maryssa bit her lip, closing her eyes against Celeste's bloodthirsty eagerness as the woman recounted yet another eerie tale of this strange, hostile land. Stories of mysteries, murders, spirits long dead who stalked the wild Donegal hills. Stories Maryssa wanted to block from her mind, holding her hands over her ears as she had as a child to shield herself when she could no longer bear her father's tirades.

Father . . . Maryssa shivered, the maid's chatter fading into the same vague background as the clack of the horses' hooves in the wake of real terror far greater than any witch's tale. What would Bainbridge Wylder say when he learned that she had been shunted back to him in disgrace, the cause of a scandal the whole of London was buzzing about? What would he do to her when he read the indignant letter Lady Dallywoulde had stuffed inside her trunk before packing her onto the first ship bound for Ireland?

Nay, Maryssa thought numbly, she'd had no choice but to act the way she had. No choice . . . Her fists clenched, she fought to banish the dread that washed over her, fought to cling to the certainty that she had done the right thing.

Even before Maryssa had spoken, there in the crowded

assembly room, she had known what the result of her folly would be—known that Sir Ascot Dallywoulde's wrath and the scorn of all of their horrified peers would crash down upon her. But to save her own soul she could not have held her tongue that night with the loathsome knight or his despicable, sadistic comrade, Lord Newley.

Maryssa's fingers crushed the edge of her muff as scenes from the party seemed to snag on the windswept branches of the scraggly trees whisking by. Images of richly embroidered cloth from India and bewigged dancers swirled across the floor of a chandelier-lit ballroom. Despite the enveloping darkness of the coach, despite the sick dread that lay like cold clay in the pit of her stomach, Maryssa's teeth clenched even now as Dallywoulde and Newley's sneering words raked across her memory. For an hour the two had pontificated on the necessity of crushing evil—evil, Maryssa thought with a chill, in the form of a honey-curled girl child with huge, frightened eyes.

'Twas too easy a death, Ascot's harsh voice had grated, *for the devil's mistress* . . . The ballroom had seemed to tilt beneath Maryssa's feet, the heat from the huge chandeliers shifting into rapacious flames consuming a wooden stake, the orange blaze devouring the screaming child bound in its agonizing embrace.

Maryssa had battled to block out the sound of Ascot's preachings. But his voice had hammered within her brain until she could bear it no longer; some unseen thread of caution and control within her had snapped. Acting before consequences could fully register in her mind, she had hastened up to the two men and the crowd of adoring fops gathered about them, and she had labeled both Dallywoulde and Newley that which they were—monsters, their souls more hideous than Lucifer's own.

The tiniest of grim smiles caught the corner of Maryssa's mouth, a twinge of pleasure cutting even through her fear as she recalled the shock on the two men's faces, the horror in the expressions of all those around them. Yet the horror had not been directed at the two noblemen gloating over an innocent child's death, but rather toward Maryssa—a woman who had dared to interfere in the affairs of men, a woman who had dared to defy one of the most honored holy men in all England.

The coach slammed over a deep rut, sending Maryssa's shoulder crashing into the inner wall, but she scarcely felt the bruising of her tender flesh. Holy? No, Sir Ascot bore more the mien of the dark angel, his eyes chill with a fanaticism that struck terror through Maryssa's very soul. He was a man who would ruthlessly crush any who dared oppose him and then take an unholy glee in watching their sufferings. And for the woman who had publicly humiliated him . . . for her there would be no mercy.

She shuddered at the memory of features contorted in fury, the cruel mouth a slash of raw hatred as his death-cold eyes pierced her with the promise of revenge. Icy fear trickled down Maryssa's spine, mingling with a primitive instinct to flee. A desperate need and a hopeless one, for no matter how far she might attempt to run, she well knew she would never escape either her father's fury or Sir Ascot's.

She possessed no skills, no money, and, Maryssa thought with a twinge of self-loathing, no courage. And by the time spring next burst into bloom at Carradown, Sir Ascot would hold the power to exact from her whatever vengeance he chose. For then he would be her husband.

Until then she would face a prospect almost as terrifying— exile here, in this savage land, where she would be a prisoner till Sir Ascot deigned to chain her to him as wife.

She let her fearful gaze rove over the moonlit landscape, the night painting eerie shadows across the wilds. The very thought of Ireland, perilous and untamed, had always made Maryssa's palms grow damp with sweat. The months her father spent attending to the estate in the wilds of Donegal were the only times Maryssa had been grateful, even glad, that Bainbridge Wylder had held her all but a prisoner on the grounds of Carradown, the land he held in England. Never once in all her nineteen years had she so much as looked upon the castle at Nightwylde or on the hills around it, which had been ground beneath the conquerer's heel. But with each lurch of the wheels along the rutted Irish roads, she drew nearer to stone turrets she had heard were mortared with Irishmen's blood. Blood that could well be mingled with her own before the sun rose.

Her spine stiffened with the memory of a score of cruel lashes dealt by her father's hand whenever she had displeased him. He had accorded the switch he used more care than he had ever given Maryssa, soaking the supple length of hickory in vinegar so that the lashes burned like raw fire while failing to leave any lasting mark. She shut her eyes, trying to blot out the memory of that switch searing her bare legs.

He had not beaten her for years now, practicing instead more subtle forms of torment. Yet in all her life she had never done anything more certain to draw his full fury down upon her. She had not only defied the man he had chosen to be her husband, but she had cast into danger the alliance of Dallywoulde's assets and Bainbridge Wylder's vast wealth.

"Father, I had to say something," Maryssa whispered, pretending to stare out the coach window as waves of misery washed over her. "The child . . . the child died. And they were laughing. I didn't mean to—to anger you."

Didn't mean to . . . A sick laugh rose in Maryssa's throat. When had that ever mattered to Bainbridge Wylder? Even her appearance had never satisfied him, and he had railed at her, as if the very force of his displeasure could change the hue of her curls from mahogany to gold and make her odd eyes remain an insipid blue. As a girl she had spent hours before the silvered glass in her bedchamber, searching her features to discover the inherent flaw her father found so repulsive.

But she had only seen a silky mass of sable curls, thick, sooty lashes fringing wide, anxious eyes as changeable as any opal, their depths sprinkled with flecks of sea blue, green, and gold. Her nose was small, her cheeks pale in a face that seemed to whisper of fairy wraiths—delicate, fragile—while her lips were the soft pink of the roses in the gardens of Carradown.

The year she'd turned seven, she had crept down to where Lucy, the stout kitchen wench, had been dying the season's wool in huge iron kettles. When the old woman had been called away, Maryssa had dragged a chair up to the fireplace and tried to dip her hair into the bubbling dye. Even now, at nineteen, the memory of her father's fury when he saw her ruined curls made Maryssa wince. And the tiny crescent scar the kettle rim had burned in one hand was but a tangible reminder of a wound that had seared far deeper.

"—tails, Miss Maryssa. *Miss Wylder*." Celeste's affronted voice cut through Maryssa's reverie, and she turned her gaze guiltily to the woman who stared at her in icy disdain.

"Tails . . . uh . . ." Maryssa flushed. Struggling to pick up the threads of conversation that had slipped through her consciousness, she grasped at the Frenchwoman's interest in the latest coiffures. "Uh . . . I'm sure they're lovely with ribbons on them."

"Ribbons?" Celeste yelped.

"Or . . . or flowers. I'm certain—"

Celeste's lead-painted cheeks puffed out, her thin lips pursing in outrage. "You think it jest, these heathens and their devil tails? The marquess of Bitner's grandfather fought under Cromwell, and he assured me every one of the rebels he dragged from the ruins of Drogheda had a tail a full six inches long!"

"Tails?" Maryssa felt a quiver go through her, the absurdity of Celeste's claim warring with her own vivid imagination. Unbidden, visions of wild red-haired Irishmen leaped through Maryssa's mind, satanic tails protruding from their ragged breeches as they whirled around writhing flames. She shook her head. "That . . . that's ridiculous," she said a bit more shakily than she intended. "You can't truly believe—"

"Oh, can't I? Wait and see when one of those savages cuts your corset strings! But then, *you* probably won't need to concern yourself." Celeste let her disparaging gaze sweep a path from the ruching on Maryssa's camlet hood to the toes of the shoes that peeked from beneath the cinnamon ruffle of her petticoat.

Maryssa plucked at the overskirt sweeping back from the quilted satin, and gave Celeste a steady look. "I assume even the Irish have some taste," she said quietly. "Of course, why *you* have deigned to stay in my company—"

"I've not *deigned* to do anything! Lady Dallywoulde paid me an exorbitant stipend or I would never even have attempted to deal with someone as hopeless as you! Make Miss Maryssa into a beauty, her ladyship said. Pah! I'd have better spent my talents on Carradown's charwoman!"

Celeste sniffed. "As if that disgusting Sir Ascot would notice a woman if she stood before him in silver gauze, with that long nose of his forever poked in God's ear."

Maryssa paled, a sick feeling stirring in her stomach as her cousin's priggish features rose in her memory—the vicious mouth whose lines took no pains to hide their cruelty, the pale, lashless eyes, like slivers of ice in the Thames. She touched the tiny swan pendant at the hollow of her throat as if it were a talisman, unable, still, to keep the quaver from her voice. "I . . . I would prefer Sir Ascot didn't notice me at all."

"Oh, he'll pay enough mind to you to fill you with his heir, no doubt. Duty, you know." Celeste poked Maryssa's stomach, her long nose crinkling in distaste. "Between the two of you, your marriage bed should be fit to freeze Hades's toes."

"Stop! P-please . . ." A shudder so violent it seemed to shake the coach itself wrenched through Maryssa as she thought of Ascot's bony white hands on her body, hands chill as a corpse . . . She bit her lip to keep from crying, but even as she steeled herself against the tears that burned her eyelids, she saw the glimmer of triumph in the maid's close-set eyes.

"Ah, yes, I'm sure Sir Dallywoulde will devise many a way to make you pay for what happened . . ."

All my life I've paid, Maryssa wanted to cry, *but I don't know why. What horrible sin have I committed? . . .*

At Lady Dallywoulde's ball, for the first time in her life, Maryssa had fought back against the pain others inflicted on her, fought the ignorance and slights, and what had she gained?

With trembling fingers she drew the curtain at the coach window wider, staring into the night as if seeking something, someone who cared. But the darkness lay empty as a madman's soul, the late-summer fragrance of wildflowers doing nothing to soften night sounds that echoed through the hills like the moans of the damned.

She braced her feet against the coach floor as the vehicle lurched again, the sound of the iron-rimmed wheels on the rutted road changing subtly, the shadows blurring past the window becoming more clear. Slivers of candlelight glowed through the wind-gnarled trees, the bulk of a tumbledown building outlined in the scant moonlight.

"Nightwylde? I . . . somehow I thought it would be . . .

bigger.'' Maryssa turned to Celeste, dread lying heavy in her throat, but for once even the maid was silent, eyes wide as she, too, regarded the light.

Maryssa swallowed hard, her gaze, against her will, drawn back to the dilapidated structure. Crumbling walls seemed to sag beneath the weight of the dirt coating the ancient whitewash, and the timbers battening the clay were as bowed as an old crone's back. Disreputable nags were tied to every available post and tree branch while, above the heavy plank door, a faded sign bearing a leering image of Satan swung from stout iron hooks: The Devil's Grin. This, then, was an inn! Maryssa's hand tightened on the feathers of her muff as she deciphered the crudely painted letters, her nose rebelling at the faint scent of fouled meat penetrating the coach's interior.

''That knave of a coachman can't mean to stop here!'' Celeste blustered, her hand going to her jeweled girdle-buckle as the coach ground to a halt.

The muted sound of male voices trickled through the window as Wickersby, the burly coachman, shouted something to the postilion. The more distant, worried tone of the boy's reply followed, eliciting a string of curses that made Maryssa's cheeks burn.

The coach door swung open, and Wickersby stuffed his head inside, his broad face flushed with exasperation and rum. ''Beg pardon fer the inconvenience, Miss Wylder, but seems my wheel rim's nigh jarred loose on these infernal roads. We've no choice but to stop an' fix it, lest we break down somewhere between here and yer father's. If ye'll just go inside a bit . . .''

''You can't expect us to—to enter that den of thieves!'' Celeste bristled. ''No proper lady would—''

''Well, you two proper ladies had better.'' Wickersby kneaded the back of his plump neck as he appealed to Maryssa. ''It's not as bad as it looks, miss. The most dangerous highwayman inside is the owner, Jack Peabody, an' the worst he'll do is charge ye three times the true price of his ale. No harm will come to ye there, especially with you bein' Mr. Wylder's daughter an' all.''

''We must be close to Nightwylde. At the last stop you said we'd reach it before nightfall.''

"Thought we would, but I been nursin' that wheel along, hopin' it'd hold. I'd keep drivin' if there was any way, but we'd break down sure, somewhere between here and Nightwylde, and the dark be full of rebels an' rogues. Heard tell just three days ago the Black Falcon's been circlin' these parts lazylike, ready to strike at the stirrin' of a feather, an' yer father'd flay my hide if I let you be that brigand's prey."

The twinge of irony Maryssa felt at Wickersby's touting of her father's parental concern was eclipsed by stark imaginings of a highwayman, his cloak flowing about his shoulders like sinister wings, his mouth savage and brutal. "The . . . the Black Falcon?" she echoed.

"Aye, miss. He's a bad one. An' deadly as 'is name. Fired Lord Thomas's storehouse but a fortnight past an' carved the word 'thief' on 'is lordship's cheek. Took the lord's mistress, too, an' the horrors the Falcon's band worked on her . . ." Wickersby rolled his eyes skyward. "A hedger found 'er wanderin' the roads pure nake—"

"Fine . . . I mean that's enough," Maryssa interrupted hastily, her fingers flying to the fastening of her cloak. "I . . . I'm thirstier than I thought." She gave her hand to the coachman and swung down from the box on wobbly knees. "Celes—"

She started to turn back to the coach, but the maid had already bounded after her like a startled roe, her face having puckered as though she had swallowed a basketful of lemons. Yet despite the ridiculous expression, Celeste managed to drag her mantle of superiority around herself. "If you're determined to go, I suppose I shall be forced to accompany you," she said haughtily. "For the sake of propriety."

Maryssa's jaw knotted as she bit back the sarcastic reply that rose to her lips. She strode to the door, hesitating but a moment, her hand freezing on the latch when the raucous shouts from behind the wood panel died as if every throat within had been suddenly slit. A shiver scuttled down her spine as the latch seemed to release itself of its own accord, the heavy door creaking open on sagging hinges.

The stench of rancid mutton sizzling over embers in the inn's stone fireplace struck her in the face like a physical blow, its greasy odor blending with that of sour ale and a score of unwashed bodies. Shifting orange light cast eerie shadows over faces glowering across the dimly lit room—like crimson-eyed wolves closing for the kill, the flames painting their savage features in gold and red.

Maryssa swallowed hard and took a step backward, but Celeste, rushing behind her, would allow no retreat. Maryssa felt the toe of one shoe snag on a splintered floorboard, catapulting her into the room. Her ribs slammed into the edge of a filthy table, her hand clutching the slippery surface as her knees crashed to the floor, her hold barely saving her from sprawling across a leering drunk's lap. Firelight danced across a wicked curved blade poised inches from her chest. The man's lips split in a toothy grin.

"Would ye be likin' me to carve ye a bit o' breast, yer ladyship?"

Quaking inside, Maryssa followed his gaze to where it was fastened on her chest, horror and embarrassment rushing through her veins. The camlet cloak had torn open in her fall, exposing the soft, creamy skin above her décolletage. The table edge pushed up her full breasts until they swelled above the meager modesty panel, giving them the absurd appearance of being some tempting culinary delicacy.

"No . . . I . . ." Maryssa clamped her hands over the bared skin, trying to scramble to her feet, but, barking a laugh, the drunken man caught her skirt in an amazingly strong grip, driving the point of his knife through a hank of her gown and pinning the fabric to the wood below.

"Come now, my little partrish. Ye wouldn' wanna fly the snare so soon," he slurred as Maryssa tugged desperately at the binding cloth.

"A snare would be the only way you'd catch a woman, MacTeague," a voice, dangerous and deep as the devil's well, offered at Maryssa's shoulder. "I prefer more gentle measures." She tried to jerk away as a strong black-gloved hand cupped her elbow, but the unseen man only hauled her back against a frame as long and tough as a wind-scarred oak, his other fist closing on the bone hilt of MacTeague's knife. "We must show our English guests hospitality," he crooned silkily. "Kindness such as they've shown us these many years."

The man yanked the knife free, and Maryssa spun to face him. Horror froze in her throat. Plumes the hue of blood swept back from a sable cocked hat, the face beneath it hidden by a black silk hood. A hood emblazoned with the silver talons of a falcon.

"Please . . . let me go . . ." Maryssa squeezed the plea through the lump lodged in her throat, her whole body shaking. "My father . . ." Eyes, so green they seemed to have stolen all the tint from the verdant Irish glens, narrowed as they regarded her through slits cut in the hood, and Maryssa was suddenly struck with what Bainbridge Wylder's daughter might mean to a savage like this—a hostage to be held for a huge ransom, a tool to be used in vengeance for lands her father had taken—used, perhaps like the mistress of Lord Thomas . . .

Her gaze darted to the doorway. Celeste had disappeared back into the darkness of the yard, but Maryssa held no false hope that the woman would bring her aid.

"Your father? . . ." the Falcon prompted. Maryssa set her teeth, cringing inwardly at the fury her refusal to answer might unleash in the man, her brain struggling desperately to grasp some plausible lie. The black-gloved hands skimmed back the folds of her cloak, then slid down to span her slender waist in a firm grip as the incredibly green eyes pierced her. Even through the layers of cloth, whalebone, and leather, the heat of him seemed to burn her.

"So you dare defy the Black Falcon?" An underlying edge bit the deep voice. "You were about to tell me, mayhap, that your father is lethal with a sword? That he will cut my black heart out and see me hang if I stain your virtue?"

"No . . . I . . ."

The blood seemed to rush from Maryssa's body, leaving her weak and shaken, as his broad palms eased up to curve just beneath the swells of her breasts.

"Come, now," his voice caressed, as his thumbs brushed lazy circles over the satin. "A woman with those eyes, those lips, surely some man before me has been wise enough to sample . . ." With a suddenness that nearly threw her off her feet, sensation swept back into her veins. He was laughing! Damn him to hell, behind his mask the cur was laughing!

Hurt washed through her, as painful as the hundreds of times her father had derided her for her ugliness, fresh as the taunts of Celeste and Lady Dallywoulde. And Maryssa hated herself, hated the fact that even now, with the danger all around her, somehow it mattered to her that this brigand, this renegade, a breath from the hangman's noose was making jest of her before the rabble.

"I assure you that my virtue is intact," Maryssa said, the hooded figure blurring through the tears that rose in her eyes.

"Is it?" There was a sudden gentleness to his voice. "That is more of a pity than you know." His fingers trailed up to the hollow of her throat, lifting the tiny swan pendant that dangled there against her skin. "Then I guess I shall have to satisfy myself with some other favor from the most winsome woman I've ever seen."

She flinched, and his fingers stilled.

"Have you ever seen a young swan, colleen, a hatchling cygnet swimming behind its mother? It's all gray down, its neck long. No one could call it beautiful. But time passes, and it blossoms into the most graceful and lovely of birds."

" 'E's goin' soft in the skull!" MacTeague's drunken jeering split the quiet. "The Black Falcon spoutin' verses like a fop! Next thing ye know 'e'll be kissin' the Sassenach doxy's hand 'stead o' beddin' 'er."

The fear that had loosened its grip on Maryssa with the Falcon's words clenched again around her chest as the green eyes behind the hood blazed with anger, and with an odd, more subtle emotion . . .

She could almost see the hidden lips shift to a wry, mocking grin. "Ah, MacTeague." The Falcon shook his head, tipping Maryssa's face more fully into the path of the drunk's bleary gaze. "I said the cygnet would blossom into the most beautiful of birds." Gloved fingers tugged at the wispy mahogany curls that had pulled free of the loosely pinned knot at the back of her head. "This swan still has a bit too much down left to heat my blood." Maryssa reeled as though he'd struck her in the mouth, a sick feeling knotting in her stomach. "I'll slake my lust with her gold instead of her maidenhead."

She pulled back, grasping the swan pendant as he reached for it. "Please," she whispered, "don't . . . don't take this. It belonged to . . ." Her words trailed to silence.

She felt his hand hesitate at the chain around her throat. "To whom? Some lover?"

"No. My . . . my mother. She died when I was a babe. If you take it—"

"I stand to forfeit much more than you this night." The rich, husky tones of his voice touched her, lulled her. The face behind the hood seemed to strain toward her, and she felt the dizzying suspicion that he wanted to touch her lips with his.

She swallowed, unaware that she had loosened her grasp on the golden swan until she felt the quick, sharp tug of the chain snapping.

"No! No! You—" The agony she had fought to hold inside since that horrible night at the ball burst forth in a sob as the broad shoulders wheeled away from her.

"Well?" He barked, cramming the necklet into a pouch at his waist. "Don't stand there gawking like striplings! Make an end to what we came for!"

As if summoned by a sorcerer's wand, a dozen black-garbed masked figures melted out of the shadows near the walls, but Maryssa was barely aware of the innkeeper's pleading, the sounds of crockery shattering and wooden casks being split as the band of rogues tore the room apart. Sticky red wine seeped through the morocco sides of her shoes, splashed her petticoat and cloak, but the sickly sweet smell of violence soured her stomach not half as much as the surge of unbridled hatred she felt for the hooded man who now stood rigid at the door of the room.

"Curse you to hell!" The sound of her own voice startled her, piercing through a lull in the din. The Falcon's men froze. The rebel himself appeared carved in stone.

With a jerk of his head he commanded his band out the door, then wheeled to stalk into the night. Maryssa's nails bit deep into her sweating palms as she saw him swing up onto a huge black stallion one of his cohorts had brought to the doorway. For what seemed an eternity those piercing green eyes glowed at her through the slits in the night-black hood.

He seemed almost to shake himself as one hand took up the reins. "You want hell, my little English bitch?" he snarled, his eyes raking the lands around him. "You've just arrived."

Two

HELL. MARYSSA BIT her lower lip to stem the bubble of wild laughter rising in her throat as, even a day later, the Falcon's words still echoed in her mind. He had thrown out disdainful barbs to wound a pampered brat. As if she'd known anything *but* hell in her life, or expected anything better . . . from Ascot Dallywoulde . . . or from her father.

The cold stone beneath her feet seeped through the carpets like the chill of a grave as she paced the huge room at Nightwylde. It was like her father to summon her to this chamber, then force her to wait, caged in the tortures of her own imagination. Three hundred years ago this chamber had served as the solarium, graced by lords and ladies, rulers of their own land. But now Satan himself seemed to dart from dark stone corners and creep beneath the velvet hangings that dripped from the walls of Nightwylde.

Stones shrouded in a myriad of ancient mysteries seemed to crush her chest until she couldn't breathe, as though the dead of five hundred years still fought to claim their own. No icings of intricate plasterwork, no gilt sconces or whimsical sculptures could mask the stark, haunting history that wove among the candle flames flickering in the shadows. It was as though the walls themselves cried out for vengeance.

"So. You've shamed me yet again." Maryssa wheeled at the slice of a razor-sharp voice through the silence. Her chin lifted but a fraction, her fingers clenching as she faced the stout figure silhouetted in the doorway, but even so, she couldn't still the hammering of her heart. The somber waistcoat denuded of any fancywork puffed out over the waistband of too tight breeches, the shirt ruffle couched beneath a double chin as stiff as the lips of the man who owned it.

"Good morrow, Father."

"Good morrow," Bainbridge Wylder mocked, yanking the massive oak door closed behind him with a plump, square hand. "Is that all you have to say, girl? I released you from Carradown into the care of that pompous witch, Lady Dallywoulde, hoping she could fashion you into a tolerable bride for your esteemed cousin, Sir Ascot, and even *she* could not bear your insolence. Tell me, miss, do you know what this letter says?"

He dug into the pocket of his rumpled coat and yanked from its recesses a wad of paper to wave beneath her nose. "Lady Olivette claims that, in the center of a ballroom you defamed your betrothed, humiliating him before his peers."

"I—I only said 'twas wrong to cast innocent babes to the flames—"

"After Sir Ascot had been touting the necessity of ridding society of its filth before they grow large enough to do evil."

"Father, they tortured—"

"I don't give a damn about aught but ridding myself of the torture of bearing responsibility for *you*." Bainbridge spun around and jammed the missive down onto the vast top of his desk, then turned to face her. "Aye, miss, and now, because of your blasted mouth, you may be a spinster instead of a nobleman's wife. A *disinherited* spinster, mayhap."

"I think I would rather be a spinster than—"

"Than wife to a noble and godly man?"

"Godly!" Maryssa nearly choked on the word, picturing her weasel-thin cousin as he had looked in the hours before the infamous ball, his nostrils pinched, his lips pursed with displeasure at having been cheated out of his afternoon's entertainment.

He had forced her to ride out with him in his sedan chair to a crowded square. Filthy bodies had crushed around them, leering and laughing as a girl of thirteen was dragged forth. A witch, Ascot had claimed, the devil's own, guilty of having lured a high holy bishop into her bed through sorcery. But Maryssa had seen no lascivious evil in the girl's countenance, only narrow, white-robed shoulders, thick honeyed curls, and eyes so terrified they seemed to swallow the child's whole face. Maryssa had pleaded to be taken home, begged to leave, but Ascot's mouth had merely curled with self-righteous glee as the executioner bound the screaming girl to the stake and piled the faggots beneath her bare feet.

Maryssa shut her eyes, the terrible stench of seared flesh still burning her nostrils. The wind . . . oh, thank God for the wind! It had rushed the flames up the girl's slight body with merciful speed, stopping the inhuman screams that still haunted Maryssa's dreams.

And Dallywoulde—*godly, pious* Ascot Dallywoulde—had raged the whole way home that the child's pain had not lasted long enough to make her pay for her wickedness . . .

"Damn, girl! You'll listen when I speak to you!"

Maryssa winced, yanked back from the horrifying memory as her father's hand clamped on her shoulder, jerking her around to meet his baleful glare. "You've heeded not a word I've said."

"I have . . . I . . ." She let her fingers stray nervously to her throat, seeking the familiar security of the tiny swan pendant, only to be flooded again with desolation at its loss. Her hand dropped to her side. "I can explain what happened, Father, if you'll—"

"If I'll what? Waste my time listening to you spin excuses? I spent three years of the most ill-advised marriage witnessed in heaven or hell listening to a woman's lies. You think me fool enough to begin again?"

"I'm not my mother!" Tears burned the corners of Maryssa's eyes as she pulled away from him, the still-fresh horror of the witch-burning causing her to flare in a rare attempt at defense. Her arms closed convulsively about her ribs, as though to guard herself against a savage, well-aimed blow. "If you hated my mother so much why did you marry her? Didn't you ever love her? Or me?"

She saw her father's lips whiten, as if she had struck him,

but in a heartbeat the fleeting expression vanished, leaving her to wonder if it had ever been there at all.

The fingers digging into Maryssa's flesh loosened, and she could see the struggle in her father, as if he were forcibly ripping them away. "Love? Mary?" With a bark of laughter he shoved Maryssa from him and wiped the palm of his hand on his breeches as if it were soiled. "Your mother betrayed me. Aye, and would have cast you aside for a fresh pair of slippers."

The words cut deep in Maryssa, searing her with their scorn, but she raised her chin, meeting her father's gaze. "And what would you cast me aside for, Father? Less even than that?"

"I've fed you these twenty years, housed you, kept clothes on your back."

"Aye, and borne me about your neck like a brace of iron weights, burning and chafing in your hate." Maryssa struggled to keep her voice from quavering. "I'm sorry I was born, Father."

"No sorrier than I."

With a choked little cry, Maryssa scooped up her petticoats and stumbled toward the door.

"Stop!" Instincts bred of a hundred like confrontations made her freeze where she stood at her father's command. "We've one more matter to discuss before you go running to your room. I've dismissed that . . . that Celeste woman you dragged here. Painted, disgusting wench! I'll not have her in my house."

Irony swelled in Maryssa's throat, her fingers clenching on the edge of a small table beside the door. "If I told you how much I hated Celeste, would you run after her, Father?" The words were scarcely a whisper, as hopeless and hollow as the corridor that echoed beyond the velvet-draped wall.

A dull bit of metal glimmered at Maryssa from among the gilded trinkets and gleaming candelabra on the polished mahogany table. She reached out to touch the object, which seemed strangely at odds with the richly furnished room. A soldier, a tiny cunningly wrought toy soldier, its blue-painted coat unchipped, the jaunty lead plume bedecking its hat tarnished with age, though it appeared never to have been touched by small fingers.

"Don't touch that!" Brittle-edged, the order bit the air and Maryssa was stunned to find the words tinged with pain.

She turned, fragile and tentative. "Father . . ."

"Od's blood! What heinous crime did I commit that I am father to such as you?" Woolly brows slashed low over Bainbridge Wylder's eyes as he jammed a blunt hand against the close-set sockets. "Worthless . . . a worthless chit cowering from her own shadow when I could have had—" The hand snapped away from Bainbridge's face, his knotted fist cracking down onto the desktop before him. "For God's sake, don't stand there gaping, girl! Leave me in peace before I'm tempted to rid myself of you by means far more permanent than marriage!"

Permanent . . .

The rage-filled face seemed to shift into patterns of raw hatred, bone-deep loathing—a loathing that might well lead to . . . murder? Maryssa felt the blood drain from her face.

"Get out!"

The furious roar seemed to clutch at her throat, cutting off breath and life. With a tiny cry she stumbled back against the table, then wheeled and fled down the dark hallway.

Escape . . . the need pounded in Maryssa's blood, a desperation past bounds of fear and wisdom, primitive and uncontrollable as sea-captured birds wave-driven onto rocky cliffs. And during the minutes it took her to make her way to the deserted stable and fling herself upon a saddled sorrel mare awaiting the groom outside its stall, she knew she would have ridden the devil himself if he had been flying from Nightwylde.

The groom's frantic cries as he ran after her, shouting warnings on the dangers of the hostile, unknown land, had only fed her need for freedom. And as the battered gray turrets faded far behind her, the savage pace of the mare flying across the Donegal hills pulsed through Maryssa's own body, primal and wild. She rejoiced in it. Rejoiced even as she feared it. Until . . .

She yanked at the reins awkwardly, attempting to turn the thundering mare down a wide path branching to the right, the other jagged-carved trail seeming sinister, dangerous even bathed in moonlight. A shudder of foreboding shot through her as she glanced at the huge boulders slicing the ground to her left, the massive chunks of stone seeming almost alive, staring at her, blank and terrifying as a madwoman's eyes.

She felt the mare veer toward the path that promised safety, and the tension that had gripped her eased, when suddenly a mass of fangs, fur, and eyes glowing red charged from the tangle of underbrush. The horse shied, her terror-sound streaking horror through Maryssa's body, the night beast lunging toward them seeming like a creature spawned in Hades.

Maryssa never knew how, in that terrible instant, she stayed on the mare's back, knew only that she clung wildly with her hands, her legs, and every morsel of her strength. The reins flew from her fingertips as the sorrel wheeled, bolting to the one path left them, crashing down the hillside with horrifying speed.

She clutched at hanks of the blooded mare's mane, terror deeper than her innate fear of horses cutting through her with a hundred daggers. What tiny fragment of control she had held shattered in the face of the mare's fright as she bolted wildly downward. And now . . . die . . . she was going to die . . .

Her numb fingers clutched the animal's mane, its coarse strands biting deep into her sweat-slicked palms as the crazed beast lunged to the left, plunging down yet another steep slope. Jagged stones pierced the tree-studded drop like gaping hungry jaws waiting for her to be hurled onto their points, waiting to snap the sorrel's slender legs and send them both catapulting into the dusk-shrouded valley below.

"No!" The word croaked through her constricted throat as sharp-thorned branches raked gashes in her arms and cheeks, the valley suddenly falling off as though gouged by a giant's hand. The sorrel dove downward, bunching its haunches, head thrown back.

The hard ridge of the horse's neck slammed into Maryssa's chin. She shut her eyes against the stinging pain, feeling the horse lose control, hoof skidding on rock, muscles straining and fighting. With a horrible shriek, the mare plummeted to the base of the valley. The crack of front hooves striding the earth jarred through Maryssa's whole body. Then suddenly the mare slammed to a halt, then reared wildly.

The coarse mane whipped through Maryssa's raw palms,

saddle leather tearing free of her shaking thighs as the mare
threw her and bolted for the safety of the hills. Maryssa
screamed as she hurtled through the air. But it was not the
rocky earth she struck. Something closed over her, crushing
her breath, dragging her under . . .

Water . . . she choked, flailing as panic engulfed her, the
weight of her soaked skirts and quilted petticoats pulling her
down. Oh, God, she couldn't swim . . .

She fought to break the surface, kicking and clawing as
the water filled her eyes and mouth. She couldn't breathe,
couldn't move, the heavy cloth tangling like tentacles about
her legs. Water rushed into her nose, a burning pain that
seared her lungs. A sob choked deep in her throat.

Then suddenly something solid was against her, binding
her, holding her. She kicked and clawed it, a muffled sound
like an animal snarl reaching her even through the now-roil-
ing water as the heel of her shoe connected solidly with whatever or whoever held her captive. The grip on her tightened
almost savagely, and Maryssa felt herself yanked upward with
power that made her head spin. Wind struck her wet face, air
bursting into her lungs in an agonizing, glorious rush. Her
nails dug deep into something smooth, warm . . . alive.

"Ow! Pull in your claws you little hellcat, or by Bridget's
cross I'll throw you back in! You all but unmanned me!"

"Can't sw . . . sw . . . Don't!" Maryssa clung to his neck
frantically. Gulps of air shot pain through her chest, sharp
objects scraping her ankles as she flailed wildly.

Her hand clenched in the hair at the nape of his neck,
feeling wet strands rip free in her fingers as the man stumbled. Cursing savagely he flung an arm over her thighs, as he
sloshed forward through the water. "Don't . . . don't throw
. . . Can't . . . swim . . ."

"You'll . . . damn well have to learn if . . . you don't quit
choking me! Ow! Damn it, now, that hurts!" The indignation
in the voice bit even through her panic as a steely grip closed
over her wrist, and jerked her hand away from his hair.

"No . . . please . . ." Great shuddering sobs broke from
Maryssa as she fought desperately to regain her hold. Her
fingers dug into the hard curve of her rescuer's shoulder, the
faintly rough texture seeping through her terror as she pulled
her body free of the water's grasping hands.

"You damn near drown us both, rake me with those infernal nails until I'm all but dead of blood loss, kick me in the—" Despite the seeming impatience of the words, they were tinted with an underlying humor that lightened their sting, the tone oddly musical as its Irish lilt softened into suppressed laughter. "By Saint Michael, I never had to fight this hard before to hold a woman in my arms."

A sudden awareness pierced Maryssa at the sound of his low, sensual voice, at the feel of the muscles beneath her fingertips rippling from barely contained amusement. He slid her down his body, her knees shaking and feet numbed as her sodden slippers touched the shore. His arms tightened about her waist as she stumbled against him, clinging as she battled to steady herself. Silvery rays of moonlight reached out to toy with an expanse of bronze male shoulder. Satin . . . she had thought it . . .

Bared by the bunched-up skirts, her legs brushed a silkier texture, warm and smooth. Perfectly honed muscle, sleek flesh, roughened by a light sprinkling of hair . . . Her gaze darted up to the face bending over hers. Arrogant, sensual, devastatingly male, the grin he flashed her sent a hundred sensations shooting through Maryssa, sparking, snapping, burning wherever he touched. The realization struck her with a force that drove the breath from her body in a single, strangled gasp.

Naked . . . The exquisitely formed male body pressed so intimately against her own was absolutely naked.

Three

"EVERYTHING MEET WITH your approval?" Night-shadowed eyes danced with amusement, their light visible even in the dim glow of the moon. With a shriek of mingled indignation and disbelief Maryssa tried to break away, but her captor pulled her tighter against his chest, the broad muscled plane brushing against the delicate skin exposed by her décolletage. Shivers of an unnameable emotion tingled from her breasts to the pit of her stomach. She jumped, a shaft of fear striking through her as one large hand found her cheek. The hand stilled.

"Easy, now. I'm not going to hurt you." Callused fingertips smoothed the wet curls back from her cheeks, and Maryssa could feel him smile. "I never accost defenseless women the evening before confession. My knees are nigh worn to bone as it is."

The lulling tone drew Maryssa's eyes up to meet his. Even his admission that he was one of the papists she had been raised to fear failed to penetrate the mist of security his words had evoked. The moonlight, in its shimmering trek from the water struck him full in the face.

Awareness such as she'd never felt rushed through her in that single instant, her gaze arrested by the most beautifully chiseled masculine features she had ever seen. Moon-glow sculpted a strong, clean-shaven jaw and a chin carved with hints of stubbornness and courage. The full, cleanly cut mouth was shaded with a subtle sensuality that made Maryssa fight the sudden urge to reach up and separate the lips to test their texture, to see them smile.

As though her wish had the power to make it happen, the corners of the man's mouth tipped up, the smile deepening with an aura of recklessness that reminded Maryssa of knights in the old romances she had read, of gleaming armor, daring charges . . . broken dreams.

Maryssa felt a tremor course through her, breath catching in her throat. What in God's name had possessed her? The man was stark naked . . . Irish . . . Catholic . . .

"Let . . . let go of me—" There was the tiniest pause as she groped for his name, then an answering flicker in his eyes.

"Tade. My name is Tade Kilcannon." An inscrutable expression darted across his features as he seemed to search her face. "Look at me like that again, my water sprite, and I may never let you go." The hand binding her waist eased up, his thumb brushing the undercurve of her breast as the deep voice thickened to an almost physical caress. "I swear by all the saints I'll make you wish I never would."

Maryssa flinched as the warmth of his fingertip burned through the thin silk of her bodice, a rush of panic sweeping through her, mingled with stirrings of anger. Complacent and bold, Tade Kilcannon stared down at her with the lazy arrogance of a man certain of his appeal to women and well accustomed to the liberties it allowed him.

And, Maryssa realized with a jab of self-disgust, she was gaping up at him with all the adulation of a dairymaid gawking at a crown prince.

"You . . . oh!" With a choked squeak, she stamped down hard on his foot, satisfaction tingling along her spine as she felt Tade's instep give just a little, her shoe biting into the tender flesh. His still-shadowed eyes widened in surprise and pain.

"Sweet Jes—" He cut off the curse, shoving her away from him, her unsteady legs pitching her backward as she struggled to regain her balance. The horrible, sick feeling of fear churned through her again as the shore seemed to give way beneath her, toppling her backward. Water splashed up around her as she broke the silver-sheened surface, but before the wetness could crash over her face, something solid and pebbly cracked into her rump. She started to struggle, stopped, arms braced in back of her. Even the tiny wavelets seemed to laugh at her as they darted in and out, barely tickling the crest of her elbows.

Her face flamed, despite the chill of the water. "It . . . it's shallow," she whispered in disbelief.

"If it were a thousand fathoms deep I'd be damned if *I'd* pull you out of it again!"

Her gaze snapped up. Tade stood at the edge of the shore, every line of his taut body etched with irritation, legs spread wide, hands planted on lean hips.

"You . . . your feet were touching bottom the whole time. I could have—"

"Walked out of the lake by yourself? Aye. And saved me a world of pain and grief. But the way you were thrashing around, you would've drowned in a teacup. If you always treat people who try to help you with such incredible kindness it's a wonder you're still alive."

"You—you wouldn't let me go. No decent man would have—"

"One of your Sassenach fops would no doubt have released you at once and let you fall back into the water you were so afraid of. We barbaric Irish have a strange custom of trying to shield our women from what they fear, although you English with your civilized, Christian ways make it nigh impossible."

"Well, we *civilized* English have a strange custom of flitting about the countryside wearing an odd new invention called *clothes*." The words spilled from Maryssa's mouth before she knew she was saying them aloud, her eyes sliding of their own volition over glistening lean hips and long, muscled legs. For the barest instant her gaze locked on what lay nested at their apex. Her eyes snapped up, clashing with his glowering ones. Horrified, she suppressed the urge to bury her face in her hands.

"I was taking a *bath*," he bit out. "And I don't *flit*." Maryssa's own embarrassment faded just a little at the defensiveness in his voice. The massive shoulders seemed suddenly a bit too stiff, his stance not quite so arrogant. If it was possible to flee slowly, Tade Kilcannon did so, walking with a controlled stride to grab up a mound of pale cloth lying on a rock. The moonlight defined muscle and sinew—bronzed, tantalizing—as he slammed his legs into the breeches, yanking what she could now recognize as supple leather over the taut curves of his buttocks.

A sudden certainty washed through her. *He* was blushing. She, solemn plain Maryssa Wylder, had been sitting waist deep in a lake three feet away from a naked man she'd never seen before—an *Irishman,* for God's sake—and they were bantering back and forth as though they were at a garden party and the hem of her petticoat was showing.

The total absurdity of the situation sang through her veins in waves of disbelief, fright, and amusement so strong they bordered on hysteria. Dear Lord, if Lady Dallywoulde could see her now . . . The picture of the skinny dowager's thin lips pursed into an expression of genteel horror, beady eyes popping from their sockets behind her quizzing glass, broke what little rein Maryssa held on her emotions. Laughter burst forth, rare, unrestrained laughter bubbling through her in wonderful, exhilarating waves.

Tade turned toward her, dark brows meeting low over his eyes as his long fingers worked the brass buttons that fastened his breeches. "You find bathing amusing?" he asked stiffly.

"Bathing?" Maryssa gasped through her laughter. "Oh . . . Only when I tumble into someone else's bathtub."

"You do that often, do you?"

"No. This is my first time." Maryssa arched her head back, oddly reveling in the feel of her hip-length tresses floating upon the water, the strands wet and silken, like the dark wisps that had escaped the thong at the nape of Tade's neck to cling to the corded muscles of his throat.

"Next time you might wait until you're invited. I prefer my community baths planned." The disgruntled tone drew fresh giggles from Maryssa.

"I'll remember that next time I'm out riding." The unaccustomed merriment palled at the memory of her terrifying flight and the realization that her mount had disappeared, but she had little time to steady her trembling hands.

"Next time?" Tade exploded. "Whoever let you ride alone this time was a damned fool. These hills are alive with rogues belly-full of hate for the Sassenach. I could be a cutthroat, a highwayman, a renegade. A lone English lady is no small prize hereabouts. Just what do you think would have happened if you had fallen into—shall we say—less hospitable hands? They might have pulled you from the lake, but I doubt they would have released your ladyship upon command."

"The lady could hardly have found more hospitable hands to fall into than yours, Tade." The voice came from the night, the brogue not unlike Tade's, yet somehow softer around the edges.

Maryssa paled, scrambling to her feet.

"Who the hell—" She saw Tade spin to the side. The mouth that had been scowling at her a moment ago dropped open, then widened into an astonished grin as a shadow separated itself from a gray boulder.

"Careful, little brother. Best not say anything you'll regret in the morning."

"Dev? Devin!" Unabashed joy rang in the deep voice as Tade hurled himself toward the shadowy figure. The two men crashed together, wrestling like enthusiastic bear cubs, slapping shoulders, ruffling hair, dealing good-natured buffets to each other's ribs. Loneliness and emptiness pierced Maryssa with a strength such as she'd never felt as she watched them.

Then Tade was forcing the other man away from him, hands still clamped on his arms, as though he were afraid the slender, blond man would vanish into the night. "Devin, how . . . how did you get here? When we couldn't trace the ship they put you on we were afraid—"

"That I had taken the penny road to heaven? It would take more than chains and hard work to keep me from tormenting you. A rum merchant smuggled me out on a cane ship from Barbados."

"But why the devil—"

"Did I come here?" Devin finished. The face Maryssa could see over Tade's shoulder grew serious and somber. "You know why, Tade. I'm needed."

"Needed? It's death if they find you. There'll be a price on your head the size of Ben Burren and the first place the cursed Sassenach will look is— Damn!" The rush of words died, and Maryssa saw Tade's long body go rigid. Her own muscles yanked tight in answering fear.

Sassenach . . . the blond Devin was obviously a fugitive, fleeing British law . . . and she . . . she was alone . . . a witness to his secret . . .

At the hissed string of oaths under Tade Kilcannon's breath, her heart snagged in her throat. The heart-stopping smile had vanished, the lines carved deep at the sides of his mouth sweeping away all vestiges of the arrogant, amused rakehell who had pulled her from the water. The face slanting toward her now glittered with a thin veneer of danger, and something more . . . Fear? That was absurd. From the first she had sensed that Tade Kilcannon was a man who courted death, laughed at it. Then why? . . .

Her eyes flicked to the tall, slender figure beside him, a shiver going through her. Merciful God, of what horrible crime must this Devin be guilty, if he was being hunted so relentlessly? To what lengths would Tade go to protect him? Devin had called him brother. Was that bond of blood to be sealed with her own? Tade and Devin's great love for each other had been evident the moment the man had stepped from behind the boulder. Maryssa swallowed convulsively. If she had a brother who loved her like that—whom she loved—she would wield a knife herself to protect him.

Her eyes leaped to Tade's face, and she was suddenly aware that even the cries of the night birds had died.

A wind-gnarled branch sheltering a break in the underbrush beckoned her with mocking fingers, promising freedom, but taunting her with the image of Tade's long, muscular legs, legs that would no doubt be swift and sure, while her own . . . Her sopping wet skirts tangled tight around her ankles. Heavy . . . the silk was so heavy . . . Every nerve in her body jumped and quivered as she tensed to run.

"Damn it, Dev, what are we going to—" Tade's face angled toward the other man for just an instant, giving Maryssa the chance she needed. The toe of her shoe bit into the turf, her skirts binding her like the arms of a terrified child as she dashed for freedom. She had scarcely taken two steps before hands dug into her shoulders whipping her around to meet a face that was hard and ruthless, yet oddly more vulnerable than she'd ever seen it.

"Where the hell do you think you're going?" Blood rushed to Maryssa's temples in a dizzying wave as her head snapped back, her face so close to Tade's rage-flushed features that his breath singed her skin.

"I . . . Please . . . let me—"

"*Let you?* Aye, and I *should* let you, by God. Let you bolt into the woods so you can finish getting yourself killed. Then you couldn't . . ." Maryssa felt his fingers tighten, and pain shot through her shoulders, yet she sensed that there was more desperation than anger behind Tade Kilcannon's big hands.

"I won't say anything," she promised. "I'll just start . . . start walking. Find a house . . ."

"A house?" Tade snorted in disgust. "It's ten miles to the nearest cottage, and every step paved with a dozen men who would cut your English throat as easily as they'd crush a flower, and do it with a good deal more pleasure. I should have saved myself the trouble and let you drown."

"Tade." Devin's soft, almost chiding voice seemed lost on the man standing before her, only the snapping taut of a muscle in Tade's jaw betraying that he had heard. The shadowed eyes flicked to the water. Devin's tone sharpened. "Tade."

"God damn it!" He seemed to hurl the words, almost in defiance, as he wheeled on his brother. "What in the hell do you want me to do, Dev? Throw her on a horse and point her to the nearest English garrison?"

"No," Maryssa pleaded, her fingertips touching the rigid muscles in his forearm. "I won't say anything . . . tell anyone. You saved my life. I give you my word I—"

"Your word?" Tade spat, glaring. "That comforts me immensely. I've heard enough English lies to know full well the value of your promise. Most likely you'd not even stop to change your slippers before you went running to the captain of the guard."

"I wouldn't. I'd—"

"Dance at my hanging? Thank you, but I'd rather not provide a spectacle for your lords and ladies at present."

"She'll have to come with us." For a moment it seemed as if Tade hadn't heard the words, and Maryssa herself doubted they'd been spoken. Then both turned their eyes on Devin. The gentle face was grave, the crude frock coat bedecking his narrow shoulders doing nothing to hide their determined set.

"Come with us?" Frustration was set in every line of Tade's face as his hand tangled in Maryssa's tumbled hair, jerking her close to Devin. "Look at her, Dev. She's English. Some rich Sassenach bastard's woman—"

"She's lost, soaked to the skin, and scared out of her wits thanks to you. We can't just leave her."

"We damn well can't take her with us! If you won't think of yourself, at least think of the others. If she talks—"

"She won't."

"Wonderful. I have a Sassenach wench's word and my idiot brother's faith. It'll make a perfect epitaph on our bloody tombstones." The hand clenched in Maryssa's hair released her as abruptly as it had grabbed her, Tade striking both her and Devin with one more killing glare before he stalked off into the shadows. The greeting nicker of a horse drifted from the darkness, followed by the creak of leather and the slap of thighs slamming too hard against the saddle. With a rush of relief Maryssa closed her eyes, waiting for the sound of hoofbeats—driving, pounding hoofbeats. Tade Kilcannon would ride out, and then she could reason with Devin . . . plead with him. But the sound of the horse retreating didn't come.

Instead, a huge bay stallion burst through the underbrush, Tade, upon its back as daunting to Maryssa as the spirited beast.

She stared up at them—both wild, dangerous, free—beings from another world—Hades, lord of the dead, astride his stallion. Tade yanked on a length of leather in his hand. A drab gray mare balked in the bay's wake, shaking her sparse mane as though disgusted by the blatant display of equine male arrogance.

"Here, brother," he grated, throwing the mare's reins toward Devin. "I assume this pathetic excuse for a nag belongs to you. If you're so anxious to get yourself killed, far be it from me to deprive you of the gallows." Maryssa felt Tade's eyes rake her and it seemed even her heart stopped beating.

The bay danced sideways. With a curse Tade yanked the stallion in a tight circle. Maryssa stumbled, trying to avoid flashing hooves, praying that both Kilcannons would ride away and leave her, but the sleek coat of the horse's barrel crashed into her. Hard and sinewed, Tade's arm locked around her ribs as she started to fall. Then suddenly the earth seemed to crumble away beneath her as he dragged her up to sprawl across the saddle.

"Nay!" She kicked and struggled, as the stallion surged beneath her, but Tade Kilcannon held her effortlessly in the viselike grip of his arms. With a deft movement he settled her astride the beast's back in front of him, her damp petticoats hiked high on her legs, her rump cradled between his strong thighs.

Maryssa clawed at the horse's mane, at Tade's arms, clinging with raw terror to the very things she feared.

"Hold still, damn you!" The light stubble roughening his jaw scraped against her cheek as he jerked her back against him, at the same instant driving his heels into the stallion's sides. The beast plunged forward and tore through the underbrush.

Maryssa closed her eyes against the wild country flying beneath the horse's hooves, against the image of Tade's dark, stormy face. But the image that rose to taunt her again was more terrifying still. Hades astride his stallion . . . Maryssa shivered. Was Tade Kilcannon dragging her to hell?

With every lunge of the powerful horse, miles seemed to pass beneath them, each smooth stride of the cantering animal's legs chafing the insides of Maryssa's thighs against the saddle leather. Raw . . . her whole body felt raw and aching . . . And her spirit . . .

Tade shifted, and she sagged closer to his body, the muscles of his chest steel-taut against the back of her wet bodice. Not a word had he spoken since pulling her onto his mount, yet had he spent every second of the ride bellowing at the top of his voice, his resentment of her would not have been more clear. With each crack of the stallion's hooves on the rocky earth, that unspoken anger grated on her, fraying the tiny threads of pride that kept her from breaking into tears of exhaustion.

Even the den of murderers she had been picturing since they had ridden out of the valley no longer frightened her. She cared not where Tade Kilcannon was taking her, only that they arrive.

"Not far now." Devin called encouragement from the gray. Maryssa could have hit him for sounding so cheerful, but her fingers, still clenched in the folds of Tade's shirtsleeve, felt far too heavy to lift.

"Devin, one last time, will you think what you're doing?" The sound of Tade's voice made Maryssa start, the anger-edged words honed with the slightest note of pleading as he reined the horse to a halt beside a stone fencerow. "Think of Rachel, for God's sake, and—"

With a snort of irritation Tade stopped in midsentence. Maryssa's bleary eyes looked up to where Devin stood high in his stirrups. His gentle features seemed to glow with a light of their own, the sensitive mouth curving in an enraptured smile as he stared at a ray of yellow flickering across the modest fields. "I never thought I'd see it again," he whispered.

"You'll bloody well wish you never had when you're rotting at the end of some Sassenach rope."

"You're wrong, Tade." Devin's earnest reply touched something deep inside Maryssa. "No matter what happens . . . no matter what comes . . . to see Ireland again . . . to see all of you . . . will be well worth the price."

"Blast you, Devin. I'd like to murder you myself." The tone of Tade's voice was that of a world-weary adult upbraiding a foolish but beloved child. With a whoop of pure joy, Devin urged his mount over the fence and up the hill.

For long seconds Maryssa watched as the gray ran across the raw fields hewn from the mountains in their fencings of stones, her gaze caught by the puffy silhouettes of a dozen sheep and eight bleating lambs as Devin's galloping mount sent them skittering to the far end of the crude pasture. Maryssa looked up into Tade's shuttered face. "Devin . . . He's . . . been gone a long time?"

"A lifetime." There was something sad and tired in the way Tade said it. Maryssa suppressed an urge to smooth away the worry lines that marred the perfection of his brow, chiding herself for being a fool as reality intruded, a flame of fear rekindling. This man was no battle-scarred knight embroiled in some noble, futile quest. He was a stranger, a brigand, dragging her off against her will to God knew where. His eyes lingered on her face a long moment; then, as if he could read her tangled, confused thoughts, he tore his gaze away.

She set her teeth against the bone-jarring start as Tade kneed the stallion forward. In the dim light ahead she could see Devin Kilcannon reining in his horse before what appeared to be a large cottage at the far edge of the field.

Rambling clay wings jutted out in three directions, seeming to embrace the slope upon which they were perched. Thin shadows of rose vines tracked across the walls, tangling upward like the trails of frolicking children to weave across thatch that promised to be gold as a new-minted crown. And the windows . . . they shone with all the open welcome of an angel's smile.

A den of thieves? Maryssa tried to focus her burning eyes on the shapes now passing before the candlelit panes. The stallion gained the cottage yard just as Devin flung himself from his mount's back.

He had not even reached the heavy wood portal before it burst open, spilling out a patchwork of shrieking, freshly scrubbed children. Maryssa gaped in amazement as, instead of the savage cutthroats she had expected, a bevy of bright-cheeked urchins, as varied in height and coloring as blossoms in a glen, hurled themselves at Devin, the tails of tiny nightshirts fluttering behind them. Only the fact that they were crushing him from all sides kept him on his feet.

In one lithe movement Tade swung off the horse, pulling Maryssa down with him. Her side skidded down the hard plane of his stomach, then the jutting bones of his lean hips, but she scarcely had time to keep her rubbery knees from buckling before he hauled her toward the door with an impatient yank.

"Quiet, damn it!" The support of his hand vanished, and she groped for it as she stumbled, catching herself on the smooth length of the doorjamb. She looked up to see Tade's palm clamping over the mouth of a boisterous ten-year-old.

"Hush you little rogues!" he hissed. "Do you want the whole blasted Sassenach army to know Dev's here? Get inside." Maryssa felt herself encompassed with the others in the curve of his arm as he herded the group through the cottage door, prodding them forward as though they were a band of lightsome colts. Her eyes swept over a welcoming peat fire aglow in a huge stone fireplace, rainbow splashes of rag rugs, and scatterings of crude handmade toys. A home, Maryssa thought, a stab of emptiness shooting through her. She slipped into the shadow of the door, even the soft sound of her footsteps seeming an intrusion.

"Next time I'll have a town crier announce that Devin's home and be done with it," Tade said wryly, giving the now-sheepish ten-year-old's freckled nose a tweak before setting the boy free.

Maryssa turned just in time to see a tall, slender girl leap up from beside a cradle. *"Devin?"* With a shriek of joy the girl hurtled across the wooden floor to battle her way through the others, all but running over a tiny red-curled waif in her path. She flung her arms around the tall man's neck, burying her face in his shoulder, as she sobbed beneath a rich curtain of spun copper hair. "I thought—thought 'twas just Tade!"

"Just Tade?" Tade feigned a look of wounded dignity.

"I—you . . . you know what I mean," Deirdre sniffled. "Oh, Devin! Dev . . . I—"

"Look at you, Dee," Devin said softly. "Last time I saw you, you had a scrape on your nose and had given Phelan Fitzpatrick the worst black eye this side of Derry." Devin forced her head back gently, brushing the curls from a face that was totally feminine, yet at the same time so like Tade's that Maryssa could scarcely believe it. Devin grinned at the sniffling girl. "Look at you now. You're a woman grown."

"Woman grown, hah!" Tade laughed. "Just last wash day she snipped the stitches in poor Phelan's breeches when they were laid out to dry on a thornbush. He went to make his bow to Aileen Nolan and split the seam wide open."

"Served him right, the way he was mincing about," Deirdre bristled, shooting Tade a murderous glare.

He winked at Devin. "The only reason Deirdre objects to Phelan's mincing is that he's not mincing around *her.*"

A door at the far side of the room opened. "Tade? Who—" At the sound of a soft voice the mass of children parted as if by magic, all the heads turning to where a woman wavered upon the threshold, a damp rag clasped in her hand. Honey-brown linsey-woolsey hung loosely around her rawboned frame, her angular face pale beneath straggling wisps of mouse-brown hair. Maryssa felt an odd sense of loss as she stared at the woman who was, from all appearances, mother to the brood of children and . . . wife to Tade Kilcannon?

His grin lit his whole face. "Rachel. How do you think my da will like the surprise I brought him?" Tade stepped out of the way, revealing Devin behind him.

"Like it? He'll . . . Tade . . . Oh, Devin!" With a sob the woman threw herself into Devin's arms. He laughed, stroking her hair, patting her shoulders until Tade grabbed her as well. The two men dwarfed her in a crushing embrace the children couldn't seem to resist. Seven pairs of arms wrapped around the three adults, the joyous babble of tears and laughter making Maryssa's throat swell shut with tears of her own.

Forgotten, she huddled against the wall, the rough clay surface pricking her skin the only thing that made her feel truly alive.

Then Tade's dark-lashed eyes alighted on her face. Crystal green, they shone overbright with emotion, strangely soft, almost tender in the light streaming from a branch of glowing rushlights. They hypnotized her as he slowly untangled himself from the others, pacing over to slip one warm palm under her elbow. Maryssa tried to hang back, feeling awkward and shy, but the fingers encircling her arm would not be denied as they urged her into the circle of children.

"Aye, and isn't that just the way of it. I survive an ordeal that makes Devin's look like a day at Puck's fair, and *he* is the one who gets all the coddling." Tade feigned such a wounded expression that the little ones dissolved into fits of giggling. Seven small faces tipped up to eye Maryssa with eager curiosity.

" 'Deal? What's a 'deal, Tade?" the red-curled waif begged, squirming free of Devin's arms.

"A 'deal is what Tade will put us through if we don't all listen to his ridiculous story," Deirdre sniffed.

"Fine. Make jest of my brush with death. Mayhap poor Phelan would like to know just how his breeches came to—"

"Tade Kilcannon, if you say one word to him I swear I'll—"

"Cut the seat out of my breeches?" Tade caught a coppery tendril with his finger and gave it a tug. "Then Phelan and I could commiserate over the viciousness of jealous—"

"Tade. Deirdre." Rachel's soft warning was cut off by an exasperated cry from Deirdre, and Maryssa could hear a shading of real desperation in the girl's voice.

"All right! All right! Tell us how we almost became so lucky as to be free of your constant torture." Deirdre's flashing green eyes flicked in a scathing path over Maryssa, and she tossed her red-gold curls. "And as long as you're tormenting us, you might be so kind as to tell us who this . . . person is."

Tade's fingers, still lightly cupping Maryssa's elbow, tightened just an instant. She could almost feel his bantering mood darken, but the smile he turned on her was warm. "This is—" His grin widened slowly, tantalizingly until even his eyes shone with blinding mirth. "I have no idea who this is, but she almost drowned me an hour since."

At the memory of the magnificent body beneath that grin, bare and glistening in the moonlight, Maryssa's breath squeezed painfully in her chest, her gaze falling to the toes of her shoes. "My . . . my name is Maryssa—"

"Maryssa . . . Maura . . ." Tade savored the sounds as though they were warm honey. "It suits you. Soft . . . sweet . . ." Maryssa's eyes leaped up to his, expecting to see shadings of sarcasm or jest, but there was no hint of derision in the incredibly green depths, only an intensity that made her body tingle as though swept by a cool breeze. A stirring of remembrance, unsettling and enticing, rippled through her as if those emerald eyes were, somehow, familiar, but in a breath all her attempts to place that raking gaze vanished as an outraged cry split the quiet.

"Sweet?" Deirdre exploded, wheeling on Tade. "Are you mad? She's *English* and you stand there mooning like you're behind a cow byre. Even now the soldiers—"

"Deirdre!" The sharp snap of Rachel's voice made Maryssa start. The waif who had stared up at her so openly buried her face in Deirdre's petticoats, the other small children darting like startled kits behind a gangly youth with the barest fuzzing of a beard on his cheeks. Maryssa squirmed under the battery of eyes fastened on her in varying degrees of hate and fear. Only Rachel's face still held welcome.

"Please forgive Deirdre," Rachel said. "I wish I could say she is not often so rude, but she takes after her brother, in tongue if not in temper. If you've suffered Tade's company for the tick of a clock you know—'' One work-roughened hand reached out, and a gasp escaped Rachel's lips the instant her capable fingers touched Maryssa's chilled skin. Rachel spun on Tade in blustering fury. "What on earth did you do to this child, Tade Kilcannon? She's as cold as a well in winter and wet through to her shift!''

"She was taking a late-night bath, and I rescued her—''

"*Rescued* her? Gave her her death of lung fever, more like! She's all but stiff with cold and you stand there spinning nonsense! Go bore the rakes at the inn and drown yourself in ale if you can't still your tongue. I'm going to get this poor child out of these clothes.''

"N-nay." Maryssa started to protest, but Tade's laugh stilled her.

"Out of her . . .'' He let his echo of Rachel's words dangle, unfinished, his eyebrow arching wickedly at Maryssa. "I'm sure I can still my tongue long enough for that. There is nothing at the Grin to compare—''

"Devin, leash your brother or I'll take a switch to him!" Rachel threatened, grabbing up a shawl to drape around Maryssa's shoulders. "Deirdre, I'll need your rose gown, petticoats, and some clean dry rags from the basket under my bed. Get them.'' With a quelling glare at the girl's mutinous pout, Rachel wrapped an arm around Maryssa and whisked her through the carved door into a smaller room.

Within what seemed like seconds Rachel Kilcannon peeled off the cloying wet layers of clothing that clung to Maryssa's skin. Maryssa tried to help, but her shaking fingers knotted the lacings, until at last she gratefully abandoned herself to Rachel's ministrations, lifting her arms and moving as Rachel asked, obedient as a child.

As Rachel pulled free yet another petticoat Maryssa's eyes roved the room, and she smiled in spite of herself. There could be no question about to whom the room belonged.

Rows of pegs driven into a strip of wood on the far wall sported an assortment of breeches and little boys' frocks, the peg nearest the ceiling boasting a branch with a fat cocoon in its fork. A wooden bedstead sprawled across most of the room, pillows stuffed beneath its coverlet at odd angles, the bedclothes rumpled, strewn with small rocks and sprigs of leaves. In her imagination Maryssa could hear the bedtime shouts of Rachel Kilcannon's sons as they buffeted each other with the plump pillows. The warm scene vanished as chill air touched Maryssa's bare skin. She hugged her thin chemise against her, clenching her jaw to keep her teeth from chattering.

"As though a body could sit on this, let alone sleep in it!" Maryssa turned her head to see Rachel scowling at the lumpy bed. "Kilcannon men!" the woman scolded with a shake of her head. "Be they four or forty, they cause naught but trouble!" Grasping the corners of the coverlet, she whipped it upward.

Maryssa took a stumbling step back as a spray of childhood treasures flew into the air, the motley assortment clattering to the floor, earth colors, spangled also with brighter, glossier hues. Something heavy thunked at Maryssa's feet, its surface catching the candlelight. She looked down to see a miniature cannon amid a host of toy soldiers, its barrel bent and battered from many a fanciful battle. Two dozen tiny swords gripped in molded hands pointed ignominiously toward the roof above painted jackets that had once, no doubt, been the pride of some small boy. The blue lacquer now was chipped and worn away, the jaunty hat plumes dented.

Strange, Maryssa mused with an uneasy stirring of remembrance; blue coats, and plumes exactly like the one bedecking the toy soldier on the table at Nightwylde. She had seen that soldier but an instant, yet she knew it had been wrought by a master, a plaything for a rich man's cherished child. These well-loved toys, battered though they were, were equally intricate; they seemed out of place in this clean, yet humble cottage.

"Warring." Maryssa was startled out of her thoughts by Rachel's wistful voice. "As if Ireland hasn't had her fill of killing these past hundred years. Seems like they train the boys up in it from the minute they leave the womb. Heroes, all of them," she said softly. "But fighting a hopeless war." One reddened hand touched the painted boot of a foot soldier still tangled in the coverlet's folds.

"Where did you get them? The soldiers, I mean?"

Rachel shook the coverlet briskly one more time, then bundled it around Maryssa.

"They were Tade's when he was a boy. His da had them made special just before his mother died and the family lost . . ." Rachel's voice trailed off. "I wanted him to save them for his own babes, but Tade, he'd have none of it. Started hidin' them about where the little ones would find 'em among the eggs in the hens' nests, in the toes of winter stockin's, even managed to bake that cannon into a pie somehow. Shane cut into the crust on his saint's day, an' his face got so bright it nigh blinded me. I—"

The door banged open, Deirdre huffing into the room in a swirl of pink gingham. She threw the cloth on the bed, stamping one small foot. "Ma, if you have to go on thus about how wonderful Tade is, at least don't do it where he can hear!" she cried, pulling a face. "Every word you said came right through that wall, and he's sitting out there so puffed up I swear I'd like to stick him with a toasting fork!"

Rachel rolled her eyes heavenward in amused tolerance as she slipped the blanket from Maryssa's shoulders, then reached for a lace-edged petticoat. "Speaking of the toasting fork, Deirdre, you'd best be sticking some bread on it and scraping together something for your brothers to eat. Devin looks half starved, and Tade—"

"Tade would eat the hide off his horse if it wasn't stuck on," Deirdre grumped. "He abuses me, and I'm supposed to make food for him? I'd like to feed him the fire irons!"

"They wouldn't taste half as bad as your bread." Tade's gibe rang through the crack in the door.

Deirdre flung the portal open and stomped out. "You . . . you—"

"Deirdre!" Rachel's cry of warning was not quick enough. The open door had given Tade a clear view of Maryssa's nearly naked body. Maryssa heard the sharp sound of breath hissing through teeth. A blush fired her skin from head to toe as her eyes locked on the source of the noise. Tade was staring at her over Deirdre's curls, his parted lips robbed of any hint of teasing. His eyes swept up trim ankles, over ribbon garters, to linger for several hot, heavy moments on the chemise that clung, in transparent wetness to Maryssa's breasts.

It was over in a few instants. She saw his jaw clench, could almost feel him rip his gaze away from her as Rachel lunged for the door, slamming it shut so quickly a blast of warm air from the peat fire struck Maryssa's chest, the heat of it spreading over her skin.

She scarcely felt Rachel's deft fingers as they fastened the borrowed gown around her, knotting the laces and tying the sashes, punctuated by muttered scoldings. Only the absence of Tade's voice in the murmurings from the other room touched Maryssa, his silence thick, laden with a tension that trembled inside her, as though his gaze had somehow drawn a part of her into himself . . . or a part of him into her . . .

A sharp tug as Rachel settled the rose gingham over Maryssa's shoulders snapped her attention back to the woman's angular face. Dark eyes flicked to the door, pale lips crumpling into a nervous smile. "I'm sorry, child, about Deirdre an' all. The girl doesn't think at the best of times, an' when she an' Tade start jabbin' at each other, well, I know to listen you'd think they were half a step from murderin' each other."

"No, I . . . it's all right. She didn't let him . . . I mean, she didn't open the door on purpose."

"She opened that door with a vengeance, but she meant you no harm. Lord knows Tade's seen more than his share of colleens in their shifts—"

Maryssa flushed, a picture of Tade amid a throng of conquered beauties flashing through her mind.

"I—I meant that with a houseful of sisters he probably scarce noticed—" Rachel stammered, stopped, her own cheeks pinkening. She turned, bustling to fish a gap-toothed comb from the shelf of a wooden washstand. When she again faced Maryssa, she gave her an open, wry smile. "I'm doin' naught but makin' it worse, aren't I, child? We'll speak no more if it. Your hair is tangled as a whaler's riggin'. Let me help you." Rachel's offer, so earnestly made, coupled with the gentle care of her hands as she plied the comb, made Maryssa want to cry.

"Thank you." She struggled to keep her voice from shaking. "For . . . being so kind."

A chapped finger crooked under Maryssa's quivering chin, puzzled light clouding Rachel's face. The woman asked no explanation for the tears welling from Maryssa's eyes, only wrapped her in arms that had comforted a thousand childhood woes and held her close. "Warm yourself here as long as you need to," she said gently.

It was as though Maryssa could feel a downy coverlet close around her shoulders, and she knew the rawboned woman offered not only her hearth but a piece of her heart as well.

Suddenly Rachel stilled as the creak of cart wheels jouncing along the rutted path outside crept through the bedchamber's open window. Maryssa peered past Rachel to see a lantern bobbing from a hook in the cart. Bits of brightness glimmered through holes pierced in the lamp's tin sides silhouetting the shape of a man.

"Kane!" Rachel's voice was joyous, reverent, and eager, her face suffused with love as the man pulled the cart to a halt in the cottage yard. " 'Tis my husband returned from tending his kerns." Formerly nimble fingers twisted at Maryssa's mahogany curls, hairpins that had clung in the thick mass slipping from hands made clumsy in their haste. Maryssa stared at the man silhouetted against the lantern's glow, confusion swirling about her as her gaze swept again the humble bedchamber in which she and Rachel stood. Rachel had spoken as though the crudely clothed Irishman climbing down from the cart were some baron out viewing his estates. Yet even in the meager light from the lantern, Maryssa could see that Kane Kilcannon's boots were most like older than little Katie, his mantle faded through countless seasons.

"Hasten, everyone! Hide!"

Her musings were quelled by the sound of Tade's voice, low and filled with mischief.

"Dev, get in here!"

Maryssa heard the sounds of the Kilcannon children as they darted to do Tade's bidding, the older ones battling to hush the younger ones, stifling giggles, and shufflings of bare feet on the floor. She could almost see them scurrying to hide themselves.

"Tade," one high-pitched voice squeaked, "Boyd sat in Ma's bread dough."

"Well, Katie's lickin' the sugar rock!"

"Ouch! Quit pinchin'! "

"You quit!"

The squabble was cut off by Tade's whispered baritone. "I'll break that sugar rock over your heads if you don't be quiet!"

The threat drew a spate of giggles from the offenders, but

the sound of their laughter was suddenly lost in the creak of the cottage door swinging open.

"Surprise! Da! Da! Devin's come home!" Whoops of laughter, shouted greetings, the heart-soaring cacophony of ten loving people speaking at once bubbled through the doorway. Rachel fumbled with the comb, grabbed for it, but it clattered to the floor at her feet.

Cupping her palm over the troublesome knot of hair at the nape of her neck, Maryssa turned to the now-frazzled woman. "Go on," she prodded gently. Rachel beamed her a grateful smile, dumping the rest of the bone pins into Maryssa's other hand.

The bedchamber door flew open. Rachel ran into the midst of the clambering group, her drab linsey-woolsey splashed with the bobbing, bright faces of the little ones, her eyes fastened adoringly on the towering figure of her husband who was crushing Devin in a hearty embrace.

Rachel had called him Kane, Maryssa remembered, staring at the man who, except for his bright russet hair, might be Tade twenty years from now. No, she amended, in a hundred years Tade would not look like his father. Tade's rakehell grin would never harden into lines so cynical; never would the dancing light in his green eyes die; and no amount of world-weariness would eclipse the beauty of his features.

Maryssa winced as she jabbed a hairpin into her scalp, but oddly the thought of Tade's face so changed stabbed more deeply.

"Da! Da!" The high-pitched voice of the red-curled waif pierced through the babble of the others. Kane Kilcannon reached down to lift his tiny daughter in his arms.

Even from the doorway, Maryssa could see the child's cheeks puff with importance. "Devin camed home."

"So he did, Katie-love," Kane Kilcannon chuckled.

"An' Tade, he brought a pretty lady, too. She gotted wet and he wescued her, and Deirdre yelled and—"

The joyous chatter died. From the open doorway Maryssa could see the eyes beneath Kane's dark brows narrow with a look that made her flinch. He turned their sparking green fury on his son. "Tade, you brought a stranger here, knowing Devin—"

Little Katie tugged at her father's hair, her tiny face puckered with worry as her gaze darted from her beloved brother to her father's implacable face. "Not stranger, Da, 'Ninglish."

"*English!* Damn you!" In one swift motion, Kane shoved Katie into Rachel's arms and grabbed for Tade's shirt front. Tade's hand flashed out and locked around his father's wrist. She saw a muscle knot in Tade's jaw, his eyes glint dangerously.

"Don't."

"Don't? You know what will happen to Devin if they catch him? They'll— By God I ought to—"

"Beat me?" Tade's challenge tore blade sharp through the threat. "I'm not ten years old, Da."

"Kane!"

"Tade!"

Devin and Rachel leaped toward them, hands clutching at arms, yanking and pulling, trying to separate the two men.

Kane knocked Rachel's hand aside, Devin's straining fingers ludicrous against the rock-hard muscles of his brother. Every fiber in Tade seemed tight in barely controlled rage, and Kane . . . Maryssa swallowed hard as his huge fist clenched.

"No! Please . . ." She stumbled forward, astonished at the sound of her voice.

Her assurances that she would cause Devin no harm withered in her throat as Kane Kilcannon spun to face her.

"Maryssa." His voice was ragged-edged, his face white. She froze, stunned that this man she had never seen before knew her name. Emotions, raw and undefinable, flashed across his face, the once-handsome features contorting with a fury that terrified her.

He wheeled on Tade, eyes wild with rage. "Christ! Sweet Christ! That's Bainbridge Wylder's daughter!"

Horror froze every face in the room, crushing Maryssa's chest. She stumbled back, the stark look of betrayal on Tade's face lashing her like the bite of a whip.

"I—"

"Wylder!" Tade's throat knotted convulsively, and for a second she thought he would strike her.

"Tade, listen—" At the fear choking Deirdre's voice, he turned, the whole family stilling to silence. Maryssa's nails cut deep into her palms, her heart hammering in her chest, taking on an odd, lurching rhythm. Her heart? No. Hoof-beats. Scores of hoofbeats.

Her gaze darted to the window just as Tade bolted over to slam the shutters. He turned, his face ash gray.

"Tade?" Rachel quavered. "For God's sake, who—"

"Soldiers." His eyes locked on Maryssa, and the menace in them shot through to her fingertips. "A whole cursed troop of English soldiers."

Four

Maryssa's head swam with the horrible sensation of being swallowed by an equine sea as the soldiers swarmed around the cottage walls, the clank of their trappings and the sound of their shouts beating against the whitewashed clay with the force of siege guns. Tade rammed home the iron bolt, nigh ludicrous as it barred the door, and in that frozen instant, Maryssa felt the warmth, security, and love of the family around her crack into shards like fine crystal, each face reflecting its own sharp-edged pain.

Kane's countenance was filled with the rage of a conquered king, set in sharp relief against Devin's waxen yet proud features. Deirdre stood frozen, stricken in the shadow of the other children while Rachel's dogged, quiet strength was laced with an inner torment so wrenching that Maryssa had a sudden feeling that she, too, was among the hunted.

But as the seconds stretched into eternity it was Tade's features that tore at Maryssa's soul—tore at it because it was as if, somehow, he had lost his own soul.

"Quick, Dev, the loft." With the first slam of boot heels on hard-packed ground, Tade shoved Devin toward a shadowed corner of the room where short lengths of board scaled the wall to an opening in the ceiling. Eyes, blindingly green and deadly, lingered just long enough to see Devin bolt up the first rungs of the makeshift ladder before Tade spun around. Snatching the babe from the cradle by the fire, he pushed it into the gangly youth's hands, mouth hard and grim as he turned the cradle over. Tiny bedclothes tumbled across the floor, the soft shushing sound lost in an odd clatter. Maryssa stared in stunned surprise as a board at the bottom of the cradle fell out, spilling the contents of a hidden compartment onto tangled muslin. The gilded crest of a sheathed dagger and the dull gleam of a pistol glinted in the firelight, their jeweled, deadly hues pillowed in the midst of the baby's cradle blanket.

Tade swooped down to snatch up the dagger and whipped it behind his back to shove its sheathed blade into the waistband of his breeches as Deirdre flew up behind him to pick up the pistol, its thick brass butt making her hands look as fragile as a child's.

"Open in the name of the king!" a voice roared inches from the bolted door. Rachel dived for the baby things, bundling the mass of muslin into the cradle and righting it just as the sickening sound of splintering wood ripped through the room. Tade's eyes locked on the pistol in Deirdre's hand, their green depths widening in surprise and fear as the iron hinges screeched, the metal tearing free of its moorings.

"Don't, Dee," he cried desperately. "It won't fire—"

Deirdre's eyes darted from the weapon in her hand to Tade's face. She fumbled with the pistol, its weight suddenly seeming too great for her fingers to hold.

Maryssa cowered back by the hearth as the battered door exploded inward and a score of red-coated soldiers poured through the gaping opening, blades drawn. She glanced at Deirdre just in time to see the last glimmer of the pistol's butt cap disappear into the pocket laced beneath the girl's dimity apron.

"Stand where you are!" a whey-faced lieutenant barked. "Any of you Irish scum twitch so much as a muscle and your rebel heads'll part comp'ny with your shoulders." Maryssa's eyes flew up, her face burning as guiltily as though she were the one with the pistol beneath her skirts, but when her gaze snagged Tade's, the expression on his handsome features drove all color from her cheeks. His mouth curled back from perfect white teeth in a smile so deceptively bland it might have greeted a friend who had stopped by for a visit, but his eyes, crystal-hard, sharp as a splintered emerald, made a shiver scuttle up Maryssa's spine. The swarm of soldiers parted, allowing a stubby peacock of a man to strut into the room. A colonel by rank, he swaggered up to Tade with the bravado of a village bully, his thick lips drawn into a gloating grin that made Maryssa think of fat white slugs feasting in rotted meat.

"What is the meaning of this!" Kane Kilcannon demanded, starting to stalk toward the man. A flash of keen-edged steel hissed through the air, its point blocking Kane's path. Maryssa saw Tade's hand jerk toward his back, freeze, then flatten against the oak table behind him.

"Things too quiet at the barracks, Rath?" he asked, breaking a piece of crust from the loaf of bread to his right and biting off a hunk. He chewed slowly, lounging back against the scarred wood as his eyes roved disparagingly from the intricately curled white wig perched atop the colonel's low brow to the glossy boots straining to encase his plump calves. The barest trace of mockery tilted one corner of Tade's mouth. "I can assure you that your method of storming cottages full of women and children remains, as always, impeccable. Of course, if you would merely have knocked—"

"And given you a chance to slip our quarry out a window? Ah, no. Far better to surround the place and kick in the door. You Irish would slide a man full grown back into his mother's womb if you thought you could hide him there."

"Aye, and you English would cut open every lass of child-bearing age in the county to find him." Tade straightened, a muscle in his jaw snapping tight. "But if you're running down some *desperate criminal* who dared say a rosary or teach his child to read, you'd best get back to your hounds. There is no one here but Kilcannons tonight, and little Ryan's not been about his cutthroat ways of late. He's a bit of a rash beneath his napkin."

"Don't play the buffoon with me, you arrogant Irish buck, or I'll show you just how deep I'm willing to cut to find my prey."

"Your prey? And just who is this fox that he takes half an army to hunt him down?"

"You know full well whom we seek and why. Your brother, fugitive from His Majesty's justice."

"Justice?" Tade chuckled, leaning over to drop the unfinished chunk of bread into the babe's tiny fist. "That explains everything. It's impossible to be fugitive from that which doesn't exist. Ryan, here, couldn't—"

"Damn you, Kilcannon," Rath exploded, his face puffing scarlet as his coat. "I'm not after babes and well you know it! It's Devin we want. And I swear I'll tear these walls down with pickaxes to find him if I have to! Men—"

The command Rath had been about to give was lost in a shriek as Deirdre stumbled forward. "Devin?" she cried. "He's . . . he's alive? Every eye in the room snapped to her face, and Maryssa watched in astonishment as the girl clutched at her throat, her thick honey-gold lashes fluttering closed as she drooped gracefully into a dapper young captain's arms.

The startled officer's sword clattered to the floor, his hands barely catching her as she sank to the floor. But the heavy, thunking sound of another metal object clunking against the wooden planks shattered the sudden silence like the crack of a musket. Maryssa stared in clutching fear as the side of Deirdre's apron bulged out, the outline of the pistol clearly visible beneath the thin cloth. It was a deadly gambit, Maryssa sensed in that instant, designed to distract the soldiers from their search in the desperate hope Devin could find some way to escape. Yet the danger to Deirdre herself . . . the scarce-concealed gun . . .

For all the girl's spirit, Maryssa could see by the twitch of her eyelids that Deirdre, who had, she was certain, never fainted in her life, was now terrified. A flash of movement caught Maryssa's eye. Tade reached for his knife hilt, and she knew in that instant that if he reached it he would die, knew, too, that she couldn't let him.

"Out of my way, knave!" She swept in front of him, knocking him off balance as though he were a cur in her path. The fingers that had been a whisper's breadth from the gilded dagger crashed against the wall, any hope Tade might have held of slipping the blade out in secret dissolving as the soldiers' eyes locked on the two of them.

"Halt, wench!"

"Halt?" Stiffening her spine in Lady Dallywoulde's most haughty manner, Maryssa pushed past the stocky soldier who had stepped into her way, stamping around him to face Rath in high dudgeon. "You dare command the daughter of Bainbridge Wylder about as though she were some . . . some Irish trollop?" she demanded, praying her pounding heart would not beat its way out of her chest. "My father will—"

"Wylder?" Rath barked a laugh. "And what would the lord of Nightwylde's daughter be doing dressed in peasant rags warming herself at Kilcannon fires?"

"The *lord of Nightwylde's daughter* was all but killed by the most disgusting mount in the manor's stables." Maryssa's chin jutted upward. "The wretched beast wandered off, then threw me into a lake where I all but drowned." She let her gaze flick scornfully about the room, her voice wavering just an instant as her eyes flashed over Tade's murderous glare.

"Considering the low company I've had to suffer since this . . . this Kilcannon person brought me here, I was beginning to wish I had drowned." She forced a disdainful sniff, patting her curls in the fashion she had seen the vapid court beauties adopt. "Can you imagine? They wanted to take me back to Nightwylde in a *donkey cart!* And now, when I dare hope that I am to be rescued from this hovel and accorded the respect I deserve from honorable Englishmen, I am slandered and degraded!"

A tiny quiver crept into Maryssa's voice, and she hoped Rath would interpret it as wounded dignity rather than the fear it was.

Revulsion prickled her stomach as his pig eyes sank deeper into their folds, their eager, slavering light skimming over her body as though it were a prime haunch of mutton. When he raised his gaze to hers, his features were schooled into a careful mask of deference and a genuine approval that made Maryssa want to retch.

"My dear Miss Wylder, what you must have endured, being stranded in such crude surroundings! Can you find it in your heart to forgive my men and me this unconscionable breach of manners?"

"I shall consider it if you will escort me to my father's estate at once. These clothes make my skin itch. Heaven only knows what kind of creatures are crawling inside them."

"My men and I will deem it a privilege to deliver you safely to your father. But first let us give you the pleasure of watching His Majesty's army ferret out an enemy to the Crown."

Maryssa felt her palms go clammy as the soldiers ringed around the room tensed, readying for the search. With so much effort she thought her face would crack, she made her lips curl in distaste, letting her gaze stray to Tade, then dismiss him. "Colonel Rath, it would be a weak Crown indeed that found an enemy in these lowly creatures."

"The Irish are most deceptive to the eye, Miss Wylder, and sometimes"—Rath's beady eyes fastened on Tade—"winning to the heart. But rest assured that the man we seek is a criminal as vile and depraved as the devil himself."

The horror that whitened Maryssa's face was real, so real it slammed the breath from her lungs, drove all sensation from her veins leaving her chilled and numb. "What . . ." She barely whispered the word, wanting to ask what Devin was guilty of, then realizing she did not want to know. She swallowed, her gaze dropping to the floor.

"Miss Wylder, have you seen anyone else here in, say, the last three hours? A man a head taller than I, blond hair, blue eyes? On last report he was wearing black breeches and a frock coat, but he might have—"

"No."

"You are certain?"

She could feel the tension in every Kilcannon, from little Katie to Devin, who was hidden away in the loft, but eclipsing all of that was Tade, the knotting in his muscles, the fire in his green eyes. He seemed to touch her, though they stood half a room apart. An enemy to the Crown, Rath had claimed. Devin . . . evil, depraved . . .

Maryssa forced her eyes to Rath's. "Colonel, I vow I've seen no one. Now, if you would kindly escort me home—"

"All in good time, my lady." Rath's eyelids narrowed, and as he scanned the room she could almost see his nose twitch, scenting its prey. " 'Twill take but a little for my men to make search before we take our leave. Something may have escaped your notice. Perhaps even now that devil Kilcannon lurks beneath a pallet or in a trunk."

"And perhaps the French army is hiding in the thatch straw," Tade observed with a brittle grin.

Maryssa hazarded a warning glance toward him, panic rising yet again in her throat as her gaze flashed back to Rath's paunchy face. "Do you judge me a liar, Colonel Rath?" she demanded, desperation choking her. "Or do you think me merely a fool?"

"I . . . no . . . I only—," Rath stammered, his neckcloth suddenly seeming too tight for his throat.

Maryssa clenched hanks of her petticoats in fists that felt too stiff to move. "I was nearly killed, was dragged off to this . . . this mud hut, forced to wear rags, and very nearly had to be trundled home in a manner that would have battered my sensibilities, not to mention certain parts of my anatomy." Tears brimmed over her lashes, burning her cheeks in hot trails of fear. "But to be humiliated—called a *liar*—by *you*, an *English gentleman*— I'll not bear one more second of this outrage! Tear the cottage down looking for phantom criminals if you must, Colonel Rath. I'm going to Nightwylde. Now. If I have to walk every step of the way!"

"Miss Wylder, surely you cannot mean— Why, every brigand in Ireland frequents these hills. Just last night the Black Falcon—"

"Perhaps the Black Falcon will prove to be more of a gentleman than you!" Maryssa spun around and ran through the door. The thin facade of control she had held over herself melted in the misty night air, terror, desperation, and guilt causing her knees to quake until she was certain they would pitch her into a heap on the rocky yard. She could merely turn around, confess everything to the soldiers, and tell them Tade had threatened her into silence.

But it was not Tade's rage that had stilled her tongue, not the specter of his revenge. Maryssa bit her lip until it bled, welcoming the stinging pain. It had been their love she could not betray—Devin's, Tade's, Rachel's. No matter what Devin's crime, Maryssa could not have borne to see the soldiers rip him away from the loving hands of his family, could not have borne the tiny Kilcannons' sobs, Rachel's keening.

Maryssa buried her face in her hands. She was aiding a fugitive from the Crown. A thief? Murderer? Traitor? No court in England would acquit her if she shielded a truant from justice. And her father . . . he would no doubt rejoice to be rid of her.

She ground the heels of her hands into her eyes, trying to stem the panic that gripped her. Were the soldiers even now discovering the ladder to the loft? Piercing mattresses, piles of cloth with their sharp-honed swords? Tade—lightsome, rakehell Tade—would never let them take Devin without a fight. A hopeless fight. A fatal one. The image of his life-blood drenching the bronzed, hard flesh that had pressed so warm against her own made Maryssa want to scream.

There was a swishing of steel and the sound of boots. Prayers whispered through her lips, half-forgotten childhood prayers, as she pleaded with what to her had always proved an icy, vengeful God.

''Miss Wylder''—Rath's stiff tone bristled with irritation as he strode up beside her—''we can hardly allow Bainbridge Wylder's daughter to go dashing off into the hills. If your comfort is more important to you than the escape of a desperate criminal—''

''At this point, Colonel Rath, I could cheerfully commit murder myself to get beneath the coverlet of my own bed,'' Maryssa said with heartfelt sincerity as Rath's command poured out of the cottage.

Yet even when the colonel settled her before him in the saddle, the soft, pudgy folds of his stomach flattening against her back, Maryssa could feel the cottage call to her. The cottage, and the green-eyed rogue inside it. She glanced back covertly at the flower-draped whitewashed walls, trying to imprint them in her memory to be taken out and savored on listless, lonely days. But all she saw were the broad shoulders silhouetted in the shattered doorway, and the solemn, seeking face of Tade Kilcannon staring after her into the night.

Tade dug his fingers into the unyielding wood of the doorjamb, fighting the urge to bolt into the yard and rip Maryssa from Rath's defiling arms. The taunts the English troops flung back as they mounted their horses found no chink in Tade's self-control, their voices only grating on his ear like those of whining children deprived of their game. In the room behind him he could feel the rage of his father as though it were a tangible thing, seething and roiling, his hatred of all things

English nurtured and tended all these years. He could hear Rachel's whispered prayers of thanks, sense the children's still-raw terror.

Yet it was the sight of Maryssa that knotted in Tade's belly, chasing the pale, frozen faces of his family into the shadows of his consciousness. Maryssa, her slight body bound in arms he knew had perpetrated a dozen separate horrors, her wraithlike face just visible over Rath's beefy shoulder. She peered back in such haunting sorrow, her changeable eyes clinging to the cottage with resigned pain, her delicate moon-kissed features shaded with a fragile beauty that made him want to pull her into the shelter of his body, destroying all who would do her harm.

Tade stiffened as Rath bellowed an order and the English soldiers reined their mounts into position behind the colonel's gray gelding. Rath inclined his head toward Maryssa, an in-gratiating smile curling his lips. As Tade's fingers clenched, a fragment of the splintered door pierced deep into his palm. Cursing, he yanked his hand back and kneaded the injured place with his other thumb. *Do her harm?* Hah! Hadn't the girl made it perfectly clear that she was no "Irish trollop" for Rath's troops to abuse at will? No, she was an *English lady* who needed only to stamp her silk-shod foot to have an entire troop of Sassenach soldiers run trailing after her like a fat old dowager's lapdogs.

She was Bainbridge Wylder's only child—daughter of the richest landholder in Donegal, in half of Ireland. Didn't she belong with Rath, with these Sassenach soldiers who shat-tered Irish lives with no more thought than they had given the oaken door that lay splintered at Tade's feet? With no more thought . . .

Tade grimaced, suddenly shamed by his own cynical mus-ings. God's teeth, he was sounding like his father, so bitter that he regarded even an act of compassion with doubt. For all her theatrics, this girl was no English belle whose nose was poked so far into the air she trampled over peasant babes that lay in her path. She had lied to protect a man she had only just met, a man she knew had broken English law.

Did she, in her highborn naiveté, have any inkling of what the gallant colonel would have done to her if his men had discovered Devin in the loft? Or had she risked all, knowing what punishment might await her? Tade shuddered inwardly at the thought of her delicate wrists cased in iron shackles. The little fool! The winsome, beautiful little fool! He wanted to hold her, wanted to shake her. And yet if she hadn't lied . . .

Tade's muscles tensed as he watched Rath knee the gray into a canter, the jarring movement nearly spilling Maryssa from the saddle. Though the space of the yard and three dozen horses lay between them, Tade felt in his own belly the terror that stabbed through her slight frame, felt, too, an almost desperate urge to tear back the veils of darkness as they fluttered closed behind her.

Damn, she could never be anything to him. She was English. A fine lady with riches and a hundred servants at her disposal, a lady who would scarce deign notice a *lowly Irishman,* regardless of the fact that the blood in his veins ran more noble than her own.

But Quentin Rath . . . he would be judged her equal, with his fine house and his commission, purchased with blood-stained coin from his admiral papa's purse. No doubt the despicable colonel would spend the whole ride to Nightwylde insinuating himself into *her ladyship's* good graces. He would be rapping at Nightwylde's door first thing next morning, his cockaded hat crushed beneath one sweaty armpit, an engraved calling card in his freshly manicured hand, and the boundaries and wealth that were Nightwylde imbedded in his greedy little brain.

And Maryssa . . . would she simper about before Rath, striking her hand to her brow and wailing about her ordeal among the barbaric Irish, as though she had been tortured in the cruelest of dungeons?

No. She had placed herself in danger to protect Devin, Deirdre . . . to protect him. She was no haughty witch, but rather a woebegone fairy who had strayed like a will-o'-the-wisp into his life, then fled back to the kingdom from whence she had come.

From the first she had stolen into his heart, her very name seeming to trail petal-soft over his lips, lodging inside him with an aching sadness akin to that he had felt the summer he turned eight and found an abandoned tinker's child huddled in the "castle" he and Devin had built in a tree. Even

Rachel's expert nursing had not been able to save the girl.
But when she closed her eyes in eternal sleep, somehow Tade
had known even in his childhood innocence that she had not
died from the buffeting of chill winds off the ocean or the
emptiness in her belly, but rather from too little love, given
too late.

Today, when Rachel and the little ones had poured out to
greet Devin, Maryssa had stood in the shadows with the same
look of haunting loneliness, so shy and frail Tade had wanted
to stroke soft roses into her cheeks, brush her lips with his
own mouth, make her smile. But when Deirdre had flung
open the bedchamber door and he had seen Maryssa framed
against a backdrop of rumpled bedclothes, her body all but
naked, golden with candleshine, he had wanted to tumble her
back onto the pillows, take all of her, and give . . . give her
things no other woman had touched inside him . . .

The stirrings of the children behind him intruded on the
dreamlike sweetness playing in his mind. He shut his eyes,
wanting to hold as long as he could the vision of tumbled
dark hair wisping over coral-tipped breasts, of wide, searching eyes. But the picture was shattered as a hand clamped on
his shoulder, spinning him around to face the rage-contorted
countenance of his father.

Tade gaped, stunned as Kane's hand arced toward his face,
shock dulling his normally keen reflexes, making him too
slow to escape the blow entirely. Pain shot through him as
his father's hard palm glanced off his jaw, pain that radiated
through his whole being with a raw agony that had naught to
do with the force of the buffet dealt him. He wheeled, fists
raised, but Deirdre leaped in front of him, her eyes wide,
tears of accusation flooding her cheeks as she glared at Kane.

"Da! How could y—"

"No, Dee. I'll be fighting my own battles." Tade shoved
her out of his path, his eyes glinting with hurt and fury as he
fought the feeling of betrayal that cinched around his chest.
An uncontrollable need to wound back flooded through him,
his words as he turned to his father intended to cut as deeply
as the lashes Tade himself had endured. "I'm a trifle too old
to drag behind the cow byre, Da," he grated. "Or did it
make you feel more a man? Ramming your fist into my face
since you couldn't bloody Rath as you wanted?"

"Damn you, if I had any sense I'd thrash you till you couldn't move! Because of your idiocy the whole family could have been cast into Rookescommon prison. That little English wench—"

"That 'little English wench' just saved our necks!" Tade snarled. "Rath must've suspected Devin was here before he rode in. If Maryssa hadn't distracted him, we'd all be trussed in chains right now, bound for a Sassenach gallows. And we'd be the lucky ones—"

"Aye, luckier than the girl would be, by far," Kane shot back. "Did you consider for a moment what harm could befall her? No. You just threw her into the middle of disaster, and now you blow up with pride as though you're a fallen hero. Do you think I want the blood of another Wylder woman on my han—"

Tade's head tilted a fraction in confusion, his eyes narrowing at the hint of bittersweet pain underlying his father's words.

The muscles in Kane's face jerked tight, throwing the stark planes into sharp relief. A shutter fell over his eyes, driving away the sadness until it seemed only shadings of Tade's imagination.

"Another? Who—"

"Another person to suffer for your irresponsibility," Kane blazed. "You're always right, no matter who you hurt! Run off at all hours to God knows where, playing catch-skirt with your rakehell friends, worry Rachel and your sister nigh to their graves, then whisk in as bold as you please, dragging an English chit behind you—"

"Tell me. What galls you the most, Da?" Tade asked, with menacing quiet. "That she's English? Or that you owe your life to a Wylder?"

"Damn you—"

"Damn me? You're the one who holds fast to hell."

"Aye, and you're the son who should be helping me battle out of it! But no, you're too busy cavorting around like a damned court fool to be bothered. You've shamed me since the day poor Patrick Dugan was dragged away, you and your reckless—"

Tade's hand knotted, fury searing through him as he swung at Kane's bared teeth. He slammed his fist to a halt bare inches from his father's face, horror rising like bile in his throat. Sweet Christ, he had almost . . . Tade wrenched his fist to his side, his jaw rock-hard as his eyes flicked to Devin's solemn face at the foot of the loft ladder. The quick, hot anger that blazed through Tade's limbs turned to stomach-twisting nausea.

Dear God, had the love he and his father shared crumbled so far that they would charge each other like crazed beasts, tearing where they were most vulnerable? Since the day fourteen years ago when Patrick Dugan had been borne away, Tade's father had never mentioned the incident . . . never torn open the scar hidden deep in Tade's soul. His father had wanted only to heal his pain and the guilt that had threatened to drive him past bearing, to wipe from his memory that horrible day, which had been the only other time in Tade's life that Kane Kilcannon had struck him. Tade looked into his father's eyes, eclipsed now by bitterness, and remembered them filled with tears.

Tade's fist tightened, dropped. "I love you, Da. God knows I do," he said quietly. "But you'd be wise to leave Patrick out of this lest you want me to forget you sired me."

"Just be certain you do no siring of your own. I marked well the way you were eyeing Wylder's wench. Get a bastard on her and he'll think no more of taking the geldin' knife to you than to a stallion in his stables."

The crystal green hardness in Tade's eyes clouded, taking on dark mysteries of forests primeval. "Da, remember the night the Fianna mare came? You tried to guard her. Stone fences, barred gates, even an iron latch on the stall. My stallion, Curran . . . he broke every one of them."

"Aye. And he was half dead himself when we found the two of them. If his foreleg hadn't healed his pleasure-taking would most like have cost him his life. You have no idea what Bainbridge Wylder is capable of. No idea. His daughter . . . Stay away from her, Tade. Or by God, you'll be no son of mine." The tiniest quaver in his father's voice made Tade's eyes snap up to Kane's. Astonishment coursed through Tade, mixed with a prickling of foreboding. Fear. His father's eyes were edged with the same fear he had shown when Devin's life had been threatened by the soldiers.

Tade's eyes widened, but the sight of Rachel's work-worn

hands fluttering up to grasp his father's shoulder in a silent plea stilled the questions stinging Tade's tongue. The soft brown eyes peering past Kane were more vulnerable than he had ever seen them. Tade forced his shoulders to relax, a half-smile twisting his lips as his eyes swept to the proud features so like his own. "You could try to deny me, Da," he said. Turning his back on his father's bitterness and on the silent pain in Devin's face, Tade paced out into the yard.

The night closed soft about him, the sounds of Rachel drawing Kane to the hearth and the family moving about, fading again into dream.

A dream so beautiful and winsome that it banished all others Tade had known, leaving in their place visions of dark hair, eyes soft and ephemeral as the mists dancing in from the sea. Tade reached down to finger a pouch secreted beneath the waistband of his breeches. Idly he pulled the leather bag from its place and slipped the laces open. After countless women, bedded and forgotten, it was only now he understood the primal urge that had driven his stallion to batter himself against stone and steel. That craving of flesh too deep to be denied. She called to him . . . Maryssa . . . with sirens' songs that he alone could hear. Spells, woven with silken threads that bound but also freed. And he would go to her, he knew, even if Kane Kilcannon chained him in irons.

Tade touched the contents of the pouch, spilling Maryssa's necklet into his outstretched palm. Moonlight toyed with the tip of one gold wing, the tiny arched neck of a graceful gold swan.

Maryssa . . . she had raged at him when he had torn it from her neck at the Devil's Grin, the blue-green sparks flaring in her incredible eyes. Yet he was certain she had not linked the rakehell Tade Kilcannon to Donegal's Black Falcon this night. Tade's lips tipped into a ghosting of smile. Aye, if she had, she'd most like have dragged Rath to him and helped knot the cursed bastard in ropes.

But in those moments within that dingy alehouse, when he had first held the golden swan in his hand, he had seen a treasure far greater in Maryssa Wylder's upturned face. He had seen there the fiery woman within her, a woman secreted behind the cocoon of childlike innocence and the timorous quivering of her sweet mouth.

What mysteries held her captive? What sorrows kept her chained? Chains . . . such fragile chains . . . Tade stared at the delicate golden links pooled against his flesh, and wondered if he could free her.

Five

MARYSSA PRESSED HER face against the mullioned glass window, the night breeze trickling through the open casement tempting her with the wild, sweet scent of mountains and the subtler fragrance of freedom. She shut her eyes, letting the cool winds soothe her eyelids, still burning from tears. Tears shed alone, into an unfamiliar pillow in a room she belonged in no more than the house full of love and children she had left the night before.

The elegant bedstead, dripping rose velvet, seemed to jut its spiraled bedposts toward the ceiling in disdain, while the barefoot, beribboned damsels frolicking across the cream silk wallpaper mocked her with their hand-painted smiles, smug in their fairy world of castles and blossom-starred meadows. What could they, with their angel-kissed faces know of the pain of being unloved . . . of being so awkward and plain that even her own father viewed her with contempt?

Maryssa touched her cheek, gingerly tracing the line of her jaw. The lower edge still swelled against her fingers, but the burning pain had faded into a dull throb that constricted in a lump in her throat. "Father . . . I almost thought you—" Maryssa whispered the words aloud, the sentence trailing into silence as she dashed away the tears that spilled again over her lashes.

For all his anger, her father had seemed almost glad to see her when Rath had brought her to the door of the castle. His wig had been swept from his balding pate, tossed in a rain of white powder onto a chair in the entryway. His face had been trekked with new lines that seemed to grow deeper still as Quentin Rath had regaled him with the tale of her "rescue."

The tiniest hope that her father cared for her a little had lightened Maryssa's heart, until suddenly Bainbridge Wylder's voice had cut Rath off in midsentence, his jowls washing the dull red Maryssa knew marked barely checked fury. "Kilcannon?" he had roared. "She was . . . You found my daughter at the house of Kane Kilcannon?"

Even now, a day later, Maryssa flinched at the memory of her father's rage. He had unceremoniously escorted Colonel Rath to the door, not even waiting for the servants to fetch the man's cloak. The stunned colonel, who had been preening in a way that reminded Maryssa of a glutted serpent sunning its scales, had scarce had time to pull his buttocks from between the heavy wood panels before her father had slammed them shut behind him.

And then—Maryssa winced as her trembling fingers tightened involuntarily on her jaw—then her father had spun on her, spitting a fury past all bounds of reason.

"Kilcannon!" he screamed. "Not in Ireland a week, and already you're whoring with a cursed Kilcannon!"

"No, father . . . I—"

"Damn you, don't deny it! You're dragged home in strange clothes after being closeted half the night with Kane Kilcannon's spawn and you expect me to believe he touched you not at all?"

"He didn't! His whole family was there. I—" Her pleading explanations had been dashed from her lips by a blow that sent her reeling against the entryway's stone wall. She had known her father expected her to crumple to the floor, to cower from him as she had in the past. But she only stiffened her spine against the smooth stone and set her mouth hard against the tears that threatened to come.

Bainbridge stalked up, his face savage as he caught her jaw

in a brutal grip. "If you so much as *look* at a Kilcannon again, girl, I swear I'll blind you myself! And, by God, you'll thank me for being so lenient. No lineage in Ireland is tainted with as many blackguards as the Kilcannons'. Their poison spreads from one end of this infernal island to the other, and they would like nothing better than to spill it upon the man who finally bested them."

"Bested?" Maryssa had echoed, remembering how Kane had known who she was though he had never seen her before, remembering Tade's face when he'd heard the name Wylder. "You . . . you do know them, then?"

"Kane Kilcannon would not be likely to forget my face, you may be certain. Or yours." The final words were softer and cryptic, as Bainbridge released her chin with a jerk, turning to retrieve his wig from the chair. He tore at the stiff black ribbons, rending then as if bent on destroying something more threatening than pomatum and flour. "Do you think Sir Ascot Dallywoulde—an English knight—would stoop to taking some Irish barbarian's leavings? That is, if Dallywoulde decides to have you at all."

Maryssa started to speak, but her father glared her into silence. With a snort of disgust, he flung the ruined hairpiece into the corner.

"It just so happens that a missive arrived from Dallywoulde after you went dashing off. He is doubtful as to whether even my properties are worth bearing a—how did he say it?—an ill-mannered bluestocking for a wife. Before this year is out, he intends to sail for Nightwylde to examine what benefits he would reap through binding himself to you. We can hope he will arrive around Allhallows Eve. And you, daughter, will meet him with what paltry feminine wiles you possess burning as bright as the peasant fires decking the hills."

Maryssa's nails had dug deep into her palms, a sick feeling gnawing in the pit of her stomach. "Sir Ascot has a great penchant for fires, Father," she returned with a spark of defiance. "But only when they consume innocents."

"Then he'll have little use for you, considering how you've disgraced yourself. But I'll make certain you understand what sentence awaits you if you dare make a fool of me again. You will remain under lock and key until I decide you are fit to be released. You may discover just how little you like being totally alone. For if you fail to lure Ascot to the altar, I'll see to it that you never set foot outside that chamber again. Mark me. You will finish out your life locked away where you can humiliate me no further.''

Grasping a handful of her sleeve, her father had yanked her up the stairway and shoved her into her room as though he would hurl her from his life if he could.

Maryssa shivered, dropping numb fingers to the cool stone window ledge as she remembered the sound of the bar crashing down across the door, the noise echoing through the bedchamber like the slamming of the lid upon a coffin.

Defiance had crumbled into dread, dread into nightmarish fear as hours had passed in which she detected not so much as the stirring of a servant on the other side of the heavy oak panel. No one had bothered to light a fire on the stone hearth, and not so much as one taper pierced the darkness that pressed around her from all sides.

When night fell again, she had all but embraced the birdlike maid who skittered into the room bearing a tray of food and two silver branches of blazing candles.

Only then had her fear changed to resentment, and she had cried in frustration at her own helplessness to battle her father, cried for the love she had tasted at the Kilcannons' before it had been snatched away.

Maryssa hugged herself, pressing her arms against the thin lawn of her night rail. The sharp tang of moors and meadow flowers wafting over her bore with it memories of a man's face, its planes and angles carved with the same dangerous beauty as the wild lands over which she had ridden.

She shivered, but the tingling sensation that crept over her skin had nothing to do with the coolness of the night wind. It was the image of Tade that set her blood to racing . . . his grin flashing, his silky mane knotted at the nape of his neck in delicious contrast to the warm, corded column of his throat.

Through everything that had befallen her this week past— her encounter with the Black Falcon, the cruelty of her father, her terror in the midst of Colonel Rath's raid—the thing that remained imprinted upon her senses most acutely was the feel of Tade Kilcannon's naked flesh pressed against her and the shape of the lips that had tempted her beyond reason.

"As though *I* could tempt any man," Maryssa muttered to herself, whisking a wayward curl over her shoulder. The rich tresses cascaded down her back in a warm, satiny curtain, their tips brushing the gentle curve of her derriere, yet the picture she presented as she turned and caught her reflection in the looking glass across the room did nothing to cheer her. When her father decided to release her from her room, it would be to entice Ascot Dallywoulde to take her to wife. There would be no handsome rake with crystal green eyes to slip the formal wig from her hair and unpin the dark mysteries beneath.

Instead there would be bony hands, icy hands using her to beget an heir . . .

Maryssa turned around, forcing her thoughts away from Dallywoulde's blade-sharp features. No . . . she wouldn't think about that now . . .

From a shelf of books in the corner she plucked a volume of myths. Then she took up a branch of candles and set it atop the small table beside the bed, then burrowed beneath the coverlet, propping her shoulders against cloud-soft pillows to lose herself again in fanciful worlds of myth and magic. But as she read the tale of Orpheus and Eurydice, it was she who sobbed for love lost, and when Persephone escaped the gates of the underworld, the face of the lord within tugged at Maryssa's soul with eyes as warm and green as the spring to which the goddess fled.

Maryssa raised her eyes to the candle flames that flickered, danced, and flirted with the night. If a Hades with dark, silken hair, and bronzed, chiseled features looked upon her with the longing her imagination had stroked into those crystal green eyes, she would forsake the earth forever, and welcome the darkness that was his.

She looked at the moonlit window, suddenly frightened by her thoughts. The image of running into the night, of welcoming arms catching her up, spinning her around, shifted to a vision of ghostly shapes, souls forever lost, dragging her down into nothingness.

"I would," she said aloud in defiance. "If he loved me, I would follow him to h—"

A sudden scraping sound on the wall outside made Maryssa jump. The book tumbled from her lap and slammed to the floor with a bang she was certain could be heard all the way to the stableyard. Her gaze darted to the locked door, then back to the window. She caught her lip in her teeth, not breathing, not moving.

Dear God, what could be out there? Some kind of animal? A brigand? Or a being of another age, still roaming the halls that had sheltered it? Surely no mortal could—

A scream choked in Maryssa's throat as the night itself seemed to vault through the window, cloak-shrouded shoulders silhouetted against the mullioned panes. She leaped from the bed, the sole of one bare foot skimming the slick pages of the open book that now lay on the floor, its leather binding skidding out from beneath her.

The scream burst forth with a vengeance as she plunged headlong toward the terrifying apparition. Gloved hands shot out to catch her. She struggled and fought as she crashed against the shadowed form, but instead of the misty softness of a specter, the fingers that closed over her mouth were very much alive. The hard plane of a masculine chest broke her fall, a warm, muscled chest that smelled of mountains . . .

"Had I known you'd be this happy to see me, I'd have climbed up hours ago." The jaunty voice was accompanied by a laugh as a finger hooked under her chin, tipping her head back to meet Tade Kilcannon's laughing eyes.

"How . . . how did you . . . What did . . . do you want?"

His mouth split in a grin, boyish, disarming, and devilishly hopeful. "Would you believe to steal a kiss from a beautiful lady?"

"No."

The green eyes widened at the tinge of defensiveness in Maryssa's voice. She tore her gaze from their questioning light, the feel of his perfectly honed body through the thin lawn of her night rail demonstrating far too clearly that his words could be naught but jest. She tried to evade his grasp, but the arm resting lightly around her waist tightened.

"Then would you believe I came to return these?" He jerked his head toward the floor beside the window where a bundle, neatly done up in a muslin bedsheet, lay on the carpet.

"What—"

"Your clothes." He arched one roguish black brow. "You left them in my bedchamber."

"It was not your bed—" Maryssa blustered, embarrassment firing her cheeks as the laugh lines bracketing his mouth deepened.

"More's that pity." He affected such an air of rueful resignation that, despite herself, Maryssa felt the beginnings of a smile toy with her mouth. "Go ahead, make jest of my plight," he accused. "With all the competition I have at home, I can never sneak a lady up the loft ladder. Everyone stops to admire the baby, and before I can turn around he's charmed them till they'll spare me not another glance."

Easing from the arms that were much too inviting, Maryssa walked to the bookshelf and traced the golden mane of one of the unicorns in its carved rosewood frame. "Somehow I doubt you have much trouble enticing women to . . . forget themselves . . . in your quarters."

"Aye, the most beautiful ladies in Ireland line the streets begging for my favors. They hurl themselves at me at the most inopportune times—in the market, on the highways . . . in my *bath*." Maryssa gasped at his unabashed arrogance, spinning around to see Tade's eyes snap emerald with devilment. "If I didn't have Rachel to drive them away, they'd nigh steal my senses. You have no idea how tiresome it is." His gaze dripped slowly; the cocksure grin began to fade, then melted into quiet, heavy longing as his eyes trailed down the flowing white of her night rail. "You have no idea . . . ," he repeated softly.

Maryssa pressed her arms to her breasts, suddenly aware of the dusky circles of her nipples just visible through the delicate fabric, aware of the candlelight gilding every curve of her body.

The stirring of the ribbon ties of her night rail made her look up. He had moved so swiftly, so silently, she had not known he was upon her until the faint roughness of his fingertips touched the satin at the hollow of her throat. His knuckles lay warm against her, brushing softly, ever so softly against the delicate arch of her collarbone beneath its meager icing of lace. She watched, enchanted, while he drew the wisp of blue ribbon through his fingers, his lips parting as if somehow savoring the feel of it.

Maryssa wanted to flee the honeyed sensations that rippled from his flesh into hers, sensations that meant naught to Tade, but everything to her. Her gaze leaped away from the strong, bronzed fingers, and sought some way to escape, but the bookshelf and the closeness of Tade's body cut her off from the rest of the room, holding her captive between the fantasy world carved in rosewood, and the man, more intriguing than any dream could be.

As if he foresaw her decision to dodge from his grasp, he captured her face in his hands, threading his fingers past her temples into the sable waves of her hair. When his eyes again found hers they were serious, dark with questions. "Maura, why?"

Maryssa swallowed, the fanning of his warm breath against her lips stealing all thought from her head. "Wh . . . why what?"

"Why did you lie? To Rath? The soldiers?"

"I . . . I couldn't . . . I don't know why."

"Yes, you do. I watched your face. A dozen fears darted through your eyes. I was sure you were going to tell them. Then—"

"Then you almost got yourself killed by reaching for your knife! What were you planning to do? Battle off a score of soldiers with only one blade?"

"I was going to grab Rath. Hold the dagger to his throat until Dev and the rest of the family had time to escape."

"You wouldn't have gotten within ten paces of Rath! There were at least five soldiers between you and the colonel. One of them would have run you through before you'd taken a step."

"Why should that matter? To you?" The green eyes narrowed until they seemed to delve into her very soul.

"I have a terrible aversion to the sight of blood," Maryssa flung back, oddly wounded by the faint edge of suspicion in his voice.

Tade started to speak, but she raised her face defiantly. "I don't know why I lied. I only knew I couldn't bear to watch them drag Devin away with all of you wreathed about. You . . . you had been so kind. Rachel, Devin, all of you. When it came time to answer, I just couldn't—"

"But Rath almost sent his troops up the ladder. If he had—"

"I'd be awaiting trial for treason." Surprise streaked across Tade's face at her words. Maryssa's lips quivered, and she hated herself for showing how much his doubt upset her. "Did you think that, being a woman, I was too feebleminded to know that?"

"No, I . . . Maura, don't." Tade's fingers feathered over her mouth, as if to sweep the sadness away, but the soft, sweet Irish name lilting from his tongue wrenched her heart like the plaintive strains of a ballad. "I never meant to hurt you," he said softly. "It's just that you're everything I was raised to hate. You're English, heiress to all of this. Nightwylde . . ." His gaze wisped over the huge bedstead, the intricately plastered ceiling, the rich carpets, and Maryssa detected a strange sort of longing in the curve of his mouth. Her chin tilted just a little as she tried to read the meaning of the wistfulness, the tinge of bitterness touching his features.

His eyes caught hers, and he released her, the barest hint of red touching his cheekbones. He turned, running his fingers over the dusty volumes on the shelf. Though Maryssa couldn't see his expression, his hands were reverent, almost loving as they withdrew a copy of the *Iliad*. He thumbed through the pages, then stopped. Maryssa listened, stunned, as classical Greek phrases, fired by the blind poet's genius, flowed from Tade's lips. His faint Irish lilt tore at her soul with a beauty that awed her as he lamented the destruction of Troy, watching the death of a kingdom, because a man had dared take the woman he loved . . .

A tiny gasp of pleasure escaped Maryssa, and Tade stopped in midsentence, looking up to give her a sheepish smile.

"We don't get many books hereabouts. If Devin were here he'd probably flay me for massacring the Greek language."

"No. It was perfect. I never knew it could sound so . . . so . . ." Maryssa swallowed hard, so moved mere words were too clumsy to explain the feelings rushing through her. "Where did you learn Greek?"

"In a cave near Penderleigh crag."

"You learned Greek in a *cave*?"

"Greek, Latin, enough knowledge to put even your high-brow Englishmen to shame. My da risked all he owned to send us there. The magistrate would have confiscated the cottage and every scrap of any worth inside it if we had been discovered. And Da . . . Da would have been thrown into prison with the rest of the felons. You see, it's against the law for us dangerous Irish Catholics to hold school. The Sassenach wager that if they keep us ignorant we'll stop fighting. For a hundred years we've battled the chains they've put on our lands. Now they want to put their shackles on our minds.''

Maryssa felt a smile tremble at the corner of her mouth. ''It seems the more they try to take learning from you, the more you crave it.''

''Aye.'' Tade gently closed the book. ''I used to plague my schoolmaster to distraction,'' he said. ''While his other charges were plodding through their ciphering, I was off with the Argonauts capturing the Golden Fleece. Many's the time Master Dugan—'' Dark-lashed lids dropped low over his eyes, not quite hiding the stab of pain shadowed beneath them.

''Your schoolmaster . . . It was he who taught you to read that way?''

''Aye.''

Maryssa flinched at Tade's sharp-edged reply as he turned abruptly and slid the volume onto the shelf as though filling the gap in the neat row of books would close out some vision lurking behind them. He hesitated, the pain Maryssa had detected fading into a distant look, tender and musing. ''But first it was my mother who made me love books. She used to let me play with hers. Build castles . . . Dev and I liked to fancy she was Maeve, the warrior queen, and she would sit in her chair for hours, a gold paper crown on her head, while we set our toy soldiers to battle for her favor.''

''She must have loved to watch you,'' Maryssa said softly, imagining Tade as an impish boy sprawled with a cherub-faced Devin at the feet of their adoring young mother.

''She did. I can still see her laughing, popping sweetmeats into our mouths from the silver bowl on her lap. Swirling around the ballroom in satin, gold as her hair.''

Maryssa tried to keep the shock from her eyes, attempting to reconcile gold satin and silver plate with rawboned Rachel Kilcannon and the humble cottage in the mountains. Within Tade's words were echoes of Rachel's claim in the cottage

bedchamber that Kane had been tending his kerns, his people
. . . Maryssa found the image of both the rugged-faced Kane
and this delicate picture of Tade's mother disturbing, yet
somehow wrenchingly right. ''What happened to her?''

Tade's face angled toward Maryssa, and despite the sorrow
touching his mouth, his eyes were hooded for the first time,
their clear depths fraught with secrets, guarded, as he watched
her. ''She died in childbed two weeks before my fourth Saint's
Day. I didn't know it then, but she had been letting go of life
for a long time. Dying one dream at a time.''

Maryssa reached out to touch him, hesitated, then let her
fingertips drift like the most fragile of snowflakes over his
sleeve. ''Dreams can be dangerous things,'' she said as the
warmth of his skin melted into hers. ''But still, I envy you.''

''Envy me?'' His eyes swept the elegant room scornfully.
''And I suppose you'd be so envious of the orphans at the
workhouse that you'd battle them scratch-and-fire for a place
in their louse-ridden beds.''

''If they've known the love of their mother, even for a little
while, yes. I have no memory of mine.'' She turned away
from him, suddenly aware that his eyes probed too deeply.

''Your mother . . . she died?''

''Aye.'' Maryssa shook back her curls, trying to affect a
carelessness she did not feel. ''When I was but a babe.'' She
could feel Tade's silence reaching out to her. She swallowed,
her voice dropping. ''So, you see, I do envy you. Every touch,
every sweetmeat, every game.''

''Maura, I'm sorry.'' His hands cupped her shoulders,
gently forcing her to look at him. She pulled away and crossed
the room to stand with her back to him, the compassion in
his face making her reckless as she battled the tears clouding
her eyes. She raked her fingers back through the heavy waves
of her hair, pulling the mass upward, then shaking it out.

''When I was little I used to make believe that my father
had lied. That my mother yet lived and was coming back for
me. Once I even tried to send . . .'' She gave a sad little
laugh. ''There was a stream that ran through Carradown, the
estate where I grew up. The gardener used to claim it ran
clear to the king of France's privy chair. I thought if I could
send a message to my mother, if she knew how much I needed
her . . .'' There was a soft sound of boot soles on the carpet

behind her, and Tade's hand feathered over her curls, gently, so gently it seemed to touch her very soul. She wanted to lean back into the comfort his body offered, seek solace in the feel of his heartbeat, the warmth of his skin, but she dared not close the tiny space between them for fear that he would ease away from her, taking away the wonder of sharing . . . actually sharing her feelings with another human being.

"You sent your mother a message?" He prodded gently.

"I thought I did. I stole a little cannikin from the kitchen, put a note inside it, and set it afloat down the stream. I watched the road every day, waiting for her to come. But of course she never did." Maryssa closed her eyes, arching her head back. "I hated her then, Tade. Hated her. And she— she lay dead."

"No." Rough-edged with emotion, his denial caressed her, soothed her. "You just . . . hurt. I don't think you even know what hate is." His hands drew her back against him, turning her so slowly it seemed as though she were moving in a dream. The face that had been so rakishly handsome with its devilish grin now held all the solemn beauty of a pagan god, his eyes blazing with emotions she had painted onto the faces of a dozen treasured heroes.

Her breath caught in her throat as his head dipped nearer, the intensity radiating from his taut body touching her before the first tentative brush of flesh upon flesh. He hesitated, bare heartbeats that seemed to stretch into forever, his gaze gently drifting to her mouth. Then he touched her, lips firm and warm as satin ghosting across her temples, the fragile curve of her eyelid, her tiny, delicate nose. Warm and moist, he brushed, just brushed, his mouth across hers in a kiss of such aching sweetness Maryssa's eyes filled with tears.

He lifted his mouth from hers, and Maryssa felt the faint roughness of his fingertips skimming her cheeks, gathering the droplets clinging to her lashes.

"Maura, you're so sweet . . . so soft . . . ," he murmured. "By Saint Michael, I feel I might crush you if I . . ." He buried his hands in her hair, his mouth taking hers with barely leashed hunger, urgent, yet gentle, as though he half expected she would bolt at his touch. Surprise shot through Maryssa at the first sweep of his tongue on her mouth, shock changing to raw pleasure as her lips parted and he slipped inside, stroking the rim of her teeth, before he delved for the deeper secrets within.

She whimpered as his tongue caressed her, wooed her, feeding fires that sluiced through her like melting honey. He crushed her against his chest, the brass buttons on his waist-coat pressing into the soft mounds of her breasts, his heart hammering against hers until she could feel the throbbing pulses in every fiber of her being. Lean and hard, his legs burned her through her night rail, the thin cloth doing nothing to hide every sinew and swell of muscle.

Of their own volition Maryssa's hands smoothed up the bronze cords of his neck, slipping back to tangle in the rough satin of his hair, her fingers tugging the thick waves free of their leather thong. Her tongue met Tade's, timidly at first, then more boldly, the pleasure-sound vibrating low in his throat, sending jolts of flame flicking through her stomach and thighs.

"Maryssa," he groaned into her mouth. "So sweet . . ." The hard heat of his palm coasted up her waist, and she felt it take in her breast as though it were a priceless treasure. She pulled back just a whisper, the shattering sensation of delight seeming too great to bear, but Tade's arm clamped around her, forcing her back into his caress with an urgency that stunned her.

"Maura, let me . . ." Tremors shook Maryssa's body as his thumb skimmed the dusky rose peak of her nipple through the fabric, his other hand slipping free the ribbons that held her night rail in place. His lips seared a path to the base of her throat, the feel of his mouth moving on her skin filling Maryssa with a wonder such as she'd never known.

"Tade . . ." She whispered his name, flinging her head back to allow him better access to the sweet mysteries he sought. The ties fell open beneath his fingers, and his mouth trailed down to where the delicate swell began, his hand eas-ing away the thin veiling to capture the creamy flesh within.

"So lovely . . . perfect . . ." He guided her back until she felt the feather bed against her thighs, then gently tipped her into its welcoming softness.

Then he was beside her, his tongue seeking the fragile rose crest of her breast in a tender fervor that spiraled ecstasy to the center of her soul. The tiny cry that breached her lips

made him break the sweet contact, pull away to look down
at her, eyes heavy with desire. His jaw clenched, and she
could sense he had torn himself away because he thought her
cry was a plea for him to stop. "Moving too fast," he rasped.
"But you . . . God, I want you—"

"Tade . . ." His name was barely a breath upon her lips
as she reached trembling fingers to trace the firm, perfectly
molded lips, his aristocratic nose, the hard curve of his jaw.
"Tade, please . . . ," she quavered. "I need . . ." She pulled
his face down to her, closing her eyes in exquisite pleasure
as his lips closed over the hardened bud of her nipple, taking
what she offered.

He ripped his mouth away from the soft mound, thrusting
his tongue deep into the welcoming sweetness of her mouth.
His tongue soothed, circled, worshiped, his hand tunneling
under her rump to pull the gentle rise of her stomach full
against the hardness swelling between his thighs. He parried
and plundered, branding as his own that which no man had
tasted. Maryssa buried herself in him, in the feel of him, the
taste of him—reckless, dangerous, incredibly sweet.

Almost desperately, she sought the neckcloth at his throat,
tearing it open with hands that trembled. Tade's breath hissed
through his teeth as her fingertips brushed his chest, her hands
curling in the crisp hairs roughening the muscled plane.

"Maura . . . oh, God, I have to—" His mouth ravaged
hers as he rolled her beneath him on the soft bed, devouring
her lips with a raging hunger that should have frightened her
but only served to drive the wild passions roiling through her
veins higher, ever higher.

She whimpered, digging her fingers in the satin-sheathed
steel of his shoulders and the bulging muscles of arms, rigid
with need. His palms swept up, catching her chin to mold
her lips into his kiss. As his fingers tightened on the fragile
curve, Maryssa cried out, pain knifing through her jaw.

"What the—" Tade yanked his head back, the night air
chilling her, deprived of the heat of his touch. She tried vainly
to recapture his mouth with hers, her passion-drugged senses
craving still more of the magic he worked upon her flesh. But
Tade tore away from her, bolting upright to snatch one of the
tapers from the candle holder beside the bed and thrust it
near her cheek. Fingers so gentle they seemed but the brush

of wind probed the swelling. She saw his eyes widen, then narrow, glinting with menacing fury. *"What the hell happened to your face?"*

The dream world he had spun around her shattered, and Maryssa struggled up from the tumbled feather bed, fear at Tade's anger and shock at her own wanton behavior firing her cheeks as she tugged her night rail over her exposed breasts. Her gaze fastened on the carpet.

"Damn it, tell me who did this. I swear to God, I'll—" A sudden noise in the hall outside made the threat freeze on Tade's lips. Every muscle in his body snapped wire-taut and alert, his eyes so savage they seemed to burn through the wood panel of the door.

"Tade, what—"

"Quiet!"

Maryssa flinched at the whispered command, then her stomach plummeted to her toes as she heard purposeful strides bearing down on her room. Blood drained from her face in a dizzying rush as a gruff voice some distance away barked out an order. "Father!" she croaked. "Oh, my God!"

Her eyes, wide and frightened, found Tade's, and she could see the realization of the truth dawn in his face. Raw fury darkened his eyes until they glittered like shattered emeralds. "It was him. Wylder. He did this to you!"

Tade wheeled toward the door, the waves of hair tangling loose about his rage-taut face giving him the primal, savage look of a Celtic warrior hurling himself into battle. A stab of fear pierced Maryssa as he reached for the door latch. She threw herself in front of him, blocking his path. "No, Tade," she pleaded, clutching his fists. "You cannot—"

"The devil I can't! By God, I'll break every bone in that bastard's body."

"The castle is alive with servants! They'd see you dead before you could land so much as a blow! For the love of God, please— He's my father!" Desperately she groped for some way, any way to stop Tade as she saw the deadly purpose harden in his face. He yanked his hands free, his palms slamming into the heavy panel. "Bolted!" Tade spun around. "That bastard locked you—"

A thud in the hall outside, followed by a savage curse tore a sob from Maryssa's throat, the memory of her father's face when he had heard the name Kilcannon filling her with terror, not for herself, but for the bold, angry man before her. "Tade, if they find you with me, they might link me to Devin's escape, arrest me for aiding a criminal—"

"Damn it, they'd never—" His eyes flicked from the door to her face, and she could see him waver. Tears spilled down her cheeks, shaking fingers reaching up to touch his granite jaw.

"Tade! Oh, God, Tade, please go!"

His own hands tangled in her hair, and she could see the raw emotion in his eyes. "All right, damn it. For you. Maura, if you ever need me"—he yanked the loosened neckcloth from his throat and shoved it into her hand—"if you ever need me, send this to the cottage. I'll come, if I have to ride through hell itself." His mouth came down on hers with savage intensity.

Tade's lips clung to hers just an instant as the footsteps stopped outside the door, then he ripped them away and lunged toward the window. He swung his lean legs over the sill, then lowered himself until only his head and shoulders were visible in the moonlight.

"Maura, I want you to know. Dev, he's no murderer, no thief." The scrape of the bolt being thrown back made Maryssa shove at Tade's shoulders in desperation.

"Go! Just—"

"Maura, Dev is a priest."

The crystal green of Tade's eyes probed hers for just an instant. Then he was gone. A hundred nightmare visions of priests hunted, tortured, and killed flashed through Maryssa's mind, horrible deaths described by Ascot Dallywoulde with fanatic glee in a dozen different drawing rooms.

She wheeled and shoved Tade's neckcloth beneath the pillow as the bedchamber door slammed open.

Six

A DOZEN BLAZING CANDLES spilled light from the drawing
room onto the marble tiles of the hall outside, the bubbling
laughter and snatches of lively chatter beyond the arched entryway seeming to tumble past the stone griffins as well, making Maryssa want to flee from the shelter of the corridor back
to the safety of her shadow-veiled room.

She peeped through the doorway, her face hot with dread
and discomfort as she glimpsed the room beyond. It was as
if the scene had been torn from the sketchbook of some elegant miss; the slender woman within might have been drawn
from some young swain's ideal. The pink satin and silver lace
robing the young woman's delicate form rustled appealingly
from the velvet-covered stool before the harpsichord, which
was just visible in the center of the room. Elegantly powdered
curls bobbed enchantingly above fingers that had just finished
a lively fugue. And as the strains of a minuet filled the room,
laughter trilled from lips as red as ripe cherries.

Maryssa's hand fluttered up to the garish handkerchief
knotted at her breast, its pumpkin and pink stripes making
her feel like an overblown poppy in a field of pristine lilies.

She tugged at her quilted petticoat, wishing she could pluck
one of the fat violet feathers embroidered across its front and

sweep away the sly-faced peacocks that spattered the skirt. Their sharp beaks parted to mock her, the orange eyes seeming to gloat that even Lady Dallywoulde's exclusive coterie had been unable to clothe her suitably.

She winced inwardly as her father's gruff voice cut into the strains of music, but the woman's laughing reply was lost to Maryssa as the brusque rejoinder was eclipsed by the memory of his words the night before.

She had quaked in the breeze from the open window, terrified that Tade Kilcannon's presence in her chamber had been discovered, or that at the very least, the fiery blush of her cheeks would stir her father's keen suspicion. But Bainbridge Wylder had spared her not a glance, merely stalking to the fruitwood wardrobe along the west wall and flinging it open to eye its sparse contents with contempt.

"It seems I have no choice but to allow you to make a spectacle of yourself tomorrow," he had snapped. "Dalton Marlow's son is dragging his bride over to make your acquaintance, there being a shortage of suitable companions hereabout for chits of your station. Not that Christabel Marlow will accept you as any but another clumsy wench she must suffer, once she sees you."

He had yanked out a gown the color of rotting squash, clumps of silk violets clinging to its bodice like plump beetles. With an oath, he had spun around, jabbing the gown in Maryssa's face.

"God's teeth, you label this monstrosity fit garb? My coin would be better spent if I pulled a crofter's daughter off my lands and sent her to the most costly dressmaker in London!"

"No doubt her tastes would run more pleasing than Lady Dal—" Maryssa had bitten off the retort as her father threw the offending garment to the floor and yanked the few remaining gowns from their pegs.

"Damnation! These rags are fit for nothing but the fire!" He had bent over, fishing the peacock-fouled gown from the pile on the rug. "I suppose Miss Christabel will be forced to meet you when you look like you've just battled the aviary at Saint-Denis," he had said. "You will don this . . . thing . . . and join us in the drawing room tomorrow promptly at two. And, by God, mark that you give me no cause to hide my head."

The final flourish of the harpsichord jerked Maryssa to the present, a round of enthusiastic applause from somewhere in the room making the pink-clad woman sweep gracefully off the stool into a curtsy. The sound of Bainbridge Wylder's clipped praises mingled with a young, hearty laugh, nearly drowned out yet another voice, its tones vaguely familiar, and somehow disturbing. She searched her memory for where she had heard it, but as the young woman beside the harpsichord turned, all thought of the others in the room fled. Maryssa's nails dug into one hideous peacock's neck as Christabel Marlow's sweetly dimpled face came into view above the foil of silver lace gracing her pale green underbodice. Maryssa started to stumble backward, wanting only to retreat, but the round blue eyes in that perfect, delicate face caught hers, the bowed pink lips tipping into a smile.

In a cloud of rustling beauty, Christabel hurried from the room, both hands outstretched to clasp Maryssa's hand warmly. The wide eyes took no note of the awful handkerchief or gown, but danced an open welcome as she said in a rush, "Miss Wylder . . . Maryssa, you have no idea how fortunate you are! You've just escaped my plunking out the musical pieces your father requires each time I entomb myself in these dreary walls. Now, if you can contrive some way to escape performing, perhaps we can chase these gentlemen into the library to tip their bottle of brandy so we can get acquainted."

Christabel struck the back of one hand to her forehead in a dramatic pose. "Horses and hurling! Faith, if I have to endure Reeve spouting off the bloodlines of his mares but once more, I shall be driven to commit murder!"

"There is only one mare whose bloodlines I am interested in at present." Maryssa started at the sound of a voice at her side. Tearing her gaze from Christabel, she stared at the man who had drawn alongside them to slip his arm about the slim satin-robed waist.

"Reeve!" Christabel's elbow flashed out, digging into his blue-velvet coat, her face, beneath its powdered curls, flushing beguilingly. The man, who stood a full three inches shorter than Christabel, sketched a bow, the smattering of freckles dusting his short nose spoiling the aura of solemn courtesy he was trying to affect.

"Enchanted, Miss—" Surrendering the effort, he allowed his wide mouth to split into a grin. "In case you hadn't guessed, my name is Reeve Marlow, the poor unfortunate who has taken it upon himself to keep this baggage out of mischief."

"To keep *me* out of—" Christabel gave him a playful shove. "I was never *in* any mischief until I met you, Reeve Marlow, and Mama vows that since the first time you asked me to dance I've not been *out* of it! Now that Maryssa is here, you may be sure I intend to lead you as merry a chase as you and your rakehell friends have led me these past months!"

Reeve wriggled sandy-blond eyebrows at Maryssa. "You see what a termagant she is? I'm trying my best to get her with child, in hope that my sons will tame her a bit."

Maryssa's cheeks burned, but instead of shrinking back, horrified at Reeve's bluntness, she smiled as Christabel squealed.

"Sons, hah! With my luck I'll have a score of daughters and we'll be driven to the poorhouse paying for buttermilk to fade their freckles!"

With a laugh, Reeve tugged on one powdered curl, leaning over to plant a sound kiss on her lips. "Daughters, sons, it matters not to me, so long as we have a dozen."

He turned to Maryssa, his hazel eyes skimming her face. He reached out, brushing one short finger over her nose as easily and affectionately as if they had known each other all their lives. "Welcome to Ireland, Maryssa," he said, with a sudden gentleness that surprised her. "You are every bit as sweet as I had heard."

Puzzlement stirred in Maryssa as Christabel gave Reeve a warning glance, but her curiosity was quelled by the sound of a throat being cleared in the entryway. Maryssa looked up to see the daunting figure of Bainbridge Wylder framed in the arch, his broad face wearing an astonishingly benign expression. Shock jolted through Maryssa when her father's mouth almost—*almost*—softened into a smile as his gaze strayed to the dainty Christabel. Then he turned, glaring back into the drawing room. "Well, man? Are you going to lurk behind me all day?"

A sick feeling knotted in her stomach as a familiar squat

form stepped into the hall. Sly, beady eyes pierced hers as Colonel Quentin Rath strode toward her, pushing past the Marlows. "I advise you not heed Mr. Marlow's flattery, Miss Wylder," he said, his thick lips twisting into an ingratiating smile. "Marlow is much practiced in weaving false tales and twisting the truth to suit his purposes." Rath swept her a low bow, grasping her hand in one sweaty paw. Maryssa tried to pull her fingers away, but he tightened his grip, turning her palm upward to plant a wet kiss in its center.

"C-Colonel Rath—" Maryssa felt her gorge rise as the blunt tip of his tongue touched her skin. She yanked her hand out of his bone-crushing grip, fighting the urge to dash up the stairs to her washbasin and bury her hand in lye soap. Grasping the embroidered tailfeather of a peacock, she scrubbed Rath's spittle from her palm with the folds of her gown.

"So you have already had the *pleasure* of meeting our *sincere* Colonel Rath?" The bite beneath Christabel's musical voice cut like a velvet-sheathed razor. Maryssa's gaze darted up, the patent dislike radiating between Christabel and the stout colonel obvious as they faced each other.

"Charming, as ever, Mistress Marlow," Rath said, flicking an imaginary bit of lint from his violet damask waistcoat. "You may be sure I am most sincere where Miss Wylder is concerned." His eyes shifted to the kerchief at Maryssa's bosom, and she cringed as the point of his tongue peeked from between his lips. "I have merely come to request the privilege of showing her about the countryside in my carriage. But, stake me, I'm half afraid every fowl in Ireland will try to attach itself to her gown."

Maryssa's face flamed at Rath's loud guffaw, but Christabel had already darted between them, bristling like a mother tigress. "You need not concern yourself, Colonel. Reeve and I have already asked Maryssa to join us for a drive this afternoon, and she has accepted. We intend to keep her occupied for quite some time."

Maryssa's mouth fell open, but her stunned reply was silenced by Bainbridge Wylder's impatient voice.

"You may occupy my daughter as much as you can bear to, Mistress Marlow, providing you teach her some manners, and"—he rolled his eyes heavenward—"please God, a trifle of decent taste! Now, if Maryssa will deign to join us, we might yet take our tea before it turns to ice.''

"I vow, I am so starved, I scarce have the strength to reach the tea cakes!" Christabel flashed Bainbridge an overbright smile, slipping her hand into the crook of his arm. "If you will aid me, Mr. Wylder?''

Maryssa felt warm fingers touch her sleeve as Reeve Marlow cut in front of the infuriated Rath, nearly causing the colonel to pitch over the heel of one glistening morocco shoe. Reeve grinned at her, his lips a bit more taut than she remembered. "Your father always filches my wife when we are at Nightwylde. May I have the honor?" He offered her his arm, and Maryssa laid her fingers upon his blue velvet sleeve. "You cannot imagine what a relief it will be for me to serve as escort to a lady who is not constantly chiding me to straighten my neckcloth!" he said, the freckles dashed across his nose seeming almost to dance as he bent to whisper: "And as for the drive we will take after tea—let me assure you, it will prove most entertaining."

"Hurling? Entertaining? Pah!" Christabel flung over her shoulder. "The only thing that will make it bearable is having Maryssa along. And Reeve—your neckcloth . . .''

"Christ's blood, how does she do it?" Reeve's hazel eyes widened, his other hand clamping on the lawn frills tumbling in disorder down his shirtfront. "I swear, she could hear me tip a mug of ale all the way in Derry."

"And I could hear your bed curtains rustle if you sailed clear to Cathay." As if suddenly realizing what she had said, Christabel gave a tiny gasp, and Maryssa could see her suck in her breath until her stays threatened to burst.

"I had quite an . . . er . . . shall we say varied youth before I met Christabel." Gold-green lights twinkled in Reeve's eyes as he caught Maryssa's gaze and nodded toward his wife's back. The delicate ivory of her neck had washed a hue more pink than her dress. Horrified blue eyes dared a glance over one satin-clad shoulder, and Maryssa saw Reeve kiss his fingertips and hold them toward Christabel as though they offered a gift. His puckish face was solemn, serious for just an instant, and Maryssa felt a jab of loneliness at the love that flowed between them.

If Tade Kilcannon ever looked at her so, bantered with her

in that bawdy, yet tender way . . . Maryssa's own cheeks flushed, the memory of his lips tasting her breasts filling her with splendorous yet terrifying wonder. *Sweet . . . so lovely . . . perfect . . .* He had touched the core of her soul with his words, awakened her body with touches that both blessed and tormented. And then he had disappeared back into the mountains from whence he had come. Never to be seen again? "Tade." Maryssa started, suddenly aware she had whispered the name aloud.

"Did you say 'plate' ?" Rath stalked up beside her, eyes narrowed suspiciously.

"No," Maryssa stammered, fear stabbing through her. "I . . . I mean, yes."

"Can you not see the poor girl is nigh wasted with hunger? 'Tis no wonder she is begging for food," Reeve quipped. He turned to her, smiling gently. "I am afraid you'll have to wait until we arrive at the banquet, little one," he said gently.

Maryssa's gaze dropped to the carpet in embarrassment, but not before they noticed something odd in Reeve Marlow's face. The boyish hazel eyes had not been bent upon the table, groaning beneath its platters of steaming cakes, but rather had roved outward to the wild, sweet Donegal mountains that whispered fey secrets through mullioned windowpanes.

Maryssa sank back against the cushions lining the Marlows' open cart, feeling very like a piece of paste jewelry suddenly thrust into the company of a diamond chain. The interior of moss-green velvet, jealously tended yet still whispering of its age, only served to make Christabel glitter more brightly as the miles rolled away beneath them. Her sincere, winning smile and affectionate ways caused Maryssa to envy the easy self-assurance that allowed this young woman to laugh aloud, to bandy words with Reeve. And when Christabel scooped up Maryssa's hand, squeezing it in delight as she gestured to a tawny-gold doe bounding through the trees, it was not at the deer Maryssa stared, but, rather at the first girl of her own age who had ever offered her friendship.

As envy prickled Maryssa it dissolved back into gratitude, for with each loving gibe, both Marlows took care to draw her into their banter, bidding her take their part in outrageous mock quarrels, listening intently to each comment she dared offer, surrounding her in their welcoming laughter.

In spite of herself, Maryssa kept watching Christabel's animated features, waiting for some subtle sign of the disdain she had experienced from the bevies of *haut ton* belles she had met in her months with Lady Dallywoulde, but there was an almost pugnacious acceptance in the face shadowed beneath Christabel's bobbing hat brim, as though she dared the wind itself to cut through the protective shield she was weaving about Maryssa.

Even the landscape that had terrified but days before now held fascination for Maryssa, its jagged rocks and untamed hills a dangerous, beckoning beauty—as dangerous and beckoning as the man who had torn her from its deadly grasp but two days before. Tade . . . Her hand tightened in the folds of her gown, embarrassment firing her cheeks as she felt her lips tingle in remembrance of his kiss.

"And just what or whom are you thinking of, Maryssa Wylder?" A sprig of leaves plucked from a low-hanging branch plopped into her lap, and Maryssa glanced up to where Reeve sat perched on the cart seat. His eyes twinkled, his imp's face more boyish than ever as he thrust his chest out with an air of wounded dignity that sent Christabel into a fresh spate of giggles. "Ever since we passed that bend in the road, you have been staring into the wilds as though you expect Brian Boru himself to dash out on a destrier and carry you away," Reeve complained. "And here I have been trying to instruct you in the finer points of hurling—"

"No wonder Maryssa has been staring off into the woods! Heaven knows I would sooner watch a spider's web catch dust than listen—"

"To the greatest hurler ever born recount his feats of daring?" Looping the reins around the whip socket, Reeve scooped up the heavy curved stick he had nestled so carefully beside him and brandished the hurley as though threatening an imaginary foe. Maryssa braced her feet against the floorboards, her fingers clenching on the cart's black-painted rim as the bay mare missed a step, ears flattening back in the age-old sign of equine displeasure. But instead of bolting pell-mell into the thinning woods, the beast merely shook her trappings, trotting on as though well accustomed to her master's antics.

Maryssa pulled her eyes away just in time to see Christabel wrinkle the end of her pert nose. "The greatest hurler ever born, is it?" she teased. "I shall be sure to insist that your opponents treat you with more respect from now on. I am certain that last week when you were sprawled on the ground—"

"That great clumsy oaf! Ran right over me. But this time the blackguard will regret his carelessness!"

Reeve parried with the hurling stick, wielding it with all the dash of a cavalier facing off in a duel. He swept Maryssa a deep bow, arching one brow in roguish expectation.

She smiled. "I must confess, I almost feel sorry for whomever you intend to . . . to hurl with that thing."

Christabel dissolved into fits of merriment. Reeve, scarcely able to speak through his laughter, scrubbed tears from his eyes with the edging of lace at his cuff. "Oh . . . Maryssa," he gasped. "You are a joy. The wretch I intend to 'hurl' is a black-hearted scoundrel I've been plagued with since we were scarce breeched. But after today"—Reeve smacked one palm with the seasoned curve of ash-wood—"I vow the rapscallion will never take to the field again."

Christabel heaved a teasing sigh. " 'Twill be a pity, Reeve, when your 'scoundrel' falls. Once you trounce him, I much doubt you'll find another full-grown man with the relish the two of you share for attempting to kill each other over a stupid ball." Christabel made a face.

"Stupid ball—" Reeve's gasp of outrage was cut short as, of her own accord, the mare turned down what looked to be merely wheel tracks branching off the road. The cart bounced across a huge rut, Reeve tumbling backward over the cart seat into a heap of flailing arms and legs.

Maryssa gritted her teeth, glancing yet again to the driverless horse, but Christabel, patently unconcerned, was already leaping to her feet in a swirl of pink satin. "Help me, Maryssa," she said, the lace at her breast fairly dancing with breathless laughter. "I shall never be able to haul this great hulk up alone, though it would serve the braggart right if the whole of Donegal saw him thus."

"Christabel, 'tis your fault I'm jammed in here in the first

place,'' Reeve warned, his voice muffled in the frills of his
shirt. ''Maligning my hurling till honor demanded . . .'' He
gave a snort of indignation. ''Help me at once, both of you,
or I'll—''

Maryssa stumbled up, self-conciously taking hold of
Reeve's wrist.

''Pull!'' At Christabel's command, Maryssa tugged, but
the second they tried to yank Reeve upward, he bounded to
his feet with the agility of a frolicsome cat and caught both
women in an exuberant hug. Maryssa tried to keep her balance, but the cart lurched abruptly to a halt and Reeve's momentum tumbled all three down into the cushions. Maryssa
caught a blur of nearby faces silhouetted against a distant
backdrop of trees, then yards of billowing pink fabric descended over her, blotting out the sky.

She struggled to push her way through them, but her overskirt seemed hopelessly snarled in Christabel's hoops which
were snagged on Reeve's waistcoat buttons. Maryssa's cheeks
fired as she felt a buckram lath of her own hoop petticoat bob
against her shoulder, the playful autumn breezes darting beneath its icing of morning gown to nip at the thin undergarments ruffled about her legs.

With stunned horror, she heard teasing voices calling out
greetings to Christabel and Reeve from the cart's rim, inches
from where they all lay sprawled. Maryssa groped vainly for
the hem of her petticoat, the sounds of a brief scuffle followed
by a yelp of indignation drifting through the layers of cloth.
Then, suddenly, large warm hands clasped her waist, plucking her from the tangle as easily as if she were a spring
flower. In one fluid motion her rescuer whisked her over the
black-painted cart edge, turning her to face him as he lowered
her to the ground.

She hardly dared raise her eyes from the wedge of bronzed
chest framed in sharp contrast by the snowy lace that tumbled
midway to the waistband of his breeches. But the well-mus-
cled plane was so familiar . . . the touch of the hands still
lingering upon her waist so sweet . . .

''Plague take you, man!'' a gravelly voice from among the
crowd pressing toward them complained. ''You have had your
arm about every pretty maiden from here to Lough Swilly.

The least you could do is allow me to help this one from the cart.''

"I would not dream of surrendering such a pleasure.'' The rich, silky tones drew Maryssa's eyes to meet Tade Kilcannon's intense green gaze. His eyes brushed downward to her lips, his hands, now hidden beneath the shielding of her cloak, drifted upward a whisper, the sides of his thumbs just skimming the undercurve of her breasts.

"T-Tade—'' Maryssa breathed his name in a choked gasp, her gaze locking on the lean planes of his face. With a laugh Christabel leaped to the ground, Reeve's bootheels slamming into the turf beside her.

"I assume tedious introductions would be a waste of breath, Mr. Kilcannon?'' Christabel's giggle tinkled on the breeze.

Maryssa saw a hint of red brush Tade's cheekbones. He opened his mouth as if to speak, but the delicate face brimming with merry insolence had already vanished in a whirl of powdered curls as Christabel whisked Reeve toward the clearing in a whirlwind of laughter. As if drawn by the ring of gaity surrounding her, the crowd melted toward the field as well, each small group turning once again to their own jests, predictions, and wagerings on the outcome of the day's hurling.

Maryssa stared after Christabel, unable to fathom either this woman who danced through life as though gifted with fairy slippers or the man, Tade, who remained at Maryssa's own side.

Daring a glance up at him, she found him searching her face with an intensity that made her palms grow damp. She swallowed, her voice quavering in her need to fill the weighty silence. "I . . . I wanted to thank you for . . . for returning my clothes last night. I—'' She flushed scarlet as a bewhiskered old woman waddling nearby chortled, her faded brown eyes sparkling with humor within puffy folds of skin. "I mean from when I fell in the lake,'' Maryssa blustered. "I—''

" 'Twas my pleasure.'' The words seemed to lodge low in his throat. "I waited outside on the ledge to make certain you were . . . safe,'' he said quietly, his fingertip tracing the fading bruise along her jaw. "You have been, I trust. Safe, I mean.''

Maryssa's fingers drifted in a self-conscious path to her cheek. "Yes, I . . . I've been quite safe. And how have you fared since . . ." She winced at how foolish she sounded, her cheeks staining berry red as her eyes locked on Tade's mouth.

The image of her wantonness as those warm lips had moved upon her flesh made Maryssa long to pull the ruched edge of her hood over her curls, to secret away both the shame and the longing that she knew must be evident in her face.

"Maura . . ." The name fell like a caress from his lips. " 'Twas all I could do not to bolt back through your window after your father had gone. I wanted to . . ." Green, green eyes trailed past her mouth, breasts, and the curve of her waist. She saw him strain toward her, lips parted, the sinews of his throat standing out in sharp relief against the satiny bronze of his skin. But the sound of muffled tittering nearby made him turn and fix an exasperated glare upon the bevy of lissome peasant girls fluttering past them.

The prettiest among them flounced her skirts above trim ankles, flashing him a blinding smile. "Ye'd best be gettin' yer mind on the game, Tade, lest they make a start wi' out ye," the girl called out.

"They'd hardly start without the greatest hurler since Finn McCool," Tade returned, tapping his chest with his fist with jocular arrogance. "And put your skirts down, Aileen Nolan. You've enough mud on your legs to fill MacConoughy Cave."

The girl yanked her skirts down, her face crumpling with the pettishness of a child caught playing in her mother's finest slippers. "Mayhap I'll be givin' the mud t' Sheena O'Toole," Aileen groused, her black eyes snapping as they flicked to Maryssa. "When she sees what ye're about again she'll probably fix t' bury ye in it."

"And if your ma knew you were mincing around with your skirts past your knees she'd lock you in the loft till you're twenty," Tade flung back. The laughter of the other girls as they skittered on toward the clearing drowned out Aileen's reply, but the name the girl had flung out echoed in Maryssa's mind, its implications reverberating through her like the tones of discordant chime.

From the moment Tade had plucked her from the cart, the eyes of every person about them had been filled either with arch speculation or with a sort of earthy indulgence, as though this same drama had been played out for their amusement time and time again.

Maryssa's whole body seemed ablaze with humiliation as her gaze locked on the ground, the delicate skin he had kissed beneath the lawn of her night rail burning as though he had seared it with a brand.

A man like Tade had no doubt had more than his share of amorous adventures. And it was patent to Maryssa that she had been added to his collection. It was as if Tade had cried his possession to everyone in the clearing, as though he wanted them all to know what he had done to her . . . what she had allowed him to do. And they accepted it as lightly as though she were a wench at one of the bawdy houses she had passed during her stay in London. Yet had she not acted the harlot? Drawing his lips to her—

"Maura?" At the sound of Tade's voice she forced an overbright smile, dragging the tattered remnants of her pride about her battered spirit. She saw Tade's eyes narrow in confusion; then a smile tipped the corner of his lips. His arm slipped through hers with a tenderness that spoke more of cherished treasure than wanton plaything. "Come on," he said with a heart-stopping grin. "There is someone here who I wager will want to see you."

"See me?" Maryssa stammered.

"Aye. To thank you in person for saving her cursed fool neck the night Rath's troopers came."

"Deirdre?"

He didn't answer, merely drew her along beside him, as he called out greetings to the people they passed, pausing in his long-gaited stride to tug little girls' plaits, to tweak the nose of a lad of five playing at hurling with the crooked branch of an oak. "Ye goin' t' grind that bloody Sassenach int' the dirt t'day, Tade?" the waif piped up eagerly.

"Aye, Owen. We'll teach Marlow to take the field against the Irish, eh?"

The child crowed with a glee unsullied by resentment or hate, despite the label of Sassenach he had placed upon Reeve. Maryssa gazed at Tade in a kind of dread-filled curiosity as she was struck by the child's tone—the innate loathing for the

Irish people's oppressors had been oddly absent, replaced, instead by a kind of amused indulgence that surprised her.

"You and—and Reeve . . . ," Maryssa began, attempting to form her confused thoughts into words. "I mean, Reeve's English, but—"

"English?" Tade grinned. "Don't let anyone else hear you say that! They'll call me out for impeaching the blackguard's good name. His great grandda might have marched with Cromwell's army, but in spite of Owen's little gibe, the mountain folk see Reeve, Christa, and all who live in Marlow Hall as nigh Irish as themselves. Since the day the laws were passed forbidding Catholics to own land, the Marlows have held in trust the estates of a dozen Catholics—men who were once nobles in their own land. Old Dalton Marlow never filched so much as a farthing from a one of them, even when his own prospects soured. And Reeve, he's done as much for the people of these glens as any man could have. If my own da had given his holdings into their hands . . ."

Maryssa saw Tade's mouth twist in bitterness for an instant, and then all shadow vanished in a wicked grin. "Of course, even if Reeve Marlow were a candidate for sainthood—which I, as his closest and most abused friend, can assure you he is not—it would fail to save him from being—how did Owen put it?—'ground into the dirt' this day."

Tade wriggled his brows with such obvious relish that Maryssa bit her lip, trying to stem the tide of merriment suddenly threatening to burst forth as they neared the gray bulk of a boulder imbedded in the rim of the clearing. But at that moment Tade's own resonant laughter rang out. His arm swept around her waist, pulling her as tight against his side as yards of petticoats would allow. She leaned against him, reveling in the feel of his warm, hard chest shaking with mirth, his unabashed joy in life releasing something deep inside her.

"For God's sake, look out you clumsy ox!" an irritated voice barked an arm's length from Maryssa's petticoats.

The laughter died in her throat, her gaze darting to where two girls sat ensconced at the flower-ringed base of the boulder.

Deirdre Kilcannon jerked the hem of her petticoat from beneath the toe of Tade's boot. She glared up at Maryssa and

Tade from beside a girl as gold and tawny as a prowling cat and half again as sly.

Maryssa peered but an instant into the girl's amber eyes, then turned her gaze quickly away, stunned to see resentment lurking beneath the long gold lashes.

"Look at what you've done, you disgusting beast!" Deirdre blustered at Tade. Clambering to her feet, she jabbed a finger at a smudge of dirt marring the sky-shaded calico of her gown. " 'Tis the least you could do to watch where you place those great hulking boots of yours."

He grinned at his sister. "A thousand pardons, fair maid," he said. "But the sweetness of your voice and your gentle disposition so blinded me I didn't notice your furbelows were spread out halfway to Derry."

"I doubt you'd have noticed if the pits of hell had opened up before you, the way you were making such a spectacle of yourself," Deirdre huffed. She cast a disparaging glance at Maryssa.

Maryssa swallowed, the joy that had kissed the bright afternoon vanishing, as if someone had driven a fist into her stomach. Guiltily, she attempted to ease away from Tade, but he only tightened his warm fingers on her waist, pulling her closer into the protective circle of his arm.

"Mayhap I *was* making a spectacle of myself," Tade said. " 'Tis a trait that seems to run in our family." His fingers swept soothing circles over the soft fabric shielding Maryssa's ribs. "But all in all 'tis fortunate I nigh killed myself upon your skirts as you are the very person I was seeking. I was certain you'd like a chance to thank Maryssa here for all she did—"

"Thank her?" Deirdre's lips snapped taut as a miser's purse string. Her eyes shot daggers at Maryssa. "I am forever in your debt, Miss Wylder. Your footman managed to return the gown I loaned you so badly stained 'twill be fit for naught but the rag bag."

"I—I'm sorry," Maryssa stammered, her cheeks flaming. "I—I'll see that you get another."

"Damn it, Deirdre." Tade took a menacing step toward her, the warmth of his arm falling away from Maryssa's waist. "If it weren't for Maryssa you'd probably be wrapped in a winding sheet instead of blathering about some blasted dress!''

"Tade's right, Dee.'' The voice was sweet as honeyed acid as the girl at Deirdre's side swept gracefully to her feet. "I know I shall be eternally grateful to Miss Wylder.'' One slender hand trailed a proprietary path down Tade's arm, stopping to toy with a button at his wrist. Maryssa fought the urge to slap the girl's fingers away, amazed at the sudden, fierce delight she took in imagining the shock that would round those slanted amber eyes.

The girl fluttered her lashes at Tade. "If aught had happened to you—any of you—I don't know what I would have done!'' she cooed. " 'Twas truly courageous of Miss Wylder to distract the soldiers. Why, think of how awkward it might have proved had she been discovered, what with Colonel Rath being such a *close friend* of her papa's.''

"If Rath had thought her involved, she would have been in Rookescommon prison with the rest of us,'' Tade hissed under his breath, yanking his arm from the girl's grasp.

Red lips dipped into a seductive pout. "Aye, and wouldn't it have been terrible for Bainbridge Wylder's daughter to suffer so.'' The girl's words pierced a lull in the voices filling the clearing, the high-pitched tones reverberating through the trees.

"Sheena!'' Tade gritted the warning from between clenched teeth, instinctively stepping in front of Maryssa as though to shield her, but it was as if the very sound of Bainbridge Wylder's name held the power to blanket the clearing with a smothering fog. A murmur rippled through the crowd, as quietly menacing as the prickling hairs at the back of a mastiff's neck. Maryssa shrank inside herself as the eyes that had been trained upon her with a kind of negligent indulgence clouded with suspicion and a very real loathing.

Yet, oddly, greater misery jolted through her at the memory of the golden-curled girl smoothing her hand across the muscles of Tade's forearm with the aura of a crowned princess beside her consort. Sheena, Tade had called her. The name the dark-eyed peasant girl had linked with Tade's own. Sheena O'Toole . . .

Warm and rein-hardened, Tade's fingers closed on Maryssa's elbow, but she pulled away from him, a sudden sick feeling clenching in her stomach. She wanted to fly scratching into Sheena O'Toole's smug face, but Maryssa only raised her chin in aching defiance, feeling the eyes of every person in the clearing boring into her.

"It might shock you to know, Miss O'Toole, just how much a Wylder can suffer," Maryssa managed in a voice that quavered.

The girl smiled up at her, venom-sweet. "It might shock *you*, Miss Wylder, to know just how much suffering your father has caused."

They heard the clacking of clog soles striking the rocks that were strewn among the grasses, and then the rustling folds of pink satin swirled into view as Christabel Marlow swept to Maryssa's side. Looping one dimpled arm about Maryssa's waist, Christabel shot Sheena a killing glare.

"Since you seem so concerned about suffering at present, Miss O'Toole, perhaps 'twould be best if you and Deirdre took your seats on the other side of the field. As you well know, I always watch from the top of this boulder, and one can never tell when my clog might slip and bruise a most embarrassing part of someone's anatomy." Christabel gestured to the field, which was now full of men wielding hurleys. "It seems that, except for Tade, the men wait ready to play. If you would settle yourselves . . ."

Deirdre bristled, brows dipping low over her freckle-spattered nose. "But we were here firs—"

"Perhaps it *would* be better at the other side, Dee," Sheena sniffed, puckering her face into a mask of blatant disapproval. "The air around here has grown distinctly unpleasant."

"As have certain dispositions," Christabel said, fixing Deirdre with a reproachful stare.

Thrusting out her lip like a belligerent child, Deirdre spun away, flouncing with the seething Sheena to a point across the clearing as far distant from Christabel and Maryssa as possible.

Clenching her fingers, Maryssa watched the girls' heads bob together, their unintelligible whisperings punctuated with nasty snickers as each sneaked glances back toward the boulder where Maryssa and Christabel stood.

Maryssa lifted her chin, what measure of budding confidence Christabel had managed to give her vanishing in the wake of Deirdre's cutting words and Sheena's achingly familiar waspishness.

"I swear, Tade," Christabel hissed under her breath. "If you marry that vicious hellcat you deserve to have your hide sliced to ribbons."

Maryssa felt a stab of some unnameable emotion twist in her stomach at the fleeting image Christabel's words evoked . . . Tade's long limbs entangled with Sheena's, her hair tumbling in disarray across his naked chest, the curled strands glistening like beaten gold in the light of a guttering candle. The defiant curve frozen on Maryssa's mouth shattered. She sank her teeth into her lip so hard she tasted blood.

"I'd make any wench a poor husband at present, wouldn't you agree?" There was the slightest hint of brooding underlying Tade's voice as his eyes followed his sister's stiff back. Maryssa glanced at his face, then away, surprised at the veiling that hid the emotions that had played upon his face. He seemed to mentally shake himself, then turned to Maryssa, eyes crystal green with concern. A hint of a cajoling smile touched his lips as he sketched her a bow. "Would milady allow me to settle her upon her throne before the match begins?" he asked, feigning the solemn eagerness of a court swain.

Maryssa turned her own eyes to his, struggling valiantly to keep the tears from flooding her lashes. "Th-thank you," she murmured in a cracked voice.

Tade's own lips softened into an expression of such tenderness that her eyes stung. As though she were wrought of fine porcelain, Tade's hands spanned her waist, sweeping her up to set her atop the huge stone. "There, Maura," he said softly, the very name a caress.

Reaching up to her cheek, he brushed back a tendril of dark hair that had escaped its bandings of green ribbons and ivory pins. Hand straying to the wisp of silk woven through her hair, Tade grasped the ribband's edge in strong, bronzed fingers, tugging it gently. Slowly, it slipped free, curling through the sable strands like the fingers of the breeze. "For luck," Tade whispered, pressing the bit of silk to his lips. The sight of his mouth pressed against the ribband still warm from her hair sent a shiver of heat skittering up Maryssa's spine.

"Luck!" Christabel's mutter of disgust filtered through the haze of sensation engulfing Maryssa. She looked down to see her friend's blue eyes still scowling at Sheena O'Toole. "The man'll need a blasted cudgel."

Tade chuckled, swooping Christabel up so abruptly the hem of her gown swished up past dainty azure garters. Her rump smacked down beside Maryssa, barely cushioned by layers of thick petticoats. A ripe oath parted Christabel's dainty lips, stunning Maryssa, but the rest of the delicate beauty's grousing was lost in a cry from the field.

"Quit yer blatherin' an' get out here, Kilcannon, or we'll be startin' wi'out ye!" A stocky man with a shock of walnut-colored hair bellowed. With a wide grin, Tade spun around and saluted the man.

"I'll be happy to annihilate you as soon as I fetch my hurling sticks, Diarmit!" he called. Eyes the exact shade of Maryssa's ribbon flashed her a wink as Tade plopped onto the ground, levering off first one gleaming boot, then the other. His fingertips skimmed the sky-blue embroidered stockings down lean muscled calves, revealing flesh the color of burnt honey and dusted with dark hair. Maryssa felt an odd lightness in her stomach as she stared at one well-shaped foot.

Tade wriggled his toes, and Maryssa's eyes leaped to his face, the flush heating her cheeks not merely from embarrassment. Hastily she dragged her gaze away from that tempting glimpse of flesh, forcing herself to look out across the rocky field where the other players awaited, their feet bared as well. Maryssa winced inwardly as she thought of trouncing about that stone-starred expanse with naught to shield the naked soles of her feet.

"You get accustomed to having your feet sliced to bits." The laughter in Tade's voice drew her gaze back to his face as he retrieved her ribbon from its nest of grass beside his boots.

"I think I'd . . . rather not."

Her hesitant reply drew a burst of ringing laughter from Tade, the sound muffled against the silk of her ribbon as Tade bound the narrow length of silk around one bicep, clamping the ribbon's end in his white, even teeth to pull the knot tight.

Springing to his feet, he tossed them each a kiss, then swung toward the broad expanse of clearing.

He loped to its midst with the careless grace inbred in generations of Arab stallions, muscles rippling beneath the thin fabric of his shirt, the green ribbon waving jauntily in the wind. And even the hostile aura of the crowd had little power to dull the tingling Maryssa felt within her breast as he swept up his hurley, smoothing his palm across it as lovingly as if it were a woman.

"Maryssa"—Christabel touched her arm, nodding toward the field—"you've just made half of Donegal cross-eyed with envy. Nigh every maiden for twenty miles would wear sackcloth on Tuesdays just to have Tade Kilcannon speak to them, let alone wear their token."

"He must have enough ribbons to fill his whole cottage, then," Maryssa said, disappointment stealing over her.

"Nay. I've never once seen him accept one. Until now." Christabel laughed. "But don't expect your Galahad to sweep about doing knightly combat. Hurling puts me more in mind of a band of warring ruffians than a jousting tourney—oh, look!" Christabel cried, pointing to the meadow as the loud smack of wood upon leather echoed through the clearing.

Maryssa gaped, fascinated and terrified as the rock-strewn turf seemed to erupt in a frenzy of slashing sticks. Thick, sinewed arms wielded the hurleys' curved blades with the deadly accuracy of infidels' scimitars, the wooden sticks driving a small leather ball through the air with blinding speed. And at the center of the murderous melee was Tade, his dark hair whipping in the breeze, mouth taut with concentration. Lithe as a great cat, he sprang and dived catching the ball upon the ashen blade with a dancerlike grace that seemed at odds with the mayhem all around him.

The other players seemed but blundering manikins beside him, the opposing team laboring desperately to keep the horsehide-covered sphere out of his reach, his own teammates trying to feed the ball to within range of his hurling stick. The only man on the field who seemed able to match him was so short he was nearly lost to sight amid the towering Irishmen. Yet that seemed the very key to the wiry Reeve Marlow's skill.

The two battled for what felt like an eternity, first one,

then the other stealing control of the ball, but neither man able to break free of the other. Reeve's hair tumbled in a ragged mass about his reddening face, while the thin lawn of Tade's shirt clung damply to the Irishman's broad chest, the planes of his face limned with a glistening of sweat.

For just an instant it seemed Tade's eyes jumped away from the ball. Maryssa felt a smile tug at the corner of her mouth as Reeve's sandy head ducked beneath Tade's outstretched arm, hurling the ball high off his blade with a dexterity that delighted Maryssa.

Christabel squealed, shrieking encouragement with all the delicacy of a street urchin as her husband dashed with the ball toward the end of the clearing. Whoops rang from the team opposing Tade's as Reeve ran toward what appeared to be the goal, but before Reeve could hurl the ball over the crossbar, Tade broke free of the other men as well. He bolted after Reeve, Tade's long strides ludicrous in comparison to the pumping of his opponent's short legs.

Maryssa saw the muscles of Tade's thighs bunch beneath his thin doeskin breeches as he sprang toward the ball, but just as his feet left the ground Reeve slammed to a halt. His foot shot out, hooking Tade's bare ankle. With an oath, Tade crashed to the ground, skidding across the turf on his shirt-front while Reeve merrily hurled the ball over the goal.

Christabel's cries of triumph were deafening, but Maryssa felt a niggling indignation as, with the pride of a David after slaying his Goliath, Reeve bowed to his whooping team-mates.

'' 'Twas not just!'' Maryssa blustered. ''He tripped Tade a-purpose!''

Christabel giggled, giving Maryssa a hug. ''If you plan to watch hurling you'd best get accustomed to it. Especially between Reeve and Tade. I vow they've been attempting to murder each other out there since they were chin high. But I must say, Tade seems a bit off his game today. Unless he starts minding what he's about, they're like to have to cart him home on a litter.''

''A litter? Can they . . . I mean, do they get—''

''Injured?'' Christabel supplied, somber for a moment. ''Sometimes. Sometimes badly. The ball moves so fast, and the sticks . . . you've seen how hard they swing them. Last spring Jamie Scanlon was struck with the ball in his leg, and even now he can scarce hobble about. And Reeve told me once he saw a man—'' Christabel stopped, plucking at the lace on her gown.

Maryssa felt a shiver of dread chill her spine, her gaze locking on the tall, dark Irishman shoving himself up from the turf. ''Don't you get scared? Watching Tade—I mean, Reeve—when he might—''

''No. The best players, men like Tade and my Reeve, have almost an uncanny sense about where the ball is. They may get grazed by it or bruised a bit, but most likely the only thing damaged on your fair knight will be his pride.'' She gave Maryssa's arm a comforting squeeze. '' 'Course, 'tis no wonder the poor man is stumbling about so,'' Christabel said, dimpling. ''I am certain 'tis passing difficult trying to hit the ball when you've one eye upon the edge of the field.''

Stunned at the implication of Christabel's words, Maryssa looked back to where Tade had bent down to retrieve his stick. The green eyes did flash her way for an instant from beneath the arc of arm and sweat-stained shirt. He straightened, and even from a distance Maryssa could sense a sheepishness in his gaze that made her lips tip into a smile. The dread knotting inside her eased as her eyes followed the dauntingly masculine lines of broad shoulders, taut waist, narrow hips—perfectly honed muscles too strong to be cut down by flailing sticks or a small leather-covered ball.

Her smile deepened at the calming thought, then widened into a grin as Reeve sauntered over to Tade and dusted off the dirt clinging to the Irishman's shirtfront with a cocksure air that sent everyone in the clearing into gales of laughter.

Tade's mouth moved as if he was murmuring something under his breath for Reeve alone to hear, but the sprightly Englishman merely danced back to the center of the field, brandishing his hurley as if it were a victor's laurels.

Maryssa let her gaze stray to the faces of those ringing the field, wanting to take this shared lightsomeness into herself and hold it. The thrill of the game and Reeve's comical antics seemed to have banished the resentment she had sensed ever since her father's name had been mentioned, yet as her eyes skimmed about, the happiness she wished to share vanished. For the first time she became aware of the distance separating her and Christabel from the crowd's excited laughter . . . from the people themselves.

It was as if a wind-witch had stolen in with her broom and swept the grass about the boulder free of its spangling of bright-skirted girls and rosy-cheeked mothers. The babes that had gamboled among the wildflowers now skirted the boulder as widely as though it were the lair of some fearsome beast, while their elders sat crowded together on the turf as far away from the boulder's base as the scrubby trees bordering the clearing would allow.

Maryssa fastened her gaze on the hurling match again, her hands balling in her lap. The roars of approval and groans of dismay from the rest of those watching still rang out with every strike of wood on horsehide. Yet as the hour passed, even Christabel's chatter and the magic of Tade Kilcannon's powerful grace as he drove the ball time and again past the goal could not hide the circle of emptiness about her. It pressed in from all sides, crushing her with a loneliness that stung hot and sharp at her eyelids.

The sun had crept halfway across the sky in its afternoon trek to the mountains when Maryssa saw Tade's gaze flick yet again to her face, as it had with increasing frequency during the seemingly endless game.

With each quick glance, the grim concentration that had furrowed his brow had shifted, his mouth pulling down at the corners in an expression of puzzled concern. Crystal green, his eyes locked on hers, clinging but a second before she saw the leather-covered ball, round and hard, slam off the blade of Reeve's stick and hurtle toward Tade with killing speed. Maryssa tried to cry out in warning. Couldn't.

As if he had caught the movement from the corner of his eye, Tade spun at that instant to meet it, swinging his hurley upward. But the ash-wood blade slicing the air never even neared its target. Maryssa stared in horror, a scream strangling her throat as the ball slammed with bone-shattering force into the sweat-sheened plane of Tade Kilcannon's forehead.

Seven

"TADE!" MARYSSA BOLTED to her feet atop the boulder, scarcely aware the name had been torn from her own throat as his dark head snapped back, the momentum of the blow driving him onto the turf with a strength that slammed the breath from his lungs. Rough-edged curses erupted from the field as hurling sticks were flung aside. Countenances that had been fierce with competition bare seconds ago were now taut and pale as the men dashed toward the tall figure sprawled on the ground.

Maryssa's fingernails gouged deep into her palms as she fought to see past the other hurlers closing in about Tade, but she caught only glimpses of lawn shirt and doeskin breeches through the maze of legs—Tade's shirt and breeches, and the blanched face of Reeve Marlow as he shoved his way through the circle of men.

"For God's sake, get out of the way, you dolts!" Reeve's worried shout split the air as his sandy head disappeared beneath the sea of broad shoulders. "The blasted man has to breathe!"

The words seemed to clutch, viselike about Maryssa's throat. Breathe! Dear God, was Tade—no!

Oblivious to the throng all around Tade, to the boulder's

rough edges slicing her palms, Maryssa scrambled to the ground. She heard Christabel call out, heard the clack of clogs against stone as her friend followed her, but Maryssa paused not an instant as she dashed onto the field with a speed she had not known she possessed.

The thick layers of her gown were scooped high in her knotted fists, the clumsy pattens on her shoes tilting crazily on the uneven ground, as she plunged through the others hurrying onto the field. But even the resentful murmurs and hissed oaths of those she passed could not slow her. Slamming her hands against broad backs and crooked arms, she pushed her way through the men still ringing their fallen comrade.

The sight that met her eyes when she at last broke through the tall shielding of bodies drove a spike deep into the pit of her stomach. His impish freckled face drawn into a scowl, Reeve Marlow bent over Tade, while Tade—vital, laughing Tade with his devilish smile and soul-melting kiss—lay death-still on the grass, the dark waves of his hair clinging to a face robbed of all color, the rich curls of his lashes fanning out in half circles on the crests of his cheeks. With a tiny cry, Maryssa crumpled to the ground beside him, drawing his dark head into the pillow of her lap.

She choked out a sob, smoothing the waving strands of hair back from pale, cold skin, the feel of slight beard stubble abraiding her palms, the scent of him, warm and alive, taunting her as she stroked the face that had tormented her dreams this past night.

"Tade . . . ," she quavered, raising tortured eyes to the man bending over him. "Oh, God, Reeve is he—"

"No!" Reeve snapped. "Damn you, Kilcannon, I didn't hit you that hard!"

"Beau'ful."

The wisp of a word was so soft it was nearly lost in the ragged edges of Reeve's voice. Maryssa's stunned gaze darted down to where Tade's head lay pillowed in the nest of her skirts.

Heavy lashes fluttering to half-mast, Tade's unfocused eyes turned up, pausing at the rounded undercurves of breasts inches from his mouth before laboriously rising to her face. Lips that had been so still twitched into a grin. " 'Ryssa," he slurred, burrowing the back of his head deeper into her lap with a contented sound. " 'S beau'ful. C' stay 'ere f'ever.''

"T-Tade?" She leaned over him to catch his murmured words, cradling his face in her arms. "Are—are you hurt? Are you—"

"Mmmm, won'ful." His eyes drooped closed and he gave a sated sigh. "Won'ful," he whispered. "If . . . if you'd—"

"If I'd what, Tade?"

The moist heat of his breath stirred the lace edging the low neckline of her gown, his words so soft she could scarcely hear him. "If you'd jus' bend . . . a little . . . lower."

In a flash his head swept up, warm lips catching hers in a quick, sweet kiss.

Maryssa jerked upright, hot fire staining her cheeks as if his mouth had burned her, horrified that the people crowding near had seen. But the only hint of humor lay in Tade's own mouth, its sensual lines tipped into a wry, wobbly grin. Eyes that had been clouded with confusion now peered up at her, a touch of their old devilment sparkling in their green depths.

She dumped his head out of her lap, taking self-righteous pleasure in his grimace of pain as the back of his head thunked onto the ground.

"Tade Kilcannon," she sputtered, "you . . . you—" Maryssa's indignant tirade was cut short by a raw curse from somewhere in the crowd, the people nearest her falling away as if an ax blade had been driven between them.

Maryssa looked up, the ire coursing through her tightening into a thin band of fear as she stared into the enraged countenance of Kane Kilcannon. Rust-colored brows slashed over narrowed eyes. His warring-king features were twisted in a way that would have turned the stoutest heart coward. And even the sight of Devin's gentle, troubled face beneath a veil of homespun hood could not still the quaking inside her at the wrath in Kane's sharp eyes. Maryssa swallowed, her mouth going dry.

A flash of pink skirts swirled toward her behind a glimpse of stocky legs as Reeve jumped over Tade's outstretched limbs to stand at her side. She felt Tade struggling upright, heard

Reeve's placating voice break in, "Good morrow, Mr. Kilcannon, sir, we were having a bit of hurling when Tade—"

"Damn you to hell, I can see just exactly what my son's been having a bit of!" Kane spat, his mouth contorting in disgust. Maryssa cringed as the elder Kilcannon's eyes swept over her with the same blatant aversion he would accord the lowliest doxy at Hell's Gate. "Bainbridge Wylder's little—"

"Da!" Tade bit out the warning in a voice surprisingly clear, the lines about his mouth whitening as he gained his feet. One hand reached down, grasping Maryssa's icy fingers to draw her up, and she could feel the slight unsteadiness still gripping him. "Da, I was struck with the ball. Maryssa just—"

"Maryssa, is it? I had no idea the heir Kilcannon had taken to calling Sassenach thieves by their first names."

Maryssa took an involuntary step back, wanting only to be free of the scathing hatred in Kane Kilcannon's face and the rumble of agreement from the crowd, but Tade's fingers tightened around hers, his face snapping taut with challenge.

"And I had no idea you put so little value on the life of your son."

"Don't you dare to—"

"To what? Remind you that we owe her Devin's life? Nay, not only Dev's but our own as well? Tell me, Da, what comfort would your damned stiff pride be with Devin under the hoodsman's knife?"

"And what comfort will your cursed dalliance be when Bainbridge Wylder strings you from his stable rafters for trifling with his daughter? Think you even Wylder has not heard of your many conquests?" A hot flush of humiliation stained Maryssa's cheeks as Kane's lip curled in disdain. "Sweet Christ, you've made yourself as legendary for your dalliances as English Charles."

Tade's jaw hardened to granite. "What I did or did not do in the past has naught to do with Maryssa."

"Damn it, Tade, look at her!" Maryssa flinched as Kane's hand shot out and clenched around her chin with a bruising grip. "She's a Wly—"

"I don't give a damn if she is child to the devil himself," Tade snarled, knocking loose his father's hand with a sav-

agery that stunned the older man. "Don't ever lay hands on
her like that again, or by God I'll forget you're my father."

"Aye, and you'll forget what her bastard father did . . .
what he stole from—"

"Damn it, Da, *enough*!" Green eyes, dangerous as splintered emeralds, shifted to Devin, then moved in a glaring
path to the throng surrounding them in uncomfortable silence. "Get him home, Dev," Tade grated. "There'll be no
more hurling this day."

Maryssa felt one hard arm encircle her waist in a grip that
seemed to dare her to balk as Tade spun her toward the Marlows' cart and stalked through the crowd of gaping peasant-
folk like a raging Caesar. Deirdre's face flashed past among
the crowd, her freckled cheeks streaked with tears, her eyes
spitting reproach and hatred as Tade paused to snatch up his
boots. Maryssa shrank inwardly, eyes blurred with tears of
hurt and humiliation as she dared a glance up at Tade's rage-
taut face.

The mouth that an hour ago had been tossing jests with
Reeve was now set in a grim line; the eyes that had shone
the warm green of a sun-kissed glen glared straight ahead,
burning with a fury that both frightened Maryssa and tugged
at something deep in her soul.

She wanted to smooth her fingers over his lips, soften them
into a smile. She wanted to bury herself in her room, never
to curse anyone with her presence again. Dear God, what had
she done? For nineteen years she had endured her father's
hatred and the scorn of those around her. For nineteen years
she had been alone. But this man wore his family's love about
him like an aged mantle, its folds mellowed with security,
faith, and a thousand cherished memories.

And in a single afternoon she had somehow ripped it from
him. The cart from which Tade had teasingly plucked her but
an hour before swam in front of her eyes, the cheery cushions
a mockery as he swung her back up into their softness. She
shrank into the worn velvet as he vaulted in beside her, his
athlete's body tense as a coiled whip.

Through a haze of tears Maryssa saw Reeve settle Christabel on the driver's bench, then clamber up himself. Hazel
eyes, dark with concern, slanted over his shoulder. "Tade,
shall we—"

"Drive, damn it!"

Maryssa winced at the harsh tones, feeling the relentless clenching and unclenching of Tade's white-knuckled fists on his thighs as if his fingers were tightening around her own flesh. The sympathy she saw as Christabel turned toward her, then quickly away, tore at her heart.

Why? Maryssa wanted to scream as the cart jolted into motion. What hideous trait lurks within me that drives people to hatred? That harms those I love? Why did I dare to taste happiness even for an hour?

She shut her eyes, remembering Tade's smile dancing up at her as he bound her ribbon about his arm, remembering the feel of his arm against her waist, the mischief in his grin as he had stolen the kiss. And now she had somehow tainted his life as well, sullying the love that had bound him to his sister and his father.

"Tade," she whispered through trembling lips.

His face angled down at her, dark brows slashed in sharp relief against his forehead. Maryssa winced inwardly at the angry bruise purpling his sleek bronzed flesh. Her gaze dropped to her hands.

"I . . . 'Tis time I went home. I—"

"No!" She flinched at his sharp reply, tears beading the corners of her eyes, then spilling free. One bronzed fist unclenched, stealing up to her cheek, gentle, so gentle. "No."

"But . . . but your father—"

"Is an old man nursing wounds that have naught to do with you."

"But don't you see? They have everything to do with me. You love him and he loves you, and because of me you were . . . were raging as if you . . . you hated each other . . ."

"Maura—"

"God knows I'm well enough used to scenes like that, but you . . . you aren't and . . ."

Strong arms, smelling of sunshine, meadow grass, and sharp male sweat circled around her, drawing her against the warm refuge of his chest. "Hush, love. Maura, don't—"

"I don't know what I do, Tade, to stir people's hatred, but I—"

"You do nothing, Maura. *Nothing*," he said fiercely. "Don't take their hate inside you and let it tear at you this way." Hard, callused palms reached down to cup her face, forcing it gently from where it was buried in his shirtfront. Fingertips smoothed over tear-wet cheeks, sable curls, quivering lips. "Let them tend the fires of their grudges until they are in their graves," he said huskily, "while we tend other flames that burn more brightly."

With infinite slowness his parted lips dipped to hers, and in his eyes she could see understanding and some other, nameless emotion that set waves of heat pulsing through her veins. The firm lines of his mouth pressed deep into the quivering softness of her own, soothing her, wooing her, as if he would take her inside himself, banishing forever the demons that tormented her. And she wanted him to, wanted to drown in the haven he offered.

Far too soon his lips drifted away. Maryssa reached up a trembling finger, touching the kiss-reddened curves. Eyes smoky, brooding as a forest primeval, bored into hers.

"Maura," he said, his voice raspy. "Stay."

The pain shadowing the scene at the clearing seemed to swell, then burst inside Maryssa. The tiniest of smiles played at the corners of her mouth as she dropped her gaze back to her hands.

Tade's finger crooked beneath her chin, tilting her face up to meet the light of his own faint grin. "And what, pray tell, is this smile for?" he asked, brushing his thumb across her lips.

"It sounds so foolish, but . . . do you know this is the first time in my life that anyone has asked me to *stay* with them?"

The smile curving Tade's sensual lips faded; his eyes were dark and serious as they searched hers. Maryssa felt them delve inside her as if they could see her very soul. She saw him tipping his face toward hers, felt his breath sweet upon her lips. But before the warmth of his mouth could close again over hers, the cart wheel lurched into a rut, almost bouncing her onto his lap.

A grin spread over Tade's face, only the slightest tautness at the corners of his mouth betraying the tension still within him as he arched one black brow devilishly. "Hit three more ruts like that, Reeve, and I should have Maura exactly where I want her," he called.

Only a hint of a blush tinted Maryssa's cheeks as Reeve

and Christabel turned their heads to look at her. The worried affection evident in their beloved faces warmed Maryssa's heart, and she vowed silently that she would not be the cause of further ruining the outing they had planned for her with such loving care. She forced her lips into a smile.

Such genuine expressions of relief crossed the Marlows' faces that the stiffness of Maryssa's lips softened. Christabel dimpled. The tiniest sparkle of mischief returned to Reeve's eyes as he turned to Tade.

"Where you want her, eh, Mr. Kilcannon?" he repeated, peering down his nose with the priggishness of a parson. "Well, you had best mind proprieties, sirrah. I have no intention of abandoning our Maryssa to a wretch such as you."

"*Your* Maryssa is quite capable of defending herself, thank you very much," Tade groaned ruefully, rubbing the back of his head. "Upon the field she dumped me out of her lap so fast I vow she gave me a lump to rival the one you dealt me."

" 'Twas no more than you deserved!" Christabel exclaimed. "You scared the feathers out of us! Tade Kilcannon, you are the most . . . arrogant . . . incorrigible—"

"Beware when she gets to 'blackguard,' " Reeve warned, rolling his eyes heavenward. "When Christabel last labeled me thus, I found my favorite snuffbox filled with Hungary water."

They all laughed, and Maryssa reveled in the sound, drinking it in as though it were some mystical, magical potion with the power to banish the ugliness of the hour before.

And when at last Reeve drew the cart to a stop in the shelter of a hidden valley, she was certain that a drop of heaven had slipped down from the clouds, spilling into this tiny corner of Ireland the greenest greens and clearest blues in all creation.

A lake rippled like liquid sapphire in its setting of lush grass while, from beneath the edges of a dozen ruggedly carved stones, the last of summer's wildflowers winked their velvet petals at the bright-winged birds skimming overhead. Three oak trees, their branches tangling heavenward, studded the steep hillside, the tallest tree dangling a weathered swing from its gnarled arms.

"I've never seen anything so lovely!" Maryssa breathed.

"It must be the sunlight." Tade chuckled. "I don't recall

your being quite so enamored of the glen when last you were here.''

''Here? You mean . . .''

Tade's gaze roved in a twinkling path to the lake, then back to hers. ''I must admit, I've never had such a diverting bath in my life. But perhaps if you'd care to go wading after we sup . . .''

Heat suffused Maryssa's face as she recalled with shocking vividness every magnificent moon-gilded line of Tade's body when he had stalked naked across the shore. The image of silver rivulets of water trickling down his broad shoulders, hair-roughened chest, and the flat, rigid muscles of his stomach below burned beneath her eyelids.

She felt Tade willing her to look at him, the smoldering remembrance within his green gaze drawing her as inexorably as the pull of the tide. Mouth suddenly dry, she wheeled around, and bustled to help Christabel tug a huge split-oak basket from beneath the cart seat.

But the image of Tade wouldn't be dispelled. It teased her as she helped Christabel spread the coverlet beneath the oak. It tantalized her in every brush of Tade's fingers on her lips as he popped succulent bites of chicken into her mouth. And as he sprawled across the coverlet when the last morsel of food had been devoured, the lazy, replete smile that toyed with his mouth whispered to Maryssa of tumbled bedclothes and lazy lovemaking. She wanted to sink down beside him, nestle against his sun-warmed skin.

But she only watched him, transfixed, as a glistening droplet of sweat gathered at the base of his jaw then rolled slowly down inside the open collar of his shirt to the whorls of dark hair dusting his chest.

''Maryssa!'' Reeve's sharp voice cut in.

''Y-yes?'' Her gaze darted guiltily across the coverlet to where Reeve sat, heaving a martyred sigh.

''I've asked you this thrice already—please mind what I'm saying. Christa and I are going to wander through the meadows a bit. Would you and the crown prince care to join us?'' He enunciated each word with the patience of schoolmaster drilling his dullest student.

Tade yawned broadly, lacing his fingers behind his head. ''Nay. You two go on, Reeve. 'Ryssa and I will stay here

and guard the remains of this delectable lunch. I've heard
the Black Falcon has been lurking among these hills of late,
and if there is one thing that brigand likes 'tis your cook's
chick—''

Reeve's face soured, hazel eyes snapping away from Maryssa to shoot Tade a hard, warning glare.

"If . . . if the Black Falcon is lurking about, mayhap we'd
best all leave." Nervously, Maryssa fingered the stitching of
her gown, seeing, instead of the delicate edging, silver-thread
talons wrought upon a stark black mask.

Reeve pursed his lips in a long-suffering attitude as he levered himself to his feet. "There's naught to fear, Maryssa.
Tade's just conjuring excuses. The truth is that after facing
my superior hurling skill today, the poor lad hasn't energy
left to take five steps. Most like you'll be forced to sit here
and listen to him snore away until—''

"Leave me to 'snore away' in peace, then, Marlow!" Tade
groaned, throwing a chicken bone at Reeve's knee. "I was
wounded upon the field of honor today, and I intend to revel
in the coddling I so richly deserve."

Reeve pulled a face. "If Maryssa dealt you what you deserve, you'd be such a mass of bruises, Rachel would spend
the rest of her life tying poultices onto that thick head of
yours." Reeve held out his hand to Christabel, helping her
up from the coverlet. "Well, enjoy your lazing, you two. We
shouldn't trouble you with our company for at least a turn of
the clock. My wife and I intend to take full advantage of this
spectacular afternoon. Milady?" He turned to Christa, offering her his elbow.

Soft powdered curls bobbed beguilingly over Christabel's
shoulders as she slipped her arm through Reeve's and started
up a narrow path that ribboned toward the valley's rim.

Maryssa watched them in silence, but the aura of happiness
she had struggled so hard to hold in their presence seemed
to drift away with them, tangled within the secret smiles of
belonging that passed between the two. Reeve's head tipped
toward Christabel's, his lips brushing hers.

"They love each other very much."

Maryssa started at the sound of Tade's soft voice beside
her. Her gaze dropped as if she had been caught stealing

something precious. "They're the kindest people I've ever known," she said. "They deserve to be happy."

"And you, Maryssa Wylder?"

She glanced down toward the dark head silhouetted against the creamy coverlet. Tade lay on his stomach, long legs stretched off into the grass beyond the coverlet's edge, his chin, resting on his knuckles as he stared meditatively into the fragile bowl of a pale rose wildflower. He plucked it, cupping it in one callused palm.

"Me?" Maryssa echoed.

"What do you think you deserve?"

"I . . . I don't know. My father says God deals us fair measure."

"And you believe that?"

"Sometimes. When I look at Reeve and Christabel, and Rachel with all her babies . . . but it seems so oft that innocents . . ." Maryssa shuddered, her thoughts turning, unbidden, to the night Quentin Rath had stormed the cottage on the mountain, his grim-faced soldiers spewing into the cozy firelit room to search for gentle, sober Devin.

When her gaze dropped to the wisp of green ribbon trailing from Tade's sleeve, Kane Kilcannon's rage-ravaged features as he faced Tade in the clearing rose in her mind. Kane's mouth had contorted in fury, yet beneath the angry flame in the older man's eyes had lurked a subtler shading: fear.

What comfort will your cursed dalliance be when Bainbridge Wylder strings you from his stable rafters . . . ? A chill scuttled down Maryssa's spine as Kane's words echoed through her. What lengths *would* her father go to to destroy Tade . . . all the Kilcannons if he discovered . . . She forced her gaze out across the wind-dappled blue of the lake, her mouth twisting in a tiny bitter smile. Discovered what? That Tade, Rachel, and Devin had committed the unpardonable sin of showing her kindness?

From the time she was a child, her father had banished all who had dared to commit such a heinous offense. The rare warmhearted housemaid, any governess who made the mistake of showing that she held aught but contempt for her charge. Maryssa closed her eyes, remembering a heart-shaped face, pale blue eyes, a full mouth with, about its corners, an endearing eagerness to please. The year she was ten Evangeline Boucher had danced into her life like drops from a fallen rainbow, scattering laughter about Carradown's nursery for the first time Maryssa could remember. For three months, while her father had been off in Norfolk, ribbon bows, lessons in flirting behind the delicate shield of a fan, and spring-kissed outings had turned what had once been tedious days into joy.

Until Bainbridge Wylder had returned and discovered the loving Evangeline's "crimes." Maryssa could still see her father's thunderous face scowling at her, could still feel the weak trickle of childish tears down her cheeks.

" 'Ryssa . . ."

Maryssa started at the sound of Tade's voice, the satiny petals of the wildflower still held between his fingers skimming a gentle pattern on her knuckles. Her eyes clung to the soft rose flower, as though to clutch at a reality far less terrifying than the hauntings of her mind. Yet the fear lingered as she turned her gaze down to where the thick rosewood-colored waves of Tade's hair were knotted at the nape of his neck. His gaze, tipped up at her, was crystal green with concern.

If her father would rip Evangeline Boucher from her life merely for being kind, to what depth would he not sink to drive Tade Kilcannon from her heart?

She jerked her hand away from the brush of the blossom and his fingers, stark misery roiling inside her. Her heart . . . dear God, when had Tade crept inside it?

Had she loved him from the moment he stood belligerently naked on the grassy lakeshore, or since the night he had stolen through her bedchamber window, his eyes snapping with a mischievous joy in life that she had never hoped to know? Or had she fallen in love with Tade Kilcannon a thousand dreams before she'd ever looked upon his face?

Fallen in love with him only to have the threat of her father's cruelty snatch him away. Desolation deeper than any she had ever known swept through her in sickening waves.

"Maryssa . . ."

She lowered her eyes to his, her gaze skimming the arrogant strength of his jaw, the full, sensual lips, eyes as green and mysterious as a druid glen. Tears trembled on her lashes, and there was naught she could do to stop them as they flowed free.

"Maura, don't let anything spoil the wonder of this day." His voice was velvet, magical, as he drew her down beside him and nestled her into the thick folds of the coverlet. "Not fools tending their hatred . . . not ghosts from yesterday . . ." The sunlight, with its first swirlings of twilight's rose, spun before her eyes, then disappeared as Tade lowered his face to hers. The warm satin of his lips blessed her tear-wet eyelids, the tiny curve of her nose, the callused tips of his fingers smoothing over her cheeks with the same delicate wonder he had accorded the wildflower. And Maryssa felt cherished, precious, for the first time in her life.

"I could not stop thinking about you," he breathed in a throaty whisper. "About touching you, watching you smile . . . You were everywhere I looked . . . in the mountains, in the pages of books . . . in my bed. I had to . . . to know you were all right . . . had to see if you could possibly taste as sweet as I remembered . . ." His voice dropped low, reverent, as his lips pressed a gossamer-light kiss upon the crest of her cheek. "You do, Maura," he murmured against her skin. "Sweeter still. I think I . . ." His lashes drifted shut, and Maryssa felt a tremor course through him.

She lifted shaking hands to his face, then trailed them in a path down the corded muscles of his throat into the crisp dark hair that fanned across the bronzed perfection of his chest. He groaned as her fingertips swept the broad plane, and Maryssa could feel his body tense against hers as one strong arm looped about her waist, pulling her deep into the lean hardness of his own tall frame.

His hand threaded through the soft curls at her temple, his eyes hot, heavy with want. "Maura . . . so sweet . . . so sad. Let me give you joy . . ."

Tade's mouth dipped down, a groan rumbling through him as his lips molded themselves to hers. She tasted of wild wind, of late summer, of sweet ripe berries bursting with warm juices, and she tasted of a despair that stole inside his very soul, robbing him of any but the fierce need to rid her of all pain. His tongue circled the satiny fullness of her lips, then parted them to pierce the inner sweetness of her mouth, and it was as if somehow he had lost himself inside of her.

Lost himself in the wonder of her innocent eyes, her fragile, wounded smile, the loneliness that welled up from within her like that of a banished angel.

He eased his palm up over the dainty curve of her waist and beyond, until the underside of her breast swelled against his hand. A tiny mewling sounded low in her throat, and Tade took the soft mound in his palm, the gentle wooing he had intended to soothe away the misery in her delicate features flaring into the heat of unbridled passion.

Her small hands burrowed beneath his shirt, smoothing the naked flesh of his shoulders and back, driving him almost mad with untutored caresses. And her eyes . . . their mystical depths glowed green, gold, and blue beneath lids heavy with newfound desire. He pressed her into the coverlet, cupping his body over hers with greedy longing. She was warm, soft, beautiful . . . so beautiful . . .

"God, Maura, I want to . . . to make love to you. Damn it, I can't . . ."

"Tade . . ." His name was a breath on the wind. He pulled back just a whisper as she pressed one soft palm against his chest. Her eyes locked with his, her small white teeth indenting the moist fullness of her lower lip as she took his hand in hers. He could feel her fingers shaking as she slipped the ribbon end of the gown's fastening between his fingertips. Passion and an odd, tearing hopelessness warred in her incredible eyes. "Please," she whispered, her lashes glossed with tears, "I . . . I want you to."

"Maura . . ."

"Make love to me, Tade. Now." Soft red lips sought his, and had she asked for his life, he could not have denied her. He took in their trembling curves, his own mouth hungry and demanding, the neatly tied cords of her gown tangling beneath his impatient hands as he tugged at them.

It seemed an eternity before folds of her dress, the dainty lawn underbodice, and the stiff corset fell free, baring warm flesh blushed soft as the petals of a primrose. Tade's mouth went dry, his eyes feasting on the silken arch of her bared shoulder, the delicate rose of her nipple, which pearled at the mere touch of his ragged breath upon its crest.

"Maura, I've dreamed about you . . . about us . . . together like this . . . until my whole body felt on fire and I'd

wake up, aching . . ." His lips dropped kisses in the hollow
at the base of her throat, and down onto the soft swell below.
"And now . . ." His tongue swept out, touching, just touching, the hardened bud tipping one snowy mound. She whimpered, and the sound shot white-hot flames through his loins.

" 'Ryssa," he moaned, his lips opening over her flesh.
" 'Ryssa . . ." He suckled her deep into his mouth, feeling
her hips writhing up against the hard proof of his sex. And
he wanted her beneath him—naked, needing—wanted to fill
her with himself, chase the desolation from her eyes.

"Maura, are you certain . . . ?"

She answered not. Her fingers, made clumsy by the haze
of desire, trailed a quavering path down his shirtfront, fumbling with the tiny buttons. The feel of her small hands baring
his skin hurtled the driving need inside Tade higher, higher.
He helped her, tearing the buttons free, his mouth never ceas-
ing its dance upon her breasts, throat, and lips. A gasp escaped her throat as he stripped the garment free and hurled
it to the ground beside them. She arched upward her trembling, moist lips skimming his hair-roughened chest.

A shudder of sensation rippled through Tade, rocking him
to the core of his being. In one swift move, he claimed her
mouth, forcing her down into the softness of the coverlet as
his tongue thrust deep. Her fingers dug into the flesh of his
back, her tongue swirling instinctively against his, mating
with his in a way that robbed him of his senses.

He worked his hand between them, struggling with the
layers of her petticoats until they wisped free beneath his
hands. The heat of her fevered skin seared his roughened
palms through the icing of fine lawn that shielded the slender
columns of her thighs, the sweet mysteries of her woman's
secrets.

Gentle, suddenly gentle, he eased the garment down over
the slender curves of her hips and thighs. "Maryssa . . ."
The soft curse he uttered was profanity and prayer. "More
beautiful than I'd ever dreamed . . ." A single fingertip
trekked a worshipful path across the silken skin of her stomach, then lower. He watched as her lashes drifted down to
grace the delicate rose of her cheeks, and the whimper as he
skimmed her downy softness seemed torn from her very soul.
"T-Tade, I want—need . . ."

"I know, love," he breathed. "Sweet God, Maura, I burn for you. Feel what you do to me." He took her hand in his, flattening it against the hard plane of his naked stomach, sliding it down to the waistband of his breeches. "Touch me, Maura," he said. "Please. I need you to touch me."

Her eyes fluttered open, and he could see her hesitate mere seconds that seemed to stretch into eternity. He swallowed, battling to force down the disappointment that tore at him. Then suddenly he felt her hand stir against his flesh. With agonizing slowness, her fingertips eased down over the soft doeskin.

Tade clenched his teeth, every muscle in his body whipcord tight as the tentative warmth of her hand brushed the tip of his sex through his breeches. The warmth retreated, then returned, testing the rigid flesh, skimming the length of him with an innocent wonder that slashed through his body with greater force than had any of a score of artful seductions beneath well-practiced hands.

The breathless sound of her voice tingled along his skin. "You're so . . . I . . ." A scarlet flush heated her cheeks. Her tongue swept out, moistening lips swollen from his kisses. She lowered her gaze, raised it, her eyes seeming to draw him inside her very soul. "I want—I want to see you."

Raw desire speared deep in Tade's belly, but no words could pass the knot crushing his throat. He nodded, moving her hand to where the doeskin-covered buttons of his breeches strained against that which made him a man. Her fingertips eased inside the taut waistband, the backs of her fingers brushing the dark ribbon of hair bisecting his stomach. Tade shuddered, his pleasure akin to pain, each tug of button sliding through hole, each delicate brush of her fingers swelling the need building inside him, until he feared he would spill his seed upon the coverlet.

The breeches fell open, the lake-cool kiss of the breeze tantalizing his fevered flesh. He closed his eyes, grimacing in an agony of waiting . . . waiting . . .

"Tade . . ." His name fell from her lips, hushed and awed. The soft pads of her fingertips trailed over the velvet heat of his flesh, the feel of her touching him pulsing torrents of desire through his hardness. "Tade," she whispered. "You're beautiful . . ."

Groaning low in his throat, Tade wound his arms around her, crushing her in an embrace that tumbled them both into the grass-scented sweetness of the coverlet. His mouth sought hers with tormented hunger as he rolled her beneath him, crushing her breasts against his chest, tangling the hair-roughened leanness of his legs with the silken smoothness of Maryssa's. Downy-soft curls damp with wanting tantalized the shaft of his manhood.

And he wanted to see her, to see every quicksilver emotion flash across her angel's features as he claimed her for his own.

His hands knotted in the thick sable swirls of hair spilling about her shoulders, his tongue thrusting into her mouth. "Maura," he moaned, "open your eyes . . . Let me watch you."

Rich, sooty lashes swept up, unveiling eyes heavy with wonder . . . dark with . . . love? Love . . . Slowly, Tade drew his lips from hers, bracing himself on his elbows to peer for long, aching moments into her trusting face. The sweet curves of her mouth quivered beneath his gaze, innocent and vulnerable, the corners tipped down just a whisper, as though weighted by a lifetime of sorrows. Sorrows that he would magnify tenfold if he took her, and then . . .

Sweet Christ, she was Bainbridge Wylder's daughter. Heiress to a fortune, with the right to grace the finest ballrooms in England. What future could she have in the bed of an Irish rogue who had been robbed of his inheritance three and twenty years past?

"Tade?" Tremulous and tentative, her fingertip reached up to touch his lips, and the torment that raged in his loins nearly made him dash her hand away as if it were a flaming brand. He rolled away from her, flinging his wrist across his eyes as he sucked in deep, steadying breaths.

"Did I"—her small voice faltered—"did I do something wrong?"

Tade dragged his leaden arm away from his face, and the hurt clouding her eyes tore at his heart. He swept up, and cupped her face in his hands, fiercely, savagely. "Nay, love. Don't even think it. You were beautiful. More than I . . . more than I ever have a right to hope for."

"Then why . . . ?" He saw the sudden crimson stain the

ivory of her skin, her endearing, uninhibited acceptance of their nakedness fading into bewilderment and shame.

"Because I can't hurt you this way. Now, this minute with the sun dripping down, the flowers, the meadow . . . now you think you want this, want me. But a week from now, a month . . ."

"I'll still want—" He stifled her passionate denial with his fingertips, pressing them tight against the lips that had given him such pleasure.

"Maura, do you think I could take you, make love to you like this, and then just . . . Damn it, think."

The wounded light in her eyes deepened, and the need to love away that pain twisted like a knife in his belly. She wrenched away from him to snatch up the clothing strewn about them.

"Maryssa, I just cannot—"

"Can't what? Make love to me? From what your father says, you've done it oft enough before." The defiant words snagged in her throat as she fumbled with the tangle of fabric. "Mayhap I'm not well schooled enough to please—"

In one, aching sweep, Tade pulled her into his arms and began to kiss her cheeks, temples, eyelids. "Damn it, Maura. This is different. *You* are different. You're not some . . . some willing dairymaid with petticoats lighter than swansdown in the breeze."

"Nay, I'm Bainbridge Wylder's daughter. You're afraid—"

"Afraid? Aye, by the saints, I'm afraid. The bastard nigh shattered your jaw because you'd been defiled by the mere presence of a Kilcannon. What think you he would do if I planted my babe within you?" His hand splayed on her bare stomach, and Tade gritted his teeth against the vision of that gentle swell ripening with his seed.

"Maura, I won't risk that—risk you. You touch me, Maryssa Wylder. Here." He took one of her small, knotted fists and pressed it against his chest. "And I swear to God, I'll not let anyone hurt you. Nay, not even myself."

Maryssa huddled deeper into the curve of Tade's shoulder as the mist of rain drizzling from the dismal evening sky groped with chill fingers beneath the layers of her cloak. It was as if each lurch of the Marlows' cart along the road that wound toward Nightwylde had spilled out the misery that gripped her very soul, darkening the sun-glossed Donegal countryside to the stark gray hues of despair.

The cart jarred to the left as Reeve murmured a command to the mare. When the green-painted wheels ground to a halt, Maryssa could feel the supple length of Tade's body stiffen against her, and her own grip about his waist tightened instinctively, as if to hold the inevitable parting at bay.

Reeve turned his rain-damp face toward his friend. "Tade," he began hesitantly, "Christa and I thought . . . well, mayhap 'twould be wise if you would—"

"Spirit my blackguard Kilcannon self back into the wilds where I belong?" Maryssa saw the slightest hint of irony twist Tade's lips as his green eyes flashed toward Nightwylde's battlements, the jesting tone of his voice sounding oddly strained. "When, pray tell, Mr. Marlow, have you ever known me to be wise?"

"Rarely." Reeve's mouth crumpled in disgust. " 'Tis just that . . ." He fingered his neckcloth, studiedly keeping his gaze away from Maryssa. "Well, Mr. Wylder might make things . . . er . . . difficult."

"Difficult?" There was an edge underlying the velvet of Tade's voice that belied the lazy tones. " 'Tis well of you to caution me. I lead such an old woman's life that—"

"Damn it, Tade, for once 'tis not your blasted neck I'm worried about. Sometimes I think if ever a man courted disaster—" Reeve gritted his teeth, a white line of irritation ringing his mouth. "Use what paltry sense God gave you. Maryssa—"

"Aye. Maryssa." The stiffness of the arms still holding her gentled, and she felt the breath ease from his taut chest in a sigh as Reeve turned again to face the darkened road. Tade lowered his mouth to the crown of her head for long moments, pressing his lips against the silken sable strands. "Maura . . ." His palm curved under her chin, raising her face so that she could meet his eyes. "It seems for once I needs must take Reeve's advice. 'Tis best if I leave you here. But I"—his voice faltered, and she could swear it was not just the mist that clung in crystal droplets to his lashes—"I want you to know that I'll always remember . . ."

Maryssa died inside, what little hope she had held that she

would see Tade again fading. " 'Tis—'tis all right, Tade,'' she said softly. "Today was the sweetest . . . the sweetest I have ever known. I'll hold it in my heart forever.''

His gaze swept over her lips, cheeks, and hair. "I'd give you a thousand tomorrows as beautiful if 'twere in my power.''

Maryssa forced a tiny smile to her lips, wanting to soothe away the worry creasing his brow. "Perhaps I would get greedy then, and not see how perfect a tiny glen can be . . . or how gentle a man—'' She stopped. Her tear-blurred gaze dropped to the damp shirt clinging to his chest. "Thank you, Tade, for—''

"Damn!'' She started at his savage oath as his mouth swept down, capturing hers in a fierce kiss and then abruptly released her. "By God, I should shove you through your father's gates and stay away from you, but I can't. I have to see you again, touch you. Maura . . .''

He pulled her against him, every sinew of his taut body burning into hers, sending life and joy hurtling through her in a rush that stole her senses. "Wait for me, love. I'll send word with Christa . . . Somehow I'll find a place where 'tis safe for us.'' He crushed the words onto her lips, his tongue delving deep into her mouth, greedily, hungrily. And then he was gone. Maryssa forced open passion-heavy eyelids as he vaulted from the cart, lifting one bronzed hand in a silent salute to the Marlows as the wheels jarred into motion.

With chilled fingers, she drew the folds of her cloak tighter abut her shoulders. *Where 'tis safe for us . . .* It was as if the wind itself mocked Tade's words, sweeping in sinister whispers off the castle's cold stone walls. Maryssa shivered as Tade Kilcannon's tall, lean form melted into the mist of the castle's brooding shadows and the gates of Nightwylde closed behind her.

Eight

THE COTTAGE DROWSED behind the veil of night, the pale
wood of its newly hewn door standing out against the time-
mellowed walls like a fresh wound, one of many inflicted of
late by Tade and the father he loved with a fierce protectiveness that had changed a lad into a man long before the years
of childhood's frolics should have passed. Wounds that had
no time to heal before the next breach split them wide.

Tade wiped his soaked shirtsleeve across his damp face,
his eyes roving to where the flame of a single candle glowed
from the cottage window, its soft light beckoning like a loving, gentle hand. From the time he was a lad of thirteen,
rebelling against his stern father to run wild in the Donegal
hills, the candle had been Rachel's way of guiding him home,
telling him all was forgiven.

And when child's games had given way to the quests of a
man, unbeknownst to the loving Rachel the taper had served
as signal to those who secretly sought the Black Falcon, telling them that the daring rebel was already one with the darkness.

Tade grimaced, tunneling his fingers beneath the rain-
sodden mass of hair that clung to the back of his neck. No
doubt the perils of the Irish highroads would prove more

peaceful than his father's hearth this night. For there could be little question that Kane Kilcannon had spent the hours since the hurling match stoking his blazing rage. Irony twisted Tade's lips. By now he should be well used to his father's temper and the bitterness that ate like poison in the older man's belly. For Kane always seemed to vent his anger on the son he saw as naught but a reckless rakehell, gallivanting across the countryside in search of fresh diversions.

If only he knew . . . Tade sighed wearily. For certainly Kane Kilcannon would claim the Black Falcon as blood of his blood with a pride he never felt in irresponsible Tade. The older man's trouble-ravaged eyes would gleam bright with the same fierce pride he reserved for Devin. He would grip Tade by the shoulders, pull him into that manly embrace.

Yet no matter how deeply the need for his father's respect ran in Tade's veins, that respect would be small comfort in return for the danger Kane Kilcannon's knowledge of his secret would bring down upon the cottage and those who lived within.

It was best for all that his father view him with contempt, and it would be well to have done with the angry scene that no doubt awaited him behind the newly hung door. Poor Rachel must be at her wit's end trying to calm the rampaging old lion.

Sucking in a deep breath, Tade squared his shoulders into a belligerent stance, forcing onto his lips the expression of bored arrogance that always served to enrage his father. Grasping the latch, Tade threw the door open, his gaze flashing immediately to the hearth before which his father always paced as he waited. But the turf fire glowed upon a room strangely empty. No solemn-eyed children glanced fearfully back and forth between the two men they adored; Rachel's gentle face didn't plead from the flickering shadows.

A needle-thin shaft of dread pierced Tade's belly. Had Rath . . . ? In three quick strides he crossed the darkened room, throwing wide the half-open door to the little ones' bedchamber. The turf fire's faint glow touched the arch of a tiny bare foot thrust out from beneath the bedclothes, mops of carroty red curls, soft dark waves, and rosy cheeks just visible above the edge of a tattered quilt. Relief washed through Tade, releasing a small measure of the tension gripping his body. Yet another row with Da suddenly seemed insignificant when matched against even the tiniest threat to the safety of the little figures sprawled across the soft feather tick.

Silently, Tade padded to the bedstead to ease five-year-old Thomas's leg back into the warmth of the coverlets. ''Ma?'' The little one's mouth gaped in a yawn.

''Nay, 'tis Tade. And I'll thank you not to be putting petticoats upon your older brother, Tamkin.''

The boy's lips curved in a sleepy grin, revealing two missing front teeth. ''Tade, I caught a wee fishy today.''

''And aren't you growing to be a fine one with the nets? By next summer you'll be leading the curraghs out of the bay.''

The boy snuffled into his pillow, rubbing sleep-blurred eyes with one small fist. His mouth turned down at the corners. ''Da made me frow the fish away. Said it would burn to an ash, it was so small.''

''Well, tomorrow I'll work you a bigger net, and by next week you'll be filling the kettle so full your ma'll have to put stones on the lid to keep it from bursting.''

''Mmhummm . . . bursting . . .''

Tade felt a ghost of a grin flutter around the corners of his mouth as Thomas sighed in sleepy contentment and rolled over on his round little belly.

Tade stroked a wayward curl back from the child's pale forehead, a curl shaded in the darkness as rich as the spun sable framing Maryssa's delicate face. A fist tightened in Tade's loins. Sons . . . Kilcannon sons . . . How many times had his father railed at him to take a wife, sire heirs to feed the fires of justice and reclaim the family fortunes. Yet always before, Tade had been content to play hero to Rachel's brood, championing their small causes, giving them playthings and much needed winter shoes, listening to their woes.

Only now did the fierce primal need to hold a child of his own blood pulse through Tade's whole being . . . a baby with eyes the shifting colors of a sunstruck sea, a babe with haunting innocence and ebony curls.

''Damn.'' A sardonic smile twisted Tade's lips. Should he ever indulge in such folly, there would most likely be a battle as to whether Bainbridge Wylder or his father put him beneath the gelding knife first. And yet . . . Tade's smile faded, the memory of Maryssa's caresses drizzling over his skin like warm honey.

Tade turned, his gaze skimming across the dimly lit room. The door to the chamber his father shared with Rachel stood tightly closed as if to block from Kane Kilcannon's vision the return of his blackguard son. That was just as well. Tade arched back the muscles of his shoulders, kneading the stiff sinews at the base of his neck. He had little stomach for Da's bitterness this night. Mayhap whatever they had to say to each other would have softened a bit by the morrow.

Tade paced back out into the light of the fire and lifted the taper from the window ledge. Shielding the dancing flame with his hand, he moved quietly to the ladder in the corner and reached up to perch the candlestick on the edge of the loft opening.

Light radiated in a golden circle past the flowered curtain Deirdre had strung across the loft. Tade climbed the ladder, then paused, his head just above the hole cut into the loft floor, and watched her anger-stiffened shoulders rise and fall slightly as she lay on her pallet feigning sleep. For the millionth time in the years since she had moved her bed into the cranny below the roof, he silently thanked God she had insisted on dividing the room with the yards of cheery calico. Otherwise this night he might be hard pressed to keep from strangling her.

Tade sighed, retrieving the candle, then pushing the curtain aside to step into his own small room. The welcoming quiet of the nook that had been his sanctuary for three and twenty years closed about him. Yet even here peace eluded him. The velvety darkness reminded him of the cloud of soft hair he had buried his face in hours before. The dried posies Rachel had hung from the rafters to sweeten the air smelled of the meadows, of rose-tinted flesh warm beneath his lips.

Tade settled the candle on the worn lid of an apple-wood chest. Maryssa . . . so fragile, so haunted . . . He had wanted to chase away her demons, to heal her, but never had he dreamed she would steal his very soul.

"You'd best strip off those wet things or you'll die of lung fever before Da has a chance to put an end to you himself."

Tade started at the sound of a soft voice behind him. Spinning toward the bed that lay tucked beneath the slope of the roof, he glared at the shadowy form perched atop the brightly patched quilt.

Gentle blue eyes peered back at him from a face lined with a sorrowful disappointment that clawed Tade more deeply than Kane Kilcannon's blackest rages.

"Devin!" Tade uttered a savage oath, darting for the small window cut in the whitewashed wall and slamming the wooden shutter closed with a force that nearly cracked the cottage walls. He wheeled on his brother, fury and fear warring in his belly. "For the love of God, are you mad, Dev, or just courting a cursed hanging? 'Twas folly enough to go stalking about at the hurling match in the light of day, but *this* is pure idiocy! Rath's been patrolling the cottage every night. If he—"

"He won't," Devin interrupted with a calm that infuriated Tade. "I was passing careful when I slipped inside. Besides, I judged there was more danger of you and Da murdering each other this night than of Rath choosing to make a search. So I persuaded Da to go to bed, while I—"

"Waited to show me the evil of my ways? Da and I did well enough tearing at each other's throats while you were away. 'Tis foolhardy for you to risk capture over something so trivial as—"

"As you roaming about the countryside with a woman who is English, Protestant, and the daughter of our family's most hated enemy?"

"Maryssa has naught to do with her bastard father. I thought you, at least, would understand."

"Understand what?" Devin pushed himself upright and walked to peer out into the slice of night visible through a tiny crack in the shutter. "That Maryssa is one of the sweetest, most unspoiled women I've ever met? That she possesses an innocence, a depth of loving that is rare indeed? Aye, and that she looks at you as though the very angels dwelt in your smile?"

"Damn it, Dev! How Maura does or does not look at me is none of your affair. I'm no blasted monk." Tade stripped off his wet shirt and snatched up a square of soft wool toweling from beside the battered washstand. "The night I gained my manhood you endured my ravings about the wonder of it for hours. Now suddenly, when I am six and twenty instead of sixteen, you crumple up your face in disapproval and sit in my room like a saint awaiting martyrdom.''

"This time it is different." Devin turned, his face solemn. "Always before you've chosen those you could not hurt in a tumble across the coverlets. Women who desired—simply, openly—as you did. You made your conquests, aye, but you left no shattered virgins, no broken hearts in your wake. But Maryssa . . ."

"You truly believe I'm blind to how special she is?" A feeling of sharp betrayal coursed through Tade, and even the forced cynicism twisting his mouth couldn't hide the pain in his face. "I thought that you—you, at least—knew better of me, but I see that Da has finally convinced you that where women are concerned I'm capable of heeding naught but my loins.''

"What are you heeding this time, Tade? Do you even know? From the time you were a child, I've seen you hurl yourself into peril to save a drowning pup or a wounded bird. I've seen you thrash boys thrice your size to spare a weaker child pain. But this time you are courting calamity such as you've never known.''

"Thank you, Father Devin, for another one of your holy sermons, but I think 'twould serve better if you saved it for the Sabbath.''

"Blast it, Tade, if I were talking to you with the robes of my priesthood, I'd have you on your knees for a full month doing penance! I'm speaking to you as a brother. Asking as a brother *why*. Why hurl yourself into something you know can only end in disaster? Because you thirst for danger? Because you need to defy Da? Or is it because in some dark and untouchable part of you, some part that you scarce realize exists, you unknowingly see Maryssa as a tool you can use to wreak vengeance on the man who betrayed our father?''

Tade wheeled, fists clenched, lips white with fury. "If any man but you had dared—"

"I know." Devin caught the stiff fingers in his hands and held them, his gentle face taut with concern. "Mayhap I deserve the sharp side of your fist. And I vow if it will make you feel better, you have my leave to whack away until you can't raise your arms. But know this: I love you, Tade. Too

much to stand by in silence and watch you destroy an innocent girl. Aye, and in doing so destroy yourself.''

At Devin's earnest, loving words, the anger ebbed out of
Tade in a rush. The day's events had suddenly exhausted Tade,
drained him. ''Devin,'' he said softly, ''I would die before
I'd do her harm.''

''Then you must not see her again. Stay away.''

'' 'Tis too late, Dev.'' Tade raised his eyes to the troubled
blue of his brother's. His fists uncurled then dropped slowly
to his sides. ''I think I love her.''

Understanding dawned in Devin's features, followed by
stunned pain. ''Tade—''

''I lay with her on the shore of the lake,'' Tade breathed
in the barest whisper. ''I touched her, desired her as I've
ne'er desired a woman before. And she wanted me, Dev. I
could feel it in her kisses, in the way she . . .'' Tade pressed
his fingertips to his eyes, the image of Maryssa in his arms
crushing his chest. ''But I folded her clothes back about her
and held her . . . only held her, because—''

A crash against the heavy door below shattered the hushed
words into a thousand fragments of terror. Tade lunged toward the loft opening, eyes catching fleeting glimpses of Devin's taut features, of Deirdre sitting up in bed, her face pale
as her nightdress. But just as Tade reached the ladder, a
clamor of voices filled the silence, their slurred tones dese-
crating the melancholy strains of a ballad.

''Tay-ed!'' someone bellowed. ''Kil-can-non! Get out
here.'' The rowdy voices changed into drunken giggles, and
there was a thumping sound as if someone's feet had rebelled
against holding his liquor-deadened body upright.

''Come ou' an' tip a glash with us, Tade,'' a tenor sang to
the strains of the tune. ''They're breakin' out butts o' whiskey
right near Derry Town, an' we're gonna drain it dry-o, we're
gonna drink 'em down . . .''

Tade heard his father curse and the sounds of the children
stirring. Going to the window, he opened the shutter just
wide enough to see into the yard below.

''Neylan? MacGary? Shut your drunken yaps,'' Tade
called, with a forced bantering tone. ''I'll be down as soon
as I find my boots, though it sounds like the lot of you won't

be able to sit a horse long enough to make it down the mountain."

There was another spate of drunken guffaws. Tade grabbed up a fresh shirt and shrugged it onto his shoulders.

"You're going?" Devin's voice was serious, his features still pale with the secret Tade had confided moments before.

"Neylan won't give me any peace until I do," Tade said lightly. "I should be gone a few days. Mayhap 'twill give me time to think on what we've discussed." He reached up, moving aside a loosened slab of the turf that formed a base for the thatch overhead. He could feel Devin's eyes on him as he slipped an oilcloth-wrapped bundle from the nook, tucked it under his arm, and attempted to replace the turf over the bared straw.

Suddenly the dark slab escaped his grasp. Tade's hand shot out, but just as his fingers touched the falling piece of turf, the weight of the oilcloth bundle slipped free. He lunged for it, catching one corner, but the thick cloth only unrolled the faster, spilling its contents to the floor. Tade swore under his breath as metal thunked heavily onto the aged wood.

Candlelight spilled over the worn floorboards, picking out the curve of a brass powder flask, a bullet pouch, and the menacing length of a pistol pillowed upon a hood of black silk. Slowly Devin bent down to ease the bit of cloth from beneath the engraved weapon. His slender fingers traced the embroidered talon of a Falcon with a resigned sadness.

"So you still break ruffians' noses for tormenting those weaker than yourself, Tade," Devin said so softly it was scarce a breath beneath the rafters. "But now you use more deadly measures than your fists."

"Devin—"

"Nay, Tade. I know. Since the day I landed in Eire, I've heard tales of the Black Falcon of Donegal. And somehow . . . somehow I knew 'twas you even then."

The shouts from the yard faded, the stirrings in the cottage below blurring in Tade's ears until it seemed that the world consisted only of him and Devin spun into the web of aching understanding they had shared since childhood.

"Godspeed, brother." Pale fingertips ghosted over Tade's forehead in the sign of the cross. "And about your Marys-

sa . . ." Devin slipped the silken hood into Tade's hand.
"May Christ be gentle to you both."

Emotion knotted in Tade's throat. "If any ill should befall
me now or . . . or in the time to come . . . you'll tell her for
me . . . tell her I—"

"I'll go to her," Devin promised.

Tade turned, swirling the folds of the black mantle about
his shoulders, and leaned down to bundle the weapons and
hood back into the oilcloth parcel.

Yet even hours after he slipped out into the night, he was
plagued by the images his mind wove in the mists. Devin,
bending over Maryssa, soothing tears from eyes dark with
sorrow. And another man, a phantom garbed in satins and
brocades, crushing her beneath him in a velvet-draped bed,
shattering the fragile dreams that had shone in her face.

Nine

MARYSSA HUDDLED IN the carved wooden chair beside the hearth, staring into the blaze with eyes that ached from a fortnight of bitter tears and nights barren of sleep. Two weeks. Had the sun truly risen and set but fourteen times since the night Tade had embraced her in the Marlows' rain-damp cart? It seemed as though an aeon had crawled past in the days since he had touched her, kissed her, vowed he would return.

He had branded his promise into her soul with the heat of his kiss, yet now even the flames unfurling bright banners of red and orange seemed to paint the words in mocking hues within the darkened chimney above: *Wait for me, love . . .*

Maryssa rose from her chair and walked to the window, flung wide to the sweet-scented Donegal air. A hundred stars winked like jewels on the velvet cap of night, their glittering blue light dancing above the shadow-veiled mountains, yet to her the landscape seemed as bleak as a gale-tossed wasteland.

Wait, he had said, and she had waited with every breath she drew, minded each minute jealously in the hope that Tade was in the next meadow, on her window ledge, around the next curve of the rutted, winding road. Yet as each day passed, empty of his smile, Maryssa felt a little of herself crumble away.

"Tade . . ." Maryssa whispered the name, tasting in its sound the bittersweet tang of hope lost. A tear squeezed itself out of the corner of her eye and trickled in a hot path down one raw cheek to fall softly onto a thick sheet of paper lying on the window ledge beneath her listless fingers.

She lowered her gaze to Christabel Marlow's delicately penned script and was surprised to find it bubbled by tears. "My dearest Maryssa . . ." She had read the message with numb detachment when the Marlow's footman had delivered it a week ago, and as each day passed, its loving, rollicking tone waxed more discordant in her ear as she skimmed the elegant lines: "Mr. and Mrs. Reeve Marlow request the pleasure of your company at a small soiree in honor of Miss Maryssa Wylder of Nightwylde, said fete to be held at Marlow Hall on Saturday evening at eight o'clock."

The day after tomorrow . . . Maryssa's eyes trailed down to the bottom of the page where Christabel's quill seemed to have fairly danced across the paper: "Reeve has finally released me from the torment of our excursion to Londonderry to purchase the sorrel brood mare he claimed he would perish without. I vow, if I was not certain of the man's distaste for orange hair, I would have fallen into spasms of jealousy, the way he was taking on about that beast!

"However, he did manage to redeem himself by purchasing for me the sweetest dress length of blue aligar in all of Derry, and another most mysterious parcel with the name Maryssa scrawled on its wrapping . . ."

Maryssa brushed the tip of one finger across the words, blurring the ink with the tears that lay on the page. No doubt Father would be stricken with appoplexy when he returned from his business in Armagh to find the daughter he despised being feted by the belle of the county. A month ago Maryssa herself would have offered every acre of land she stood to inherit for just one moment of the joy of Christabel's friendship. But now even the Marlows' generous insistence that she spend the fortnight after the soiree as their guest at Marlow Hall served only to add yet another shade of melancholy to the fire's curling flames.

"Witling!" Maryssa hissed at herself, digging her nails deep into her palms. "Most like you were staring up at Tade like a moonstruck calf and he had not the heart to humiliate you." She swiped her knuckles savagely across her eyes, grinding hot tears into the stinging softness of her cheeks. "He pitied you, Maryssa. Pitied you. Stop crying after a man who—"

She bit her lip, then sat back down in the chair and pulled her knees tight against her chest. A man who gave you life, who took a hundred bleak yesterdays and sprinkled them with bliss, her mind screamed. A man whose merest touch banished all your pain, giving you hope for tomorrows struck through with sunlight.

He had held out joy, poured it into her cupped hands, and she had sipped from it, then watched helplessly as its silvery glow dripped like crystal water through her fingers.

Maryssa rested her burning cheeks against her knees, pressing her face into the limp brown petticoat she had not had the energy to shed in favor of a night rail. "If only he had let me drink full measure once . . . just once." She whispered the words aloud, capturing in her mind the sweet, heavy weight of Tade pressing her down into the coverlet she'd spread on the grass of the glen.

She wanted to cry some more, but the rest of her tears were dammed up inside her breast, lodging there with an emptiness borne upon the breeze that crept in through the open casement. Maryssa shifted on the hard seat of the chair, her stiff muscles shooting a dozen sharp needles of pain down her spine. Raising bleary eyes to the night-veiled mountains beyond the window, she drank in the scent of wild heather and sea-swept darkness. Then she stared into the night until the stars flickered out beneath her heavy lashes and loneliness draped itself around her in dark gray folds of despair.

Maryssa burrowed deeper into the warmth enfolding her, her sleep-numbed brain struggling groggily to understand how the rosewood chair that had cut into her shoulders moments ago could suddenly cradle her with such delicious comfort. She had been cold . . . so cold . . . She had felt the chills scuttle beneath her skin, yet her eyelids had seemed weighted with bits of lead, far too heavy to open even enough to allow her to stumble to the bed, but six steps from the chair on which she had fallen asleep.

But now . . . sensations crept up her fingertips. She was suddenly aware of the sleekness of finely woven cloth, downy soft warmth snuggled about her shoulders.

Maryssa's eyes flew open, and she shoved herself upright, her gaze darting about her in stunned surprise. The partly drawn bed curtains let in trickles of sunlight to frolic among the bedclothes tucked about her with the greatest of care, one bright ray darting up her wrist to where the lace cuff of her nightdress ruffled out over her hand.

Maryssa's fingers fluttered to her throat to touch the buttons that ran down her breast. The heavy corset and layers of petticoats were gone. Each tiny ivory button on her night rail had been slipped through the loop that held it. A hazy memory of the faintest of sensations stirred inside her, as if the mountain breeze had flowed over her sleeping body in dreamlike whispers. Had the chambermaid come in after she had fallen asleep, taken pity on her, and helped her into bed? No, she had barred the door, unable to endure the thought of even that stout old woman bearing witness to her misery. Had—

A sudden chill gust of wind surged into the room, setting the bed curtains whirling in heavy sweeps against each other. Maryssa jumped from beneath the coverlets and scurried toward the open window. She slammed to a halt, and froze, her fingers a hand's length away from the window latch.

Elation and disbelief bubbled inside her as she stared at the ledge, blanketed now in a tumult of riotous color. It was as if wood nymphs had stolen great armfuls of happiness and strewn them upon the ancient stone in the guise of every wildflower that grew on Donegal's hills. Palest rose, butter yellow, crimson, and purple, myriad blossoms crowded one another among tender fronds of meadow grass, the stems of one nosegay bound with the loveliest piece of lace Maryssa had ever seen.

She couldn't breathe, couldn't speak as she reached shaking fingers toward the square of paper tucked beneath a half-blown primrose.

"Maura-love"—Maryssa felt her heart flip over, then slam against her ribs as the boldly scrawled words leaped up at her. "You are softer and sweeter than any angel when you sleep, but watching you, holding you, makes me want to sweep the dream dust from your eyes and fill them with wonder. Let me, Maura. Come to the lake when the sun is high. I will be there. Waiting."

Clutching the note to her breast, she whirled in a dizzying

circle, a joyous laugh rippling in her throat. Tears spilled freely down her cheeks, but she welcomed their healing wetness, welcomed the bite of the paper's edge in her palm, as if the sensations could convince her it wasn't a dream. Tade had returned, kept his promise. He had scaled the wall to her window and . . .

Heat suffused her skin beneath its thin icing of lawn at the thought of Tade's dark fingers peeling away the layers of her clothing as she slept, then easing her into the nightdress that flowed in a thin veil about her nakedness. She scooped up an armful of flowers and buried her face in their fragrant brightness.

"Asleep?" Maryssa giggled to herself. "I must have been nigh *dead* not to feel . . ." A delicious shiver of anticipation raced up her spine. Her gaze swept out over the mountains to where the sun climbed, a sphere of liquid gold set in a cerulean sky. "I'll have to make haste if I want to be ready."

She danced to the elegant washstand in the corner and swept up the silver-backed brush to smooth it through the waves of hair tumbling past her hips. Coiling the luxuriant strands in a glistening crown about her head, she hummed a sparkling little tune, half-remembered from a day Evangeline Boucher had taken her out berrying.

Anchoring the last wayward strand with a hairpin, Maryssa turned back to the blossoms she had set on the washstand. She would weave them through her hair, splashes of brilliance against the dark tresses. A crimson bud, all but buried among butter-colored flowers seemed to beckon her. A smile touching her lips, she plunged her fingers into the bouquet seeking the stem.

Pain drove itself into her thumb. With a cry of surprise, she yanked her hand away, spilling the blossoms across the thick rug. Bright red, a drop of blood welled up on her skin. Maryssa's gaze flashed to the tumbled flowers. There, tangled among their satiny petals, lay a tiny spray of thorns—danger bathed in beauty. She reached down, lifted the sharp spikes, and gingerly held them in her cupped palm. Danger . . . Was that not what Tade faced in sending for her? And she, in running to meet him?

Her gaze straying to the elegant silver-framed looking glass that hung on the wall, Maryssa stared for long minutes at the image peering back at her. The happiness setting her eyes asparkle could scarce hide the dark circles smudged beneath them, and the blush of pink now tinting her cheeks only heightened the pallor that two weeks of sleeplessness had stroked into her skin.

No. Maryssa banished the thought of danger, tipping her hand to let the thorns fall onto the stand's embroidered cover. Today would hold only joy. Yet when she spun back to the window, the smile that curved her lips was touched with defiance.

The sun was nearly halfway to its crest, and heaven lay in wait for her beside a shimmering lake.

"Blast it, Dee, you nigh made me lay open my jaw with this thing!" Tade jerked his razor away from his skin, steadying himself as his sister swept past him. His exasperated voice cut through the clamor of the crowded room as he wheeled away from the basin of steaming water, brandishing his razor at the thunderous countenance of his sister. "You know cursed well I need to finish in haste."

"Scrape that thing across your face with any more haste and you'll slice your nose clean off," Deirdre snapped, pushing past him. "Though I vow the loss of it might be an improvement, the way you're always poking it into the air."

Tade grinned, jerking the towel from around his neck and snapping the damp length at her skirts with a well-practiced aim. He winced, gritting his teeth against the sudden stab of pain that shot through his arm at the quick movement. But even the soreness that throbbed up into his shoulder and the serious, questioning weight of Rachel's gaze upon him could not quell his amusement as Deirdre skittered to one side. Her foot snagged on a pair of pudgy legs sprawled out from the overturned stool behind which Brody and Tamkin lay dragging wisps of twine beneath the paws of three mischievous kittens. Tade couldn't resist a burst of laughter at Deirdre's black curse as she stumbled and pitched scowl-first into the heaping willow basket at the side of the washstand.

"Plague take you, Tom and Brody!" she sputtered, extricating herself from the soiled clothing. "I've told you a hundred times to take those infernal beasts out into the yard before you kill someone! And you, Tade Kilcannon"—she wheeled and shot Tade a killing glare—"can go straight to blazes!"

"According to most of Donegal, I'm going there as quick as I am able, thank you very much," Tade said with mock solemnity. "Of course, if you know of a shorter route . . ."

"You . . . oh!" Deirdre's small fists clenched in fury, her face washing red as her hair. "You are the most disgusting, arrogant bast—"

"Shame, shame," Tade teased, clucking like an old dowager. "Talk like that and a fairy is apt to come steal away your tongue. Mayhap if you could uncross your eyes but a trice, Dee, you'd save getting your freckles flattened."

"I wouldn't dream of robbing the high-and-mighty Tade Kilcannon of so much amusement gleaned at my expense," Deirdre snapped, stooping to snatch up the travel-stained clothes strewn on the floor. "Mayhap you should follow me down to the stream and watch me while I wash your filthy clothes. You might be fortunate enough to see me fall into the water and drown. That would send you into pure spasms, no doubt."

"Aye, no doubt, since you swim like a gannet and the stream is knee deep," Tade agreed, chuckling as he turned back to the mirror. "Now, if you'd permit me to finish my shaving before the soap turns stone-hard, I do have a most important assignation in but an hour's time."

Deirdre muttered another oath, and Tade struggled to keep from nicking himself as he drew the razor across the lines of merriment crinkling about his mouth. An hour's time . . . His smile faded at the memory of satiny skin beneath his fingertips, firelight glossing rose-tipped breasts, slender legs. Maryssa . . . Every muscle in his body was taut with the wanting . . . waiting . . .

Tade started, the image of fireglow and soft, yearning lips vanishing as something hard jabbed into his ribs. He looked down to see Deirdre rubbing her elbow, her mouth drawn into lines of acid contriteness.

"A thousand pardons for disturbing you. I didn't mean delay you from your assignation! Tade the magnificent! The great high king! Not burdened by the rules of the household like the rest of us poor lowlings," she trilled, dipping him an insolent curtsy.

"Last Monday when Shane forgot to throw his soiled bawneen into the willow basket before I went to the creek, Ma made him suffer a whole week without it. But you? Oh, nay. You sashay in after two weeks—*two weeks*—and she expects me to spend half a Friday afternoon washing your stinking—"

"For shame, Dee." The tiniest edge to Rachel's ever-gentle voice made all eyes in the room turn to where she leaned over the cradle. Her angular features were creased with concern, and Tade could feel her gaze sweep the slight thickness of the bandage hidden beneath his shirtsleeve. He shifted, to hide the telltale bulge from her view. Yet it was as if those soft brown eyes could see through the layers of fine linen and bloodstained cotton to the gouge a Sassenach bullet had carved beneath.

Rachel turned to Deirdre, the patience that usually glossed her features marred by tight lines about her lips. " 'Tis a fair enough exchange, I think," she chided. "An hour of washing clothes for the shoes Tade brought you from Derry."

"Oh, aye," Deirdre sniffed, her mouth quivering with resentment. "And such lovely shoes they are, too. Heavy as a cow's hoof and well nigh as appealing. I may die of gratitude every time I don them. Most like you scarce had time, though, to spend at the cobbler's, what with the hours you must have wasted plying confectioners with your coin." She glared at where little Katie leaned chubby elbows on the table's edge, her round baby eyes wide with delight as she stared, transfixed, at the sugar swan gracing the center of the table.

Tade turned, a smile tipping one corner of his mouth as his eyes skimmed the cunning creation. But it was not the sugar swan he saw, wrought as perfectly as a sculptor's masterpiece amid carefully unfurled petals of thick wrapping, but rather its image reflected back at him in eyes as fathomless as the deepest lake, alive with the wondrous hues of his mountains.

"Don't pay her any heed, Tade."

The vision of Maryssa's face faded at the sound of Brody's call, and Tade turned to see the ten-year-old thrust his head from beneath the stool. "Dee's been cross as a stinging bee since Phelan took Aileen t' the dancin' at the Dalys'. An' I heard her brag t' the other girls that you went t' Derry 'specially t' buy her somethin' that'd turn Aileen sick with envy.''

"Brody Kilcannon if you don't close you're mouth, I'll—''

"Come, now, Dee, I could hardly know you wanted frills and furbelows when you didn't see fit to tell me,'' Tade interrupted in his most cajoling tone. "And I doubt Phelan would be smitten with a girl who lost her toes at first frost.''

"*You* seem smitten enough with that dull English dishrag of a girl to make a complete dolt of yourself. Perhaps if I minced about with my eyes fixed on my toes and my mouth barely peeping open to whisper 'aye, sir,' and 'nay, ma'am,' Phelan would hurl himself at my feet.''

"Well, little sister, at least if he does, he'll not be staring at bare skin.'' Tade nodded toward the sturdy new shoes, which lay in an ignominious heap in the hearth corner. He grabbed up the towel and wiped the remaining lather from his lean cheeks, then draped the length of linen over one shoulder. He grinned as his gaze strayed to the table where Katie's tiny nose was a hair's breadth from the sugary temptation of the swan's outspread wing. The child's pink tongue peeked out of her mouth.

"Nay, nay, Katie, treasure, that sweetie is not for you,'' Tade said gently, sweeping the child up in his arms. "I brought that back from Derry town for a very special lady.''

"See-na?'' the child asked dejectedly, her little face crumpling. "See and De'dra 'll never give me a lick.''

"Well, neither one of them will get so much as a taste of this treat,'' Tade said, tweaking Katie's rosy cheek. "That swan is for the prettiest lady in Donegal, next to you.''

"Pwitty?'' the imp echoed.

"Aye. Her name is Maryssa, and she has the sweetest face God ever put on a woman.''

"You—you didn't drag home that sugar monstrosity for that cursed English witch?'' Deirdre gasped, jabbing a finger at the swan.

A frown touched Tade's brow, and only the sudden hint of fear in the girl's eyes saved him from anger. "Nay, I dragged home that sugar monstrosity as a gift for the gentlest woman— English *or* Irish—I've ever known,'' Tade offered with forced lightness. "But 'tis obviously most fortunate I had the confectioner slip a packet of peppermints for you in with the sugarteat I brought back for Ryan. Your disposition is in great need of sweetening.''

"Tade, you—you can't mean to—to woo Wylder's daughter! He would . . . will . . .'' Deirdre gulped.

"Mayhap perforce become accustomed to seeing a Kilcannon once again about Nightwylde?'' Tade finished, shooting Deirdre a mischievous grin. "What think you, Dee? Would I not strike a fine figure standing on the turrets? Or should I say dangling from them?''

He saw Deirdre flinch, her face becoming tinged with gray. A small hand tugged on his open collar, and he turned away to where Katie's eyes feasted on the swan's sugary wing, their wide blue depths bright with wistful yearning. "Tade, is your 'Ryssa gonna eat the sweetie on the terpets?'' she asked.

"Nay, love. I'm meeting her at the lakeshore. Most like she'll nibble on it there.''

"Where y' taught me an' Tamkin how t' puddle about?''

"Aye.'' Tade's mouth widened in a smile. "Come to think of it, I vow Maura could use a few lessons in puddling herself.'' The sun-drenched memory of Katie and Tamkin splashing about in the water shifted, and Tade could almost feel the cool water lapping at his naked flesh, feel Maryssa in his arms, warm, sleek, and willing . . .

"Tade?''

He mentally shook himself, vaguely embarrassed as though the child could somehow see the scene he had imagined and sense the tightening in his loins. "Aye, Kate?''

"Does your 'Ryssa like little girls?'' she asked in a tiny, hopeful voice.

Tade looked down into her round little face for a long moment, then grinned and brushed one finger over the tip of her nose. "Aye. And if she were here, I'm certain she'd break off a wee piece of the wing for my favorite little sprite,'' Tade assured her, reaching down with one hand to chip a delicate scallop from the base of the swan's wing. He popped it into Katie's mouth, whispering in a voice just loud enough for Deirdre to hear, "Maryssa has a much more agreeable temperament that either Sheena or Dee can boast.''

Tade stifled a laugh as Deirdre snatched up the laundry basket with a vengeance. One bentwood handle slammed into the washbasin, sending the metal container careening to the floor, spraying soapy water to the four corners of the room. Yowling noisily, the kittens streaked out the open door, Tom and Brody shrieked and scrambled up from the floor, their sopping wet shirts and breeches rimed with soapsuds, and little Ryan set up a piercing wail that set the very rafters shaking.

In an instant, Tade had set Katie down upon the edge of the table and grabbed a fistful of clothes from Deirdre's basket to swab up the mess. He looked up at her, words designed to tease her into laughter on his lips. But the jests stilled at the oddly stricken expression on her face.

He watched as Deirdre's tear-bright gaze swept from the graceful swan, safe upon the table, to the rivulets of water running merrily across the newly scrubbed boards to stain the leather of the shoes in the hearth corner. Tade dived for the shoes and whisked them out of harm's way, then turned, holding them aloft with a smile. But Deirdre only flung him a look of stark betrayal and then, clutching the basket, spun and ran out the door.

Tade stared after her, scarcely noticing when Brody and Tom stomped into their bedchamber to peel off their sodden clothes. "I warrant I should have told her about the gown I sent back with Reeve," he said, turning to Rachel with a rueful sigh. "But I hadn't time to match slippers to it, and Christa promised—"

"She'll see the dress soon enough, Tade." Rachel scooped up Ryan and cuddled him to her shoulder. "Some days I know not what that girl needs more, a good shaking or a month's worth of hugs."

"Well, whichever it is, she's of a certainty not gaining it from me," Tade said, moving to scrub the last of the dampness from the floor. "It seems that she spends every minute I'm home either shrieking or staring at me as if I'd just drowned her pup. She used to romp and laugh, flinging back just as good as I dealt. But now every time I open my mouth she bursts into tears or—"

"She misses you," Rachel interrupted with a sad smile. "We all do."

"But I stay home as much as possible, and even when I'm gone, 'tis for but a few week's time. I have to—"

"I know." Rachel bent to lay Ryan in his cradle. "But

each time you go, it shows us how empty this cottage will be when you finally leave for good. We've always depended upon you so—me, the little ones, and especially Dee. It seems to her that you've committed the most unforgivable sin of all. You've grown up, Tade, and left her behind.''

Tade pushed himself to his feet, a sudden ache of loss in his chest. ''Rachel, I—''

''Don't.'' Rachel held up her fingers to stop him. ''No one knows better than I how deeply you love this cottage and all of us. But you can't stay forever, despite the ties that bind you. And you can't wed Sheena to please either Dee or your father.'' Rachel's voice softened. ''But we fear for you, Tade. All of us. And this fascination you have with the Wylder girl—''

''She has a name.''

''Aye. Wylder. And yours is Kilcannon. Think, Tade, what that name means in these mountains. For three hundred years it has graced earls, rulers in their own land, and before that, kings.''

''It means naught now but one more cottage full of Irish fighting to scrape a livelihood from beneath the heel of the Sassenach.''

''Nay. When your father rides Nightwylde's lands, 'tis to him the people turn with their loyalty and honor, not to Bainbridge Wylder. They leave baskets of vegetables, chickens, aye, even coin they can ill afford, as if they were yet tenants on Kilcannon holdings. You were too young to remember how your da tried to stop them after . . . after Wylder stole the land. Kane railed at them, saying he had naught to offer them in exchange now—now that he was no longer the earl. But the mountainfolk only started leaving their baskets of treasures on the doorstep at night, so there was no way your da could know from whence they came, nay, nor return them.''

''I know of the bond between da and the people, and God knows he does what he can, to ease their burdens, but—''

''He does more than that, Tade. He makes their burdens his own. Betimes—betimes I grow jealous of his love for those who were his kerns, of the hours—sometimes days—he spends away from the babes and me, tending to them . . .'' Rachel's voice trailed off, her rawboned face suffusing with an aura of quiet pride. "But I'd ne'er clutch him to myself, to this cottage," she said. "For he gives the people the one thing the Sassenachs cannot take away from them. Aye, and so do you and all the babes. To the people who live in these hills, Tade, 'Kilcannon' is the word for hope."

" 'Tis naught but a name, Rachel. It can't warm your bed at night or bear your children." Tade paced slowly to the open door and stared out across the rock-studded slope that dipped down to a winding ribbon of stream. The laundry lay abandoned on the turf. Deirdre, her scarlet petticoats tucked into the waistband of her skirt, stretched up on the tips of her toes, shielding her eyes as she peered down the path that wound up the mountain. Tade tensed, his instincts suddenly alert as Fagan O'Donal's lumbering dray horse galloped into view, its rack-ribbed sides heaving with exertion.

The strapping O'Donal leaned down to Deirdre, calling out something Tade couldn't understand before wheeling the horse about, slapping the reins against its neck with a force that sent the staid animal plummeting down the path as if pursued by demons.

Tade was halfway to the stream by the time Deirdre had splashed back across it, her petticoats tumbling down as she dashed up the slope toward him.

"Dee, what the devil—"

" 'Tis Fagan's wife, Leah! She's borne their babe, but Fagan says 'tis too tiny. It can scarce breathe, and—"

"I'll take Rachel to her right aw—"

"Nay, Tade," Deirdre burst in, her face oddly flushed. "I . . . Leah's ma and sisters are with her. 'Tis Devin they want, to baptize the babe in case—"

"Devin? Where in blazes is he?"

"He was riding out to the O'Cahans', I think, or . . . or was it the Fitzpatricks'?"

"Damn it, Dee, they're on opposite sides of the mountains. Which was it?"

"Both," Deirdre said almost too quickly. "He was to say mass for the O'Cahan's sick mother, and at the Fitzpatricks' . . . I . . . well, I don't remember, but—"

Tade spat a curse. "He could be anywhere within a full fifty miles. I hope to God I can find him before . . . Damn!" His eyes flashed toward the valley below, finding the distant break in the trees that sheltered the hidden glen. "Dee, you'll have to go to the lake for me. Tell Maryssa what happened. That I'll come to her as soon as—"

"I will. Now go!"

"And, Deirdre, tell her I—" Tade stopped at the strange look on his sister's upturned face, a fist twisting in his stomach as the words he had wanted to whisper to Maryssa snagged in his throat.

The green of Deirdre's eyes washed bright with tears and terror, and he could see that she sensed what he had been about to say. Pressing her knuckles to her lips, she spun away from him and stumbled down the hillside.

Tade took one step after her, then, spitting a curse, wheeled and raced toward the byre where his stallion waited.

The flowers were dying. Maryssa slipped a drooping blossom from her hair and fingered the once-crimson petals that now lay wilted to the hue of dried blood. She had waited since the sun was at its crest, watched it as it sank inexorably toward the scraggly tops of the trees. And with each gossamer sweep of clouds that drifted above the grassy rise on which she sat, the joy that had sung within her stilled a little more.

"He will be here. He *will*," she had told herself a hundred times. But with every rustle of underbrush, every snap of twigs, every breath of wind that failed to bring with it Tade's laughing face, the doubt within her unsheathed its velvet claws.

And as twilight dripped jeweled colors across the glen, the very breeze seemed to whisper of the dangers lurking in the hills that had seemed touched only with beauty when graced by Tade's smile.

Maryssa shivered, remembering the horror in the stable boy's peaked face when she had ordered him to saddle a horse. "Ye—ye can't be mane-in' t' go ridin' off alone, miss," he had stammered. " 'Tis lucky ye are that ye weren't carried off or murdered or worse the last time ye went gallivantin' off, what with the rabble that roams here'bouts. Why, it hasn't been but a bit past a week since the Black Falcon was a-raidin'."

Maryssa twisted her fingers together, remembering the night at the foul-smelling inn, when eyes as green as Tade Kilcannon's had glared at her from slits in the night, but those eyes had been cold and dangerous, reflecting none of Tade's easy warmth and tenderness, and none of the devilment that sparkled from within him. She bit her lip, dread rippling through her that had nothing to do with the stable lad's babblings.

No, it was impossible, she told herself, quelling the niggling thought. The Falcon had stalked into the inn full of menace, as sharply honed and as lethal as an infidel's blade, while Tade . . . She pictured the mischief in his grin, the delight he took in the smallest of pleasures. Yet instead of comforting her, the image tightened the unease that gripped her, casting across her mind the memory of an instant—an instant when a certain odd tenderness had shone in the brigand Falcon's eyes. She glanced apprehensively at the liver-colored mare that stood cropping grass at the lakeside, then back to the waning sun. Perhaps it would be best if—

Suddenly she started, instinctively scrambling to her feet at the sound of something passing through the brush behind her. Tade? Or . . . Hope, dread, and fear roiled inside her as she whirled around, half expecting to see a black silk hood and a sable cocked hat with plumes red as blood.

But instead of the Black Falcon's sinister countenance or the ruggedly masculine visage of Tade, it was Deirdre Kilcannon who flounced into view. Her freckled nose was crinkled in disdain and grains of sparkling sugar clung to her lips as she munched on what looked to be a delicate scalloped wing.

"D-Deirdre?" Maryssa stammered. "What . . . what are you doing here?"

The girl licked one sugary finger. "Tade couldn't quite manage to keep your little tryst this afternoon, so . . ." She shrugged, letting her voice trail off.

"Deirdre, is . . . is Tade well? Safe?"

"He's well, most certainly. But safe?" Deirdre smirked, then took another bite of the confection. "When last I left him he seemed in the gravest of danger."

"Danger?" A sharp, sick feeling stirred in Maryssa's stomach.

Deirdre's laugh tinkled on the air. "Aye, he and Sheena O'Toole were roving off on horseback, but I vow they were in more of a mind to tumble in the grass than race over it."

Pain and betrayal crushed Maryssa's chest; then a sudden fierce spark of denial flared up. "I don't believe it."

"And just where do you suppose I got this?" Deirdre held up the delicate piece of sugar, smacking her lips. "Tade brought it from Derry, and when he gave it to Sheena, why, I vow, she could scarce wait to carry him off somewhere private to . . . uh . . . thank him."

Maryssa stared at the confection, then raised her eyes slowly to Deirdre's face. Satisfaction glinted in the girl's green eyes, and her mouth was pursed into sharp lines of smugness.

Maryssa lifted her chin. "You must be mistaken. Tade told me to meet him—"

"Here? Oh, aye, I know. That did make things a bit awkward. I mean, what with you lingering about at their favorite spot. But I'm certain they found somewhere to . . ."

A wave of nausea gripped Maryssa as her gaze darted to the flower-spangled bit of glen upon which the coverlet had lain weeks before. *Their favorite spot* . . . Had Tade truly tumbled Sheena back into this sweet meadow grass? Kissed her, loved her . . . here where he had given Maryssa a glimpse of heaven?

No! Yet how could Deirdre have found this glen? How could she have known that Maryssa waited here, unless . . .

Much as she fought against it, the image of the honey-haired Sheena running her fingernails over Tade's chest, kissing him with a practiced skill that made her own untutored fumblings seem all the more clumsy, seared itself into Maryssa's brain with sickening clarity.

"Come, now, Miss Wylder, you mustn't look so distressed."

Maryssa's eyes leaped to Deirdre's face, the girl's smile, so like Tade's tearing at her heart.

"Even you must agree 'tis only right Tade should first take a gift to the girl he is bound to marry," Deirdre chided innocently. "And I am most certain that he brought some little trinket back from Derry for you as well. No doubt he'll dash it off to you as soon as he's able."

Maryssa clenched her teeth against the pain welling up inside her. She wanted to scream, to drown out the sound of Deirdre's voice, but her throat was blocked by tears.

"Of course you must be patient," Deirdre rushed on. "It

may be quite some time before he can reach you, considering all the other deliveries he has to make. My da claims Tade needs a dray to haul home all the trinkets he buys to satisfy his mistresses—uh . . . I mean, ladies.''

Maryssa spun toward the lake, forcing her quavering voice through the sobs constricting her chest. ''Well, you may tell your brother he need not trouble himself delivering anything to me. I wouldn't . . . wouldn't want—''

''Oh, 'twill hardly be any trouble.'' Deirdre waved a slender hand in dismissal. ''After all, an English heiress is quite a grand conquest, even for Tade, and since you allowed him . . . er . . . access to your charms a fortnight past, why, I am certain Tade is fairly chafing to be with you.''

Maryssa wheeled to face Deirdre, and even through the white-hot shards of torment exploding within her, she could see the girl falter beneath her stricken stare. ''Tade . . . Tade told you . . . ?''

Deirdre started to speak, then stopped, her face paling a tinge beneath her freckles. ''About the afternoon here on the lakeshore?'' she asked, stooping to swoop up a small twig and examine it as though it held the answer to some mystic riddle. ''Why, of course Tade told me. I've been privy to his confidences since I wore short skirts. And . . . well, I must confess, 'tis ever so much more entertaining to hear about grand passions than about boyhood pranks.''

Maryssa felt a knife twist deep in her stomach as a sense of betrayal sharper than any she had ever experienced ripped through her. Shame, humiliation, and mind-numbing agony crashed in smothering waves over the memory she had cherished, grinding to ashes the images of blossom-starred meadows and hot, hungry kisses. She raised her gaze to Deirdre's face, but the girl swung away.

''You . . . you needn't be dismayed. I mean about my knowing your secret,'' Deirdre faltered, busily snapping off bits of the twig. ''Tade has filled me with so many *affaires de coeur,* that, I vow, by Allhallows Eve, I'll most like forget I ever heard this one. After all, 'tis not as if there is much to remember, what with Tade halting before he—''

''No!''

Deirdre winced at the strangled cry, the raw torment in Maryssa's features burning into her memory as Maryssa

wheeled and stumbled toward the horse tethered nearby.
Deirdre watched, guilt and vague horror at what she had done
stirring inside her, as the English girl flung herself astride the
beast and pressed her heels into its sides with a clumsy recklessness that threatened to pitch her onto the jagged stones
below. The horse plunged up the hill, nostrils flared, eyes
wide as it tore up the slope toward the treacherous and wild
lands beyond.

" 'Twill be the last we see of that English witch," Deirdre
whispered to herself. "I'm glad. *Glad.*" Yet the feeling of
triumph she had expected to soar within her rang hollow as
she remembered Maryssa's waxen face. The girl loved Tade.
Her love was carved in every line of her face. And Tade . . .
Deirdre tried to swallow but couldn't, the image of his face
before he had run to the byre flashing before her eyes. He
had looked so solemn, serious, yet oddly touched with greater
joy than ever before. If he discovered what she had done . . .

Nay. Deirdre's fists knotted, her nails digging into the soft
flesh of her palms. It mattered not whether Maryssa Wylder
loved her brother or if he cherished some budding tenderness
for her. She could bring him naught but danger . . . death.

Closing her eyes, Deirdre struggled to conjure in her mind
the image that had haunted her for hours. Yet as the ancient
stone of Nightwylde's turrets rose in her mind, the silhouette
of a body dangling from their peak, it was not Tade's face
she saw contorted in death throes, but the delicate features
of Maryssa Wylder whose eyes screamed their pain in a dozen
shattered hues.

Ten

TADE NARROWED HIS eyes against the half-light of dawn, his mouth a hard line as he hauled himself up the rungs of the loft ladder. The first waking birds twittered from their perches on the thatch, the banked peat fire gilding the room with the glow of its tiny embers. Yet within his stiff, sore body roiled a barely leashed anger that threatened to rage like wildfire.

Deirdre. For five miles he had ridden like a madman, anticipating the bliss of wringing her spoiled little throat with his own two hands. Sweet God, when he thought of what her foolishness had almost caused this time . . .

Tade vaulted through the loft opening and stamped across the darkened room to the small window at one end. With a muffled curse, he grasped the shutter handles and threw the heavy wooden panels open with a force that sent them slamming against the walls. Dim light spilled across the worn rag rug and tumbled in pearly rays across the rumpled pallet beneath the eaves.

"Deirdre!" Tade snapped the name, spinning around to yank the mound of coverlets from the narrow bed in which she lay. Yet instead of sleep-blurred features beneath her tousled hair, he saw red-rimmed eyes peering up at him with the watchful gaze of a cornered mouse.

She struggled upright, a too-bright smile pasted on her lips. "Tade! You needn't rouse the whole house. I—I was waiting for you."

"Aye, and I'll just wager you were. After all, you'd not want to miss the pleasure of seeing the fruits of your little plot, would you?" Tade blazed.

"P-plot?" He saw Deirdre flinch, a guilty flush staining her cheeks. "I don't know what you—"

"Damn it, don't play the innocent. I've spent the whole night tearing through the mountains like the very devil was on my heels, and I have no stomach for your lies. Just tell me, do I look worn enough, filthy enough, angry enough, for you to feel as though you've reaped full justice for my horrible sin of daring to return from Derry without a cartful of baubles for you? Or can I look forward to a like performance in the future?"

"What . . . what do you mean? I only gave you Fagan's message! He said the babe was in danger, and—"

"Blast it, don't cram untruths into someone else's mouth! I saw the O'Donal babe with my own eyes. A girl it is, weighing a full nine pounds, hale as a well-born filly. But you know that, don't you, Deirdre? You knew it from the moment Fagan reined in his horse."

"Nay! I—"

"Just like you knew that Dev was nowhere near the Fitzpatricks' or the O'Cahans'," Tade accused. "The whole time I was riding, nigh driving Curran to his death, Devin was just three miles from home, at Liam Scanlon's, helping to arrange a way to smuggle young Jamie off to school in Bordeaux."

"Scanlon's?" The feigned shock in the girl's face made Tade want to slap her.

"Devin told me he left word with you as to exactly where he could be found, in case old Patrick Mahoney took a turn for the worse. You knew—"

"Nay, Tade, I—"

"Damn it, Dee, quit lying!" Tade cut the denial off with a snarl. "This time your little game near ended with consequences too great for even you to bear. A mile from O'Donal's, Dev and I ran afoul of a contingent of Rath's guard dogs."

"R-Rath . . ." Deirdre blanched, her freckles standing out in stark relief against her pallid skin.

"Aye, Rath. By the time I found Devin, I'd been tearing about the countryside half the night, thinking a babe lay dying, maybe dead. And Dev . . . when he heard how long I'd been seeking him—" A muscle in Tade's jaw knotted at the memory of Devin's face, a mask of solemn desperation as they rode toward Fagan O'Donal's cottage. "The way we were racing across the mountain, 'twas a miracle I saw the soldiers at all, let alone managed to ride Curran into Penderleigh Cave before the bastards spied us. You lied, damn it, and—"

"I don't care!" Deirdre's chin quivered, her eyes spitting defiance. "I'd do it again!"

"Again? You'd risk Devin's life because I failed to bring you a damned dress?"

"Nay! It wasn't the dress!"

"Then why? Why the bloody hell did you—" Tade froze, the look in Deirdre's eyes—anger, betrayal, resentment—striking him like a fist in his belly. "Maryssa," Tade rasped the name, knowing . . . somehow knowing . . . "Damn it, Dee, what have you done?"

"I fixed it so that Sassenach witch will never see you again!"

"You what?" Tade's hands shot out, crushing Deirdre's arms in a bruising grip.

"I told her you were with Sheena," Deirdre flung back. "That you'd no doubt get to Nightwylde after you'd finished with your other mistresses. But is seems the high-and-mighty Miss Wylder is not wont to be just another in your string of women, because she—"

"Damn you!" Rage coiled within him as he imagined the agony tearing at Maryssa's fragile heart. "Deirdre, I trusted you and—"

"I did it for you!" Deirdre clutched at his shirtfront. "A score of girls in Donegal would forfeit all they own to wed you—*Irish* girls, *Catholic* girls, prettier by a thousandfold than that Wylder chit."

"I don't want them. I don't *love* them."

The defiance that had burned in Deirdre's face faded into

desperation as a ragged sob was torn from her throat. "Tade, she's not worth dying for!"

"Aye, Dee. She is."

Gripping her wrists, Tade pulled her fingers free of him, then strode to the opening of the loft.

"She'll not see you, Tade!" Deirdre shrieked, stumbling after him as he climbed down the ladder. "She'll never forgive you!"

"Tade! Deirdre!" Tade caught a fleeting glimpse of night rail as the lank white-robed form of Rachel threw open the door to her bedchamber. Barefoot, she rushed across the room to catch the sobbing girl in thin, gentle arms.

Deirdre clutched at her mother, childlike tears flooding her frightened eyes. "Mama . . . Mama, don't let him go!"

The piteous cries tore at Tade's heart, but he could not go to her. He felt the pull of Maryssa like that of the moon, wooing the tide onto jagged cliffs at the gray sea's edge.

Tade paused at the door, unable to sever his gaze from the terror in Deirdre's face, the silent pain in Rachel's soft brown eyes. Then he turned away from all he had loved and walked alone into the dawn.

The walnut-paneled dining room of Marlow Hall was stifling with the heat of three dozen candles, their waxy fragrance blending in a sickening mixture with the stench of heavily perfumed bodies and the aroma of rich food. Maryssa pricked at a bit of roast duckling with the tines of her fork, unable to imagine how she would ever be able to swallow with Quentin Rath slurping and guzzling bare inches from her elbow.

The odious colonel had all but shoved Reeve Marlow into the punch table in his effort to gain Maryssa's arm when the footman announced that dinner was to be served. And in spite of Christabel and Reeve's valiant efforts to maneuver her out of his grasp, Rath had brazenly plopped his broad buttocks into the chair beside Maryssa and barked for the liveried footman to spoon dizzying portions of meat and gravy onto his delicate china plate.

Maryssa hazarded a glance at him from the corner of her eye. His sloppily powdered bag wig sat askew on his florid sweat-dappled brow, while great rings of dampness seeped through his flowered velvet coat in malodorous half-circles.

Maryssa felt her stomach churn as he shoveled half of a baked capon into his sauce-stained mouth. Her eyes leaped away from his smacking lips, bile rising in her throat. But as her gaze skittered across the table, it snagged on Christabel's blue eyes, which were fastened upon her in loving concern.

Maryssa managed a smile and hastily popped a piece of roast duck between her lips. The succulent meat clung to her mouth like wet cotton as she struggled to force it past the knot in her throat. She wished for the thousandth time since alighting from her father's carriage that she had been able to hold true to her plan.

She had arrived the night before, wounded by Deirdre's words, weary, and without so much as a valise in her hand. Maryssa had fully intended to explain to the Marlows that she could not bear to be introduced into Donegal society the next evening and would even be poor company for the fortnight's visit Christa had cozened Bainbridge into allowing Maryssa to accept. But when the footman had ushered her into the salon, Christabel had fairly flown over to clasp her in a joyous embrace.

"I vow I could cheerfully murder Tade Kilcannon for declining my invitation for tomorrow evening!" Christabel had bubbled. "Reeve's been nigh wearing the carpets to shreds, pacing about in a fury to give him the news, and I thought 'twould be forever before you arrived!"

The pain in Maryssa's chest had wrenched tighter at the mention of Tade's name, the knowledge that he must be, in truth, avoiding her twisting like the blade of a knife. But Christabel had merely tightened her silk-clad arms about her, saying, "Now we have two things to celebrate tomorrow evening, Maryssa. My finding a best friend and—" The shy blush that tinted Christabel's beautiful face set her aglow with happiness. "And," she continued breathlessly, "well, it seems that Reeve's penchant for breeding has finally brought results."

"Breeding?" Maryssa had echoed numbly.

"Yes. I . . . Reeve and I are going to have a baby."

Despite the torment Deirdre Kilcannon's words had hurled within her and the pain of yet another proof of Tade's rejection, Maryssa had not shed even one drop of unhappiness on the rainbow of joy enveloping her friends. She had instead forced a weak smile to her lips and explained that her new maid had neglected to see her trunk loaded into the coach.

Maryssa's throat constricted convulsively, the bit of meat finally squeezing its way through the tightness as she gazed miserably past the heaping platters of food to where Christabel crowned the head of the table like a sparkling goddess. The joy that had lit her friend's delicate features the day before had deepened during the night, leaving her smile softer, gentler, her eyes brimful with a completeness that jabbed Maryssa with sharp pricks of envy.

A babe . . . How many times in her lonely childhood had Maryssa vowed that she would have a babe of her own someday? A girl, tiny and dewy-soft like the one Jenny, the scullery maid, carried with her in a split-oak basket as she went about her chores. Maryssa could almost hear herself sobbing into the pillow of her narrow bed at Carradown that she would love her baby just as Jenny did, even if it always cried, even if it was awkward and had strange eyes and ugly dark brown hair.

Maryssa closed her eyes, the face of the babe she had always imagined rising in her mind, but the golden curls and sky-colored eyes of her childhood dreams shifted, changing to hair the color of polished rosewood and a gaze as bright green as the Irish hills. Tade . . . the thought of him, of his child, struck her like a hidden dagger to the heart.

Suddenly the vision shattered, something hard and damp slamming into her back with a force that nearly pitched her bosom-first into her plate. She turned her gaze to where Quentin Rath bent over her.

"Miss Wylder, are you all right?" he asked, his palm still flattened against the ivory damask of her gown. "Stake me, but I thought you were nigh about to strangle yourself on that bit of meat you ate, your face got so pasty."

"I . . . I'm fine, Colonel Rath. Just . . . 'twas just the heat, and—"

"Well, if you'd take yourself bites of size to chew on, perhaps you'd not be so overcome. 'Tis little wonder you wax so frail, the way you pick at morsels scarce large enough to tempt a linnet. Take this advice from one who has dwelt on this infernal island near all his life," he chided, eyeing her breasts as greedily as he had eyed the capon bare moments before. "Eat hearty. You'll need your strength to battle this crude land and its witless inhabitants."

"Oooo, Miss Wylder, do mind the colonel, here," a voice edged with a constant whine crooned at her shoulder. Maryssa turned to where the close-set eyes of a girl Christabel had introduced as Jacinth Levander blinked up at Rath adoringly from above her decidedly hooked nose. "Colonel Rath has had no end of heroic exploits, protecting us from these barbaric Irish." Jacinth's skinny fingers reached up to pluck at the gravy-splotched sleeve of Rath's coat. "Why, he was off pursuing that devil the Black Falcon but a week since."

"The heroic Colonel Rath has been off pursuing the 'witless' Falcon nigh on two years now without success," Reeve Marlow observed dryly, lifting his wine goblet to his lips. His words pierced a lull in the buzz of voices about the table, and a sudden quiet fell over the room.

Rath's fingers went stiff on her back, and Maryssa feared his buttons would burst as his chest swelled out in indignation. "True, in the past the rogue has eluded me," Rath grudgingly admitted. "But I trow the Falcon will not be soaring for a while this time."

Maryssa saw Reeve's face go suddenly still. "Not soaring? What do you mean?"

"A ball from my pistol struck his left arm. Saw him jerk, I did, and the blood. But even wounded, the bast—I mean, blackguard—can ride like the devil himself."

Maryssa felt an odd squeezing in her chest at the thought of the Falcon falling beneath Quentin Rath's bullet, the rebel's swirling black mantle marred with blood, the piercing green of his eyes . . .

Eyes . . . Sudden dizzying waves of fear swept over her as Tade's face rose in her mind, his gaze so incredibly green it shone like polished emerald. She bit her lip, seeing his grin as he tossed his baby sister high in the air, his lean body cutting naked through the cold blue waters of the lake, his long legs hurtling him across the meadow in pursuit of the horsehide covered ball . . . No, lightsome Tade, with his laughter and his teasing, could never change into the implacable hooded rebel known as the Black Falcon. Could never . . . Why, then, did the thought torment her so? She shoved the thought away and turned her eyes to Reeve's taut features.

"He did escape, then?" Reeve stifled a yawn, but Maryssa could detect lines of tension about his lips.

"Aye. Fled like a coward into the mountains. But most like the bullet I buried in his flesh will clip his wings long enough to keep him holed up in his nest until his new adversary arrives."

"You're bringing in a new man?" Reeve asked.

"Aye." The hair at the nape of Maryssa's neck prickled at the eagerness that slackened Rath's thick lips. "The finest huntsman of human quarry in all of England. He will arrive in Lononderry upon Allhallows Eve and has vowed that within the month he and his hounds will ferret out every brigand and papist priest who lurks within these hills."

Maryssa's fingers tightened on the handle of her fork, driving its silver scrolls deep into her palm as she remembered Devin's pale, gentle face. "Surely you can't mean to set hounds on priests?"

"Aye, and great sport it will be, too. Wilier than wolves, they be, these priests, and thrice as dangerous. Why, just last month I found one secreted away in a hole carved into the wall of Tiernan MacCarthy's hovel. Before my men could rout him out, MacCarthy nigh slit my throat."

" 'Tis hardly a wonder," Christabel said, an edge to her voice. "The priest was Mr. MacCarthy's son."

"Well, both sire and his spawn have got their just punishments," Rath said, spooning up a glob of potato cake and gravy. "MacCarthy lies rotting in Rookescommon prison, and his papist son . . ." Rath guffawed, then stuffed the heaping spoonful of food into his mouth. "I vow he lies rotting over half of Londonderry."

"Over half of—" Maryssa stammered. "I—I don't understand."

"A chunk here, a chunk there. Drawn and quartered he was, and by the time the horses were done with him—"

Maryssa's stomach turned inside out, what little food she had managed to choke down rising in a sour ball in her throat. She saw Christabel's face take on a greenish cast.

"Rath! Enough." Reeve snapped, his gaze flashing to his

wife. "No one at this table has any interest in your barbaric *sport*."

" 'Tis not so barbaric." Rath shrugged. "Even in England priests are sometimes hunted. And here on this cursed island the papist poison runs far deeper. Their clergy fester like a cancer, spreading foul, sinful lies to these brainless peasants. 'Tis the duty of all God-fearing men to cut it from their hearts."

Maryssa looked up at his sagging jowls, his face puffed with self-righteousness. "Odd," she said softly. "Your words are near echoes of the claims made eighteen hundred years ago."

"Your pardon, Miss Wylder?" Rath's mouth was set in a line of displeasure, and all eyes about the table had fastened on Maryssa.

She leveled her suddenly steady gaze on Rath. "I said, the men who murdered Christ used much the same excuse."

Forks froze midway to a dozen separate mouths, faces washed with lead paint waxed whiter still as shocked silence fell over the room. Maryssa saw Reeve's mouth twitch into a smile as Christabel lifted her chin with pride.

"Miss Wylder," Jacinth's high-pitched voice trilled, her eyes bugging out in horror, "surely you cannot compare those foul beasts to Colonel Rath. Why, after all, this is *Ireland*. He is but ridding the land of . . . of vermin who—"

"I doubt Tiernan MacCarthy considered his son vermin, Miss Levander," Maryssa challenged.

"And I doubt that your father will be pleased to be informed that he harbors one so sympathetic to the Catholics' plight," Quentin Rath snarled. "Especially since 'twas at Bainbridge Wylder's prodding that we sent for Sir Ascot."

Maryssa felt something snag in her breast. "Who?"

"Sir Ascot Dallywoulde, the most ruthless priest hunter ever to loose his hounds."

Maryssa gripped the edge of the table so hard her fingers ached, the pain that had torn through her at Tade's betrayal deepening to a sick horror as she pictured her cousin's fanatical eyes. A priest hunter, an animal who tracked down men like Devin—gentle men, men who believed . . . "Father?" Maryssa croaked. "Father knew Sir Ascot was—"

"Miss Wylder, you look most distressed at the thought of

these brigands being brought to justice,'' Rath observed in frigid tones. ''Just when did you acquire your sympathy for papists? While you were in England? Or was it perhaps during the night you spent at the Kilcannons'?''

A murmur swept over the table, and Maryssa could feel Christabel bristle. ''Colonel, how dare—''

''The night your soldiers smashed in the door, Colonel Rath?'' Maryssa cut Christabel's sputtered words off, the horror that had wrenched her moments before giving way to blazing anger. ''That was most heroic of you!'' she bit out. ''An entire troop of soldiers raiding a cottage full of babes.''

''Not all babes, eh, Miss Wylder?''

Maryssa struggled to keep the guilty flush from her cheeks as Rath's eyes skimmed over her décolletage. Her chin tipped up, eyes clashing defiantly with Rath's cunning gaze.

''Just what are you intimating, Rath?'' Reeve challenged, his eyes hot with anger.

''Merely that 'tis most unusual for a well-born English lady to wax so . . . er . . . pugnacious in defense of low-born peasants like the Kilcannons.''

''The blood of kings ran through Kilcannon veins when our grandsires were still mucking out swine huts,'' Reeve said.

''That may be true, but I doubt 'tis their royalty which holds such allure for Miss Wylder.''

Maryssa's stiff fingers fluttered to her breast, and she felt as though the despicable colonel could almost see the tracings of Tade's lips upon her skin.

Reeve hurled his napkin onto his plate, bounding to his feet in barely coiled fury. ''By God, Rath, I'll—''

''Nay, Reeve. 'Tis all right.'' Maryssa drew herself up haughtily as she faced Rath's sly leer. ''I care not whether Rachel or Tade or any of the Kilcannons were born in the lowliest ditch in Ireland. They were kind to me, loving . . . They took me in when I was lost and frightened and—'' The words caught in Maryssa's throat, the cunning light in Rath's beady eyes making her feel naked, vulnerable.

''I beg your forgiveness, Miss Wylder.'' The apology slipped like oil from Rath's tongue, his lips curving into a knowing smile. ''Until this very moment I did not comprehend the full extent of your . . . *loyalty* to the Kilcannons.''

Maryssa flinched, feeling the jaws of some invisible trap snap shut about her throat. A sudden primal need to escape gripped her.

Her eyes darted to Christabel's worried features. "I-I'm sorry," she said. "I've a bit of a headache. Perhaps if I could withdraw . . ."

"I'll go with you." Christabel started to rise.

"Nay, I'll not be long. Mayhap a turn about your garden will help to clear my head." Maryssa rose, struggling to affect a calm mien beneath Rath's cold, assessing stare. "If you'll pardon me, Colonel Rath?"

"Pardon you?" A smile slithered across Rath's lips, his voice dropping to the hiss of a snake. "That entirely depends upon the seriousness of your offense."

Maryssa felt a chill prickle her skin. Squaring her shoulders beneath the ivory damask of her gown, she walked to Christabel's side to give her friend's hand a reassuring squeeze. Then Maryssa turned and swept away through the ornately carved doors.

The night was sweet, heavy with the scent of darkness, as Maryssa fled into the garden's warm embrace. Yet in spite of the scores of paper lanterns bedecking the moonlit maze in a dozen glowing colors, it seemed to Maryssa as if the garden's precisely trimmed hedges pressed about her like the bars of a jail.

Rath's silkily voiced threats seemed to lurk within the night-shadowed pathways, lashing her with coils of panic, driving her ruthlessly through countless shifting images that seemed to dart across the darkened sky like scenes from some macabre play.

Tade . . . Maryssa clenched numb fingers in the lace that tumbled past her wrists, the starched patterns rasping against her palms. She cared not if he took a thousand women to his bed, if she never again felt the wonder of his touch—if only he was safe. Yet even as she fought to banish the nightmare visions from her mind, they roiled onward, giving her no hope, no peace.

Hounds pursued their quarry through dream-hazed mountains. Devin, his slender wrists bound with stout rope, lay stretched beneath brutal hands, face contorted in agony as the executioner's knife bit into his flesh. And a midnight-black mantle shrouded Tade Kilcannon's broad, lifeless shoulders in its scarlet-stained folds as green eyes, glazed in death, stared up at her through slits in a black silk hood.

The bullet I buried in his flesh . . . Maryssa shut her eyes against the hideous image Rath's words painted, but the rich imagination she had cultivated during childhood proved her betrayer, casting across the canvas of her mind a hundred vivid images of Tade, the pistol ball tearing his hard bronzed flesh, his lean body crumpling, falling . . . dying.

"He's not the Black Falcon! He's *not!*" Maryssa pressed her knuckles against her teeth, tasting the salt of tears. "Deirdre said nothing of Tade being wounded. He's hale. Safe."

Yet in the darkest corners of her mind echoes of horrifying laughter rose to torment her, fanatical tones honed with a blade-thin edge of evil. Dallywoulde . . . Maryssa's flesh crawled at the memory of his colorless eyes, cold and treacherous as ice veiling a churning sea, eyes satanic with a soulless hate, their eerie light greedy as he watched a child devoured by flames.

Maryssa shivered. From the first moment she had squirmed from Tade's arms upon the lakeshore, seen his achingly handsome features and his reckless grin, she had known he was a man who courted Dame Death with the same bold abandon with which he had wooed scores of other mistresses. But this evil . . . Dallywoulde . . . was spawn of another world . . . dark and stygian as the face of Satan, yet far more dangerous because he cloaked himself in the guise of righteousness.

And nothing would give him more pleasure than to slash his hatred into the very souls of the only people Maryssa had ever loved.

"Nay! I won't let him," Maryssa cried fiercely, panic licking tiny flames through her veins. "Ascot and my father will not take this from me, too. I have to . . . have to warn Devin and Tade . . . while there is still time—"

Time for what? A tiny voice jeered within her. For them to run? Hide?

"Aye!" Maryssa dashed the thought aside with the defiance of a hysterical child. "I'll make them hide! Make them understand that they have to."

She spun back toward the hulking stone shadow of Marlow Hall, its windows, topaz with candleshine, glaring at her like great disapproving eyes. Silks and satins of every hue wafted past the open casements and she could hear the quartet Christabel had hired striking up the strains of a minuet. 'Twould be but a few moments before Christabel or Reeve or—Maryssa shuddered at the thought—Rath came in search of her. Did she dare . . . ?

Maryssa's gaze darted toward the place where she knew Reeve's stable stood with its back to the brooding mountains—mountains teeming with cutthroats, brigands, long dead spirits from a hundred haunting tales stalking the night. Yet even as claws of fear pierced Maryssa's throat, the toes of her satin slippers dug deep into the pebbled path, hurling her through the darkened maze toward the stable.

The hedges caught at her petticoats and sleeves; the crimson ribband woven through her dark curls pulled free, sending the heavy mass of her hair cascading down her back. Yet still she ran, ran as if the very night pursued her, as if somewhere in the mists Ascot Dallywoulde lurked beneath the shroud of darkness, his pale eyes watching, ever watching, his thin lips twisted in unholy glee.

A sob choked in her throat as she rounded yet another bend in the intricate maze, her slipper snagging on something veiled by the night. She stumbled, thrusting out both arms as she sprawled on the ground. Her palms struck the path, the tender flesh tearing on sharp-edged bits of stone. But despite the stinging pain, she paused not an instant, only shoved herself to her feet, pushing herself the last steps toward the opening of the maze, where an ancient oak split the garden pathway, its branches as black and twisted as Dallywoulde's soul.

Suddenly Maryssa froze in terror as the branches of the oak seemed to reach out for her. Fingers swept out to clutch her arms and yank her against a hard wall of muscle. She screamed and kicked, her fingernails gouging flesh as she raked their sharpness against a beard-stubbled jaw and the soft, fragile skin below an eye. A callused palm clamped over her mouth, stilling her cries. The sound of a curse hissed in her ear as she sank her teeth deep into the fleshy mound beneath her attacker's thumb.

"God's wounds, Maura!" A voice battled its way through

the haze of fear enveloping her. "At least let me explain before you make me faint of blood loss."

A sob of relief snagged in her breast as light from a delicate lantern limned the achingly familiar curve of a lean bronzed cheek, marred now by thin tracks of blood.

"T-Tade!" She sobbed, collapsing against his chest. Strong, comforting arms crushed her tight into his muscled frame, the hard heat of him searing warmth into her fear-chilled skin.

"Easy, love, easy. Of course 'tis me. I swear to God, I didn't mean to frighten you." Soothing, incredibly gentle, the words wisped through the curls at her temple. "I was going to wait until the soiree was over, then come to you and explain, but when I saw you—" The tender rumble of his voice stopped, and she felt him suck in his breath. "Damn, you're shaking like a reed in a gale. What the hell—"

"Tade, I-I had to find you . . . warn you. Devin . . . Devin's in danger, and you—"

"Devin?" Moonlight touched a menacing hardness in Tade's jaw.

"Aye. C-Colonel Rath—he's bringing in a priest hunter. A man from England."

"That doesn't make any sense. I know Rath wants Dev, but for the bastard to go to the expense and trouble of dragging in a master huntsman . . ."

"Rath isn't hiring him especially to find Devin. The hunter is to stalk the Black Falcon, then clean out any . . . any other priests hiding in the hills."

"Odd," Tade said with grim amusement. "In all the tales I've heard of this Falcon, I never guessed he was a priest."

"Tade, 'tis no jest! Ascot Dallywoulde—"

"Dallywoulde?" Tade rolled the name off his tongue as if it were a bawdy riddle. "*Ascot Dallywoulde* is the name of this savage huntsman?" Tade threw back his head and let his rich laughter dance on the darkness. "By God, the name alone is enough to send me hieing into the hills. Perhaps Dev had best fear Rath's huntsman after all. No doubt the second the Black Falcon hears that a man with such a fearsome name is stalking him, he'll cast aside his hood forever."

A knot of raw terror yanked tight in Maryssa's throat as

she saw the heedless twinkle in Tade's eyes. "This man is no buffoon," she cried desperately. "He—"

"He's a priggish spidershanks with a bulbous nose and a case of gout, I wager," Tade teased. "And most like he's so cross-eyed he can scarce hit the side of a ship with a musket ball. No doubt the Falcon will be well pleased to sink his talons into such a vicious adversary. I vow, I'm nigh tempted myself—"

She clutched at his chest, tremors shaking her to her very core. "Nay, you can't! He can't . . . Tade . . ." Sobs of near-hysteria racked her body, and her quaking knees suddenly refused to bear her weight.

"Maura!" Uttering an oath, his voice raspy with concern, Tade caught her as she sagged against him, sweeping one muscled arm beneath her legs and scooping her up into his arms. She felt him tense as if in pain; then the tautness in his muscles eased slightly as he carried her to a curved marble bench hidden in the maze's thick shadows. He lowered himself onto the seat, cradling her against his hard body, his hands stroking the tangled hair back from her moist brow. "Damn, you're cold. Shaking."

"Tade . . . Tade, oh, God, you have to listen to me!"

"I will, love. I will. Hush, now." He pressed the firm warmth of his lips into her hair, skimming kisses sweet and light as spun sugar against her cheeks and lashes.

"If Dallywoulde finds Devin—"

"I won't let anything happen to Dev, Maura."

"But you, Tade, if aught were to befall you—" The horror of the imaginings that had tormented her minutes before—of Tade's lean body broken, bleeding—crashed in about her. She closed her eyes against them, a tiny cry breaching her lips as she arched her head back, reaching, seeking, needing the hot sweep of Tade's tongue upon hers. His mouth descended, hard, moist, and pulsing with life, upon her lips. A groan rumbled low in his chest.

"The bullet's not been molded that could steal my life away. Not now, love . . . now that I—" He dragged his mouth from hers, catching her face between his palms. "Maryssa, look at me." Her eyes fluttered open, his heart thundering beneath her hand for long seconds that seemed to stretch into forever. "Maura, I love you."

Maryssa gaped at him, the words splashing over her like a molten rainbow, searing, blinding, far too bright for her to touch. An overwhelming sensation of disbelief, elation, and anger rioted inside her, dashing away the tight-strung coils of fear that had bound her, replacing them with bands that cut more deeply.

"You . . . you love me?" Maryssa's eyes locked on his face, expecting to see mockery, jest, some tinge of the bored, accomplished rake who must have murmured the same words to countless others. Her throat constricted, bitter tears threatening to spill over her lashes. "And just when, pray tell, did you make this great discovery? When you and Sheena O'Toole were out riding? Did she . . . did she fail to thank you thoroughly enough for the gift you brought her?" Maryssa tried to pull away from his grasp, but his arms tightened around her.

"Gift?"

"Aye. The sugar swan. Sheena was most generous. Deirdre was munching on a piece of the confection when she came to tell me where you were." Maryssa turned her face away from him, unable to keep the hurt from her voice.

"Damn Deirdre! I'm going to flay her alive!" Tade growled savagely. Then his fingers caught Maryssa's chin in a determined grasp, tipped her face up toward his. "I brought that swan back from Derry for *you,* Maura. Deirdre knew it."

"It seems she knew a lot of things. That we—" Maryssa stopped, her cheeks burning with anger and humiliation at the words that had almost slipped from her tongue.

"That we what?"

Maryssa spun away again, her mouth set in a defiant line. " 'Tis of no consequence."

"No consequence? I tell you that I love you and you fly in my face, clawing like a half-crazed kitten. And then you won't even deign to tell me why you're in such a temper? Deirdre lied!"

Maryssa gave a bark of bitter laughter. She leaped to her feet and wheeled on him, shocked at the depth of fury racing through her, stunned still more as it burst free. " 'Twould have been passing difficult for her to have concocted this particular lie, her words were so close to what I know as truth."

Tade rose and clamped his hands about her arms, holding her captive.

"Damn it, Maryssa, I'm not letting you go till you explain—"

"You told her!" Maryssa accused. "Told her what happened between us on the lakeshore."

"What?" Tade's fingers tightened, his eyes searching her face as if she'd gone mad.

"She said you told her about all of your—how did she say it?—*affaires de coeur.*"

"Damn it, Maura, do you really believe that I would tell my fifteen-year-old sister about my dalliances with women?"

"She described *this* dalliance in great detail."

"How the hell could—" His face paled. "That night I talked to Devin . . . she must've overheard."

"Overheard what? Your recounting of your latest conquest? She knew everything, Tade. Where we were, what we did . . . how you stopped before we—" Maryssa hated herself for the tears that flooded her lashes.

"Before I came into you?" Rough-edged, ragged, the words seemed embedded deep in Tade's chest.

Maryssa's gaze flew to his face. He peered down at her—solemn, oddly vulnerable, the planes of his face taut with a look of exquisite torment. One thumb skimmed over her cheek, its callused tip gathering her tears. "Leaving you without making you mine on that lakeshore was the hardest thing I've ever done," he said.

"I—I don't believe you." Maryssa forced the words from between stiff lips, the icy wall of anger she had built around herself weakening.

"I scarce believed it myself at first . . . Love was just another game I played at, slipping about like a lad at a banquet, stealing nips of pleasure until I had nigh made myself sick with it. But you . . . " He ran his fingertips across the soft petal of her lip, and Maryssa felt the reverent touch in every nerve of her body. "From the moment I saw you staring up at me with those eyes, love stopped being just another frolic. There was something . . . something about you that buried itself in my heart."

"T-Tade," Maryssa choked out his name, feeling the tearing pain within him as though it were her own. But his fingers gently stilled her words, his eyes locking on hers with a fierce intensity that rocked her very soul.

"I wish"—Tade's voice caught in his throat—"that I could come to you untouched, as you come to me, but I can't. All I can do is swear to you that never have I spoken these words to another: I love you."

Maryssa felt the earth vanish from beneath her feet, the rainbow that had burned her mere moments before now embracing her in all its glowing shades, hues of joy and wonder, made only the brighter by the tiny black rim of doubt that still bordered their edges. Tears rolled down her cheeks unchecked as she hurled herself against Tade. She delved her hands in the thickness of his hair as he crushed her in his arms, every muscle, every sinew of his lean, hard body melding with the fevered heat of hers.

"I was so afraid when . . . when you didn't come to the lake. I wanted to . . ." The agonized words died on her lips as she sought Tade's mouth, opening to him, drinking in the heady feel and taste that was Tade's alone. "I love you," she sobbed into his mouth again and again. "I love you."

She felt an answering groan low in his throat as his tongue thrust deep, mating with hers in a wildly erotic kiss that left them both quivering, clinging. One hand slid up to cup her breast beneath its layer of cloth, his other palm riding down to her derriere, its gentle curve obscured by the layers of petticoat. His fingers clenched in the fabric, pressing her tighter against the muscled length of his thighs, the hard heat of his loins.

Maryssa whimpered in frustration, wanting to tear away the thicknesses of cloth that held them apart, wanting to touch the warm satin of his naked skin as his mouth again covered hers. Her hand tunneled inside his open shirtfront, hungry for the strong arch of bone, the rippling muscles padding his wide shoulders. She felt his flesh jump beneath her hand, the mat of hair on his chest delighting her, the small, beaded point of his nipple spinning heady sensations through her fingers as Tade's own hands wove their magic about her breasts. Of their own volition, her fingertips moved lower.

"Maryssa . . . oh, God." Tade's head arched back, his face nigh a grimace of pain as her soft fingertips swept down the line of hair that divided the taut muscles of his belly, her hand brushing the waistband of his breeches. Tade's fingers closed in a bruising grip about her wrist, dragging her hand from beneath his shirt, forcing her back slightly away from him. He leaned there, against her, his breath ripping from his chest in short gasps, his fingers shaking as he buried his face in the curve of her neck.

Maryssa tried to nudge his jaw away, to find his lips, but Tade pressed his face more tightly against her, his voice a hoarse whisper. "Don't. Don't move, Maura love. Touch me like that again and I'll tumble you back into the grass and love you here and now."

Confusion and the same horrible hurt that had roiled through her on the lakeshore curled about her. "Tade, I—I want you to . . ."

"Nay, love." He raised his face from her shoulder, threading his fingers through the silken curls that framed her face. "When we . . . when I love you, I want our first time to be perfect. More than just a hurried coupling in the shadows with the chance of God knows who stumbling upon us. I want candleshine, coverlets soft with swansdown; I want the scent of wild roses, and strings of golden hours in which to kiss you, stroke you, see you smile. I want so much for you, Maura, *mo chroi*."

The glow from a pink paper lantern bobbing on a hedge caught the misty green of his eyes, and the hurt that had washed over her faded. Maryssa felt cherished, loved, the driving need he had stirred in her body dissolving in the promises his words wove within her soul. She blinked back tears of joy, her fingers stealing up to the muscled column of his throat, feeling the warm pulsings of his life's blood beneath his skin. "Tade, it doesn't matter where or how, she quavered shyly, "as long as 'tis with you."

She felt a shudder go through him. Then his mouth widened in a dazzling smile.

"I'll come for you on the morrow, then. Don the dress I sent you from Derry, and—"

"Dress?"

"Aye. 'Tis wrapped up among Christabel's things. Ask her, and—Damn, how will I ever wait until dawn?"

His mouth swept down, claiming hers in a kiss—hungry, haunting, flooded with honeyed promise. "I love you, milady," he breathed. "More than life itself. God help me, but I do."

More than life . . . The night wind echoed his words as the hatred in the faces ringing the Marlows' table, the rage and warning in Kane Kilcannon and Deirdre, filled Maryssa's heart. Her hands slid away from the corded sinews of Tade's neck; the throbbing veins therein suddenly seemed terrifyingly fragile. Fear rocketed through her, her fingertips freezing in their path upon Tade's arm.

Maryssa tore her hand away, not wanting to feel or think. But as Tade vanished into the darkness, the knowledge she had fought to hold at bay pounded relentlessly into her mind as Rath's gloating words broke over her in fresh waves of terror: *A ball from my pistol struck his left arm. I saw him jerk . . . and the blood . . .*

"God help us both, Tade," Maryssa whispered. But even the slice of her nails in her flesh could not banish the sensation burned into her palm—the feel of woven cloth beneath a lawn sleeve. The thick-woven cloth of a bandage.

Eleven

THE DAWN MELTED over the horizon like rich cream, gilding the weathered walls of the Marlow stables in patterns of mellow gold. Maryssa smoothed her sweat-damp hands over the full skirt of the gown Tade had bought for her, astonished yet again at how perfectly the garment's tight jacket molded itself to her breasts and waist. It was as if some fairy had charmed the seamstress's needle, forming the yards of satin into a gown fashioned for Maryssa alone. Yet whoever had sewn this wonder of silver lace and fine, glistening cloth had never set eyes on Maryssa.

Had the fit been but an accident? A casting of luck? Or had Tade, indeed, marked with his hands and heart every curve and swell of her body? Had he charted them exactly and held them in his memory all the way to Derry? Maryssa felt a warm surge of delight at the thought and could not restrain herself from twirling about like a child in the deserted stableyard.

Yet she had scarce wheeled about once, when the sound of unseen hooves pounding near flung her joy still higher. Maryssa's fingers knotted into a fist, pressing against the bounding pulsebeat at the base of her throat as she strained to see the rider just cresting the sweep of hill to the west of the stable.

The sunlight glinted off massive bay flanks and midnight-black mane as Tade's stallion raced down the slope, its noble head tossed high in the wind in an equine expression of the same pure enjoyment that shone in every line of its master's lean body. Maryssa's breath caught at the picture they made—the magnificent horse and Tade astride it. A scarlet-lined cape streamed behind Tade's broad shoulders, the wind molding his shirt to the muscle and sinews of his chest. And as the stallion gathered his haunches and sailed over the high fence surrounding the yard, the unsullied joy in Tade's face filled Maryssa with such love and longing she thought her heart would burst.

Even when the horse thundered toward her, she knew no fear, and as Tade reined the beast to a halt scarcely three arm's lengths from where she stood, she felt her lips curve into a smile.

"Good morrow, Miss Wylder." A current of huskiness ran beneath the teasing in Tade's voice as he swept his scarlet-plumed hat from his head. " 'Tis little wonder the dawn has burst forth with such glory this day. No doubt the sun sprites rousted all their fellows from the star beds to view the loveliest sight in all Christendom." Green eyes roved in a lingering path from the top of Maryssa's silk hood to the toes of the soft kid slippers that peeked out from above their shielding clogs.

Maryssa felt his gaze burn her, firing a blush in her cheeks and on the skin veiled beneath the satin as well. She groped for something witty to say, but words eluded her, and she could only fix her gaze on one of Curran's oiled hooves as a quivering excitement stirred deep within her.

She saw a flash of tight leather breeches as Tade swung from the saddle, then heard the crunch of his boot soles as he came lightly down before her.

"Maura."

Rough and warm, his fingertips brushed her chin, raising her gaze to meet his, and it was as if the full force of what she—they—were about to do had stolen her tongue. But then her gaze caught the heat of his green eyes, saw within them not only desire but also a tenderness that made her knees tremble. She raised her fingers and laid them, feather-soft upon the moist warmth of his lips as she blinked away the droplets that clung to her lashes.

"Tade, the gown . . ." She forced the words from between trembling lips. " 'Tis the most beautiful thing anyone has ever given me."

"I'd give you heaven, Maura, if I could," Tade breathed against her fingertips, his own eyes overbright. "Let me try." He swallowed convulsively, his thumbs sliding up into the curls at her temples, his large palms cupping her cheeks. "There is a place high in the mountains, a place Devin and I built as lads. We vowed we would hold it secret until the day we died, but for you . . . for what this morning holds . . . I trow I'd break a vow to God himself if keeping it meant I could not . . . make you my own."

" 'Tis all I've thought of and dreamed of since we parted." Maryssa's hushed admission seemed breathless even to her own ears. "But I—I'm afraid . . . afraid I'll not please you."

"Afraid you'll not please *me*?" Tade's lips parted into a smile of such sweetness it pierced Maryssa's soul. Gentle, so gentle, his laugh rippled across her skin. "Do you know, Maura *mo chroi*, how precious you are? Not one woman I've e'er known has held more than a paltry concern that *I* feel pleasure in the loving. They cared only about taking pleasure, gaining whatever they could. But you . . . always, in all things, you seek to give . . ." His head tipped down, his lips blending with hers in a kiss of infinite sweetness and bridled passion.

He released her slowly, reluctantly, molding his rein-hardened palms about her waist and swung her up onto the stallion's back. Maryssa knew she should be prey to the raw terror that had gripped her each time she had faced a horse since the night of the wild ride that had thrown her into Tade's arms. But the web of security and love his words and caresses had built about her shielded her from even that fear as he lifted her high and settled her on the horse's back.

In one lithe, graceful movement, Tade swung up behind her and cupped her hips between his hard leather-encased thighs. And as she leaned back against the muscled plane of his chest, Maryssa smiled, remembering that night not so

long ago when a terrified, unloved girl had thought Tade Kilcannon was dragging her into hell.

"We'll ride through the wilds," Tade said in her ear. "You
need not fear anyone will see us."

Maryssa didn't even answer, just laid her cheek against his
smooth-shaven jaw in a gesture of complete trust, reveling in
the scents that clung to him—wildwood, sea breeze, saddle
leather.

The movement of Curran starting forward jarred her deeper
into the curves of Tade's body, and as the stallion loped
smoothly away from Marlow Hall, losing them in the untamed beauty of Tade's mountains, Maryssa cast the last vestiges of her doubt and unease into the sunrise.

The countryside seemed to open its arms to her, embracing
her in bright splashes of wildflowers and stark juttings of
stone lovelier than any carved by a sculptor's hand. And the
low rumblings of Tade's voice as he pointed out a roe drinking from a crystal stream or a soaring bird skimming the
treetops only served to heighten the anticipation that tingled
through Maryssa's veins.

When the narrow trail on which they had been riding disappeared into naught but turf beneath Curran's hooves, Tade
grew suddenly silent, the tension in his muscles building
against her. Maryssa felt as if a fist were tightening inside
her, every brush of Tade's body against hers so exquisitely
pleasurable it was almost painful. At the rim of a tiny valley
ringed with jagged stone, Tade reined Curran to a halt and
dismounted.

Maryssa felt a shiver work unbidden across her skin, the
absence of Tade against her making even the sweet, sun-
warmed breeze seem chill as it played among the clouds.
Then there was only the feel of his hands lifting her down,
his strong arm curving beneath her knees, pulling her, like a
child, against his chest.

She started to move, intending to gain her feet, but his grip
about her tightened. "Maura, let me hold you, carry you."
His request set her pulses racing. "I want you in my arms
when you see my secret place."

She wrapped her arms about his neck, and it touched her
to see that instead of the usual leather thong, a midnight-
black silk ribbon caught up the thick strands of his unruly

hair. As he strode down into the valley, she buried her face in the ruffles at his throat, terrified that she would ruin the magic hours of their loving by sniffling and weeping in her joy.

But he had taken no more than a score of steps before Maryssa lifted her head, tempted away from her tears by a fragrance so tantalizingly delicate and lovely that it seemed to have been borne on angels' wings.

Her eyes swept the tiny valley, searching for the source of the wonderful scent, but the glen was spangled by only a few late-blooming flowers. Hardy grasses struggled to gain purchase on what little soil clung between the wealth of jagged rocks scattered across the east side of the valley, while a single gnarled oak tree, larger than any she'd ever seen in Donegal's wilds, thrust its mighty branches skyward from the center of the glen.

Maryssa hazarded a glance up at Tade's expectant face, confusion niggling at her as she tried to imagine them somewhere in this rocky hollow. But as they drew near the towering oak, confusion gave way to disbelief, then amazement, as her gaze followed the massive trunk up to the lacy foliage above. She gasped, dazed, as her eyes locked on what looked to be a fairy castle tangled so high amid the oak's lush leaves it seemed to touch the very sky.

The low walls of the wooden haven were draped with cascades of wild roses, their heavy blossoms festooned with ribbons of pale blue satin. And even from her low vantage point Maryssa could see the waxy whiteness of a dozen unlit tapers set among the blossoms.

She tried to speak but couldn't as she thought of the hours he must have spent gathering the roses, tying the ribbons so that they would hang so perfectly among the delicate flowers.

"Tade, 'tis so beautiful," she whispered, "how . . . how long did you work to . . . to do all this?"

"Think you I could sleep, knowing that in the morning I would be bringing you here, touching you?" His soft words twisted in her heart. "Look, love. You'll not even have to climb the branches to reach it. I fashioned a carriage fit to bear my lady up into her kingdom." She turned to look in the direction he indicated, seeing, partially obscured by the tree trunk, what seemed to be a wooden swing, the ropes that anchored it to the tree castle twined with delicate green vines and sun-colored blossoms.

"That will carry me?" A tiny quaver of doubt edged her voice as her gaze traveled from the sturdy wooden seat up through the branches to the platform. " 'Tis . . . 'tis so high . . ."

Tade's laughter rumbled deep in his chest. " 'Tis the tallest tree in these mountains, I vow. When Dev and I were lads we used to love the tale that was spun around it." His mouth crooked in an amused grin.

" 'Twas said to be Badb Catha's haven, the place of the druid goddess of war. She and her three sisters supposedly had aided in battle one Preanndaigh the Red, crushing his enemies, but one enemy warrior, Cian of the Sea, showed courage so great that Badb Catha could not bear to see him die. Disguised as crows, she and her sisters tore out Cian's heart and buried it here within the glen. And, legend claims, the oak born of his life's blood grows great with his courage."

Maryssa shuddered. "He—he must have had a great—great deal of courage for the tree to grow so—" She craned her neck back, peering up fearfully into the branches.

"Tall?" Tade's voice fell gentle. "Maura, I'd ne'er let anything hurt you." He strode to the swing and eased her down onto the seat, the tenderness in his face spiced by an imp of mischief. "Of course, once I hold you captive in my castle, I may never let you come down." He dropped a kiss upon the tip of her nose. " 'Twill take me but an instant to make ready once I reach the top. Then I will pull you up. Hold fast to the ropes."

Her fingers had scarce closed about the hempen cords before Tade's muscled arms and legs carried him up among the spreading branches of the oak. A moment passed, then two, but though she peered up into the tree, he remained hidden from sight. She was about to call out to him when she felt a strange sensation of weightlessness. The ropes tightened and she began to rise upward like a leaf drifting on a breeze, being carried higher, ever higher. She arched her head back, feeling the velvety caress of leaves against her skin, feeling the playful wind thread its fingers through her hair.

The glen spilled out beneath her, dappled gold, spangled

with emerald grasses. Maryssa drank it in like honeyed wine, wanting desperately to hold the jeweled shades and sweet scents fresh in her memory for all the endless tomorrows that stretched before her. Moments later, the swing broke through the branches, and the wonder of the glen faded beneath the soul-wrenching beauty of Tade Kilcannon's face.

The smile that had shone upon his countenance as he scaled the tree was gone, his eyes now solemn, brimming with a vulnerability that touched her. She felt as though he had bared for her his heart, his dreams, and had tried to create here in this crudely built castle a tangible symbol of his love for her. Maryssa released her hold on the rope and placed her hand in his outstretched palm. His fingers closed over hers, steadying her as she stepped from the swing into the wood nymph's bower.

The foliage blocked out most of the sunlight, dimming it to the soft gray of twilight. The weathered wood that had been fashioned by a boy's hand long ago was iced now with velvety petals, the tapers set among them now glowing with soft orange light. In the corner of the surprisingly large floor nestled a basket, the aroma of spiced cake and wine emanating from beneath the cloth that covered it. And beside it were spread five thick down comforters, layered atop one another to form a soft bed amid pools of candlelight.

"You said once you wanted to give me heaven," Maryssa whispered. "But heaven will seem a dismal place compared to what you have given me here."

The brush of his fingertips as they untied her hood made her knees feel like water, and as he cast the bit of camlet aside and slipped free the pins that imprisoned her curls in a loose chignon, waves of desire crashed over her so sharp and deep that she had to grasp his hard-muscled arm to keep from sinking to the floor.

He ran his long fingers through the sable mass of her hair, smoothing it past her waist, stroking it as though it were the finest silk; then he bent down to retrieve from the coverlets a single perfect rose. "For milady." It was as if he had laid all that he was in her hand at that moment. And she wanted to offer him something . . . something beautiful in return.

She lifted her hand to trace the planes of his face with her fingertips, memorizing each arch of cheekbone and jaw, the tiny crinkled lines fanning out from the corners of his eyes the result of a lifetime of laughter. Then she rose up on tiptoe and touched her lips to his mouth in a kiss blushed with all the love that filled her bursting heart. Her fingers slid down to grasp the folds of his shirt; then she sank onto the coverlets, drawing Tade with her. He eased her back, his muscled forearm curving beneath her to pillow her head as his mouth moved over hers, and she could feel him shaking against her, could feel his need.

But he gently broke away from her, rising up on his elbows to peer into her face. "Maura, you don't have to . . . I mean, I didn't intend to carry you up here and—and bed you before you had time to catch your breath. There is cake here and chilled wine, and—"

His words died in his throat, drowned in a gasp of pleasure as her fingers slid beneath his neckcloth of lace, unfastening it to bare a triangle of hair-roughened bronze flesh. "Tade, I'm not . . . not hungry for aught but . . ." Assailed by a sudden wave of shyness, she let her words trail off, but she moistened her lips, tipping them up to touch the corded muscles of Tade's throat. A groan rumbled deep within him, and he caught her face in his hands, burying his lips in hers with a hunger that sent jolts of raw desire searing, jagged edged, through every inch of her body.

Maryssa parted her lips to the hot sweep of his tongue, and he plunged inside, his mouth possessing her in a wildly primal dance that presaged the mating of their bodies. She felt his fingers fumbling with the fastenings of the blue satin gown and the laces of the stiff corset beneath. Maryssa whimpered in exquisite torment as he removed both garments and let her breasts spill into his hands.

"Lovely . . . so lovely," Tade breathed against one hardened coral crest. His moist lips skimmed once, twice, over her straining nipple, worshiping, caressing until Maryssa could bear it no longer. Her trembling fingers knotted in the thick waves of his hair, drawing him fiercely down to her heated flesh, and he took the delicate bud into his mouth, his rough, wet tongue tracing hot patterns on her skin.

Maryssa's hands skimmed at the hard muscles of his chest, then opened the loose cloth of his shirt and pulled it down over his shoulders to glory in the rough bronze satin of his bared skin. Tade winced, and she heard air hiss between his teeth as she yanked his left sleeve from his arm. But the momentary flash of pain that crossed his features did not halt for even an instant his deft fingers from their hurried task. Tade's hands skimmed her body, ridding her of her petticoats and undergarments, his fingers slipping the bows of her ribbon garters and easing down the silk stockings that clung to her thighs. His knuckles brushed the downy swell at their apex, and a shattering need filled Maryssa.

She tore at his breeches as she kicked free of the rest of her clothes, her careless haste sounding in popped seams and torn lacings. Breath catching in ragged gasps, she fumbled with the stiff fastenings that clasped the soft leather about his hips. Her fingers dug into the hard bulge of his sex pulsing beneath the breeches, a sudden hissed curse stunning her as her nails bit overdeep.

A sick silence gripped Maryssa as she mentally cursed her clumsiness, embarrassment joining with the fear that her wantonness had somehow dulled the edge of Tade's desire. Most likely he thought her little better than an awkward child or a faded, plain spinster desperate for a man's touch.

But she *was* desperate, more desperate than she had ever been in her life. Desperate to hold on to this brief moment of being loved, knowing that with the turning of the seasons she would have to release Tade again to his mountains while she lay caged in English society as Ascot Dallywoulde's bride. As abruptly as the surge of impassioned freedom had gripped her, it vanished, leaving her shaking and uncertain.

"Go on, sweeting." Tade's voice brushed over her, his eyes sparking with an imp of mischief. "Don't stop now. My breeches but pinched what strains beneath them to reach you."

But the soothing words could not brace her flagging confidence. Unable to meet his gaze, she fastened her eyes on the snowy band of cloth tied about Tade's left arm, a wisp of dread, a sense of danger, flowing through her at the evidence of the dark secret that might well lurk beneath the face of her lover. She clutched the coverlet to breasts still tingling from his kisses, but he would allow her not even that shield. His gentle hands drew the downy folds from her grasp, slowly, so slowly.

"Maura." His voice was harsh with leashed desire. "I want nothing between us this morning. Not the coverlet. Not fear."

Her gaze flitted up to his. " 'Tis just that I . . . I don't know what to do. I've . . . touched you before, on the lakeshore and—and in the garden, but you've—you've loved so many others who were far more beautiful than I and skilled in the ways to pleasure a man. And I—"

"Nay, Maura. I've loved only you." He took her hand in his, then flattened her palm against his naked chest. "Feel," he said, low in his throat. "I'm trembling like a raw lad. Shaking with want of you. Let me lose myself inside you, Maura. Let me . . ."

With a choked sob, she opened her arms to him, tumbling them both back down onto the soft coverlets. She never knew how he shed the rest of his clothing, only felt his lean body flame against hers, its hard sinews trembling as they molded themselves against her answering softness. He kissed her everywhere, his mouth sipping her throat, her breasts, the soft swell of her stomach. She whimpered and writhed as his lean bronzed fingers traced a sensual path up the fragile skin of her inner thigh to part her gently, so gently. The green of his eyes glowed like shattered emeralds, hard and bright with passion, and his breath touched her there, moist, sweet.

"Maura . . . sweet God, Maura . . . so delicate, so sweet. I need to taste you . . ." A current of disbelief washed through her as he lowered his mouth to press his lips against the velvety folds. She started to protest, her cheeks blazing, but then his lips parted and the rough wetness of his tongue against the center of her desire drove all doubt from her mind, leaving her drowning in a sea of fire.

She cried out, clutching at his muscled shoulders and dark hair as his mouth worked its magic. She was swirling, soaring, into a million tiny sun drops of gold. She tried desperately to reach out . . . catch something she did not understand. But suddenly Tade's mouth left her, his lean hips crushing her down into the coverlets, his sex iron-hard against her stomach.

He braced his arms on either side of her head, his face whip-taut. "Maura, open yourself for me, love . . . my love . . ."

Maryssa's hips arched up, seeking the rigid proof of his maleness, her fingers digging deep into the steely muscles of his buttocks. She felt him probe the entrance to her womanhood, heard his primal growl of pleasure mingled with an odd reluctance. " 'Ryssa, you're so—so tiny. I don't want to hurt you.''

" 'Tis—'tis all right, Tade. Please . . . I love you so much. I want—want to feel you inside me.'' She felt his fists knot in the sable curls that pooled upon the coverlet, his eyes darkening with passion. His mouth pressed down on hers in a fierce, wild kiss, his hips driving forward in one mighty thrust.

There was a sharp twinge of pain as the delicate membrane tore, but the stinging sensation was lost in rippling wonder as the proud heat of him filled her, touching her very womb. A sob tore from Maryssa's throat as the expression on his face seared itself into her memory—the magnificently carved planes and hollows now contorted in agonized joy. He lay there motionless for long minutes, his breath coming in ragged gasps, his lips kissing away the tears that clung to her lashes.

"Maura . . .'' His fingertips brushed a wayward curl from her forehead. His voice was choked with emotion. " 'Tis . . . 'tis so very precious, what you have given me.'' He tore his eyes away from hers, their emerald hue mysteriously bright as he buried his face in her tumbled hair. "Did I hurt you?''

"Nay.'' Maryssa raised her hands to trace with her fingertips the arrogant curves of his cheekbones, the tangled waves at the nape of his neck. " 'Tis more beautiful than I'd e'er hoped or dreamed,'' she breathed, searching desperately for words to describe the splendor that she felt. " 'Tis as if I can touch your soul . . . carry it with me always.''

" 'Tis yours, Maura. I'd cast it into hell and welcome in exchange for just this moment. I love you, Maryssa Wylder, I vow, until I die.'' Tade's rasped pledge made Maryssa's heart ache with a joy too great to hold. And as he started to move within her, her heart burst, showering her in a rainbow of rose petals, kisses, and laughter, such sweet laughter.

With infinite slowness he held the curves of her hips, molding her against him, guiding her as he buried himself deep inside her again and again. Maryssa's hands clutched at his shoulders and chest, the sensation of his satiny hardness throbbing inside her turning her wild with need. Her mouth pressed fiery kisses on his shoulders and neck, her teeth nipping at hard flesh, sharp with the tang of sweat as she fought to bring to him a wisp of the magic his hands and body were weaving about her. Her hips writhed against his, meeting each white-hot stroke with her own primal need.

She raked at his back with her fingers, her head thrashing as he drove himself into her body faster, harder. She was the ocean, breaking in waves upon jagged cliffs, a bird soaring toward the sun. Her teeth sank into her lip as she was propelled toward the blazing fire of his passion, wanting to warm herself near its raging heat. She dug her fingers deep into Tade's hard buttocks, clinging desperately to her tormentor and savior as the torrent of feeling he had loosed inside her hurled her higher, higher, until suddenly the earth and sky exploded into a million jewel-hued fragments of sensation.

Maryssa's heart soared at the splendor of it, the joy of it as Tade's body went rigid atop hers. He cried out, a cry of triumph, wonder, as he buried himself deep inside her. Then he collapsed against her naked breasts, the tremors of their loving still coursing through them both.

" 'Ryssa . . .'" He raised his head, his green eyes dark with a longing she had not seen there before. "If I could, I would make you my wife before another dawn—take you into my life, my bed, forever—fill your arms with my babes." His voice dropped to a hoarse whisper. "If I could."

Tears flowed free upon Maryssa's cheeks as she stroked his face, his hair, and she was stunned to find the hot wetness born of her joy and sorrow mingling with Tade's own tears.

Twelve

MARYSSA NUZZLED CLOSER into the warmth of Tade's body and fought to shade her sleep-blurred eyes from the increasingly insistent rays of sunshine. With a soft grumble, she burrowed beneath the coverlet Tade had pulled over their naked bodies after their last loving, reveling again in the spicy scent of his skin, the tenderness with which he held her, as though, even in sleep, he sought to treasure her. This was so new, so special, this sensation of being safe and loved, that tears prickled again at Maryssa's eyelids.

The sting of salt in eyes already tender with weeping chased the velvety haze of drowsiness from her, but she gave it up gladly, pressing her lips against the dark hair roughening Tade's chest. It would be folly, she thought, to waste even a moment of the time fate had granted them to remain hidden here, away from the world that waited to pull them apart. She wanted to savor every breath of mountain air, every rose, every expression that graced Tade's face, wanted to hold each perfect moment like a pearl in her hand and string them into a chain of memories to wear around her heart forever.

For even as Tade had swept her again and again into heaven during the long hours they had laughed and loved within the rose-draped bower, his face had held the shadow of parting, a desperation and hopelessness that had made each brush of his hands and lips a blending of wonder and torment.

And before he had at last fallen into an exhausted sleep, he had drawn her against him, holding her as if he would never let her go. Maryssa swallowed the sudden tightness in her throat, her eyes fluttering open in the dimness beneath the coverlet. She nudged the soft folds away from her face, blinking sleepily against Tade's shoulder as her eyes grew accustomed to the light.

Tade's low, sated sigh at the brush of her lashes against his skin drew Maryssa's gaze to his face, but the bronze planes still lay in soft lines of slumber beneath the golden rays of the waning sun, the rosewood waves of his loose hair tangling about his face.

She shifted away from him but a little, loving the contrast of his hard muscles against the downy coverlets, his bronzed skin against the soft ivory of hers. It was pretty—her hand against the sinews that rippled across Tade's chest. Aye, pretty. And the dark tresses that had always made her feel hideous in her father's presence curled now in seductive waves over Tade's arm, the hip-length strands as soft as silk.

A shiver of delight, of newness, trickled over Maryssa's skin as she slipped carefully from the circle of Tade's arms, drawing the coverlet over her breasts and curling her legs beneath her as she had when she was a child. Tade had promised her in their lovemaking a joy such as she'd never known. And he had given it to her . . . given her so much that she would never again be the lonely, awkward, frightened girl who had endured Celeste Ladonne's insults in the coach so long ago.

She reached over to break a chunk from the half-eaten spice cake, grinning at the memory of how Tade had sprinkled rich crumbs of it on her skin, then cleaned them away with teasing nips and tickling sweeps of his tongue. She had laughed—laughed and laughed—squirming beneath him, learning to play lightsome games that led to a passion as consuming as the fire in Tade's eyes. Never before could she remember having laughed aloud, not even as a child at Carradown. But in Tade's arms she had already learned so many things. Laughter, yes, and the sweetness of his loving teasing, but most of all . . . Maryssa touched her fingers to her cheeks, feeling, for the first time, that they were soft, feeling that she was pretty, aye, pretty, because she *was* pretty in Tade's eyes.

She smoothed the coverlet over his broad chest, the words he had said drifting back to her on the wind: *If I could, I would make you my wife before another dawn . . .* Maryssa's tongue tasted of bitterness and of a longing so deep it threatened to tear out her soul. It was unjust. Unjust that the world, which had offered her nothing but scorn, should rob her of this one pure joy, snatch from her this man who had wooed her away from despair and made her feel richer than any of the court belles who had looked upon her with such disdain.

She reached out, her fingers whispering breath-soft across the thick, spiky lashes that lay in rich crescents on Tade's cheekbones. He had wept when he had first come into her body. She had tasted the salt of his tears, felt his trembling as deeply as she had felt her own. He loved her. And in that loving he risked as much as any rogue riding the High Toby. For if Bainbridge Wylder ever discovered that she had lain with Tade . . .

She shuddered, remembering Kane Kilcannon's face twisted in rage as he bit out his warning on the hurling field, remembering the hate in Quentin Rath's slack features as he spat out his loathing of the Kilcannons. Justice in Ireland was clasped in the fists of the landlords and the soldiers. In truth no court of justice would interfere if the powerful Bainbridge Wylder chose to dispose of one of the "papist vermin" infesting the land. And no Englishman, laborer or gentry, would fault her father for drawing the blood of the "lowly Irish scum" who had dared despoil his daughter.

Even Christabel and Reeve feared for them. Maryssa sensed it, though neither had ever spoken of their concerns. And yet, to release Tade, to hurl away the love he had given her . . . A knot tightened in Maryssa's stomach.

If they were careful, shielding their lovemaking in the branches of this tree, confining their meetings to the dark garden walks during the hours before dawn and after nightfall . . . Her fingers dug fiercely into the coverlet. They had so little time to taste of each other, so little time. Surely her father's god would not be so cruel as to snatch away these brief moments of happiness before he condemned her to the hell of being Ascot Dallywoulde's wife. For Satan himself could devise no worse torture than forcing her to feel those cold white hands on the flesh Tade Kilcannon had made beautiful. Still, she would endure the marriage, endure it gladly, in exchange for these days of Tade's loving.

"Maura-love?" The sound of his voice made her gaze dart down to meet eyes unsettlingly clear of sleep, their green depths allowing no veilings or deceptions. "Maura, what is amiss?"

"Amiss?" Maryssa struggled to soften the clenching of her jaw, loosen the fingers clutching at the coverlet's downy folds. "I but awoke hungry, and—"

"You have the look of someone about to face the gallows." Tade levered himself to a sitting position and let the snowy white coverlet slip down the taut plane of his chest to pool between his thighs. Doubt twisted the corner of his mouth. "Maura, did I hurt you somehow or do aught to bring the sorrow back to your eyes?" His hand reached out, his fingers curving beneath her chin, tipping her face up to meet his worried gaze.

Maryssa closed her eyes against him, her lips quivering. "Nay, Tade. 'Tis—'tis none of your doing.'Tis my own idiocy that—"

"Is it regret that tears at you?" he asked, his voice laced with a sadness of his own as he pulled her gently into his arms. "Regret that you gave yourself to naught but a landless Irish—"

"I could never regret making love with you," Maryssa said fiercely, her eyes wide, blazing into Tade's. "Never. But I want it . . . want you forever, and I know . . . know I can never have you." A sob escaped from her throat, but Tade crushed it against his chest as he pulled her, coverlets and all, into the strong warmth of his embrace.

"Maura . . . oh, Maura," he breathed against her wet cheek. His arms tightened about her as he murmured sweet Gaelic love-words, stroking her hair, rocking her as though she were a baby. She could hear the threadings of torment in Tade's voice, feel it in the way he clasped her to him. His sorrow seemed only to feed her own aching emptiness as his fingers delved into her hair, pressing her gently into the sleek muscles of his chest.

"Listen to me, *mo chroi*. If I could have you forever, what would the future hold for you? A daub-and-wattle cottage on some barren mountainside? A patch of dirt to grub in for the rest of your life so that our babes wouldn't starve? And a husband two steps away from the hoodman's hands?''

Maryssa raised her damp face from his chest, dread twisting inside her at Tade's words. His mouth was curled in bitterness, his gaze, fixed on the distant horizon as if on some specter he alone could see.

"The . . . the hoodman? Tade—''

His eyes snapped back to her face, the lines carved about his mouth deepening Maryssa's dread, but before he could speak, the faintest of sounds penetrated the hushed glen. She could feel Tade stiffen as his eyes swept the valley, his mouth compressing into a grim line.

"Tade, what is it?''

"Quiet.''

Maryssa flinched at the sharpness in his tone, coils of fear unfurling in her belly. Heedless of his nakedness, Tade sprang up from the coverlets, crouching at the edge of the platform to peer through the foliage. '' 'Tis a horseman,'' he hissed, "riding like his mount's tail is afire.''

Maryssa's eyes widened, horrible visions of her father and Rath flashing through her mind. "But you said no one knew of this valley or of this tree castle. Whoever it is will but ride past.''

"Mayhap. But there is naught else for miles on this mountain, and a man would have no reason to brave the wilds at that pace, unless—'' He turned to snatch up Maryssa's clothes and thrust them into her hands. "We daren't take any chances, Maura, what with Curran tied in full view. Blast it, I should've known better. But I thought—damnation!''

With a spate of oaths, Tade grabbed up his breeches and jammed his legs into the soft leather. But his hands had barely closed the fastenings when the approaching rider crested the rim of the valley, drawing rein with a haste that nearly set his mount onto its haunches.

Panic boiled up inside Maryssa, her fingers tangling in the laces of the corset as she struggled to draw them tight. And the shout from the horseman as he swung down from the gray fairly made her leap from her skin.

"Tade!"

The vaguely familiar voice was laced with urgency, and through the shielding of leaves, Maryssa glimpsed a simple brown cloak, its hood pulled close over features she could not see.

"What the—" Tade bolted upright, one fist tearing back the branches that hid the platform. The expression on his face chilled Maryssa's soul. "Christ's blood," he roared at the figure rushing toward the oak. "What is it? Rath? Are the hounds—"

His cry was cut short by the rider's reply. "Calm yourself!" the man called up. " 'Tis naught to do with me. 'Tis but a message I bear from Neylan and the others."

"A message? By God's feet—" Tade's broad shoulders sagged with relief, but eyes as green as a hidden glen snapped with irritation. "For Christ's sake, couldn't it have waited?"

"For you to come to confession?" The exasperation in the sweet tenor was discernible even to Maryssa's ears. "Or mayhap, with the entertaining you're about up there, we'd best pass the confession and get you straight to your knees."

"C-confession?"Maryssa quavered, drawing farther into the shadows, visions of thumbscrews and floggings whirling in her head. "Tade, who? . . ."

He turned, his mouth pale, thinned with tension, but as his gaze fell on her ashen face, his eyes softened. " 'Tis but Devin come to torment me," he said, the rueful smile he forced his lips into etched with an unnerving shading of grimness. "Catching me here as he has, he'll most like keep me at my Hail Marys till next Whitsuntide."

Maryssa's cheeks flamed. "D-Devin . . . " She clutched the billows of soft blue satin against her, certain, unreasonably, that the solemn holy man could pierce the veilings of leaves with his eyes. She caught her lower lip between her teeth, astonished at how much Devin Kilcannon's good opinion of her meant and sure that she would lose it. "But . . . but how did he know we were here?"

"*I* bloody well didn't tell him, if that's what you're thinking," Tade snapped, thrusting his arms into his shirtsleeves. Then he turned to her, his smile thawing from its icy grimness. "I vow the wretch has more eyes than Cerberus when I want to avoid him. But don't fear. I'll take his blasted message, then tell him to hie himself off somewhere. He'll never suspect 'tis you here."

The words were meant to comfort her, but Maryssa felt something wilt inside her. "Who?" she managed with a sick little laugh. "Who would he suspect?"

"Maryssa, I—" His gaze flashed from her face to Devin below. "Just stay quiet." He brushed her lips with a kiss before he swung down through the tree's branches.

Maryssa stared after him as he dropped lightly to the ground and closed on Devin while the slender man strode through the rocky outcroppings toward the tree.

The hood that had concealed Devin's features had fallen back against his shoulders as he walked, and, even from a distance she could see that the usually gentle, solemn features were sharp with the same sparkings of temper she had oft seen in his brother.

She pressed her knuckles to her lips as an angry rumbling drifted up to her, the words unintelligible but the tone unmistakable. Unconsciously she drew into the farthest corner of the platform, wishing she could melt into the garlands of fading roses. But even huddled into the pools of darkness, she was not spared the sound of voices from below.

"Damn it!" Maryssa made out Tade's curse. "I told the cursed fools never to come to the cottage . . . endanger Rachel and the babes."

"Where *were* they to seek you?" Devin shouted back. ". . . will hang in two weeks . . . take time to find a way into—"

"Hold, curse you," Tade cut him off. "I know how blasted long it takes to break into a jail." From her hiding place Maryssa saw Tade turn, driving his fingers back through the tumbled waves of his hair. His eyes flashed up toward the tree where she lay hidden, and Maryssa could see the anger and frustration in his granite-hard jaw, could see him battle to leash his temper.

He lowered his voice, and his words were again muffled when he turned back to Devin. The holy man's gaze shifted up to the tree. Pale blue eyes seemed to lock upon her bare arms and legs, the curve of her breasts swelling above the cloth clenched in her fingers. She flinched as Devin's hand shot out, gripping Tade by the arm. Her nails dug deep into her palms as Tade dashed the hand away from his open shirt, leveling a murderous glare at Devin.

For an instant she feared Tade would strike Devin or that Devin would raise his hand against Tade, but the priest's fingers fell limply to his side, the slender shoulders sagging beneath the coarse cloak. A second passed, two, but although the brothers' exchanges were now hushed, Maryssa could see the rift between the two widen.

What was Devin saying? As a priest, would he be bound by conscience to bar Tade from the sin he had just committed with her? Was Devin prating of God's punishment? Or only of the folly of Tade's flinging himself into a liaison with a woman who could well get him hanged? And Tade . . . ?

She shut her eyes, wanting to blot out the anger she could still detect in the low voices. Tade would no doubt rise to her defense, mayhap closing his heart to the brother he loved so deeply.

Her fingers dug into the blue satin still pooled in her lap, bitterness surging through her. It was cruel! Unjust that even what little she had hoped for in the moments before Tade had wakened had been a fool's dream. It was as if some evil presence lurked on the edge of her life ready to snatch away any love, any pleasure, Maryssa dared take. Snatch away even this one day of magic and sully it with pain.

Maryssa fought back the tears that balled in a hot lump in her chest, her fingers fumbling with buttons and laces as she struggled to don her gown. But as she drew about her body the shielding of blue satin, she pulled about her heart the veils of hopelessness, hurt, and doubt that had tormented her since she was a child.

She reached for her hood, her knuckle snagging on the rose garland, her flesh tearing on a thorn. She almost laughed, a tiny, anguished, wild laugh, as she stared at the blood welling up from the little cut. It was as if the awkwardness she had shed like a chrysalis in the warmth of Tade's love had returned to encumber her, taking the hand that had looked so delicate against his bronzed flesh and turning it clumsy once more.

And she wanted nothing now, nothing except to flee the wilting garlands, the crumbled spice cake, the remnants of a dream now shattered in some bawdy masquerade. She wanted only to secrete herself away within the walls of her bedchamber, to be hidden from eyes snapping with fury or weighted with disappointment and disgust.

Almost without thinking, she swung her legs down off the platform, the bark digging into one tender palm as she grasped a branch and lowered herself into the gnarled limbs. She was halfway down when she heard Tade curse, saw his furious visage through the dappled shadows of the leaves as he sprinted toward the tree trunk.

"God's teeth, you little fool!" Tade growled, yanking her from the lower branches, his hands bruising her waist. "Did you mean to break your witling neck?"

Maryssa blanched at the anger in his voice, saw his teeth clench with fury.

"Of all the idiotic, witless things to do—"

She fought to steady her wobbly knees as she pulled from Tade's grasp. "I but thought to save you the time of coming to fetch me down," she managed, driving the quaver from her voice. "I couldn't help but—but hear some of what you and Devin said. 'Tis patent you must leave, and I want to get back to Marlow Hall." She turned away, letting the veil of her hair fall forward to shield her face from Tade's burning glare and Devin's gently sorrowful expression.

"Maura." She felt Tade's hand on her shoulder, heard the strain in his voice as he battled to chain his anger.

"Nay, 'twas monstrous thoughtless," she said, "my—my not staying to attend Christabel . . . " The words dwindled to a broken whisper, and Maryssa could feel herself melting into a pool of humiliation. She started to speak again, but the words lodged in her throat, escaping only in a choked sob. Hating herself for her weakness, she spun away from the brothers, dashing the tears from her eyes with one satin cuff.

Tade's breath came out in a harsh, weary sigh, and with gentle pressure, he turned her to face him. "Maura, I wish I could stay to explain to you why—why I have to leave," he said. "But there isn't time enough. All I dare say is that I have to go, and that I'll be gone nigh a month. Mayhap more."

"A month?" Maryssa echoed. "But I— What if Father's sent me to England by then?" A tiny web of hysteria caught at her, and she couldn't keep the tremor from her voice. Her gaze flickered to the silent Devin. She swallowed hard, looking away.

"Dev . . . " Tade's gaze flicked to his brother, then to the rim of the valley in an unspoken plea. Devin turned, withdrawing to where his horse stood beside Curran. Tade watched his brother walk away, one large fist knotting and loosening upon his leather-clad thigh.

"Damn it, Maryssa, do you think I want to leave you now? Like this?" His gaze swept her face, furrows digging deep into his brow. He caught her hands in his. "I know you're hurting, damn it. I feel it. But I have no choice. I vow I'll hasten to Nightwylde or to the gates of London itself to find you as soon as this business is done."

"This business of breaking into jails?" Maryssa demanded, fear churning in her stomach. The blood drained from Tade's face, and his hands, gripping hers, turned suddenly chill.

"Maura, I have to go." The words were deathly flat, wrapping Maryssa's heart in cold tendrils of fear. "Dev will take you as close as he dares to Marlow Hall."

"I can find my own way," Maryssa protested. Tade raked his hand through his hair, and she could feel every muscle in his body grow taut, could sense that his temper was held by a thread.

"You don't even have a horse," he grated. "And I'm not about to let you torment poor Curran the way you did that unfortunate beast you were riding the day we met." He cupped one hand around her cheek, and she could feel a measure of tension drain out of him as his palm was dewed with her tears. "Maura," he said, "don't."

She started, confused at the sudden change in his voice. The anger was dulled with tenderness and regret. "Don't bind yourself up in your fears again, love. Don't hide away in a dream world."

"Dream worlds are fragile things," Maryssa whispered brokenly. She scarce felt the brush of Tade's lips as he kissed her. She only fixed her gaze on a jagged stone piercing the side of the glen as he retrieved his boots and cloak from the tree castle.

He dropped to the ground again and paused a breath away

from her, his own voice tight with anguish. "I love you, Maura."

Maryssa bit her lower lip to keep from crying, her nails gouging her palms as she battled the urge to run to him, to stop him no matter what the cost.

His voice drifted back to her, and she felt tears burn her eyelids. "Take care of her, Dev," he said. Then all sound was lost in the pounding of Curran's great hooves as Tade set him at a run down the mountainside.

Maryssa watched him as he rode away, his scarlet-lined cloak streaming behind him, his hair, still unbound, whipping in a dark brown tangle about his shoulders.

"Maryssa . . . " She turned to find Devin Kilcannon standing beside her, his blue eyes brimming, not with contempt, but with a gentle understanding and sadness.

Hurt, loneliness, anger, welled up inside her, the mixture of emotions overwhelmingly sharp. Of its own volition, Maryssa's hand pushed back the tangled curls that still tumbled about her shoulders in disarray, and she was suddenly painfully aware of how disheveled she looked and of how obvious it must be, even to a man pledged to celibacy, that she and Tade had made love in the tree castle.

She lifted her chin in a show of defiance, vowing she wouldn't cry. "There are coverlets above," she said. "You'd best take them back to Rachel."

No sparking of censure came to Devin's eyes; his sensitive mouth softened even more. "I'll come back for them after I've taken you to Marlow Hall."

He gripped her elbow in a thin, firm hand and guided her through the stones in a silence not weighted with the disdain she had expected. But she felt as though his very kindness had been a blow, numbing her as he aided her onto his horse and kneed it to a trot in the direction of Marlow Hall.

And with each clop of the horse's hooves, each darkening of the lengthening shadows, her fears and doubts seemed to reach out their poisoned tendrils and bind her in a hundred chains of despair.

When at last the night-shadowed outline of Marlow Hall was visible from the skirting of woodland surrounding the estate, Devin drew rein and slid down from the gray. Maryssa felt his hands curve about her waist, helping her to gain her balance as she slid stiffly from his mount.

The gentle concern in Devin's face chafed her raw feelings. " 'Tis but a little way down the road," he said. "Would I could take you right to the door, but Rath . . . he has eyes and ears everywhere, even among those we know as friends."

" 'Tis all right. I wouldn't want you to take risks when 'tis obvious you disapprove of—of Tade and me." Maryssa pulled her camlet hood closer about her throat.

A melancholy smile tilted Devin's lips. " 'Twould be a bit much to expect a priest to approve of his brother dallying with a lady out of wedlock, Maryssa Wylder, would it not?" The words were spoken so gently, they were more blessing than chastisement.

Yet instead of soothing her pain, Devin's words made her want to lash out at him, lash out until he dealt her the condemnation he most likely thought she deserved. Maryssa steeled her spine, her eyes unflinching as they met Devin's gaze. "I love him, Devin," she said. "And he . . . Tade loves me."

Devin straightened, squaring his thin shoulders as though to bear a heavy burden. "I know."

"There is naught wrong in what we do. We hurt no one, ask naught but what few stolen moments we can share."

"And after? Tell me, Maryssa. What will happen when you are forced to return to England, to the life you were born to, and Tade must go on here in Donegal? Will your few stolen moments cause him no pain?" Devin pressed his fingertips against his brow. "Tade has wooed more than his share of women, but his heart—"

She saw Devin's mouth dip into a wry smile. " 'Tis strange for you, I know," he continued, "to think of Tade speaking to me thus, making me privy to affairs a priest should view with righteous horror. But I was Tade's brother long before I donned my robes. And from the time he was a lad setting the hedge school awry with his pranks, half the maids on this mountain have been vying for his attentions."

Maryssa felt again the twisting of jealousy at the thought of all the women who had known Tade's touch, but with Devin's next words, even that pain faded into a despair that seemed to drag her deeper into the hopelessness that threatened to engulf her.

"But you . . ." Devin reached out, catching her hands in a caring grasp. " 'Tis different with you. He's given you his whole heart, Maryssa. And your eyes shine with such love for him, any would have to be blinded not to see it there. Priest I may be, but I have a man's body, a man's needs. I know what you both suffer. God help me, I do. But 'tis wrong, Maryssa."

"Why? If it is such sin why did your God bring us together? Did he make us love to but jeer at us and say 'tis evil that we—"

"I know not." Devin's sigh echoed her own pain. "I wish . . . wish that I could give you an answer that would soothe away the grief tearing at you both. But I lack the wisdom"— his voice dropped low—"and mayhap the faith."

Maryssa looked into the gentle countenance beneath its halo of gold hair, aware of a sudden that it held a silent suffering of its own.

"Still, I do know this," Devin said softly. "The love between you and Tade can do naught but cause you harm. Even if you could endure the censure that would result from a union between a poor Irishman and an English heiress, there are a hundred more barriers your love could never surmount. Your children would be outcasts, Maryssa, despised by the mountainfolk and by the English as well. Even legitimacy would be nigh impossible to give your children, for there are laws forbidding marriage between Catholic and Protestant. Any holy man who dared to hear your vows could be cast into prison for years, while all you stand to inherit from your father would be snatched away."

Maryssa wanted to scream at Devin, to block his words from her ears, from her heart, but they drove themselves into her with the force of daggers, lodging in the center of her being. She spun on him, defiant, despairing. "What does it matter? Any of it? The lands, the wealth? My father's estates and his power at court have brought me nothing but pain. And even your God cannot offer Tade more love than I do."

"Maryssa—"

"Nay!" she cried, her words tearing out in a sob. "Save me your preachings about your cruel God. He has snatched happiness and love from me as if my life were some twisted game. But he'll not take from me what little time I have left to spend with Tade. He'll not rob me of that, Devin, even if he casts both Tade and me into hell for all eternity.''

She glared for endless seconds into the fine patrician features, the brow creased with trouble. But Devin fastened his gaze on the distant wilds, his voice soft, low. ''He won't have to,'' he said.

She turned to look out into the tangled shadows of trees, the rugged outline of the mountains into which Tade had vanished, and it was as though the wind carried from the sinister depths beyond laughter . . . the chill, soulless laughter of specters a hundred years dead. Dead, but still thirsting for the heart's blood of those who had stolen their land, and willing to regain it at any price—even the sacrifice of one of Ireland's own.

Thirteen

MARYSSA STARED LISTLESSLY into the gilt-framed mirror, the silvered sheen of the looking glass doing naught to soften the ravages six weeks of waiting had worked upon her countenance. Eyes, huge in the translucent oval of her face, peered back at her from bruised circles. The once-bright depths held the numb suffering of a wounded fawn, while her cheeks were hollow, their curves shrunken by the sick churning that so often beset her. It was as if, with each melting of night into dawn, all love, all hope fled, leaving with the last wisps of darkness the agonizing certainty that Tade lay upon the stones of some nameless jail, cold and dead.

She raised trembling fingers to eyes that were hollow from endless nights spent leaning against the window casement searching the fathomless night for any sign that an emerald-eyed rogue with a flashing smile still roved through the wilds. But as the weeks had passed, September giving way to the winds of October, hope withered into despair. And when one of the Marlows' frequent visits was interrupted by Quentin Rath—come to gloat with her father about the capture of the "insolent wretches" who tried to free the papist Andrew Muldowny—desperation had driven her to risk riding to the Kilcannon cottage before dusk fell.

She could still see Christabel Marlow's cornflower-blue eyes, wide with sympathy, as she insisted upon accompanying Maryssa into the mountains. Could see the fresh-hewn oak door of the cottage swing wide to reveal Deirdre's peaked face. For an instant there had been a spark of shared fear and misery between Maryssa and Tade's sister, but in a heartbeat it had vanished, leaving Deirdre's tear-swollen eyes hard with loathing.

"Go away!" the girl had ordered shrilly. "Have you not caused enough sorrow?" She had burst into racking sobs and slammed the door in Maryssa's face with a force that all but shattered the precious panes of glass set in the cottage windows. But before Maryssa could raise her hand to knock again, the portal had flown open and a pallid, harried Rachel had appeared within its weathered frame.

Her brown eyes darted between Christabel and Maryssa with a wariness that drew their frayed nerves almost to the breaking point.

"Good—good morrow," Rachel had said, her thin lips twitching into a mockery of her usual warm smile. " 'Tis . . . 'tis a most pleasant surprise to see you again after all this time. Is there aught we can do for you?"

"I was wondering if you have had any word from Tade. If you've seen him, or heard—"

"Tade . . ." Rachel's hands had fluttered to her throat. "When last we heard, he had dashed off for Dublin with a brace of his friends. I—I think he said 'twas some sort of . . . There was a horserace he was hoping to see."

"A horserace at a jail?" Maryssa asked, pleading edging her voice. "Rachel, I was with Tade when Devin came to give him that message a month past. Please, if you can spare any mercy, tell me how Tade fares. Have you heard any news of him?"

Rachel's hands had fallen down into the folds of her threadbare apron, but the dark rings beneath her eyes were more eloquent than any words could have been. "We've heard naught of Tade since that day."

"I overheard Colonel Rath telling my father that some men had been captured while trying to rescue one Andrew Muldowny from hanging. Think you Tade was among those men?"

Rachel caught her lip between her teeth, avoiding Maryssa's eyes. "Tade is scarce solemn enough to involve himself in political happenings." She gave a weak laugh. "Most like he's taken it into his head to bolt off for Kilkenny to see some horse he's heard well of or to match his skill against that of some other renowned hurler. God knows he ne'er takes the time to tell us where he's off to."

Maryssa stared into the pinched features, carved with worry and mistrust. Mistrust, not of the soaked urchin whom Tade had dragged, half-drowned, to the doorstep so long ago, but rather of the daughter of Bainbridge Wylder, the English heiress who, with one sweep of her privileged hand, could destroy not only Tade but the rest of the family Kilcannon as well.

Slowly she had reached out to lay her fingertips on Rachel's thin wrist. "I understand, Rachel. Truly," Maryssa said. "If I discover aught about Tade from my father or anyone else, I'll ride to tell you at once." Stunned at the sense of strength stirring within her upon offering comfort to one Tade loved, Maryssa had forced an encouraging smile to her lips, then walked with Christabel to their awaiting horses.

In the days that followed, she heard little news about the daring rescue of Muldowny or about the men who had been captured while trying to free him. And when Maryssa dared to ask questions, her father only sneered and told her to keep to her mindless woman's games, reminding her that when last she had meddled in the affairs of men she had nigh been ostracized from polite society forever.

Only through Christabel and Reeve had Maryssa heard any news of the Muldowny rescue. Five days after her visit to the cottage, the Marlows had come with the news that Muldowny and his would-be rescuers had been freed from prison by the notorious Black Falcon when they were but moments away from the gallows. It was said that the outlaw and his cohorts had appeared from nowhere and had released the prisoners from the grasp of the soldiers before the officers knew what was afoot.

Maryssa shivered at the memory of the pointed little face of the Irish housemaid who had darted in to stir up the fire just as Reeve finished his tale. She had tossed them a smug smile and whispered some tale of a cloak the Falcon bought from the devil, a magic cloak that could shield him from sight and make him as invisible as the wind. Reeve had snapped at the wench to hold her tongue, his freckles standing out in stark contrast to his drawn cheekbones. His voice had been low and tight as he had glared at the retreating wench, saying that the cloak must have failed the Falcon, then, for the price of Muldowny's rescue had been the lives of three of the high-wayman's own men. No one knew how many of the rene-gades had been injured during the fray or how many had died on the highroads as they attempted to make their escape.

Half mad with worry, Maryssa had wanted to demand that Reeve tell her whether Tade Kilcannon and the blackguard Falcon were one, but the stricken look on Marlow's face when she broached the subject had silenced her, leaving her to be torn by the teeth of her fears.

Maryssa turned away from the mirror in her bedchamber and closed her eyes, shoving the memories from her mind as her fingers curled about the tiny bottle of jessamy Christabel had given her. The delicate scent, which had been intended to cheer Maryssa, wafted up to her, soothing and sweet— very like Christabel herself, Maryssa thought glumly. If it had not been for the ever-present concern in her friend's beautiful face, Maryssa knew well she would have gone mad with this waiting. Now, alone in the crushing silence of her chamber, she could find no comfort, only the sensation of helplessness, the kind of terror a fox kit must feel amid a pack of hounds closing for the kill.

The cut-crystal bottle dug into her palm, and her eyes darted to the stiff envelope she had shoved to the far corner of her dressing table. The gilt edges of the missive winked evilly in the light of the single taper, the broken seal of the house of Dallywoulde clinging to the paper like drops of blood.

She glanced at the precise script that had directed the letter to Nightwylde six days past, her name penned there in thin slashes as if a razor had cut the ink into the paper. She could almost hear Dallywoulde's voice, cold as a winter grave, see his eyes, pale caverns echoing with fanaticism.

Her skin crawled at the image of his hated face, yet the vaguest whisperings of relief stirred within her as she recalled the reprieve that had been scribed within the lines. ''I am most distressed to find myself detained from your enchanting company," Ascot had written, "but as a humble servant of God I have no choice but to put off my excursion to view your dower lands until I can give my valued testimony at the trial of that blasphemous wretch, Jeremy Bludgeon . . ."

Maryssa shuddered, despising that part of her that was able to know a feeling of deliverance that Dallywoulde's sojourn to Nightwylde had been postponed, when the reason for his tarrying in London was to see some miserable innocent suffer. Yet in spite of the prayers she whispered for the poor accused Jeremy, she clung to the certainty that the trial would take time, as would the execution.

A chill coursed down her spine. Ascot would not be cheated of the ultimate pleasure of watching the poor wretch suffer. And every moment her hated cousin labored in his "godly duty" was one more in which Devin Kilcannon would remain safe from the diabolic priest hunter, and one more Maryssa could spend fighting to discover what had become of the green-eyed rogue she loved.

It was that knowledge only—that she had time, precious little time—that kept the tiny thread of her sanity from snapping, leaving her prey to a hysteria as wild and terrifying as that of any inmate of Bedlam.

The cut-glass bottle, which had been clutched in Maryssa's numb fingers, clattered to the table, the scent spilling onto the polished wood. Maryssa started, then grabbed a crumpled lace handkerchief from the cluttered tabletop. Her eyes burned as she righted the bottle and swabbed up the rivulets that ran in sweet-scented paths to drip onto the rich carpets.

Dropping the bit of lace to the floor, she buried her face in her hands. "Dear God, what am I going to do? If Tade doesn't come . . . If Devin . . ." She shut her eyes, fighting to blot out the haunting image of Dallywoulde's empty gaze. "I will have to—to warn them when Ascot . . . if Ascot arrives. But I don't know how or where to find them."

She fought desperately to cling to the memory of Tade's strong arms enfolding her, struggled to picture the mischievous flash of white teeth, the pure devilment that shone in his smile. If he were here he would cajole her, tease her, until he drew a smile. He would kiss her and say, " 'Tis not so terrible, Maura-love. Naught can be so terrible." And she would believe him. Aye, if only she could look into the rich green warmth of his eyes . . .

She shivered, the chill from the open window creeping beneath the quilted satin dressing gown she had drawn about her shoulders. She had left the casement open these many weeks, braving the drafts in the hope that, if Tade passed Nightwylde upon his return, he would see the candlelight in her window, see the panes thrown wide, and know that she was waiting.

But with every turn of the golden hands on the clock that graced the mantel, Maryssa doubted the more that she would ever see again that rakish grin, taste the lips that had taken her to ecstasy in the dream he had woven for them both. For even if Tade did return unharmed, even if he scaled the stone walls of Nightwylde to come to her arms, it would be for but a heartbeat of time to bid her farewell. Yet she would welcome it gladly, embrace the agony of having to watch him stride out of her life forever, if she could but know that he walked the same earth as she, alive and strong.

She walked on weary feet to the mullioned window. A stool, carved with fanciful creatures spawned of ancient myth, sat in the shadow of the window ledge, an abandoned coverlet lying in a pool of ivory satin at its feet. She stared at the fluffy folds, a mute reminder of the hours she had spent curled upon that stool, beneath the blanket. Endless hours she had watched the dawn play at hoodman blind, until it had swept its bright colored ribbons of light from between the night's black fingers.

Sinking down onto the stool, Maryssa drew the coverlet about her shoulders, huddling deep into the comforting folds to begin anew her vigil.

Folding her arms on the hard stone of the window ledge, she pillowed her cheek in the crook of her elbow, the sable masses of her unbound hair tumbling about her in a waterfall of silk. She closed her eyes, remembering Tade's fingers charting sensual paths through the heavy strands, remembering his lips as they gentled her, loved her. Remembering as she at last surrendered to an exhausted sleep.

Something was crying. Maryssa heard it, soft and pitiful, felt the brush of warm wetness that could only be tears. She struggled to reach it, shake off the heavy bindings of sleep, but white-haired sorceresses seemed to keep her weighted with a score of magic spells. Cruel spells that whispered to her in the beloved tones of Tade's voice, brushed her with the sweet warmth of his lips, his callused fingers.

She whimpered, feeling, even through the numbness of sleep the fierce, twisting pain of needing him, yet the insistent crying thing would allow her not even that peace, intruding on her senses until it sounded in her very ear.

Maryssa stirred, pressing one hand against her ear to blot out the sound. But when her fingers encountered something soft and furry—something *alive*—wriggling upon the sill, she came suddenly awake, a scream rising in her throat.

She tumbled off the stool, her rump thudding onto the floor, her eyes flashing wide, expecting to see some creature of dream or of nightmare seated on the stone ledge. But instead of some night demon, her gaze fell upon what looked to be a puff of mist with whiskers and huge tilted eyes of the most brilliant blue she'd ever seen.

Too startled to move, she stared at the tiny kitten, which was now cavorting ever nearer the edge of the windowsill, its wide eyes fixed on a night-moth that kept dancing just out of reach. But when the tiny feline hunkered down on its little haunches, tensing to spring, Maryssa bolted up from the floor and snatched it from the ledge just as it made ready to dive into the night.

With a decided lack of gratitude, the furry beast wriggled in her grasp until it faced her, its pink mouth sending forth a most affronted mew. Maryssa peered down into the impish face, feeling her fear drain away, leaving in its wake a flush of tenderness.

" 'Twill serve you no purpose to begin caterwauling." Maryssa scolded gently. " 'Tis passing dangerous for a wisp of fur the like of you to be climbing about castle walls! Does not your mistress mind what you're about?"

"I fear the little rapscallion is sadly irresponsible, milady, and is given to wander at will. But since you show such promise in taming renegades, I thought perhaps if you were to give Odysseus, here, a firm, loving hand . . ."

The deep, rich tones seemed to have been born of her dreams. Her eyes struggled to pierce the darkness outside the window; then she wheeled, her heart leaping as her stunned gaze took in the lean, jaunty figure lounging against the bedpost. A cry of joy rose in Maryssa's throat.

"Tade!" Still grasping the kitten, she hurled herself at the tall form, nearly toppling him into the huge feather mattress. She felt the kitten being plucked from her hands, and dropped into the fluffy mounds of pillows, as Tade's sinewy arms closed about her.

He swept her high, twirling with her clasped to his chest while his lips caught tastes of her throat, her brow, the curve of one shoulder bared by the slipping of her dressing gown.

" 'Tis . . . 'tis truly you!" Maryssa gasped, reveling in the hard expanse of his shoulders beneath the black mantle. "Truly! I scarce believe—"

"Aye, my Penelope, and I hope you're not accustomed to anyone else ascending through your bedchamber window while your Odysseus is away." His eyes held emerald sparkles of joy. "Of course," he mused, planting a kiss on her nose, "sound as you sleep, I vow the whole of the Trojan army could tramp through here without you stirring an eyelash. Tell me, Maura-love, were your dreams sweet?"

She winced at the remembered torment of hours before, but his palms swept up to frame her face in tenderness, driving the fear away.

"My dreams were sweet, *mo chroi,"* he breathed into the curls that brushed her temple. "Passing sweet. Filled with garlands of roses and the touch of lips so soft they stole my very soul."

Maryssa buried her face against his chest, clinging to his lean-muscled frame, the hoarse, passion-thick tones of his voice robbing her of all strength. "T-Tade"—she squeezed his name through a throat roughened with joy and banished fears—" 'twas so awful, and I was so afraid. I didn't . . . didn't know where you were or if you lay wounded . . . dead . . ."

He crushed her against him, soothing her, gentling her with his hands as he tried to hush her broken words. "Think you the Sassenach musket ball has been molded that could cut down the heir Kilcannon?" he cajoled.

"I've never—never known a musket ball to be particularly discriminating," Maryssa snuffled into his shirt.

She was rewarded with a laugh, rich and loving, as he lifted her high against him, her hair tumbling in a silken cascade about them. "By the saints," he gasped, flinging such a comical expression of feigned shock toward the gamboling kitten that Maryssa felt a smile tug at the corners of her mouth. "Odysseus, I vow she made a jest!" He plopped her down on the feather bed in a tangle of twisted night rail and bare legs, to the delight of the kitten, which pounced on her toes. But Tade spared the little rogue not a chuckle. Instead, the tall Irishman strode to the open window and leaned out into the night. "Come, horned god, take me," he cried. "I can die without regret. Maryssa Wylder made a jest!"

A shaft of disbelief and panic shot through Maryssa as the sound of his voice echoed into the castle yard. Nearly toppling the kitten off the bed, she leaped toward Tade and clamped her hands over his mouth, yanking with all her strength to drag him away from the window. "Dear God, are you crazed?" she chided, spinning to close the windows. "Half of Donegal could hear you!" She leaned against the wall, quakes of fury and raw fear bounding through her.

"The whole of Donegal lies asleep," Tade said, crossing his long legs and offering her a totally unchastened grin. "And any who rove about this late are most like so far in their cups they'll think it was a banshee wailing."

"I much doubt my father believes in your banshees. And the servants . . . if any heard—"

"Whist, Maura, 'tis the risks that set your blood pounding that let you know you are alive."

"Then 'tis a miracle any who love you are yet sane!" Maryssa ground out, suddenly struck by the audacity of the wretch before her. He was so devastatingly handsome as he took up one of her hair ribbons and trailed it across the pillow to the infinite satisfaction of the frolicking kitten. The planes of his face showed not the slightest trace of sleeplessness or concern; his grin seemed totally unaffected by what, for Maryssa, had been six weeks of pure hell.

"Damn you, Tade Kilcannon!" she bit out under her breath. "How dare you vault through this window with your jests and your kisses when I've been nigh wild with worry for six weeks, while no one—not Rachel, not Reeve, *no one*— had any idea whether you were alive or dead!"

The ribbon fell from his long fingers, and he paced toward her, the devilment that had graced his features darkening into something solemn and disconcerting—a passion that made Maryssa's tongue seem to fuse to the roof of her mouth, made her knees feel as weak as water.

"Christ," Tade murmured low in his throat as his hands curved about her ribs, the thumbs warm against the undersides of her breasts. "Is that anger flashing in your eyes? Turning them to blue-gold fire? God's teeth, look at you, Maura . . . look at you!" His mouth came down on hers, hungry, hot with leashed desire, but she thrust the heel of her hand against his chest, still clinging to her anger.

"Tade, don't you dare try to distract me. I want to know—" Maryssa battled to keep the words from coming out in tiny breaths.

"Believe me, Maura, there is naught I'd rather do than distract you." Tade caught her wrists, pinning her hands against the ruffles at his throat. He kissed the hard bumps of her fists. "Yet I am sorry for every moment you spent afraid. I'd not cause you one moment of pain if I could help it. But know this: The grave has not been dug that could keep me from you, love. I left, having tasted only once of your sweetness, and I vow to you that since the instant I rode from your side, my heart has known naught but the need to hold you again. The need to see if 'twas possible our joining was as beautiful as I remembered."

"So beautiful you were able to just ride away? Leave me half mad with worry?" For all her anger, her words sounded broken and plaintive, as though she were a good wife berating a thoughtless husband, or a village lass hurt by her swain. Maryssa hated the sound of her voice, the raw pain in her words. For in truth, though she had once shared his body, known the wonder of his practiced caresses, Tade Kilcannon belonged to her no more than did the Donegal mountains or the hawks that swept its wide slate-hued skies.

She turned away, fixing her gaze on the roguish bewhiskered face of the kitten, Tade's gift to her. "I'm sorry, Tade," she whispered. "I had no right to snap at you."

"Maura . . ." His hands were achingly gentle as he grasped her shoulders and turned her into his embrace. "You have the right to all things with me—the loving, aye, and the anger as well. They are both but emotions—different sides of the same coin. I wish I could spend the rest of my years watching your eyes kindle to flame, only to wash away the hurt with my loving.'' He pressed a kiss to her stiff lips, his mouth wooing hers, coaxing hers in a way that was at once a plea and a demand. ''Let me love away the pain, Maryssa,'' he breathed. ''Please . . .''

Maryssa drowned in the tenderness in his voice, the earnest curve of the lips that had just parted from hers. And with a low cry she strained against him, whimpering as her mouth caught his. She felt herself being tumbled back into the pillows, her body crushed by the welcomed hardness of Tade's. And as his hands and mouth wove their magic about her, it was as if, indeed, he were trying to wipe away the nightmare of the weeks without him, to banish all from her heart but this moment . . . this mating.

But even as he swept her into a passion as fierce as any gale, she felt like a captive in the tempest, lost among the savage tides tearing at them both. Mysteries, dark and dangerous, lurked within his eyes, secrets that could destroy him, aye, and her as well. And when at last they lay quiet, the fierce hunger of their bodies sated, the fires in their souls yet unquenched, she stirred against his chest, then sat up to curl her feet beneath her and peer into his face.

His mouth, still red and swollen with kisses, parted, one bronzed finger reaching up to trace her cheek. ''I love you, Maura,'' he said, running the callused pad over her chin.

''Do you?'' she looked away, turning her head to avoid his touch as an odd, dry dusting of bitterness fell over her.

''Aye, Maryssa, I do,'' he said, his voice edged with strained patience. ''I rode like the devil for three days over damnable muddy roads to reach you. Now come, love, back into my arms.''

Maryssa struck the covers away, nearly treading on the tail of the disgruntled kitten as she slid from the bed. Scooping up the dressing gown pooled upon the carpet, she jerked the garment about her. ''If you forced yourself here at that pace, you must be passing weary. You had best rest.''

''By Satan's beard, what is amiss now?'' Heaving a sigh, Tade levered himself up with his elbows, propping his back against the carved headboard.

"Amiss? What could be amiss? You had to leave. You conducted your business at whatever jail Devin sent you off to. Now you are home, alive and safe." Maryssa felt the catching of tears in her throat. "God knows I prayed—prayed that you were." She wheeled back to him, all the helplessness and fear crashing over her. "You're my heart, Tade, all of it. All the joy I've e'er known I found in your arms. But until now I ne'er understood that joy, aye, and even love mean but little without trust."

"Trust?" Tade's eyes darkened with a disarming hurt. "Christ, think you I spent the nights dallying with some lightskirt? Since the day we met, I've taken no other."

"Nay. I know you'd not do that. 'Tis that other part of you that deals me pain, the man you hold apart from me. The one I catch glimpses of only when you think I am not watching."

He started to dismiss her words with a laugh, but it was a hollow sound.

She turned away, hurt washing over her. "Aye, hide it away again," she said softly. "Ne'er let me know where you ride, what mantle you don when you melt into the night. I'm the enemy, even now, Tade, am I not? The Sassenach bitch you named me that first night when I tumbled into the lake."

She flinched as Tade levered himself upright and stalked to the carved mantel to stare into the flames. The sinews and muscles of his thighs glistened bronze in the orange light, the steely curves of his buttocks rigid in his anger. "Damn it, Maura, you don't know what you're asking," he bit out, his mouth and jaw hard, his eyes wary slits of green. "Don't force me to thrust you into danger when—"

"Danger? And what is this? Trysting with you here within my father's walls—my father who hates your family with such fury."

Tade wheeled, and Maryssa's stomach clenched at the flashings of barely leashed fury in his eyes, but as the glinting emerald gaze fell upon her, the stony sparks softened, gentled. "Aye," he said at last. "I'll vow you courted danger with a vengeance when you entrusted your heart to me."

Tade raised his hand to his face and pressed his fingers against his eyes. "But the hate between the Kilcannons and the Wylders has naught to do with you and me. 'Tis a rage that goes far back, nigh the time when you were born." A misty, distant look drifted across his face, and Maryssa felt enthralled by it, held captive by some delicate, unseen thread as he touched the gilded horn of one of the unicorns dancing upon the bookshelf.

"This was my mother's room when I was but a lad," he said softly. " 'Tis a wonder it still stands, the way Dev and I used to tear about it with our wooden swords and our leaden soldiers."

"Your . . . your mother? Here? Tade . . ." Maryssa stared at him, confusion spinning wisps of the past about her, sweeping away all awareness of the delicately painted walls, the huge bed, even the tiny kitten nosing about on the dressing table.

"Aye. This was the place she loved best in this drafty mound of stone. She was beautiful, and she remains beautiful, Maura, in my memory. Even now, when I pray to the Blessed Virgin, 'tis my mother's face I see—her hair all struck with gold, her eyes so kind . . . blue as a mountain stream . . ."

He stared into the fire, and it was as if he had forgotten that Maryssa still stood near him, as if he had forgotten all but the memory of his mother's beloved face. Maryssa was about to touch him, unable to bear the bitterweet flashes of love and loss in his countenance, but he straightened his shoulders, as though righting himself beneath a heavy burden.

"I was but five years old when she died," he continued. "Even so, I still remember the sorrow in her face. 'Twas like that in the statue of the Madonna she kept beside her bed— full of courage, yet lacking the power to stop . . . stop whatever threatened her peace."

"She must have been beautiful," Maryssa said softly.

"The old people claim she was the most beautiful noblewoman in all Ireland, with the blood of a hundred kings flowing in her veins. And my father—he was the mighty earl of Nightwylde then, heir to one of the few Catholic peerages to survive the thieving of Queen Elizabeth and the scourge of Oliver Cromwell. Father . . . he loved this castle, these lands, and those kerns who worked upon it. He bought their safety with his sword, aye, and his wits." Tade gave a bitter laugh.

"He even managed to hold Nightwylde when that coward, Catholic James, cast Ireland to the devil at Boyne."

Maryssa's nails dug deep in her palms, a sick knot forming in her belly. "Then what . . . what happened?"

"The Crown decided to crush Ireland forever by turning the entire nation into ignorant wretches so poor they could think of naught but attempting to feed their starving children. They outlawed our religion, made it a crime to educate any but the cursed Protestants, and snatched all property from Catholic hands."

"That, then, is how . . . how you came to lose this castle?"

"Oh, nay. 'Twas not a cut so clean as that. For six years after his title was stripped away, my father thought Nightwylde safe. His boyhood friend, Bainbridge Wylder—"

"My father and yours were . . ." Maryssa's voice trailed off in disbelief and dread.

"*Friends,*" Tade continued. "Wylder had offered to have the property transferred into his name—the name of an Englishman, a Protestant—with the vow that Kilcannons would rule Nightwylde lands forever. 'Twas common then, trust born of desperation. Reeve Marlow's father still holds title to the properties of Catholic friends—properties that, for all their financial difficulties, no one at Marlow Hall has ever touched."

"But *my* father . . . ," Maryssa interjected in a hushed voice, her mind filling with stark images of her father's hatred for all things Irish, his loathing of all who bore the name Kilcannon. The dread within her twisted tighter in her stomach, and she wanted to clasp her hands over her ears, to block out the truths she knew were to come.

"I know not what happened between him and my own father," Tade said. "All I am certain of is that, whatever your father's original intentions or my father's rights, the plan they had contrived crumbled. Mayhap that was my mother's secret pain . . . that she saw disaster rolling ever toward us but lacked the power to stop it." Tade's voice fell, hushed. "She died but three days before we left these walls forever."

Maryssa padded across the floor to him, reaching up to touch his broad shoulders.

"Know you," Tade went on, "I can still remember running through the corridors screeching battle cries as I darted into the rooms. Nowhere was forbidden me, even the rooms your father . . .'' Tade looked away.

''The day after my mother's wake, I remember . . . remember hearing them, my father and yours, shouting at each other in the library. Dev had been trying to distract me from the whisperings of the mourners by playing with me at lead soldiers, but he was older than I and understood what death meant . . . that Mother would ne'er again sit in her gilt chair pretending to be queen of the mock tournaments we held.

''I can hear myself laughing at Dev when he tried to explain her death, telling him over and over not to be such a dolt, that Mother loved us and would ne'er let anyone cover her up in the ground and keep her away from us forever. But somewhere, deep inside, I must have suspected . . . feared . . .''

Maryssa stared at him, silent, aching at the pain in his face, yet clasped in the grip of some hideous terror, some sense of the truth yet to be revealed.

''I ran into the library, still clutching one of my soldiers, meaning to demand that Father and Mr. Wylder awaken my mother at once. But a pretty woman—your mother—caught me up. I remember her holding me before your father, asking him if he could . . . could steal more than he already had from such a tiny lad.''

Maryssa swallowed hard, seeing in her memory, a tiny leaden soldier amid the clutter on her father's polished table, seeing the stricken expression on Bainbridge Wylder's face when she touched it. But even that was lost in the subtle picture Tade's words had painted of the mother she had never known.

Tade raked his hand through his hair, squaring his shoulders, the muscles rippling beneath his bronzed skin. ''I remember my father dragging me from the woman's arms, saying that Bainbridge Wylder had already taken my mother's life. That he could steal Nightwylde as well and be cursed for it.''

A gasp tore, jagged-edged, from Maryssa's throat, pain twisting deep.

''I knew then that what Devin had told me was true. My mother was never going to wake up. Life was never going to be the same again. I was afraid, suddenly, so damn scared of my father's rage, of Bainbridge Wylder, of the pretty woman. I hadn't cried since I was a babe, but I remember sobbing then, screaming, as my father carried me down the hall.''

"Dear God," she whispered, a sudden sharp loathing of and shame in the man who had sired her sweeping over her. "No wonder you—you hate us so. How could you have been so kind to me—you, Rachel, Devin—knowing who I was . . . what my father had taken from you?"

Tade of a sudden seemed to remember where he was, who she was, and the pain his words must have caused her. He gave her a wistful, loving smile, his eyes searching her face. "I would have loved you, Maryssa, if you were given to me from the devil's own hand. From the first moment I saw you, touched you, my heart was bound to yours. You looked so fragile, so haunted, I wanted naught more of my life than to spend it making you smile—shielding you from whatever or whoever had put the sorrow in your eyes."

His hands molded themselves gently to the curves of her cheeks. "My father clings to his bitterness," he said softly. "But Devin sees you as the gentlest of souls, and I . . . the love I feel for you will last until Nightwylde's stones are but dust."

He threaded his fingers through her hair, breeze-soft and warm. "You ask me to trust you," he said. "Well enough, then. I'll keep nothing from you, Maura. I'll give you all of what I am. When morning comes, tell those who ask that you are off to the Marlows', that Christa has asked you to go to church with them. Then slip away and meet me beside the lake. I vow, then, I'll show how much faith I put in you."

He turned away, his eyes sweeping to the mullioned panes, the wilds beyond. "Pray God these truths you crave do not destroy us both."

Fourteen

THE LEATHER REINS cut deep into Maryssa's palms. Her pulse was pounding despite the sorrel mare's sedate pace as it followed Tade's stallion up the rocky trail. It seemed as though they had been riding for hours—winding along trails grown over with brambles, picking their way along cliffs, poised, it seemed, on the brink of some gaping unseen maw that threatened certain death for those who fell upon the jagged stones below.

Once, as they had journeyed, Tade had reined in his mount to point out the mouth of a cave, all but obscured by vines and gorse. And the face that could be so lightsome grew harsh and dark as he told her that it was within that cave that the children of the Catholics met with schoolmasters whom the English hunted with hounds.

A trickle of icy fear ran down Maryssa's spine as her gaze flitted from Tade's broad shoulders to the steep, stone-pierced mountain that fell away from the path. "Tade," she had whispered as she glanced from the shadowed entry to the cave to the rough land surrounding it, "if the soldiers did come, where would the children go?"

Tade's mouth had turned bitter hard as he said, "To the devil."

The mare stumbled, and Maryssa's heart caught in her throat as she yanked on the reins with an awkwardness that would have sent a more spirited mount skidding down the mountainside. Tade turned his head, his face a mask of unaccustomed grimness, and for the hundredth time since they had ridden away from their meeting place at the lakeshore, Maryssa wished she had not pressed him into resorting to this excursion.

Where was he taking her? To some highwayman's lair bursting with stolen treasure? To some den dug deep into the earth, like the cave they had passed? She must have been crazed to have badgered him into dragging her off to reveal to her truths she would have preferred to leave unknown.

She glanced at the rippling black of his mantle, a chill creeping beneath her own camlet hood. What would she say if he took her to a hideaway? If he yanked from some battered chest the silk mask she remembered from that horrible night at the Devil's Grin? Would she weep and accuse him of having duped her? Played her for the witling? Or would it matter not at all whether he lived but a breath away from the hangman's noose?

She fixed her gaze on the mare's flowing mane, cursing herself for being a fool. Of course it would matter if Tade was the Black Falcon. The outlaw played no child's game of seek and dare. He rode into the night bent on terror—stealing, destroying property, and maiming people—English people.

She stared as the mare drew abruptly to a halt, her placid nose almost thumping right into Curran's rump.

"We must tie the horses here, out of sight," Tade explained, swinging down into the spindly shadows of a dead tree.

Maryssa tried to slip down from the mare's back, but before she could manage it, Tade strode to her side and helped her to dismount.

"Where are we?"

A tiny smile crooked Tade's mouth. "Christ's Wound."

"Christ's . . . ? I don't understand."

" 'Tis a hollow in the mountain, hidden as though in the palm of a hand. The ancients say that when one of Donegal's own dies defending the land, the soil here bleeds."

Maryssa felt the hair at the nape of her neck prickle; her

gaze darted about the countryside. "Bleeds . . . ," she echoed, feeling a tinge of nausea.

" 'Twas thought to be a place of evil . . . or of great magic. But few dared brave the mountain to discover which." He took her hand and gazed down into her eyes with an expression of mingled dread, defensiveness, pride, and love. "You asked me where I ride when I disappear into the night. But I can't tell you that, Maryssa, until you see with your own eyes *why* I ride."

Her fingers felt numb against the heat of his hand as he led her the last few steps to the edge of the hollow. Maryssa looked down into the rugged valley cupped in the mountain's stone hand, all visions of thieves' lairs and stolen treasures obliterated by the sight that spread beneath them.

A huge flat boulder dominated the far end of the depression. Behind it stood the slender, solemn figure of Devin Kilcannon. Before him a score of people knelt upon the stony ground, their bowed heads catching the light of the sun.

Not one among their number could boast a gown or bawneen less than four seasons old, but from the tiniest child in short skirts to the most crabbed old crone, there was about them a sense of faith, of closeness to God, that Maryssa had not seen in the most magnificent cathedrals in London.

Her gaze swept the tiny, hunted congregation, picking out Rachel amid her brood, the faces of those who had glared at her suspiciously during the hurling match, the countenances even of some of those who served her father at Nightwylde. Even the glossy-tressed head of Sheena O'Toole was bowed as she knelt beside Deirdre Kilcannon in the waning October breeze.

Because of the distance between herself and the priest, Maryssa heard only a few of Devin's words as he offered his tiny congregation what little he himself possessed: faith in the God who had seemingly deserted them and the strength that could be found only in unity, love, and the hope that someday, in some glorious future, all men—be they Protestant, Catholic, English, or Irish—would live together in peace.

Maryssa stood on the brink of the hollow called Christ's Wound, feeling as if, in truth, she were looking into the gentle Savior's greatest sorrow. All who knelt there, whispering prayers in Latin, feeding babes threatened with poverty and ignorance upon dreams, risked everything they owned and even their lives to drink of their faith.

"Some have ridden all night to reach here." Tade's voice, low and solemn, stole into her thoughts. "They bring their nurslings to be christened, their dying to be shriven, their lovers to be wed. Sometimes no priest can meet them here, when the fangs of the hounds snap too close behind them. But the people still come . . . wait . . . hope . . ."

She turned her face up to his and saw a solemn strength in his features, a stubborn pride that made the bronzed planes she had always loved seem suddenly strange, yet more beguiling than ever before. " 'Tis the perfect place to feel close to God," she said softly, lifting her eyes to the broad sweep of sky, the clouds so low she was tempted to reach out and touch them. " 'Tis so high here . . . so close to the heavens . . . that no one would dare defile it with the petty warrings of men."

Tade's eyes sought hers, the green depths as warm as a sun-drenched meadow. "I fear, Maryssa love, that men would defile God's very gates if they could but reach them," he said gently.

"Have the hunters come here before?"

"Seven times since I was a lad the soldiers have come to other mass rocks in other glens. Most times our sentries give warning, and the people are able to steal away before the hunters reach them. But thrice I've seen blood spilled upon the very stones where the host has been offered up, and once, when I was but seven, I watched as they hanged the priest who had served us."

"Watched . . . but why?"

"Rachel had taken Dev and me to mass. I can't recall why. Mayhap Da was off to Derry or tending to something that couldn't wait. She was heavy with child, and I remember her wanting Father Dominic's blessing for the confinement to come. But he had scarce opened his mouth in prayer when the sentries cried out. The others ran. But Rachel was so heavy she could scarce walk. I remember hearing the horsemen, being afraid. Father Dominic saw us and, instead of fleeing with the others, thrust us up into the branches of an old tree.

"Rachel didn't want to leave him, but he charged her to care for Devin and me, for we were the hope of all who dwelt upon Kilcannon lands." He paused, wiping the back of his hand across his eyes. "We were the hope of all those poor ragged wretches, two boys scarce breeched. I know not how Rachel managed to gain the tree's lower branches, but I remember her face, all raked with scratches. I remember her crying. Crying without making a sound. Then the soldiers burst over the rise. I remember Father Dominic standing there, praying to God to forgive those cursed Sassenachs for what they were about to do."

Maryssa felt choked by unshed tears; her eyes burned with the torment on Tade's face.

"They hanged him, Maura," Tade whispered, a tear glistening on his cheekbone. "Hanged him from the tree where we were hidden. I remember Dev, sitting on the branch above Rachel and me, his eyes big, his face white. Rachel, had to hold on to me, because I wanted to aid Father Dominic. Even now I can remember the hideous—hideous feeling of the tree jerking beneath his weight as the rope snapped tight."

"Tade . . ."

"I vowed even then that someday, somehow, I would find a way to keep the people safe—the priest, aye, and the people who for generations have served my name."

"Surely they are safe here. 'Tis so far up the mountain and so well hidden. No priest hunters could find them."

Tade's jaw hardened, and Maryssa saw his keen emerald gaze sweep the horizon. "They'd have to be led by their greedy Sassenach noses, and among the hunted there are few betrayers. The Wound, here, is well hidden in the wilds, and the soldiers fear to tread too far into the mountains." There was a glint of savage satisfaction in his eyes she'd never seen before, a menacing set to the mouth that could be so gentle.

Maryssa felt suddenly cold, the breeze sweeping up the side of the valley weaving beneath the shadowy folds of her hood. A fist seemed to tighten in her stomach, her fingers trembling as her eyes swept the ragged worshipers, the stone altar, the hard face of the man beside her.

"The soldiers," she said, her voice scarcely a whisper. "They fear the wilds because of you?"

"Nay," Tade said, slipping the knot of the soft leather pouch that never left his waist. "Because of a phantom their own guilt has created—a rider, fools claim, who wears a cape that can turn him to mist, and a hood of black and silver marked by a falcon with its talons spread." Tade took her hand, but she could scarce feel his fingers, her own were so numb. He turned her soft palm upward and carefully emptied the contents of the leathern pouch into her cupped hand.

She felt something cool and smooth slide into her fingers, but she dared not look at it.

"You asked for all that I am, Maura. Everything. No dark shadows hidden. And I'm giving it to you. Now."

Slowly, so slowly, Maryssa dragged her gaze down over the folds of his mantle, past the brown hands that had taught her to love and laugh, then across her own slender fingers to where a fine gold chain pooled against her skin.

She stared at the familiar curves of a swan's golden throat, arched gracefully over delicately wrought wings. The pendant that had belonged to the mother she had never known. The chain that had been snapped from her throat by a silk-masked brigand with eyes of emerald fire.

The necklet seemed to swim before her eyes, but instead of the horror and revulsion she had expected to feel in the event of such a revelation, she felt only the hollow sorrow of a knight's lady sending him off to do battle. A battle of honor, for what was noblest in men. In that instant she hated the brutes such as Quentin Rath and her own father, who had forced a man such as Tade to rove the highroads—not to seek a fortune cut from the purses of innocents but rather to shield those who had nothing to protect them but the few rags their conquerors had left them.

Shame for the nation that had bred her and for the father who had shown her only scorn surged through her, and it was all she could do to meet Tade's eyes.

She knew not what she had expected to find there, in those dark-fringed depths—hate for her and all her kind, or the savage arrogance that had glinted from the slits in his hood that long-ago night at the inn. She only knew that the tender hopefulness, the solemn, gentle pleading for understanding that shone in his face stole away all words, leaving only the silent tears to slip down her cheeks.

"Maura, I never meant to dupe you. 'Tis just that I feared putting you in danger." His eyes flicked to her hands, a dark flush tinting his cheekbones. "Aye, and in truth I feared, too, that I would lose you forever if you knew that the man who dared to love you was not only a landless Irishman but a common thief as well."

"Common!" Maryssa could feel the blaze in her own eyes. "Nay, Tade Kilcannon, you are far from common. You are not only kind but brave as well, and willing to cast away your own life for the safety of others. You are even good enough to put away your hatred for the man who wronged your family and to love that man's daughter—"

"Maura . . ." He pulled her to his body with a force that drove the breath from her lungs, but Maryssa reveled in it, losing herself in the hard heat of his mouth as it plundered hers, claiming her with a fiery possession that branded itself forever on her heart. His hands swept up, driving the folds of her hood back from her hair, to frame her face in his callused palms. " 'Ryssa, I was scared . . . so damn scared you would hate me if you knew . . ."

"Hate you?" A tiny laugh tore from her throat. "Before this moment, I ne'er would have believed it possible that I could hold a love deeper than that I already felt for you. But now . . ." She pushed herself up on her slippered toes, her lips brushing his with a reverence more binding than any vows. "I love you Tade, more than my life, more than—more than Devin's gentle God or my father's cruel one. No matter what the future holds, no one will ever steal away the place you hold within me."

Tade's eyes were tear-bright, and the firm lips that had brought her such ecstasy were quivering with emotion. "I want you . . . want you for my wife . . . want to fill you with my seed, my sons. I want to hold daughters with ebony curls in my arms and make love to you until no demon can haunt you."

Maryssa laid her fingers on his lips, her own tears flowing free. "Aye, love," she said. "I know." Her other hand tightened about the swan pendant. "You held this once as a secret remembrance of a terrified girl you scarce knew." She raised her eyes to his, incredible strength and confidence springing from some well of love within her. "Wear it now, openly, as a token from a woman who would . . . would give you the world if 'twas in her grasp . . . a symbol that whatever the fates may bring, you'll e'er be . . . be bound to me as husband in my heart.''

Love and a fierce sense of protectiveness toward this bold man and the people he sheltered flowed through her as she reached around Tade's neck to fasten the clasp of the thin gold chain with fingers that trembled. The swan lay in the bronzed hollow of his throat, glistening against the warmth of his skin.

She raised eyes shimmering with tears, full of the emotion that seemed about to burst her heart, and the love that shone from Tade Kilcannon's face seared deep into her soul.

''I have no—no token to give you,'' he said in a choked voice. ''Except this vow.'' His eyes pierced hers. ''One day you'll be my wife, Maryssa Wylder. Mine. For naught—not the laws of men or of God himself—will keep me from binding you to me. I swear it on my mother's grave.''

He started to seal his promise with his lips, but suddenly it was as though a tempest in all its fury had whirled down upon them. ''Your mother's grave,'' a voice snarled. ''I vow you're not fit to spit upon it!''

Maryssa cried out in shock, her stomach plummeting to her toes at the hate-filled tones as Tade wheeled toward the man who stood but an arm's length away. She could feel his muscles jerk whip-taut, like those of a warrior readying for battle, the pallor of his face attesting to the fact that Tade, too, had been oblivious to the sudden silence that had fallen upon the hollow, unaware of the crunch of boots charging toward the place where they stood. Maryssa saw Tade's jaw set hard, proud, and defiant as his eyes swept the sea of hostile faces closing in on them, his gaze locking with the murderous glare of Kane Kilcannon. But for the first time she saw beneath the proud earl's rage and fury to the pain that weighed upon his heart.

''Mr. Kilcannon,'' Maryssa began, fighting to stay the storm lashing between father and son. ''I—forgive me if I disturbed your worship. Tade was but—''

''But placing every man, woman, and child who dared

come here in danger?'' Kane snarled. ''Dragging the daughter of English Wylder *here,* to the one place that was safe?''

''Da''—Tade's voice was hard and cold, a warning as he grasped Maryssa's hand in his own—''don't say things you'll later regret.''

''Regret?'' the earl blazed. ''The one thing I regret is having spawned a son who would cast to the devil a man's courage, a man's honor. Christ, you're my son—my heir. These people are yours to protect, to defend, and you throw them into danger to amuse some English bitch you've been rutting with?''

''Damn it, Father—'' Tade's eyes flashed deadly fire. A fiercer anger than Maryssa had ever seen now burned in their depths.

''Damn you to hell!'' The bellow of rage was rife with a desperation and helplessness that tore at Maryssa's heart as Kane Kilcannon's features contorted into a mask of torment. ''Don't you dare defend her to me!'' One powerful fist knotted. Maryssa screamed a warning, fighting to break Tade's grip on her arm and leap between the two men. She caught a glimpse of Devin running through the crowd, but they were both too late. Kane's fist arced in a savage path toward Tade's jaw, and the hard knuckles connected with a sickening thud. Tade's head snapped back with the force of the blow. He staggered a step back, his own fist flashing ready, then freezing in midair.

Someone in the crowd shouted. A baby set up a wail. But Maryssa saw only the white imprint of Kane Kilcannon's hand on Tade's skin and the thin trickle of blood dripping from the hard line of Tade's mouth. Yet even that physical evidence of the rift between father and son filled her with less horror than did the raw hatred that flashed between them.

''Kane! For the love of God!'' Rachel's cry of distress mingled with a harsh-spoken ''Hold!'' as Maryssa stumbled backward. She felt a hand flash out to steady her and knew it as Devin's when he propelled her out of the path of the angry men. In her stead he stormed between them, his slender body seeming but a reed trapped in the joining of two raging rivers.

''Stop it, Da!'' Devin's voice cut clear and strong through the rumbling of the crowd.

The bitterness that twisted Tade's mouth tore at Maryssa's heart. "You might as well spare your breath, Dev," he said, turning his glare upon his father. "You've ever been ready to strike me, have you not, Da? To wreak your punishment on me for the sin of being a failure as your son? Fine, then, take your fill of it if you have half as much courage as you have hate."

Maryssa flinched as Kane gave a cry of fury, but Devin's hand dug deep into his father's bulging arm, holding him with astonishing strength. The holy man's mild eyes glinted with sorrow and pain tainted with blade-sharp indignation. "Enough, both of you! This is no highroad suited for a brawl! 'Tis a place of God."

" 'Tis a place for the heir Kilcannon to be dallying with his English witch, more like!" someone in the crowd dared.

"Well, I vow we'd best leave the glen to those a-trysting, then, if this is any example of the reverence with which you treat the saying of mass," Devin blazed, his challenging gaze sweeping the faces about him.

The grumblings of the ragged parishioners died to a murmur, and the eyes that had been boldly glaring at Maryssa were now fixed upon the ground, the cheeks of most flushing pink at Devin's reproof. "Look at you, all of you!" he went on. "Aye, and most especially you, Da! Charging up here with your hate, casting it like stones at a woman who has done naught to you." The mutterings of the crowd rose, the catlike face of Sheena O'Toole peeking out from the rest, dripping hatred.

"Done naught to us? This woman is the daughter of the man who stole your father's lands!" she sniffed.

Devin wheeled on the girl, his face deathly white. "The English have left us but little. They've taken our lands, our churches, the food from our mouths, but by God, don't let them take our common decency! I know Maryssa Wylder, and I would stake my life on my trust in her."

"You may well be called on to meet that wager," the earl snarled, "at the point of the hoodsman's knife! If she leads the Sassenach hounds to this mountain, sets Rath upon us—"

"Maryssa has proven her loyalties where Rath is concerned," Tade said between gritted teeth.

"I hate Rath's cruelties as much as any of you do!" Maryssa choked out. "I would never harm you."

"Harm us?" Kane Kilcannon's lip curled in raw hatred. "You've done more than harm us, my fine English lady. You've ripped one son from my heart, aye, and you may well send the other to the gallows. And I hope to God you burn in hell for it beside your traitor father!"

Sick horror twisted inside Maryssa's belly as she saw Tade lunge toward his father, his face taut with black fury.

"Nay, Tade!" she shrilled, diving toward him, but before she could reach him, Tade froze, his muscles standing out like bands of steel.

Seconds seemed to stretch into eternity, every person in the valley strung to the snapping point of tension. Tade's eyes glinted like splintered emeralds. "You needn't consign only Maryssa to hell, Da," he said. "You'll not rest happy until all of us—Dev, Rachel, the little ones, aye, and myself—burn there with you."

He straightened, his eyes seeking out Rachel's tormented, tear-streaked face. "I'll have my things out of the loft before you reach the cottage," he said softly.

"Tade! Tade, no!" Rachel pleaded, clasping his wrist.

"Let him go!" At the sound of Kane's harsh voice the brood of Kilcannons, from wee Katie to little Ryan, crumpled into wails, the older lads battling their tears behind pathetic, torn faces.

"Da, you can't—can't hurl Tade out." Deirdre stumbled to her father, her copper hair streaming about a face suddenly childlike. "You can't!"

" 'Tis long past time I left, Dee," Tade comforted softly, pausing to touch his sister's tear-streaked cheek.

"Nay! Tade! Me wants Tade!" Katie's piteous shrieks rose above the others.

"I'll bring you a present when next I visit, Katie darlin'," he said through a throat thick with pain. "Mayhap a sugar swan . . .." Tade straightened, and Maryssa could see it was as though his very soul were being wrenched from within him, but he turned to her, offering his hand. Nay, Maryssa thought, her heart rending. He was not offering only his hand. He was offering her his life and all the love he had known.

She stared at the long bronzed fingers, unable to take them, to rob him of a birthright far more treasured than any castle built of stone. But he only curved one arm about her waist and led her through the silent crowd. With each step he took, Maryssa could feel pieces of his life shattering—memories of the past, friends long cherished, a family who had been his heart's blood until this day.

Mothers tugged their children out of her path as though she were marked with the lesions of a leper while their menfolk raked Tade's tall, proud shoulders with the scorn reserved for the foulest Judas.

Maryssa cast but one glance over her shoulder as Tade led her away, her eyes catching the pain on Rachel Kilcannon's face, the loathing darkening Sheena O'Toole's sharp features.

Yet even as Tade swung her onto her mare and spurred his own mount down the path they had trekked a lifetime ago, she could not banish the images from her mind. She held them with Tade's silence as the two horses made their way across the stony ground. Even the wind tangling through the wilds seemed to mourn as they neared the lands that had once been Tade's birthright.

And as the daunting stone walls of the castle rose before them, Nightwylde itself seemed to jeer at the fierce revenge it had exacted, not only from the usurpers who had raped the land but from the true heirs who had failed to hold it.

Maryssa's gaze swept the gray turrets that pierced the sky, making the heavens bleed broken dreams. "Tade," she whispered as he reined Curran to a halt in the shadows, "I can't let you cast aside your father and the rest of your family."

His face tipped down toward hers, his eyes full of such solemn sorrow that tears welled up on her lashes.

"You're my family now, Maura. 'Tis long since over between my father and me," he said. "I could never be the son he wanted, could never tell him I rode as the Falcon. To keep the family safe, I had to let them think I was naught but a heedless rake. And Da believed the worst so easily, Maura. The facade was all he ever saw. I needed him to sense who I was inside, to have faith that I could not be so shallow as to watch others suffer and do naught but guzzle ale and play at catch-skirt.''

His words were a knife twisting in her breast. ''I know,'' she said brokenly.

''Maura, I need but a little time to think . . . to be alone. I—''

''Shh!'' Maryssa reached out to where his fingers still clung to his reins, her voice quivering. '' 'Tis all right, Tade.''

''Nay.'' Tade's gaze shifted to the stone gate. '' 'Tis not all right. 'Twill ne'er be all right for us in this place, this time. But my father's hate changes none of the vows I made to you. On Allhallows Eve I will come for you, take you to the celebration fires, aye, and farther still, if you dare.''

Icy fingers seemed to creep beneath Maryssa's skin. ''Nay! 'Tis—'tis too dangerous for you to come to Nightwylde now. If any of your enemies should tell my father what happened in the glen . . . I'll steal away and meet you at the cross-roads.''

He opened his mouth as if to protest, then compressed his lips, his mouth a hard line. '' 'Twould end our plans right early if I were seen at the castle,'' he allowed. ''Very well. I'll await you at the crossroads until midnight. If you've not been able to escape by then—''

''I'll be there, Tade. I vow it.''

His emerald gaze seemed to pierce her, and in it she caught a glimmer of the fire and a shade of the hardness she had seen in their green depths that night at the Devil's Grin. ''Till Allhallows Eve, then.'' He reined his stallion in a circle, his mantle streaming out behind his broad shoulders like liquid midnight as he spurred Curran away.

Her eyes strained after him, his words, his promises, echoing within her. But as she watched the man she loved melting into mist, the faces of the peasants in the glen rose before her—their ragged forms helpless, with naught but Tade's courage and wit to shield them.

''My rogue,'' she breathed on a sob, ''my gallant rogue of the night.'' Despair seemed to clutch at her, but she clawed it away, tearing loose as well her hold on him. ''Nay, not mine, Tade,'' she whispered. ''No matter how much we both wish it.'' She closed eyes filled with tears.

On Allhallows Eve I will come for you . . . His voice seemed to breathe the promise on the wind. And he would come, Maryssa thought, clenching her fists in torment, but he would carry away with him naught but his mantle of legend.

Fifteen

MIST SWEPT ACROSS the mountain, swirling in ghostly dances as twilight crept over the craggy earth. Allhallows Eve, the church called it, renaming the ancient druid celebration in an effort to banish the memory of pagan rites. Yet still it was Samain in the hearts of the Irish, the night of evil pucas, cavorting with demons, the night of the dead walking again upon the earth. Tade shifted against the dark mouth of the cave, the stone on which he had been leaning the hour past suddenly feeling cold against his back.

Samain. From the time he was a lad, toddling about the bonfires the mountainfolk built to drive away the devils, he had gloried in this night, so ripe for the pranks and jests he adored. Always he had dismissed the lurking mysteries and dangers that filled the others with fear. But tonight the crude shelter he had shared with Devin since the altercation at Christ's Wound seemed alive with menace. Neither the presence of Devin's robes, abandoned now upon the straw tick beside the cave wall, nor the crudely carved crucifix propped reverently near the bundle of Tade's possessions seemed to hold the power to banish the stirrings of evil born of this night.

" 'Twill be a fine night for the fires," Devin said softly as he joined Tade.

"Aye." Tade turned his gaze away, hoping his brief answer would signal to his brother his need for silence, as it had unerringly in the days since they had lived together in the cave.

But for the first time, whether as a result of impatience with his morose companion or the conviction that Tade had brooded long enough, Dev failed to heed the warning. "Do you remember the year you strung a skeleton together with old twine?" he asked, hunkering down in a way that indicated quite clearly he meant to stay. "You rummaged around for bones in every rubbish heap from here to Derry, and at midnight you rigged it with string and made it dance over my pallet. I almost died of terror."

"Aye, and Da bloodied my backside with a butter paddle."

"Only because you gave him a fright, too. I mean, poor Da, rushing up that loft ladder, with me screaming as if the devil were carrying me away, and you . . ." Devin chuckled at the memory. "I vow, Tade, Da would have thought the jest a grand one if you hadn't made the creature swoop down on him, toppling him from the ladder."

Tade made no reply, just stared out to the distant crossroads where tiny flickerings of orange flame were beginning to splash the dusk.

Yet Devin, it seemed, was bent on bedeviling him, stirring childhood memories that now only brought Tade pain. "Remember the night you scaled the roof and moaned and screamed into the chimney like a cursed banshee?"

"Aye. I remember. I tumbled in and nigh set the seat of my breeches afire in the embers Rachel had banked on the hearth before bed."

"Well, 'twas lucky the worst of it was a few blisters on your hinderparts. By rights you should have broken your fool neck."

"Mayhap 'twould have been more gladsome for Da if I had."

"Blast it, Tade, that's not true and you bloody well know it." Devin shot to his feet, exasperation in every line of his pale face. "Despite the fact that the two of you have spent the last six and twenty years ramming your stubborn heads against each other, Da loves you. And you love him. If you'd both but open your eyes and your hearts, strip away your cursed Kilcannon pride—''

"Kilcannon pride?" Tade's mouth twisted with irony. "Is that not all that matters to him? He's had naught but contempt for me since the day Patrick Dugan was murdered." The tiniest catch in Tade's voice betrayed his pain, the infinitely patient, wearily amused face of the long-dead schoolmaster rising in his memory.

"Tade . . ." Frustration had vanished from Devin's tone, and the fingers that had dug into Tade's flesh grew gentle. " 'Twas naught but a child's mistake you made. Master Dugan would not have blamed you. And Da has long since forgiven you."

Tade hated the stinging in his eyes, the haze that transformed the horizon into images from of the past, which centered on the memory of a hank of fleece all dyed gold, its edges sewn together with a boy's awkward stitches. "That child's mistake cost Patrick Dugan his life."

"You only wanted to surprise the man with the gift you had made, to thank him for the joy he had shown you in giving you the book."

Tade gave a bitter laugh. "Oh, aye, I thanked him right well for putting the story of Jason and the Argonauts into my hands. I abandoned my post as sentry—''

"To retrieve the fleece you'd made from its hiding place. Blast it, Tade, you were but a child!"

"Aye, but I was a Kilcannon." Tade tasted bitterness on his lips. "Kilcannons are allowed no mistakes, no frolics. Know you that when I cried for Patrick Dugan the night they cut him down, Da told me that if I'd had Kilcannon honor— if I had stayed at my post—I would have been able to give the schoolmaster fair warning, and Bridey Houlihan's treachery would have come to naught?" Tade closed his eyes, the features of the bitter informer who had caused Dugan's death filling his memory.

" 'Twas her choice to betray Master Dugan, 'twas *her* plotting, Tade. Not yours." Devin raked one thin hand through his pale hair. " 'Tis hard . . . hard to understand what moved Da to wax so harsh about the happenings at the cave that day, but his honor, Tade, is the only legacy he has left to give his sons, the only thing that has not been crushed in him or stolen from him. He knew you had no way of knowing that the schoolmaster had been betrayed.''

''Betrayed . . .'' The terrifying memory of the child merged with the righteous rage of the man. ''I vow, if Bridey Houlihan hadn't fled to France that very night, I would have found a way to repay her in like coin for what she did that day, even though I was but a lad.'' Tade's fists knotted, his nails cutting into his palms. ''But she was gone . . . gone even before the soldiers rode in to do their butchering. 'Twas a cursed lot of blood the vindictive bitch spilled because poor Patrick Dugan dared to love his calling more than he loved her.''

''Passions can be like a madness in our souls—love, jealousy, hate, rage.'' Devin turned his gaze to the steady banner of flame now unfurling from the distant bonfire. ''Trapped within those passions, we can be less than the most savage beast that stalks the wilds or, rarer still, we can touch such splendor as angels seldom know.''

''What am I, then, Father Devin? A beast because I dared to mate with a woman I would die for? A woman I love and who loves me? Are Maryssa and I accursed, then, because of some paltry law thought up by some pope sitting on a gilded throne in a gilded palace a hundred years ago?''

'' 'Tis no paltry law, Tade, especially here in Ireland. I wish I could tell you to take your Maryssa, cherish her as I know you would, but the faith we hold is much battered in these times. 'Tis a war we fight here, without weapons, and each of us must be certain about which side we are fighting on.''

''I've fought your cursed battle since the day I turned seventeen, but I fought it *with* weapons, Dev. I bought your God's safety with my blood. But now''—Tade's eyes flashed up to meet the pale blue of Devin's—''I'm casting down my sword. I'm taking Maryssa away. Away from her bastard father, away from Ireland.''

''For God's sake, Tade, you can't—can't mean that!'' Twilight painted bruised hollows in Devin's thin face. His eyes looked stricken, stark with disbelief and despair. ''Where would you go? How would you feed her, clothe her, keep her from her father's grasp? Think you Bainbridge Wylder will let you simply sweep away his only daughter without taking rash measures to stop you?''

"I doubt Wylder will even know Maryssa is gone, unless he turns to beat her. And if he does give chase, 'twill gain me the greatest of pleasure to return to the cursed bastard good portion of the bruises I saw on Maryssa's cheek.''

"Despite the fact that Wylder has used her harshly, she is still his only child—heiress to all he owns. Even if Maryssa would willingly go with you, he'd hunt you down.''

"By then 'twill be too late. She'll be my wife, Dev, may-hap with my child growing inside her.''

"Tade—''

"Nay, Dev. I'm taking her, riding to the coast, and from thence setting out for Cannes. Once I wed her, I'll contrive some way to build a life for us there. Mayhap French Louis has need of a strong sword arm among his armies. If that fails, I'll ply my skill at coloring gaming cards.''

"And when you get shot for cheating some drunken Gaul, what will happen to Maryssa?''

Tade's voice dropped low. "She will still be my wife, Dev, joined to me as one. And if ill befalls either of us, 'twill be worth the pain to have known that bliss.'' Tade raised his gaze to Devin's, needing desperately for this brother, whom he had tormented and teased, but whom he loved more deeply than any other member of the embattled Kilcannon clan, to understand.

Devin cleared his throat, and the eyes that darted away from Tade's were filled with tears. His chin dropped to his chest. "When I was in the cane fields and the Barbados sun was beating down on me like the devil's breath, I used to make a game of remembering your pranks,'' Devin said softly. "I recounted them all, Tade, in the months I slaved there. 'Twas those memories that held me strong—aye, more, sometimes than the faith to which I am pledged.''

He raked one slender hand slowly through his moon-gold hair. "I thought you would ne'er change. That you would always be a half-wild boy, driving us all mad with your scrapes.''

"I vow I'll have to be getting myself out of them without your help from now on,'' Tade said. Throat knotting with emotion, he unfastened the pouch at his waist and withdrew a thin silver crucifix affixed to a loop of dulled beads. "I want to give you something before I sail," Tade said, turning the rosary in his hand. "Most like 'twill be years before . . . before Maryssa and I can return to Ireland."

He fixed his eyes on the rosary, knowing that he might well never return home. "When I'm gone, MacGary and the others will continue to ride—to guard the mountain. There is a man coming, an English huntsman named Dallywoulde, whom Maura warned me about. I've told Neylan and MacGary about him. They'll be waiting at the ready."

"I'll depend upon them."

"You can, Dev. I'd not go if I didn't believe that you—all of you—would be safe. If you should e'er find yourself in need of aid, send this to Reeve Marlow. He'll know how to reach the men I leave behind."

Devin took the rosary into his hand and ran the tip of one finger over the engraving that graced the back of the crucifix. "A falcon," he said softly as the waning light touched the carved image, bathing its patina in a rose glow.

"Aye. I fear 'tis far from polished, what with my neglecting my prayings so much of late. But 'tis one of the few things in my possession I've not gained by slitting some rich Englishman's purse or by dicing at some inn."

Devin's fingers closed about the gift, his sensitive mouth quivering in a smile full of love and sadness. "I'll use it to pray for your blackguard soul," he said, attempting to lighten his tone. "But mayhap Maryssa will have more luck in saving it than I have."

The jest had a hollow sound. Unable to bear the feelings of love and loss that were dragging both him and Devin down, Tade strode into the cave that had been home to the brothers these last days. From a niche in the stone wall, he pulled a blanket-wrapped bundle bound with strips of leather, which he slung over one broad shoulder. It contained the possessions of a lifetime. Crude forbidden weapons he had seized during his raids, the leather mittens Deirdre had worked for him last Christmastide, one ragged-bound book, its embossed letters long ago worn away by grubby hands and a boy's tears, and one faded leaden soldier.

He turned back toward Devin, seeing the twilight carve

deep shadows into the beloved face that had once seemed so serene. Tade swallowed a lump of pain in his throat, feeling as though, somehow, he were cutting away a part of himself in this leaving, deserting this man who seemed now, not the steadfast priest filled with strength, but rather an innocent, groping in some abyss Devin alone could see.

"Tell Rachel and the babes I love them," Tade said. "And Da . . ."

Devin raised his hand as if to bless Tade, but the pale fingers froze in the air. With a choked sound, Devin lunged forward and crushed Tade in his arms. "Go with God, Tade."

Tade caught his brother tight with his free arm, feeling he had abandoned Devin to some private hell. "Dev," he began, "if there is aught troubling you, Maryssa and I . . . we can wait—"

"Nay." Devin gave an empty laugh. "The demons I wrestle this night can be bested by me alone. 'Tis time for you to think of yourself before any other. 'Tis growing dark, Tade, and your love will be waiting."

Torn and confused, Tade shifted the burden to his other shoulder, his fingers worrying the end of one leather thong. But as though Devin sensed the turmoil loosed within his brother, he divested Tade of the bundle and strode with it upon his own narrow shoulders to where Curran stood tethered. Tade watched, silent, as Devin fastened the rolled blanket behind the saddle.

Giving the leather strips one last tug, Dev took hold of the bay's reins. "Beware the ghosties as you ride," he said, his mouth twisting in a crooked smile as his eyes swept the faraway flickering of the bonfires.

"I will." Tade's fingers felt chill and numb as he gripped the saddle and swung up on the bay's back. "Don't forget to say farewell to Rachel and the babes for me. Aye, and Da."

"You'll not be telling them yourself?"

"How can I?" Tade's fingers clenched on the reins, the pain at not being able to see each round child's face, Rachel's loving smile, or his father's proud countenance washing over him afresh.

" 'Twould prove a mite awkward, now that I think on it." A flat laugh broke through Devin's lips and died there. "I'll give them your love. Be happy, Tade." Devin's face turned up to meet his gaze, the rising moon casting a translucent pallor over the gentle, beloved features. "I need—need to believe you are happy."

Tade felt loss claw into his heart, as though half of his soul were being wrenched from his breast. But though he wanted desperately to tell this man about the special place he held in his heart, the words seemed to snag in his throat. "Dev, all these years . . . you . . . I ne'er told you how much I—"

"I know, Tade." Devin's smile widened, the tiniest flicker of strength touching his gaze. "I know." His words were a blessing, a benediction. A farewell. "Now, go tend to your Maryssa before she sets after you with a butter paddle for being late." Devin raised one hand and gently slapped Curran's glossy rump.

The stallion jolted into motion, driving its way through the undergrowth. But Tade spared the horse's path not a glance. He swiveled in the saddle, straining his gaze back to the inky opening of the cave and the man silhouetted against it. A shiver of foreboding prickled his scalp as the waves of the Samain darkness broke over Devin's gentle face, the gnarled mountain trees casting over the pale features the shape of a cross.

Maryssa drew deeper into the shadow of a jagged boulder, her numbed fingers clutching the folds of her cloak more tightly about her throat. Despite the heat emanating from the tongues of flame writhing up from an Allhallows fire a little distance from where she stood, she felt naught but the chill of despair and the jeering touch of the wind soughing down from Tade's night-shaded mountains.

In the days since the mass at Christ's Wound, she had been torn between railing at the fate that ever rent her and Tade apart and succumbing to the temptation to disregard all except the passion she felt for him, to but meet him here at the fires and clutch to her a future bright with the love that he had promised.

Yet whenever the tug of a future at his side pulled too strongly, she had but to close her eyes to quell it, conjuring in her memory an image of the ragged cluster of mountainfolk in the tiny glen or the remembered image of Kane Kilcannon's ravaged face.

She twisted a tendril of hair that had slipped from beneath her hood, and bit her lip to still its trembling. She had no right to steal Tade away from those who needed him so desperately, who had no other champion to stand between them and disaster. And yet, to turn her back on the promise of such joy, when her own life had been so barren of pleasure, to exchange Tade's offer of happiness for the chill promise of Ascot Dallywoulde's bed . . .

Maryssa shuddered, clenching her teeth. Even if she never again knew the sweetness of Tade's touch, even if her father railed at her and beat her, she could never become Dallywoulde's bride. And yet, if she were to ride away with Tade this night, would not the years hence prove but a more subtle torture than any her father and Ascot could deal her?

Always she had sensed the honor Tade possessed, the pride and soul-deep nobility that gave his lightsome features such inner beauty. What would become of that pride during years of playing the fugitive from her father's wrath? How savagely would the lash of his honor flay him in some foreign land, bound by the knowledge that he had deserted those who needed his strength and courage so desperately? He would come to resent the woman who had dragged him away from his duty, perhaps even come to hate her . . .

Shrill laughter pierced the rollicking music of harp, pipe, and fiddle, and Maryssa's gaze flicked to where the ring of dancers writhed and whirled about the bonfire's flames, which clawed at the black curtain of the night like the fingers of Maryssa's own dread. No, she thought, it would be far better to drive Tade's love for her from his heart with a clean, hot blaze like that of the Samain fires, banishing the emotions that tempted him to betray his own soul—and in so doing, condemn her own to the fires of a hell far worse than even Satan could devise.

She clenched her mittened fingers as she caught a glimpse of Deirdre Kilcannon's bright hair. The girl, her shoulders drooping, sat huddled beneath a shawl some distance away from the dancers, her face almost as forlorn as Maryssa knew her own to be. She steeled her spine, wishing she could go to Tade's sister and comfort her, but knowing that Deirdre would fly into her face, searing her with hatred. All Maryssa could do was to return to the girl that which Deirdre felt she had stolen—the love of the brother Deirdre adored, the peace of the family that had cherished the copper-haired firebrand from the day she was born.

Tade Kilcannon had given Maryssa so much—love, a budding faith in herself, the wonder of days spent in such beauty that the memory of their joy would hold her through a lifetime. Now he needed only her strength to let him go.

Her eyes caught the lithe, sensual movements of Sheena O'Toole's sleek form as the girl twirled around the leaping flames, and Maryssa bit her lip, her eyes burning with unshed tears.

Of all the agony to come—her loss of the tender ecstasy Tade's love could bring—the greatest would be the knowledge that Tade would need to find someone else on whom to shower his abundant love. He would need a wife and a cottage full of babes to kiss and cuddle and hold in his arms. In time, he would forget the plain English girl who had not had the courage to risk all for his love, and he would take another to his bed and to his heart.

A steel blade twisted in Maryssa's breast, tearing her with a sharp edge of jealousy and hopelessness. But she fought it, forcing her chin high, clenching her teeth against the sob that swelled within her chest. Above all, Tade Kilcannon had blessed her with strength. Though she lost all else, she would cling to that one special gift.

The sound of more revelers approaching drew Maryssa's gaze to the shadow-shrouded ribbon of road winding off toward the base of the mountain. Shouts of recognition and ribald greetings were flung to a rider as he burst forth from the night astride a huge bay stallion.

Maryssa swallowed hard as the rider spun his mount in a prancing circle, firelight glinting off of its sleek flanks, the swirling folds of a black mantle, and the flashing white of Tade Kilcannon's rakehell grin.

One long, booted leg swung over Curran's withers as Tade leaped from his mount's back, calling some teasing jest to a lad decked out in an Allhallows Eve mask fashioned of old hide. Maryssa saw Sheena O'Toole glance toward him, her gyrations in the dance growing immediately more seductive, her full breasts thrusting at the low-cut bodice of her gown, her hips undulating in a rhythm that issued an invitation to the man now tethering his stallion to a nearby gorse bush, an invitation to join her in a dance far more primal than the one she was now engaged in.

As Tade offered the hot-eyed girl no more than a fleeting nod of greeting, Maryssa saw in his fire-limned features something that filled her with a dread far deeper even than the knowledge that she would be abandoning Tade to Sheena's practiced wiles. The bronzed planes of Tade's face were drawn into a mask of trouble and indecision, emotions Maryssa had never known to mar the innate confidence he had always worn about him with the same careless ease with which he wore his dashing black cape.

The glow of the fire cast eerie patterns of light and shadow on lines etched deep at the corners of his mouth and furrowing the brow that had always been as smooth as a rollicking lad's.

Maryssa felt an unreasonable twinge of hurt and betrayal at the thought that Tade might be having doubts of his own about the flight he had urged her to. Her mouth twisted in tormented irony. Somehow, sending her knight errant off to fulfill his noble quest had seemed far easier, believing, as she had, that he held fast to his desire to sweep her away. Now, already feeling the horrible wrenching of Tade pulling away from her, she knew the full agony of the emptiness his absence would leave within her, and of the wound—soul deep, never healing—she would carry for the rest of her life.

She stepped from the shadow of the stone into the flickering fingers of light that crept out from the fire, just as Sheena O'Toole trilled out a greeting to him. But he saw neither of them. For at that moment Deirdre's gaze locked upon her brother. Any doubt Maryssa still felt about freeing Tade vanished in a twisting pain as the girl let out a cry and dashed forward to fling herself into his outstretched arms.

Though the sounds of the music and the shouts of the dancers drowned out the words that passed between Tade and his sister, Maryssa could see the child's shoulders shake with sobs, could see Tade's large hand tenderly smoothing the tumble of red-gold curls as he clutched her close. The light from the fire splashed with merciless clarity over the anguish that was carved into Tade's face, the white, tortured line of his mouth, his eyes, squeezed shut against what Maryssa sensed were tears.

Then his eyes opened, and Maryssa could feel the intensity of his green gaze on her own shadowed form. Tade straightened, his face schooled into lines filled with strain as he brushed Deirdre's cheeks with a kiss. Maryssa saw him tug the girl's hair, then hook one finger beneath her stubborn Kilcannon chin, lifting it, as if to infuse her with his strength.

Deirdre's eyes flicked toward Maryssa, tear-bright, reddened with hours of crying. The girl pressed one small fist to her mouth and then wheeled to dash back into the darkness.

Then Tade was striding toward Maryssa, his broad shoulders squared, his face burdened with sorrow. And a solemn hope burst in anguished waves through Maryssa's soul.

He paused but a step away from her, hesitating, with something akin to shyness as the beloved curve of his smile parted in a mockery of his smile. "Good morrow, Miss Wylder," he said, raising one finger to caress her cheek. " 'Tis rumored you are off to be wed—that within a week's time you'll bear some blackguard rogue's name."

Maryssa tried to speak, but couldn't, for her throat was strangled by tears.

" 'Tis an old name, though, and a noble one." Tade's other hand came up to cup her face. "A name borne with honor and courage through the ages by ancient Irish earls."

His piercing emerald eyes searched her face, and in those green depths she could see every agony that had torn at him these past days, see the warring loyalties within him, including the love he felt for her. She turned away, shame stealing into her cheeks.

"Then 'tis . . . 'tis far too grand a name to give to a coward," she managed, battling the sobs that crushed her chest like iron bands.

"Maura, what the—"

She spun around, nails gouging deep in her palms, the confusion in Tade's eyes flaying her. "I came here tonight to—to bid you farewell."

The planes of Tade's face turned suddenly brittle. "Farewell?" he grated, grasping her arm in a grip that hurt. "What the devil do you mean?"

"Ever since that day in the valley, I've been warring with myself—wanting to go with you, and yet afraid . . ." She fixed her gaze on the dirt, unable to meet Tade's eyes. "Afraid of my father and of . . . of places I don't know and . . . and people . . ."

"Maryssa, for God's sake, I love you." She felt his body stiffen. "You have to know I'd give my life to keep you safe."

"I know, Tade," she said, with a choke in her voice. "But I was never meant to go off adventuring. You—you thrive on it, on battles of wits, aye, and of swords and pistols. 'Twill all be a grand frolic to you, but to me . . ." The words trailed off, and she knotted her fingers in the folds of her cloak to keep from flinging herself against him, kissing away the torment now etched on his face.

"I was meant to spend my days curled in a hearth corner with my books and my dreams."

"Books? Dreams? Your father kept you imprisoned in that cursed castle like some fairy-tale princess, chained away from love and life. You belong in my heart and in my bed as my wife, not in some stone grave that bastard Wylder has buried you in!"

"Nay, Tade. I belong at my father's side—at Nightwylde and Carradown—as his heiress. And you . . . you belong here in Donegal."

She flinched at the savage curse that tore from Tade's lips as his eyes spat fury at her. "I belong wherever you are, damn it," he snarled. "Breeding sons and daughters, carving out a home. Even now your womb might hold my child."

The possibility that Tade's baby might flourish within her cinched bands of pain tighter still about Maryssa's breast, the feelings of queasiness that never left her taking on new meaning. Yet she pushed relentlessly on.

"You belong here, astride your stallion, Tade," she said, "with your silken hood and your pistols firing. Have you given a wisp of a thought to what would become of these people if you were to run off somewhere with me? Of Rachel? Deirdre? Devin?"

"Damn it, I've thought of little else since we decided to sail away! Think you it is easy for me to turn away from those I love, knowing . . . knowing that at any moment Rath might—" Tade drove his fingers through his hair, his broad shoulders quivering with rage and hurt. "But I would cast them all to the winds, Maura, to hold you . . ." His voice was low, thick with emotion, his mouth twisting with pain. "I thought . . . thought you loved me with the same—"

"Our love is not the same, Tade." The words were torn from Maryssa's breast. "My love for you is real, but 'tis a timid thing lurking in the shadows beside your love for me—a love that makes you willing to risk all, forgive all. My religion is but a stiff duty while yours runs deep in your blood. My father and I merely tolerate each other while your family is rich in loyalty and affection." Maryssa's eyes turned to the writhing flames, and it was as though she were seared within their depths as she took up one last weapon with which to crush the love Tade had blessed her with.

A bitter laugh bubbled up in her throat, her eyes spilling hot tears. "I had not even the courage to be honest with you when you put yourself in such peril to endow me with your loving."

"Honest?" the word rasped from Tade's tongue.

She forced herself to gaze at his devastated face, knowing that this last blow would have the desired effect only if she had the courage to meet his gaze. "Aye, Tade. From the time I was in the cradle, I—I have been betrothed to my cousin."

The fierce light in Tade's eyes made her falter, and she found the will to hold his gaze in some reserve of strength she had not known she possessed.

"Betrothed," Tade bit out. "All this time we—I thought you loved me, you were pledged to another man?"

"My vow to him has naught to—to do with love. 'Tis a binding of properties, fortunes, and rank."

"*Damn* you." Tade's fingers bit deep into the flesh of her arms as he yanked her against him, his emerald gaze searing her in its fury. "I offered you my heart . . . my soul. I defied my religion, incurred the wrath of my own father for you—and you stand here prating about fortunes and land? You tell me that even when you lay with me you were planning to go to another man's bed? Christ, what a witling I've been, what a cursed besotted fool!" His bitter laugh raked her.

"You claim that you lack courage," he spat. "Fine, then, *Maura-love*, slink away to your safe castle, parade about in your bloody velvets and silks, and take between your legs a man whom you can scarce endure. 'Twould be a shame if you dared to dirty your cursed Sassenach hands by *living* like the rest of us.''

Maryssa couldn't stay her hand from reaching out to touch the whip-tight muscles in his arm, but Tade yanked away from her as though she were filth, his lip curling in a grimace of disgust that scarce hid the desolation in his eyes. He reached up to his throat, his fingers closing on glinting gold, and jerked savagely on the chain she had placed there but days before.

"Here," he said. "A woman gave me this. A woman I loved . . . thought I knew. But it seems her vows were as false as those of her father." Tears blinded Maryssa as he jammed the necklet into her palm; the swan's delicate wings gouged into her flesh.

"Farewell, Miss Wylder," he mocked her, his face savage. "We'll not meet again, unless of course 'tis on the high-roads."

He spun away, his mantle swirling, his long stride filled with fury and danger as he stalked around the circling dancers. Maryssa took a stumbling step toward him, wanting to cry out that she would storm the very gates of hell if she could stay at his side. But he never so much as glanced back. She winced as she saw Sheena O'Toole break from the ring of dancers and reach out her arms to ensnare him. Her lush curves pressed against the taut plane of Tade's body as her full lips strained to press seductive kisses along the rigid line of his jaw.

Yet Tade seemed not even to see the girl; he merely pushed her hands aside with suppressed violence and brushed past her, not seeing the fury that lit the girl's tilted amber eyes, not seeing that the mouth, which had been parted in hot invitation, was now pursed into a grimace of outrage and humiliation as those nearest her burst into guffaws and taunting laughter.

But Maryssa saw it as she watched Tade stride out of her life and into the grips of the fate for which he was destined. She stumbled to where her own mount was tied, no longer able to stem the racking sobs that ripped at her breast. He had believed her, accepted her whinings of fear. He now held her in contempt and loathing. Someday, when his wound had healed, he would remember her as only a weak-willed child who had cowered from the reality he embraced with such reckless abandon.

Yes, Maryssa thought. Tade would despise her. But she would love him more than her own life for all eternity. Her numb fingers opened over the gold chain, letting the pendant, still warm from Tade's skin, slip to the Donegal stones— abandoning the tiny swan to his mountains along with her own shattered dreams.

Sixteen

SHEENA O'TOOLE GLARED at the broad back of Tade Kilcannon, her cat-gold gaze seething with humiliation and outrage
as he strode out of the circle of light cast by the flames. The
sniggers and cutting mockeries of the dancers, who had seen
her fling herself on the chest of the heir Kilcannon and had
witnessed, too, Tade's dashing her aside, ate like acid at the
lush curves of her body. Her fingers curled into claws as she
fought the urge to rake the sly, sneering expressions from the
faces of those nearest her, or to fling an orange-hot brand at
the disappearing back of the man all of Donegal had once
expected her to wed.

There was a kind of triumph in the sparkling gaze of the
other girls now ringing the fire—those lowling chits over
whom Sheena had played the queen in the days when Tade
had come to take her riding or caught up her hand in the
dance. It had been fitting that the son and heir of the greatest
Irish Catholic family in Donegal should mate with the daughter of the O'Toole. Both families had desired the marriage;
the mountainfolk had expected it. And the fact that Tade Kilcannon cut the most dashing figure in all the mountains had
but fed Sheena's confidence that he would choose from among
Donegal's eager maidens the most beautiful of all.

She dashed the flowing tawny curls back from her shoulders, her flawless complexion flushing crimson. She had even burdened herself with the adoration of that tiresome child, Deirdre Kilcannon, in an effort to gain Tade's loyalty. And it had seemed that Tade was at last ready to throw aside his rakehell ways, to do his duty, and to provide heirs to the Kilcannon legacy, sons to battle for the lands that had been stolen from them, sons to rule the mountain wilds. Aye, Sheena thought fiercely, sons in whose veins would flow the blood of the O'Tooles as well. He had been nigh to taking her to wife until that Sassenach witch had twined him in her spell.

Sheena cast a fulminating glance at where the Wylder bitch stood, her hair straggling about her pale cheeks. It could only be black arts that had lured Tade to Maryssa Wylder's side, Sheena thought, her eyes narrowing on her rival's stricken face. What else could there be in those plain features, that pale skin, those wide, frightened eyes that could hold a man the like of Tade?

On the day of the hurling match, Sheena had quelled her irritation at Tade's attentions to Maryssa Wylder, dismissing them as but another of his numerous passing fancies, full certain that before the sun set whatever spark of attraction he might have felt for the girl would be smothered beneath the Sassenach doxy's mealymouthed shyness.

And when the distraught Deirdre had fled to the O'Toole cottage, railing that Tade claimed to be in love with the Wylder heiress, Sheena had but gritted her teeth, clinging to the knowledge that naught could come of such a mésalliance and that this English witch would soon flee back to her candlelit ballrooms and her perfumed beaux.

But when Sheena had glanced up at the hillside at Christ's Wound and seen Tade bending protectively over Maryssa Wylder's slight frame, his incredible eyes glowing as though she were an angel dropped into his palm from the heavens, Sheena's hauteur had vanished, leaving in its place desperation and a raw, burning fury.

She had boasted for months of Tade Kilcannon's favors, dangling her tales of his attentions before the other mountain girls' noses like a honeyed confection before the starving. She had seen their eyes narrow with envy, had loved pricking at their vanity while puffing up her own. Yet always she had comforted herself with the knowledge that once Tade did betroth himself to her, none of the girls she had goaded would dare to even whisper against the wife of the heir Kilcannon.

Yet now—now that all in the parish had seen Tade dare to incur the wrath not only of the mighty owner of Nightwylde but of Kane Kilcannon as well in order to shower Maryssa Wylder with the love plain-written on his handsome face— Sheena's bragging would be held up to ridicule. Those whom she had slighted would take the greatest pleasure in smearing her with their jealous snipings, jeering at her from behind their hands, whispering their joy that Sheena O'Toole had been brought low.

Her jaw clenched as the lame Jamie Scanlon raked his bow again across his fiddle strings. The dancers, stilled by the spectacle Tade had created, started their feet to flashing in time. The gay music seemed but a grating reminder of the other women's joy, the sound more infuriating still as it blended with the trilling laughter of Caitrin MacVee. The rival beauty shook out masses of rich brown hair, her pixyish face fairly bursting with triumph as she swirled past Sheena's rigid form.

"Tade seems to have lost his lust for the flames, Sheena," Caitrin giggled, "be they Samain fires or otherwise." The girl's blue eyes swept Sheena from lips to toes, and she tossed her head as Brian MacGary caught her in his sinewy arms.

"Most like poor Brian will be singed enough for all of us before the night's past, the way you're hanging on him," Sheena snapped. But even Caitrin's gasp of irritation brought her no pleasure.

Gold eyes flicked to Maryssa, hate sluicing through every pore of Sheena's skin. Nay! She would not be cast out like yesterday's wash water in favor of some English slut—even if the cursed witch's father owned half of Ireland!

Sheena moved farther away from the fire and closer to the slumped figure in the shadows. The flickering light dripped gold on the Sassenach girl's cheeks, stroking orange into the moisture that clung there, revealing in stark relief that delicate mouth contorted with . . . what was it? Tears?

Sheena's feral eyes narrowed, her lips pulling taut over

small white teeth. Perhaps it was time to close in on the weakling bitch and teach her the danger in snaring a man already spoken for.

Holding her chin high, she paced toward the shadows, eager to breed in Maryssa Wylder the same tearing humiliation to which Sheena herself was now condemned, but she had scarcely stepped out of the fire's glow when a hand closed on her arm, staying her.

"Leave her alone."

Fresh rage surged through Sheena as she wheeled, and she was stunned to see the tear-swollen eyes of Deirdre Kilcannon, her tangled coppery locks curling about a face torn with confusion, sorrow, and an unsettling shading of guilt.

"Leave her alone?" Sheena sneered. " 'Tis time the witch was taken to task for dangling after Tade! 'Tis a wonder she's not gotten your fool brother hanged by now, or worse! I vow she'll regret the day she—"

"Leave her alone."

Sheena's jaw dropped at the steely Kilcannon stubbornness glinting from beneath Deirdre's dark brows, the chin, so like Kane Kilcannon's, jutting out in a dangerous line.

"Deirdre, by Saint Jude! You should want her to pay—"

"For loving Tade?" Tears welled up in Deirdre's eyes. "I vow I'll hear no more of your poison. Both—both she and Tade have already paid overmuch!"

Indignation ripped through Sheena as she glared at Deirdre's face, the desire to slap the cursed Kilcannon pride from her countenance nearly overwhelming her. "You had no trouble supporting me these weeks past! You aided me in foiling your precious Tade's grand passion."

"Aye. I lied to my brother and nigh got Devin captured by the priest hunters. Tade wanted to murder me after I sent him out to gather fool's wool when he got back from Derry, and he had every right to slip a noose around my neck. My idiocy nigh put one around Devin's."

"You stupid—" The sound of retreating hoofbeats brought Sheena's head snapping around, her tirade dying in her throat as her gaze locked upon Maryssa Wylder's mare vanishing into the shadows.

With a cry of fury, Sheena yanked herself from Deirdre's grasp, all pretense of friendship and sweetness gone as she turned on the girl. But with the same arrogance as her brother, Deirdre Kilcannon had spun away from her and crossed the ring of light with the same innate pride that had been in Tade's broad shoulders moments before.

Sheena started to stalk after her, but the laughter of Caitrin MacVee drifted in the air. Nay, Sheena O'Toole would not be subject to ridicule yet again this night at the hands of a Kilcannon. She'd find a way to make them all swallow the insults they'd dealt her this night—Caitrin, Deirdre, Tade, aye, and that Wylder witch with her pale skin and her fears.

Sheena chewed on her lower lip, a dozen schemes darting through her mind. There must be a way . . . some way to regain Tade's loyalty while shattering any illusions of love he still held for the Sassenach slut. Theirs 'twas an alliance ripe to be corrupted by betrayal . . . and by hate.

The sound of Deirdre's voice above the music rasped across Sheena's taut nerves, and she glanced up to see the girl running to embrace Devin Kilcannon's tall, slender figure, his hair a pale halo in the firelight.

Sheena's eyes narrowed to slits. Yes, there was a way—a way to be a heroine to all the mountainfolk, a way to win Tade's gratitude and love. And yet . . . A shiver coursed down her spine, as if she had been kissed by a dark angel. She would be throwing into peril not only her life but her immortal soul as well. If aught went awry . . .

No, she would take care . . . be clever, cunning, do no lasting harm to any except the English heiress who threatened to steal the man who rightfully belonged to an O'Toole. Sheena tore her gaze away from Devin Kilcannon's gentle face, shifting her eyes to where Maryssa Wylder had stood moments before. Her amber eyes caught the tiniest glint of gold on the ground. She stepped toward it and snatched it up, holding the delicate swan high in the firelight. With a sneer of disdain, she flung the fragile necklet into the writhing flames and smiled.

If she was cunning and clever, she would stand as Tade Kilcannon's bride before the seasons turned, and the heir to Donegal's wildlands would look upon Maryssa Wylder, not with the adoration reserved for an angel, but with the contempt set aside for a witch born of Satan himself.

* * *

Maryssa forced her chill-numbed feet up the steps to the wide
oaken door, slipping one shaking hand from beneath her be-
draggled cloak to turn the heavy latch that barred the entrance
to Nightwylde. With all the stealth her aching limbs could
muster, she forced the portal open, terrified that some servant
kept late at his duties might hear the creak of hinges, or that
her father, hovering over his ledgers and accounts, might still
lurk in the library.

Still, she thought, it would be worth incurring her father's
wrath to huddle beneath her coverlets, bury herself in her
pillows, and sob out the grief that threatened to tear her in
two—a grief she had borne for hours as she had ridden aim-
lessly among Tade's night-shrouded vales, a grief she knew
well she could never escape.

She stepped out of the rising wind. The tapers set in
sconces in the wide stone hallway oozed inky shadows along
the floor, the candle flames fluttering as the midnight breeze
crept around her cloak, batting at the wicks.

The very stones of Nightwylde seemed to taunt her, as if
the spirits loosed on this demon night were cackling on the
rising wind, mocking her. Yet even the devil-spawned specters of Allhallows Eve could not torment her more than did
her own tortured heart, which was crying out for the healing
touch of Tade Kilcannon's strong hands. For as she had
watched Tade stride into the embracing shadows of his mountains, Maryssa had known that he carried with him every joy
she had ever known—the promise of a future bright with his
loving, sharing his bed, bearing his children, babes he would
cherish and guard with the same fierce tenderness he had
lavished on Maryssa.

Here, among the stones of Nightwylde, and even in the
gardens of Carradown, there would be no haven to turn to,
no succor except what strength he had left within her, and the
unspoken, half-wild hope that his seed might have taken root
in her womb.

One hand fluttered down to her stomach, savage joy
springing forth at the thought that a child born of their love
might even now be clinging to life inside her—a part of Tade
no one could ever take from her, a part of him that would be
hers forever, that she could shower love upon during the dismal days that seemed to stretch into eternity.

It had been more than two months since she had had her last bleeding, yet never had she considered that she might be with child. The queasiness that had beset her during the weeks of Tade's absence had seemed spawned of terror that he might lie dead, the excruciating sensitivity of her breasts evidence that every nerve in her body was yanked wire-taut with the tension of waiting. But now . . . Tade's words echoed in her mind and heart, blossoming into hope: *Even now you might carry my babe . . .*

Maryssa started, berating herself for her careless preoccupation as the latch clacked shut behind her, the metallic sound ricocheting off of the entryway walls. Her pulse leaped as she scooped up her skirts and darted for the safety of the wide staircase as the sound of fast-approaching footsteps filled the hall from some distant doorway.

Her slippered toe had touched the first step, her cloak unfurling behind her, when suddenly a hard fist knotted in the billowing folds, jerking her to a stop. Unable to stifle a scream, she wheeled toward the hand, her gaze fixing upon the raging visage of Bainbridge Wylder.

"F-Father!" she stammered, her skin stiff with fear. "I—"

"Where, by God's blood, have you been?" The words hissed through her father's teeth, his lips blue with fury, his face mottled red.

Maryssa searched desperately for some excuse, some lie to save her from the menace beneath those woolly brows. "I— I wanted to see the Samain fires, and—"

"Those satan fires! You—"

"I overheard the servants whispering about them," Maryssa interrupted despairingly. "And it—it sounded so curious I decided to ride out to see them."

"Hold your lying tongue, girl! You expect me to believe that you, who possess not an ounce of courage, hied yourself off in the middle of the night to watch a horde of pagan wretches dance about fires?"

"Father, I—" Maryssa winced as the blunt fingers closed on her arm, cutting deep into the soft flesh. "I but thought to see—"

"You'll be seeing the rough side of my hand before this night is o'er unless you can conjure a more believable tale than that," Bainbridge snarled, ripping the tie of her cloak loose with a force that burned her throat. "Unfortunately, I haven't time now to tend to you as I'd like. You've kept our guests waiting far long enough." He hurled the cloak into a heap on the stones, his eyes raking in a derisive sweep over her linsey-woolsey petticoats, honey brown against the muslin modesty piece set in her plain bodice.

Maryssa's stomach wrenched, her eyes flicking to the block of light from the arched doorway of the library. "G-guests?" she repeated. "At this time of night?" Her fingers nervously smoothed a wisp of hair back from her temple. "Father, who—"

"The good colonel, Quentin Rath, has driven over from Roantree," Bainbridge snapped. "But more importantly—"

A footstep echoed along the corridor, and it was as though the chill of the night had suddenly seeped into the walls.

"But more importantly," echoed a voice as cold as the scales of a serpent, "your eager bridegroom has come to wait upon you."

The sickeningly familiar voice crawled over Maryssa's flesh, and she felt it like the brush of a corpse's hand. Dread and fear knotted in her stomach, then were forgotten in a surge of savage protectiveness. She folded her hands across the slight swell of her abdomen as an almost unearthly sensation of evil seemed to permeate the corridor. Reluctantly she dragged her gaze from her father's face to where Sir Ascot Dallywoulde's rapier-thin body slashed the candlelight.

The shadows of the night clung to his death-hued skin and to the sparse blond hair clinging about flesh as shrunken as any cadaver's. His thin lips parted in a cruel smile beneath eyes that burned with hellish zeal.

"Sir . . . Sir Ascot . . ." Maryssa choked, battling the hideous feeling that those fanatical eyes could pierce her very soul, gaze through the folds of linsey-woolsey into the sanctuary of her womb. She leaned against the carved banister in an unconscious effort to shield her stomach from Dallywoulde's sight. "You—you're supposed to be—"

"Watching Jeremy Bludgeon's execution?" Ascot paced toward her with a dangerous stride. "The cowardly villain decided to cheat his judges out of their due. He hanged himself in his cell the evening after sentence was passed."

Maryssa stifled a sick gasp. "How—how horrible!"

"Horrible? Aye. He robbed us of an afternoon's pleasure."

"I meant that the poor wretch was so desperate he—" Maryssa cut the sentence off, seeing the varying degrees of anger, disapproval, and disbelief on the faces of the two men.

Dallywoulde shrugged. "In any case, Bludgeon's well-deserved death enabled me to conclude matters in London sooner than I had hoped, so 'twas possible to be reunited with the woman who made the season past in London so . . . memorable. I assure you that I hastened to your side the moment my business was concluded." Light glinted off his small, sharp teeth, and Maryssa shuddered at the hate that was scarcely concealed in those ice-pale eyes. She forced herself to meet and hold the Englishman's gaze.

Stiffening her quaking knees, Maryssa forced her lips into what she prayed would pass for a smile. " 'Tis a pity you tired your horse so. I can't tell you what a comfort it was knowing that you were being so satisfactorily entertained—so far away from me that I could not be forced to join in your revelry."

Sir Ascot's thin lips curled in menace, icy anger staining his cheekbones with color. "Oh, I intend quite a revel, my dear, after you wed me. I shall exact from you just retribution for the sins you committed at Thorndyke Place."

Maryssa flinched, then steeled herself, refusing to give him the satisfaction of seeing her jerk away as his bony fingers closed over her hand, lifting it to his damp lips. She felt the sharp edges of his teeth beneath their thin veil of flesh, felt the barely hidden threat within as Dallywoulde's eyes glowed like pale slits in his white face.

"I assure you I have a passing long memory." Ascot smirked. "And your father, in giving me your hand in marriage, has made clear his desire that I curb your wayward impulses and crush you into womanly obedience. Uncle Bainbridge has allowed you too much license, cousin, but I vow that once you are under my rule, you will learn your place."

Maryssa glanced at her father's face, expecting an outburst of anger directed at Dallywoulde for the insult just paid him, but Bainbridge Wylder's craggy features were as impassive as stone. " 'Tis her mother's blood that taints her thus," he growled, his eyes narrowing on Maryssa. "But I have faith that you, Ascot, have a will strong enough to crush her cursed rebelliousness with as much ease as you do the lowly scum who stir violence in these lands.''

Dallywoulde's lips stretched into a wintry smile. ''Aye, by the time I sail for England, I will have had much practice in snuffing out rebelliousness—what with clearing the country-side of priests, aye, and snaring the Black Falcon in my noose. 'Twill be child's play for me to quell the sinful stubbornness of one mere woman.''

Maryssa felt her cheeks grow pale and her throat constrict at the vision of this satanic knight hunting down Tade and gentle Devin, but she firmly pulled her fingers from his grasp. ''Mayhap, Sir Ascot, you will find your quest not so simple, once you brave the Donegal wilds,'' she said, leveling her gaze on his empty, evil eyes. ''And I promise you, tearing out my 'sinful stubbornness' will prove a worthy challenge, once you have murdered your way through these lands.''

Her father's furious gasp mingled with a menacing hiss from Dallywoulde, and Maryssa's courage nearly faltered.

''By God, you impertinent—'' Her father's beefy hand flashed out to strike her, but before the blow could land, Ascot Dallywoulde's tensile fingers closed around her chin, digging deep into the tender flesh.

''Nay, Uncle Bainbridge.'' Dallywoulde's moist breath dampened Maryssa's skin. '' 'Twill be my task to drive the wickedness out of this vassal of the Dark One. Always it has been thus—men, carved in God's image, preyed upon by temptresses with their sinful bodies and lying smiles. But I promise you that as soon as the papist scum that infests your land lies rotting in hell, I shall drag your daughter through cleansing fire as well. Make her a humble servant of the light.'' Dallywoulde's gaze flicked to the furious countenance of her father. ''If you would leave us for a little, good uncle.''

Maryssa cast a pleading look at Bainbridge Wylder's implacable face and felt anger snap through her at her father's scorn. With a grunt of disgust, he spun on his heel and stalked back toward the door, where a cunning-eyed Quentin Rath lurked.

Resolve coursed through Maryssa, born of the new strength and sense of worth Tade had blessed her with, and of the knowledge that she had little left to lose. She flung her head back, the heavy seal ring on Dallywoulde's finger gouging her cheek as she broke his hold on her chin. "I have nothing to say to you, sir, be it in the company of my father, or here, alone," she said, stiffening her spine. "I'm far grown from the shy girl you terrorized at Thorndyke Place."

Dallywoulde's eyes glinted, his lips stretching into a sneer. "I have found that cleansing sins from the souls of the fallen is much like breaking men upon the rack, milady. When one level of suffering no longer suffices, I but need to twist the wheel tighter."

Those evil eyes flicked in a cold path down her body, pausing for terrifying seconds on her slim waist. It was as though some devil had given his minion the power to see every sweep of Tade's hands on her skin, as if those chill white lips sneered at a union of the flesh, which this cold knight regarded with naught but revulsion.

Maryssa felt the stab of those pale eyes, fear tearing like talons at her courage. If Ascot Dallywoulde suspected she had joined her body with Tade's . . . if he knew of the child she might carry, he would shower her and her babe with vengeance in the name of his wrathful God, crushing them beneath the weight of his fanaticism.

Fear, sharp and slashing, cut through her as she turned and fled up the stairs, the hideous sound of Sir Ascot's laughter filling her with dread.

" 'Twill not always prove so easy to elude me, milady," Dallywoulde said. "Soon 'twill be my estates through which you flee, my power that will hold you captive." Ascot licked his lips, a twisted pleasure stinging along his veins as he watched Maryssa's slender form dash up the huge stone stairway. The wench had always seemed but a milksop of a chit, her eyes round with fear, flinching when he had dragged her to his favored spectacles at Tyburn Tree and within Newgate's walls. Never had he expected his whey-faced cousin to turn on him like a raging kitten, claws spread. He steepled his fingers upon his brocaded waistcoat, a sensation of eagerness stealing over him.

Dallywoulde had decided to wed the chit in exchange for Bainbridge Wylder's vast wealth. He had taken pleasure in dealing twisted cruelties to Maryssa, tormenting her, watching her writhe on the blade of his justice. How much more entertaining it would be to watch the budding spirit he had seen within her fade and die, crushed beneath his boot heel when she was in truth his wife.

His dearest cousin had a secret, Ascot thought slyly. He had seen it in her eyes, which were now shadowed with fear. But then, Ascot mused, taking his snuffbox from his pocket and flicking it open with a manicured finger, the most dreaded priest hunter in all Christendom was most adept at ripping from people their secrets.

A knock on the outer door made Sir Ascot stride to the portal and fling it open.

There on the step stood a weasel of a man decked out in Quentin Rath's livery. "Beg pardon, sir." The man gave a stiff bow. "I bring a message for my master, Colonel Rath."

"Give the message to me. I'll see it reaches his ear."

The man squirmed, his cheeks turning a dull red. "F-forgive me, sir, but I vowed I'd give it to the colonel himself. 'Tis a most important matter . . . one that I dare not trust to any but—"

"Symington?"

Dallywoulde's teeth clenched as Rath's voice grated along his nerves. The incompetent peacock was striding toward the servant with a look of such pomposity Dallywoulde had an urge to boot the colonel in his wide buttocks.

"Aye, sir." Symington's pointed features revealed his relief. " 'Tis a message, sir, I dared not hold until you arrived back. 'Tis regarding an informer who—" Symington bit his lips, glancing nervously at Sir Ascot, and the knight couldn't resist frightening the oaf with one of his most chilling stares.

Rath glanced from his distressed servant to Dallywoulde, and Sir Ascot could see understanding dawning on the colonel's dull face.

"Pay no heed to Sir Ascot, Symington," Rath said, then faltered as Dallywoulde turned his frigid gaze upon him. "I— I mean, Sir Ascot Dallywoulde is privy to all that concerns the affairs hereabouts. The most noted priest hunter in England, he is, and kind enough to journey here to aid us in crushing that scoundrel, the Black Falcon."

" 'Tis no act of kindness," Sir Ascot cut in. "Your cursed highwayman is but another scrap of filth to scoop into the devil's basin. 'Tis the priests' blood I hunger for. Now, what message is it this lout has dragged in?''

Symington's Adam's apple bobbed in his gangly throat. "Sir, I am told that an informer awaits you at the Devil's Grin."

Rath snorted. "More oft than not these informers are but beggars expecting the Crown's good coin."

"Nay, sir, this one . . . I heard tell that this one is different. A woman, sir. Aye, and a Catholic."

Dallywoulde's eyes narrowed. "A woman," he said, fingering the gold cross dangling from his watch chain. "Naught can be more vicious than a woman, Colonel Rath. Aye, and no beast of prey proves more eager than a member of the gentler sex to sink its fangs into another."

Rath started to bark a command to a sleepy-eyed footman, but Dallywoulde's harsh voice cut him off.

"Nay, good Colonel." The knight's lips snaked over his teeth. "This time there will be none of your bungling."

Rath blanched, his cheeks puffing with outrage, but Dallywoulde plunged on, scenting the kill. "You have emptied a sizable purse into bringing me here to flush out the vermin that beset your lands. 'Tis time I began to ply my craft." Dallywoulde turned and strode to where his mantle hung. "This papist informer," he said, swirling the gray folds about him, "I vow to you she'll betray to us even more than she suspects. She'll betray her own mother before I have done with her."

Dallywoulde drew the mantle closed about his skeletal form, sensing the fascinated fear emanating from the colonel and his servant—the same sinister fear he had engendered in scores of secret Catholics—and in the changeable eyes of Maryssa Wylder. He gloried in it, reveled in the terror he could spawn. He threw back his head, and rare, grating laughter echoed through the corridor as he stepped into the night.

Seventeen

TADE, POSTED AS sentry, stared down into the valley at Christ's Wound, his throat raw from the two dozen leathern jacks of ale he had drained the night past, his eyes burning with a bitterness that seeped into his very soul. The spirits of Samain were banished, the demons cast back into their holes of hell, and the bonfires' brands lay cold, ground to ashes beneath the cart wheels that had grated through the crossroads. But even here, with the November sun blessing the hidden glen and the ragged crowd of faithful who had come to attend the Allhallows Day at mass, Tade could gain no peace. He doubted he would ever know peace again, tormented as he was by the memory of haunted eyes flecked with sea green, sapphire, and gold.

"Damn her!" he cursed beneath his breath, his eyes stinging with hurt and betrayal. "Damn her to the same hell she consigned our love to, condemned me to. 'Twas her choice to leave me, her choice to turn coward and run."

Yet, even as he cursed the day he had placed his heart in Maryssa Wylder's hands, he felt a horrible emptiness within his very soul, as though his heart had been ripped from his chest, leaving only a barren wasteland—a wasteland filled with memories of sable hair spilling over breasts the hue of alabaster, of a tremulous mouth tipping up in a smile, and of laughter, such wondrous laughter, all the sweeter because he had been the first to draw it from her.

His gaze blurred, casting the bowed heads of the worshipers, Devin's earnest face, even the mass rock with its crude wooden crucifix, into a haze of pain. The first . . . aye, he had been the first to make Maryssa laugh, to romp with her and tumble her in sweet meadow grass, to lie with her beneath the coverlets and coax from her cries of ecstasy. And in bringing these wonders to her he had gained for himself a greater joy than he'd ever known, a passion so fierce, so consuming, that he had stood willing to sacrifice all he loved— the wildlands, his family, aye, even his honor, to carry her away with him.

"But she stood a coward," Tade growled under his breath. "A coward, who dared skulk about in the bushes, mating with me like a furtive creature of night, but lacked the courage to throw off the veils of secrecy, to declare our love before all, and to cleave to me as my wife."

Why should she take a landless wretch to husband when she was already betrothed? a voice mocked inside him. *Betrothed to a velvet-bellied popinjay with perfumes and silver to shower down upon her.*

Steel talons seemed to claw at Tade's belly, twisting and tearing as he shut his eyes against the remembrance of this last, most agonizing betrayal of his love. During that long-ago night, when he had woven garlands of roses to bring Maryssa joy, when he had drawn her into the fairy world he had formed for her as a gift of love, she had belonged to another man. Pledged to wed since she lay in her swaddlings, she had claimed the union was a matter of properties to be joined, wealth to be gained. Well, damn it, Tade Kilcannon had no wealth to offer her except the pistol jammed into his belt. The lands that had been his to inherit were now clutched in Bainbridge Wylder's thieving hands.

A bitter laugh tore at Tade. What a sick, twisted irony it was that the lands he should rightfully have inherited were to bind the woman he loved to another. Aye, the very stones his ancestors' kerns had hewn would no doubt be Maryssa Wylder's marriage portion; the lands in whose defense his father and grandfather had spilled their blood would be her dowry.

Would Tade, then, in years hence, be forced to watch her driving in her fine carriage up to Nightwylde's gates and alight there upon the arm of the man who was her husband?

A curse breached his lips, the oath so savage that he heard Greenan O'Toole's grunt of disapproval and caught the censure in the golden eyes so like the man's eldest daughter's. Tade's gaze flashed away from the glowering older man, fleetingly aware of the absence of Sheena's tawny head from among the O'Toole brood. His mouth was set, grim. It was a relief to him that the chit was not there to turn upon him her injured pout, to gaze at him with infuriating reproach, as though he had played her foul. That would be all he needed to drive him past sanity.

Pain twisted in Tade's throat, his eyes burning with a misery that would not be denied. If affairs had gone as planned the night past, he would now hold in his arms Maryssa's delicate form, so warm and soft, her cheek pressed trustingly to his shoulder, her eyes shining up at him as though he were some hero of legend come real.

But that could never be . . . It was but misty fantasy, as unrealistic as the tales his mother had spun for him in her castle room a lifetime ago. From the first he had known that his love for Maryssa was impossible, and he had defied the fates, God, aye, even his father to grasp at a dream. But like the warriors in the bards' ancient tales, he had been left with nothing except his honor, his quest, and the keen edge of his sword.

His fingers tightened on the butt of the pistol secreted beneath the folds of his mantle, and his gaze swept out toward Nightwylde. Nay, he thought, even if Maryssa did return to Ireland in some distant future, chance held that by then the Black Falcon would long since have taken the penny road to heaven, having failed to rob the gallows of its due.

His eyes swept the crowd below, espying the O'Donnel twins, Ryan Moynihan, and the three O'Byrne brothers in the midst of their families. All but four of Tade's rebel band knelt on the ground in prayer, their knives and pistols tucked beneath their threadbare clothes.

Tade clenched his teeth. They had lost three men in the raid that had freed Muldowny, and since then the Sassenach soldiers had been hot for vengeance against those who had shown them as fools. How long would it be before the English wolves closed tight the jaws of some trap to rid them of the Falcon forever? How long before some tiny mistake or miscalculation threw the rebels into the Sassenachs' grasp? Tade's fists knotted, his gaze shifting away from the men who had entrusted him with their lives.

A blur of movement in the distance made him curse, as he recognized Greenan O'Toole's gray mare cantering toward the rise, Sheena astride its sway back. But his irritation vanished as his eyes narrowed against the sun, fighting to block out the sharp spikes of brightness that obscured the hillside to the west with splashes of color—vivid color that stung his eyes, the crimson of fresh-spilt blood.

Red . . . A sick, knifing sensation drove itself into Tade's gut as the hill seemed to move, rushing forward amid flashes of black, bay, and roan. "Christ," Tade hissed, as the forms snapped into sharp focus. "Sweet mother of God!" He caught a fleeting glimpse of Sheena wheeling her mount around, assumed that she had been riding to warn the tiny congregation and knew she was too late. Aye, too late, as his own warning would come. Tade bolted toward the valley, sliding down the hillside as fear surged through him, horrified at what his mind's wanderings had allowed to come upon the quiet glen.

"Raid!" His voice shattered the sound of Devin's gentle Latin. "Flee, for God's sake, 'tis a raid!"

Never in his life would Tade forget the faces that turned up to him, pale, terrified, frozen for an instant with a horror too great to comprehend. He saw Devin grab up the crucifix, his voice, resonant with authority, urging the people to scatter, run.

Gun barrels glinted in the hands of the O'Donnels and the O'Byrnes. Ryan Moynihan dashed with them to shield the retreating crowd as the vale, so tranquil but a heartbeat before, erupted into madness. Mothers scooped up babes, fathers fought to herd their families toward what safety might be found in the rocky countryside. Strong arms locked about the aged, the crippled, and the young.

Tade caught a glimpse of Rachel among the sea of humanity, struggling vainly to cling to Tom and Brody, while Kane Kilcannon forged ahead, his arms weighted with a wriggling, sobbing Katie and tiny baby Ryan. Even through the screams of fear, Tade could hear his father's gruff voice shouting encouragement to Shane and Deirdre, could see Kane battling to shore up the courage of the little ones.

Tade called out to Devin, seeing his light hair farther ahead in the crowd, the crucifix still clutched in his hand. "Damn it, Dev, run!" Tade cried, desperation sending fire through his muscles as he surged forward. He turned, yanking the pistol from his belt as the wave of soldiers crested the hill. A dozen weapons blazed, spitting death into the ragged crowd as the horsemen charged down on them.

With a cry of rage, Tade leveled his own pistol at the raiders' leader in a desperate hope that if he could down the stout Rath, the troops would fall into confusion. He felt the powder flare to life as he pulled the trigger, saw the blaze of orange, and Rath's hands closing over his belly.

But there was scarce time to feel even the feral rush of pleasure in killing the man who had tormented the Catholics for so long. For even as Rath tumbled from his mount, Tade's eyes locked on another man, a man who was bearing down on the crowd like a rider from the Apocalypse. Tade stared at the figure but an instant, yet in that wisp of time the rider's face burned itself indelibly into his mind—eyes empty and fanatical, fleshless lips taut over sharp teeth, and a face, so thin, so evil, it seemed to have been spawned by the Dark Reaper himself.

Then suddenly a cry of pain from the rear of the retreating crowd drew Tade's gaze to tumbling copper curls and a tangle of skirts. Deirdre. Sick horror wrenched his soul as he saw Rachel stumble to Dee's side, saw his sister battle to gain her feet.

"Rachel, nay!" Tade shouted, racing toward them, dodging pistol fire and the wounded who had fallen. "I'll get her!"

Scarce pausing in his flight, Tade snatched up the small form of his sister, her cry of pain tearing at him as his hand closed over the hot flow of blood from her shoulder. He gritted his teeth, burying Deirdre's sobs of terror in his chest as he ran into the wildlands that would prove their only hope—praying that the others whom he loved had been spared the soldiers' wrath as well.

* * *

Tade bit the edge of muslin, rending his bedding into strips with which to bind the wounds of the soldier's victims. The cave that had been Devin's haven seemed now a scene wrought from the Last Judgment—masses of the damned clawing hopelessly at stone, writhing in pain, cowering in terror, or worse still, staring at the wall with faces blank of all emotion, devoid of all hope.

They had been straggling in for the past hour, some scarcely able to crawl, others nearly hysterical as they searched for their loved ones in the crowded cave. Tade yanked at the cloth savagely, gritting his teeth against the most horrible sounds of all . . . that of mothers crying for their children and of little ones, their faces stiff with fear, sobbing for parents who would never come again. He glanced again at the cave opening, tortured by his own fear of loss. The Kilcannon family had been among the first to reach the cave. Rachel and the little ones had spread out the coverlets to form beds for the injured; Kane had barked orders to the men as they arrived.

Tade had seen the scarlet stain on his father's side the moment the earl had charged into the cave and had hastened to him, meaning to bare the wound and tend it. But the earl had roared at him to aid the others first. Tade's fears for his father's life had eased, and he had turned to help the others, certain that his father's wound must be but a trifling one. Yet as he labored over the slashes and bullet wounds left by the Sassenach onslaught, the absence of one Kilcannon grew increasingly terrifying—Devin's golden head and solemn, gentle face were nowhere to be seen . . .

Tade's gaze flashed back to the bandaging, and he gritted his teeth. The last survivors of the massacre in the glen were still making their way toward the cave, winding through the wildlands like terrified deer as they tried to evade the patrols the soldiers had doubtless formed to sweep up any who had escaped. Devin had to be among them somewhere, aiding those who had been hurt, shepherding them toward safety. Yet with each moment that his slender form failed to darken the cave's entryway, the coil of dread tightened in Tade's belly.

He started, his eyes leaping to the figure beside him as a shaky, pale hand grabbed the bandage from his fingers, his gaze fixing upon the strained countenance of Deirdre. A score of freckles stood out stark against her chalky skin and her mouth was set in resolve as she turned to wrap up little Andrew MacGary's wounded leg.

"Damn it, Dee, I told you to lie down," Tade snapped, snatching the bandages away from her. "That shoulder could well get infected, or break open and start to bleed again."

" 'Tis only a scrape," Deirdre shot back, but the tremor in her voice betrayed the fire Tade knew must burn in the fresh wound. "There are scarce enough to aid the others, and someone . . . someone has to . . ."

Little Andrew looked up at them with sorrowful eyes, his tiny mouth puckering in a way that wrenched Tade's heart. "Dedra, hurts," he whimpered. " 'Drew hurts."

Tade saw a huge tear glisten on Deirdre's lashes, saw her mouth tremble. "I know, Andy love. Deirdre will fix it right up." She knelt down beside the child, and Tade felt a twinge of sorrow as he saw the carefree impish face he had loved and tormented grown suddenly far older than her fifteen years. He put the bandages into her hand, his voice catching in his throat as he chided, "don't push yourself too hard, Dee. 'Twas no scrape Rath dealt you, and you'll do no one any good if you're stricken with fever or exhaustion."

She nodded, her tangled curls falling in a curtain about her face as she bent over the child. Tade pressed his fingers against his eyelids, remembering Deirdre's courage as he had cleansed the slash the pistol ball had cut into her flesh, remembering the rigid clenching of her jaw as she had insisted that he allow her to walk, claiming he'd need his strength later to tend to the victims of the raid.

If there had been in Maryssa Wylder but a shading of such bravery he'd be halfway to France by now, not buried here among filth, blood, hopelessness . . . Tade drove his fist into the cave wall, feeling his skin split on the stone. *You belong here, astride your stallion* . . . Maryssa's tortured words echoed in his mind. *With your silken hood and your pistols firing* . . . *What would become of these people if you were to run off with me . . . ?*

The pain in her words penetrated even the misery all around him, filling his chest with a bursting agony. How could he have been blind to her pain as he stood in the glow of the bonfires? He had been too deeply engulfed in his own feelings of anger and betrayal to hear what Maryssa had been truly saying to him. Perhaps she really was afraid of dashing off into the unknown. Perhaps she truly feared her father. But beneath her fears, in the depths of her changeable eyes, he had seen an understanding of his soul far deeper than any he had ever known.

Tade glanced about the shadowy cave, clenching his teeth as his eyes swept Rachel's bent head and his father's bare arms, stained red as he labored over Caitrin MacVee's shattered ankle. He knew now that even for Maryssa he could never have abandoned them to this brutality. He could not have lived with himself had he done so.

The sound of dragging footsteps nearing the cave's mouth drove Tade to wade through the huddled masses toward the shadowed opening, a wild hope gripping him, coupled with sick desperation.

"T-Tade?"

The quavery voice of young Brian MacGary made Tade stumble down the path and put his arm about the youth to support him. Thick, sticky blood clung to Tade's hand, and Brian uttered a guttural moan of pain as Tade's fingers brushed torn flesh.

"Caitrin . . ." Brian choked out the name. "Is Caitrin MacVee . . .?"

"Aye, she's inside," Tade said, bracing his body more firmly against the lad's sagging weight.

"I couldn't find her . . . looked for her . . . Oh, God, Tade, I went back and—" A sob tore its way out of the boy's throat.

"Whist, now. She's been hurt, but she's alive and safe."

But Brian seemed not to hear him as shudders racked his lean frame. "I went back, Tade," he sobbed. "Blood . . . there's so much blood . . ."

Tade's jaw clenched, his stomach churning. "Brian," he said in a bracing voice, grasping the boy by the arms, "when you went back or . . . or when you were fleeing the soldiers . . ." A knot rose in Tade's throat, nigh crushing the words, but he forced himself to go on. "Did you—did you see Father Devin?"

"Father—Father Devin?" Brian's glassy eyes fixed on

Tade's. "When I—I was running . . . when the soldiers came,
I saw him—saw him run to Ma Bedelia . . ."

Tade battled to keep himself from shaking the injured boy,
battled the terror that writhed like a hundred serpents in his
chest. "And then what did you see, Brian?"

"The—old woman was so slow . . . so lame . . . Father
Devin couldn't reach the wildlands before—before they fell
upon him. I saw the man . . . the evil man . . . plunge his
sword into Ma Bedelia and—"

"Damn it, Brian, what happened to Devin!" Tade hated
the harshness of his voice, hated the raw terror that surged
through him.

"I didn't . . . couldn't see . . . I ran. Oh, sweet Mother
of God, Tade, there was so much blood!"

Pain, fury, and hate raced through Tade's veins, turning
him white-hot with rage. Blindly, he scooped Brian into his
arms, stumbled back into the cave with the injured boy, and
settled him on one of the makeshift pallets.

Deirdre rushed over to him, her face stricken, as though
somehow she knew . . .

"Tade—" The word caught in her throat, and he could see
the terror in her eyes.

"Take care of him, Dee." Tade's anguished gaze flashed
from Brian's pain-ravaged face to the stiff shoulder of Kane
Kilcannon, whose movements were now disturbingly slow
and awkward. "I'm going back to the glen."

"The glen . . . Tade, 'tis too dangerous! The soldiers—"

"Damn it, Dee, I have to find Devin!" The words were
torn from his throat, their sound akin to a sob. He heard her
cry of confusion and protest, felt her hand try to stay him,
but he shook himself free of her grasp and bolted from the
hellish cave.

Later on, he could not remember anything about his race
through the rugged Donegal hills except the burning of the
muscles in his thighs, the blood pounding in his heart, and
the dread and rage that gripped his vitals. A dozen times his
boots skidded from beneath him, sending him crashing against
a jagged boulder or a sharp stone, but he felt neither the
bruising and tearing of his flesh nor the warm trickle of blood
from the gashes scoring his skin.

The blood, Brian had sobbed, *so much blood* . . . Tade

could picture the devout old Ma Bedelia, her silvery head bent, her gnarled fingers plying the worn beads of the rosary that never left her hands. And he could see Devin struggling to shore up those feeble legs, battling to shore up the woman's deep faith as the soldiers' steel bit flesh.

"Nay!" the denial tore itself from Tade's throat as he crested the rise that had once held the glen so serenely in its meadow-grass palm. His stomach wrenched, bile rising in his throat as he staggered down the hillside. Fragments of the old ones' tales of Christ's Wound darted through his horror-hazed mind, tales of the soil bleeding . . . bleeding . . .

Twisted, rag-clad bodies littered the ground, red stains standing out against flesh that was already blue with death. Small forms of children lay curled protectively in the lifeless arms of their mothers while men, caught battling to protect their fleeing families from the soldiers' onslaught, lay clutching, even in death, what few crude weapons they had possessed.

Tade's gaze skimmed over Timothy O'Donnel's dark head, his death-stiffened hand caught about that of his fallen twin. Ryan Moynihan and the O'Byrne brothers lay nearby, their spent pistols beside them, their eyes glazed with death, while Greenan O'Toole's broken body was curled around that of his smallest daughter, both of them reeking of gore and of death.

"Sweet Jesus," Tade choked out, "what . . . what kind of monsters could do this?" The words trailed off as his eyes caught a glimpse of silver set against the meadow's green. The silver of Bedelia O'Friel's hair. It was as if every sword thrust, every musket ball that had struck flesh, buried itself in Tade's body at that instant, driving through him a terror and horror such as he'd never known.

Half-blind with tears, he stumbled toward the place where the old woman lay, a cart's length away from the stone altar. Forcing himself to gaze at her lifeless body, he felt his knees give way beneath him, and he sank deep into the blood-sodden ground. Like a gaping, hideous leer, her breast had been laid open, slashed through by a Sassenach sword, while beside her . . .

Tade's fingers reached out and closed stiffly on the crude object that lay there, stained with blood. It was a crucifix—the tortured body of Devin's beloved Jesus upon the cross—

which Tade had fashioned for him and given to him on the day Dev had donned his priest's robes. The same crucifix Tade had seen Devin snatch from the mass rock as the soldiers plunged into the valley.

His eyes swept grass, defiled now with the blood of innocents, as he searched desperately for the golden halo of Devin's hair, the crumpled heap of his robes against the hillside, but it was as if God had reached down and plucked his servant from the midst of the carnage, banishing all evidence that Dev had ever been there.

"Devin!" Tade's eyes blurred with tears of desperation as he struggled to stand. "Dear God . . . Dev!"

The thunder of approaching hoofbeats scarcely penetrated the haze of agony and helplessness that gripped him. He wheeled, praying it was the English who neared, thirsting to avenge himself on the murderers who had wrought these horrors. But instead he saw the taut familiar faces of a dozen mounted men, their eyes savage and expectant as they reined their horses to a halt.

"Phelan Fitzpatrick staggered into Ballyshea Inn an hour past. He told us what happened," Gilvarry Beagan explained, handing Tade the reins of the huge midnight-black stallion he had led. "We rode straight to the caves, pistols loaded, swords ready, but Deirdre said you'd come here."

"Aye." Tade's mouth curled grimly as he regarded the men he had formed into the most feared rebel band in all Ireland.

"MacGary stayed at the cave," Beagan said. "So many of his family lay injured . . ."

" 'Tis where he belongs." Tade shoved Devin's crucifix into the waistband of his breeches, then swung up onto the prancing stallion.

"Tade . . ." Revelin Neylan nudged his gray gelding forward. "They've taken Father Devin."

Tade's gaze leaped to Neylan's steely eyes. "He's still alive?"

"Aye. But not for long, if the Sassenachs have their way. Word has it that some bastard named Dallywoulde is taking him to Derry as a cursed example." Neylan's gaze faltered. "They're going to execute him, Tade. Put him beneath the knife."

Eighteen

THE GARDEN OF Nightwylde was like a vanquished knight's lady, grieving for a lover who would never return. Rose vines, many seasons dead, straggled over crumbling stones, their withered tendrils whispering of remembered beauty, while weeds encroached upon what had once been a path of such whimsical loveliness that it clouded Maryssa's mind with visions of the delicate lace on a maiden's gown.

She hugged her arms tight against her middle, trying to gain more warmth from the folds of her cloak, but the winds seemed to play at darting beneath the wrap, taunting her with the knowledge that she must soon abandon even the garden's meager haven. Abandon it to condemn herself to the surly company of her father and the more menacing society of Ascot Dallywoulde. She bent over to scoop up Odysseus as the rollicking kitten pounced at her feet, but the little wretch evaded her, bounding into the lengthening shadows. The expression of pure feline delight he shot her from beneath the drooping vines should have made the most staid of mistresses smile. But instead the kitten's antics brought only a renewed mistiness to Maryssa's eyes, as she remembered the night Tade had brought him to her.

It seemed as though three lifetimes had passed in the endless hours since she had left the Samain fires, and the future stretched before her like a bewitched ocean, endless, gray, unbroken by any joy except the hope that . . . Maryssa's fingers fluttered to her abdomen, cradling the babe she was certain thrived within. She lifted her chin, resolve and strength flowing through her. All in her life from now on would revolve around the child she would bear. The babe she would love, nurture, and protect with her own life if need be. Tade's child.

She closed her eyes, picturing in her mind a soft, blanket-wrapped bundle with angel-kissed cheeks, a tiny, eager mouth, and eyes as green as the Donegal mountains. Even her dread of her father's black fury could do but little to dull her happiness in the coming child. Yet thoughts of Ascot Dallywoulde—his chill outrage, his thirst for vengeance—filled her with a fear so primal and savage that she was stunned to know such emotions lay hidden within her.

Maryssa's hand tightened over the slight swell of her stomach. When she refused to accept the loathsome Dallywoulde as husband—and broke the betrothal, exposing him to scorn and humiliation throughout London—would not the fanatical Dallywoulde lurk about, eager to tear this fruit of "sin" from her arms? Would he not seek to punish a child he would regard as the get of the devil?

Maryssa turned her gaze to the castle, seeing the odd moving glow of a candle as some servant moved about the rooms, touching flames to the awaiting tapers. *Aye,* an eerie voice whispered inside her, *he will wreak his vengeance at any cost* . . . She felt an unbidden shiver course down her spine as the spectral glow from the castle windows insinuated gold fingers into the night, as though Ascot's own bony hands were stretching out, seeking to find her and crush her in their grasp.

She shivered, knowing even as she pulled her cloak more tightly about her that it was not the wind that had chilled her. The garden of a sudden seemed quiet—too quiet. Even the breezes seemed to have died; the rustle of the withered leaves, the rattle of dead vines, and the sounds of Odysseus's frolics had been stilled.

She started at a kind of thump at the far side of the garden, as though something had tumbled from the wall. Her heart stopped as she struggled to listen. "Odysseus?" she called softly, battling the sudden instinct to flee to the castle. "Odysseus, come here!"

The snap of a fallen branch beneath something heavy made Maryssa spin around, her eyes focusing on a shadow rising up against the far wall.

"Who goes there?" She forced the words through lips stiff with fear, her voice surprisingly steady.

She resisted the urge to step backward as the silhouette moved from the shadows, the waning light falling over a stained, torn dress and fiery hair. She gasped in shock as her gaze fell upon the face of Deirdre Kilcannon. Maryssa shook her head as if to clear it; the image before her was so unlike that of the spoiled, thoughtless child who had caused her such pain. Torment was etched deep in the impish curves of the girl's face, and even in the sparse light, Maryssa could see the tears in Deirdre's eyes.

Maryssa's hands clenched in her skirts. It was as though the agony in the girl's waxen face were a great stone crushing Maryssa's own chest.

"Deirdre," Maryssa managed, rushing toward her. "What . . . what is it? Tade?—''

"Nay, 'tis not . . . not Tade," Deirdre sobbed. "I—I mean it is . . . They'll kill him, and Devin, too, and I . . . you have to help me!"

"Deirdre!" Maryssa attempted to take the shaking girl in her arms, terror striking deep, but Deirdre jerked free, regarding her with a horrifying mixture of mistrust and stark desperation. "Tell me what happened," Maryssa prodded. "Now, Deirdre, or I can't aid you."

"Da—Da says you already know. He said—said you sent the soldiers down upon us. He thinks that because Tade brought you to Christ's Wound, you—''

Nausea twisted in Maryssa's belly, a sick horror stirring to life. "Soldiers? Dear God, Deirdre, please—'' Her words were a plea for the girl to end the anguish of not knowing, the anguish of understanding perhaps too full well.

"I—I don't believe you could—would throw us to the priest hunters—''

"Nay, Dee, it matters not what people think," Maryssa broke in, desperate. "Just tell me what befell you."

"We were at mass when they came," Deirdre choked out.

"Murdering . . . killing babes and—and the women, aye, any who fell in their path. Tade . . . he had to help me. Carry me. A bullet struck me, and—and I couldn't run." Deirdre turned tortured eyes to Maryssa. "But some Sassenach named Dallywoulde captured Devin and took him away. They . . . they mean to kill him."

Dallywoulde. Terror clawed at Maryssa's soul, obliterating the joy that had surged through her at the knowledge Tade still lived. Her fingers clenched, bruising Deirdre's arm, as images of Devin Kilcannon's solemn, devout face swirled before her eyes. Devin in the hands of the satanic knight . . . "Sweet God," she breathed. "Of course I'll help . . . I'll do whatever I can. I know not what I *can* do, but tell Tade and your father that I will try my best."

Instead of easing the agony in Deirdre's face, Maryssa's offer of aid brought a burst of tears and sobs from the girl's slender body. "Da lies nigh dead of a fever. The wound he took at the Englishmen's hands festered until . . ." She looked away. "He can't even open his eyes, can't move. And Tade rode off with some other men to try to free Devin. But Rookescommon prison is so—so huge . . . They'll be slaughtered before they can find him."

Maryssa bit her lip, fighting to block out the image that rose in her mind. Rookescommon. When she had traveled through Derry with Celeste Ladonne, the maid had taken great relish in pointing out the massive prison, its barred windows glowering out at the streets below like malevolent eyes. It had seemed to Maryssa that hell must look the same—impenetrable, evil, offering no hope of escape. If Devin was indeed locked away in Rookescommon bowels . . .

The memory of the raid Tade had staged to rescue Andrew Muldowny haunted Maryssa. Three of the Falcon's band had been killed, but the religious leader Muldowny had been snatched from the gallows. The resultant rage of the soldiers' superiors had rocked military circles all the way to England. No warden of any jail in Ireland had known peace since that raid, and even Maryssa, cut off as she was from the news, had heard Colonel Rath vow that every turnkey and every soldier stationed on Irish soil had sworn that he would not be the next to be made the fool by the rebel Falcon.

With the jailers thus spurred to alertness, there would be

no time for Tade's band to seek one prisoner among the hundreds who crowded the massive stone prison.

But if Tade knew exactly where to find Devin . . .

She felt a twinge of revulsion as she recalled the day Sir Ascot had dragged her to an amusement much favored by London society. Decked out in their grandest silks and brocades, the bewigged gentry had gained entry into an asylum to titter at the antics of the insane and then had gone to a prison to view renowned cutthroats and brigands as they dropped from the gallows.

Maryssa bit her lip as a shocking idea entered her mind. If Sir Ascot Dallywoulde had captured Devin Kilcannon, might it not be thought natural for his betrothed to want to see his caged quarry? And if she could get into the prison and be taken to Devin's cell, Tade might have a chance . . .

Maryssa cupped the sobbing Deirdre's face in her hands, brushing aside a tangle of curls from the girl's cheeks. "Listen to me, Deirdre," she said. "I think there might be a way to help Tade, aye, and Devin. You'll have to come with me, take me to Derry. Then we'll have to find Tade—get word to him somehow."

"Tade . . . Tade left a message for Brian MacGary to meet him at a place called the Hangman's Fool. But how can we—"

"Leave that to me." Maryssa shoved back her hood, feeling suddenly confined inside the walls of the garden. "I'll be at the crossroads as soon as all here in Nightwylde lay asleep. Be there, Deirdre, astride a horse. Don't fail."

"I—I won't." Deirdre rubbed the tears from her eyes with one grimy fist. The shuddering sobs had ceased. "Maryssa"—the name sounded natural on the girl's trembling lips—"I was wrong to hate you . . . wrong to try to—to tear you and Tade apart. You love my brother, I know that. I could see it on your face last night at the fires. 'Tis . . . 'tis that which gave me the courage to come here and beg you—"

"You need beg me for naught, Deirdre," Maryssa soothed. "Whatever aid I give, I give freely." She forced her voice to remain calming and steady, but the acceptance by Tade's beloved sister now, when it was too late, tore at Maryssa's heart.

"Hasten now," Maryssa told her. "I have to go make ready."

Deirdre nodded, then headed toward the wall she had climbed minutes before, but she stopped and darted back to catch Maryssa in a hard embrace.

" 'Twill be all right, Deirdre," Maryssa said, smoothing a hand over the girl's tumbled curls. "I promise you." Deirdre nodded, her face showing a small brightening of hope; then she spun and swung herself up over the wall with the same easy grace ingrained in her brother.

Maryssa stared for long seconds at the place where Deirdre had disappeared, wishing she could indeed be certain all would be well. But a hundred fears and doubts gnawed at her stomach, all overlaid by the evil in Ascot Dallywoulde's pale, soulless eyes. Scarcely realizing she did so, she turned and scooped up the kitten that had curled up beneath a dying shrub. Her nerves tingled with an odd sense of exultation at the knowledge that she was facing the ill fate cast her, attempting to divert calamity instead of accepting it as though she had no choice. And yet fear—for Tade, Devin, Deirdre, and, aye, herself—sharpened her senses, making her feel like a whipcord strained taut.

The door that led into the castle from the garden was in disrepair, its hinges protesting as Maryssa hustled inside. But she had barely swung the door closed behind her when she felt the change in the atmosphere of tension and anticipation that had haunted the corridors earlier in the day.

Cradling Odysseus in her arms, she paced down the narrow hallway, drawn as though by some sorcerer's spell. A laugh, hideous and grating, sounded from behind the half-open door of Bainbridge Wylder's library, and Maryssa froze, seeing inside the room a pair of blade-thin shoulders and a cruelly twisted mouth.

"Drink, Ascot! This is my finest wine." The heartiness in her father's voice seemed oddly brittle despite the cheerful words. "And you well deserve it after this day's work."

One midnight-black sleeve rose up, touching a crystal goblet to pale lips. " 'Tis but God's work I do," the chill voice said. "And 'tis far from finished."

"But you said Devin Kilcan—" Bainbridge seemed to stumble over the name, and she could hear in the sharp-edged tones something akin to . . . was it discomfort? "I mean, the papist scum lies in prison, his death assured."

Dallywoulde's low chortle made Maryssa's skin crawl. "Aye, one cursed priest. Yet I vow our Father Devin might be more important than even I suspected."

Bainbridge Wylder's inquiring grunt was muted by a rustling, as though Sir Ascot were rummaging among some objects. "Important?" Bainbridge snorted.

"Ah, here it is."

Maryssa drew deeper into the shadows along the walls, her heart pounding.

"What see you here, good uncle?"

" 'Tis naught but a cursed rosary. All the blasted Catholics carry them."

"Aye." Maryssa could hear the triumph and eagerness in Dallywoulde's sneer. "But how many papists do you know who carry a rosary with a *falcon* engraved on the back of its crucifix?"

Talons seemed to tear at Maryssa's stomach, her blood running ice.

"A falcon?" her father interjected. "Bloody Christ, think you Devin Kilcannon—"

"Nay. That whey-spirited wretch is no rebel raider. But whoever the Black Falcon might be, he holds this priest in high regard. If 'twere not sin to wager, I'd vow upon my life that we've just captured a lure with which to draw the Black Falcon from his cliffs"—Dallywoulde's voice dropped low—"and into our waiting chains."

Maryssa sagged against the wall for support, feeling her confidence fade. It was one thing for Tade to storm out of the night and strike swift and hard with surprise as his greatest weapon. But if Dallywoulde was but lying in wait . . .

"Then your men," her father said, "are prepared to seize the rebel scum?"

"More than ready."

Maryssa saw Dallywoulde's lip curl.

"Double the usual guard is posted over that devil priest; the men are under the command of Captain Marcus Langworth. He is a right able leader when he's not out chasing petticoats. But I vow he'll not be tempted by Salome herself, after the threats I left thundering in his ears this night."

" 'Twill be passing good when the righteous here in Donegal can again drive the highroads in peace,'' Bainbridge grunted.

The righteous . . . Maryssa closed her eyes, seeing again the serene hidden valley and Devin preaching to his flock. Her stomach tightened as she envisioned a scene from a nightmare—soldiers spilling into the hollow, slashing the helpless with their swords.

Then even that bloody scene was overlaid by another in her imagination, that of a faceless captain, hungry for advancement, and with a weakness for the ladies . . . a captain who might prove her only hope of gaining entry into Devin's cell and having a moment alone with him.

The fingers of one hand fluttered up to the haggard curves of her face. She was no Salome, no temptress who could entice a man to neglect his duty and yet . . .

Still cradling the sleeping kitten in her arms, she stepped away from the doorway and hastened toward the curving staircase. Her meager feminine wiles were all that now stood between gentle Devin, reckless Tade . . . and the gaping, brutal jaws of death.

Chill as the core of a tomb, the labyrinth of passageways twisted into the stone belly of Rookescommon; the oozing walls reeked with the stench of excrement, rotting flesh, and three hundred years of despair.

As Maryssa wound her way through the passageway, which was thick with guards, ripplings of dizziness set the blackened stones, the guttering torch, and the lascivious smirk of Captain Langworth to turn in slow spirals before her eyes. One hand fluttered up to the goose flesh sprinkling the partly exposed curves of her breasts as the scent of jessamy and the eager heat in Marcus Langworth's gaze nearly overwhelmed her.

''Miss—Mistress Maryssa,'' Deirdre's anxious voice slowed the swirling of the corridor as one of the girl's icy hands closed gently around Maryssa's arm, ''are—are you certain you don't want your cloak about you?''

A warmth swept Maryssa at the very real concern in the girl's voice, a concern that had been present in all the endless miles of riding to the ancient walled city, and present as well in the hours they had spent searching for a gown daring enough to suit their needs. But Maryssa secreted away the budding affection she felt for Tade's headstrong sister, and forced a laugh to her lips, appearing to dismiss the girl with an arrogant sniff.

"Maidservants!" she said, giving the captain a glance of commiserating disdain as she swept on down the corridor. "Just mind you don't be dragging the hem in the muck, girl," she snapped at Deirdre. "I can assure you I am feeling naught that is *cold* in these halls." Her gaze flicked over the captain's broad shoulders as though the braid on his uniform were woven of spun sugar.

Langworth puffed out his chest, the torch in his hand wavering as he raked her breasts and waist with his bold gaze. " 'Tis the light of your beauty that brightens these halls, milady," he said. "I vow 'tis a pity to waste it on that bastard Kilcannon."

Maryssa heard Deirdre suck in her breath, felt a flush of embarrassment and revulsion mingling with the anger in her own breast, but she battled it down, daring to lay one hand on the captain's sleeve, in the hope of drawing his attention away from Deirdre's too-readable expression.

" 'Tis my hope that the papist scoundrel will look upon my—er—attributes with the same gallant favor as you do, Captain Langworth." Maryssa lowered her lashes, affecting a simper. "For I have come solely for the purpose of trying to tempt Father Kilcannon to abandon his vows."

"Abandon his—" Langworth halted abruptly, mouth agape, his worldly face registering shock. "Miss Wylder, surely . . . surely Sir Ascot has no desire for you to—to—"

Maryssa forced a laugh from between taut lips and arched her neck to expose the creamy column of her throat as she drew him on down the hall. "Oh, nay, Captain! Tell me you did not think that—" She pressed her palms to her heating cheeks, then ran the tips of her fingers down to the swells of her breasts in a movement calculated to be seductive. "I certainly wouldn't soil myself by allowing a—a vassal of Satan the like of Devin Kilcannon to lay his hands on me! If my betrothed even believed that you had hinted at such a thing . . ." She let the sentence trail off, thankful for the sharp tang of fear that flashed into the captain's expression.

"But then," she said with a sugary smile, "you may depend upon me for complete secrecy."

The captain's gaze flickered away from her, and he cleared his throat.

"After all," Maryssa trilled. "You will benefit as much as I if the little surprise I'm attempting to arrange for Sir Ascot is successful." Scooping up her ruffled petticoats, she swirled around, displaying her charms. "Come now, Captain, think you some turf-cutting peasant will be able to resist giving me the information I seek, be he priest or no? When I leave that cell this night, I will carry back to my beloved all this lowling knows of that rogue, the Black Falcon. Sir Ascot will be able to ride out and chain the brigand and all his band, and you and I, Captain Langworth, will earn my betrothed's eternal gratitude."

The captain's gaze flashed back to Maryssa, the twinge of fear she had seen there receding slightly beneath a wave of what she knew as ambition. Langworth licked his lips, almost thumping into the wall as he turned a sharp corner. "I am certain Sir Ascot will be—er—most appreciative of your attempts in his behalf. Yet . . ." His voice trailed off as they reached the end of the winding corridor and paused before a doorway flanked by four burly guards. Langworth's voice dropped to a whisper. "Yet I cannot but think he would be furious if any ill befell you at the priest's hands. If you would allow me or one of my men to remain at your side . . ."

"Your concern is most touching and chivalrous, Captain," Maryssa said, dimpling, "but I scarce think one lone prisoner amid an entire garrison of soldiers would dare so much as lift a finger against me. And, in truth, you can scarce expect even a dolt of an Irishman to divulge any information that might be of use to us if he is peering at the sword hilts of you and your brave comrades."

"Miss Wylder, I—"

"Nay, Captain, you needn't make yourself pale with worrying. I shall have my maid beside me. And though she is somewhat dull-witted, even for an Irish wench, she is strong of limb and will see that the good Father can do me no harm."

Langworth fidgeted with the gold tassel bedecking his sword, his gaze darting skeptically from the key at his waist to the heavy iron-banded door.

Maryssa held her breath, sensing that the soldier was weighing the promotions to be gained with her success against the wrath that could follow failure. The prospect of sporting a major's laurels won out.

"Very well, then," Langworth acceded, heaving a sigh. "Your maid will be with you, as you say, and if there should be any difficulty, she need but rap on the door and my men will be inside the cell before Kilcannon can draw another breath."

"I have total faith in their strength and in your alertness," Maryssa said, battling the rolling dizziness that still tormented her. "And you may be certain that, once I am back in Sir Ascot's presence, he will know full well your part in this plan and will reward you most handsomely."

A heavy clanking of iron against iron drew Maryssa's eyes to where Langworth struggled with the heavy ring of keys at his belt. "I but hope Sir Ascot fails to reward me by relieving me of my head," the soldier muttered, driving the key into the massive lock with unnecessary force.

The key grated, the rusted lock protesting as it was snapped free. "Kilcannon!" the captain bellowed, swinging the door wide. "You have visitors."

Maryssa heard a shuffling from within and strained to get a glimpse of what lay beyond the heavy door, past Langworth's broad shoulders, but she could see only weak light and filthy straw until the captain stepped aside to allow her entry.

She heard Deirdre following just behind her and wanted to reach out a hand to reassure the girl, but her fingers froze midway to Deirdre's azure-sleeved shoulder. Her fist knotted and fell to her side. It was all she could do to stop the cry that rose in her throat as her gaze locked upon the figure battling so valiantly to sit up in the moldy straw.

The torchlight dripped orange across features so brutalized Maryssa wanted to retch. The curve of Devin's sensitive mouth was all but obliterated, the lips split, swollen. The high, patrician cheekbones that had hinted at ancestors born of kings, were bruised; the eyes, once so serene, now reflected the anguish of the damned as they peered out from bruised circles.

Maryssa bit her lip to keep from crying as she saw a tear

glisten in those gentle eyes. Angling her body so that Deirdre, who stood behind her in the narrow opening, could not see the full wreck of her brother's face, Maryssa cast a mockery of a smile at the captain. "Th-thank you. I—'twill be but a little while until we—we summon you to open the doors."

The soldier stalked over to Devin and yanked on one arm until the shaky prisoner gained his feet. "Take care you treat the ladies politely, Kilcannon," he bit out, "else we decide to make you do further penance."

Maryssa heard Deirdre's tiny cry, felt her pushing forward, but she reached out and caught the girl's hand in a warning grip. "The papist rogue will do penance enough full soon," she said, certain her fury was reflected in her voice.

But Langworth only smiled and offered her a stiff bow. He threw her an absurd compliment or tossed a crude insult at Devin; she never knew which. She only knew rage and then relief as the captain stepped back into the corridor, the heavy door scraping shut behind him.

The instant the portal closed, Deirdre broke free of Maryssa's grasp, hurling herself at the wavering Devin with a sob.

"Dev . . . oh, dear God, what—what have they done to you?" She wrapped her thin arms about him as Maryssa helped her support him on his quaking legs.

"I should think 'twould be passing obvious," Devin managed through swollen lips. "Some Englishman took exception to my face." His mouth twitched into a pathetic smile, his obvious attempt to gain Tade's air of jesting in the face of danger tearing Maryssa's heart the more. Deirdre buried her face in his chest, bursting into racking sobs.

"Don't—don't try to jest when—"

"When I've just been given the gift of seeing your sweet face one last time?"

Maryssa let her own hands fall away from Devin's shoulders, meaning to withdraw into the shadowy corner of the tiny cell and offer Devin and Deirdre what privacy she could, but Devin's fingers closed over hers, gently staying her as he soothed his sister.

The other thin, bloody hand reached up to smooth the tangle of Deirdre's coppery gold hair. "You should't have come."

"How—how can you say that?" Deirdre cried. "With you

in this horrible place and—oh, sweet God, Dev, half the king's army is standing guard about the halls!''

''I had no idea they thought me such a dangerous prisoner,'' Dev attempted to tease.

'' 'Tis not you they fear. 'Tis Tade . . . They await the Black Falcon. They think he'll attempt to free you, and—and I'm going to lose both of you,'' Deirdre wailed, ''both of my older brothers . . . They'll kill you!''

Maryssa's heart wrenched at the pain in Deirdre's voice, her own terror bounding at what she had seen in the endless trek down Rookescommon's halls.

Devin's bruised eyes rose to capture Maryssa's over Deirdre's tangled curls, and for the first time she saw fear in the savage depths. ''Jesus Savior, Tade can't—can't come here!''

Maryssa's throat knotted, tears starting to her own eyes as she turned away from Devin's tormented gaze. ''You know he will try anything to spare you,'' she quavered. ''He loves you, and—''

''That is why he *must not* come.'' Devin released Deirdre and struggled to remain standing. ''They wait out there to murder him, Maryssa. They plan to ensnare him because of his bond to me.''

''I—I know, but he will not just let you die—''

''And what, pray God, does he think I'll gain by watching him meet his death as well? This Dallywoulde can do naught to my flesh that would be as horrible as that.''

''Dev—''

''Nay, Dee. Listen, both of you. You've seen how they hold me here; you've seen the guard. God knows I don't want to die, but 'twould take a miracle to save me now''—Devin's fingers raked back through his lank blond hair—''and I fear God has been full short of them of late in Ireland.'' His eyes were overbright and full of pleading. ''Yet I can meet my fate, aye, with courage, if I but know that Tade, at least, is safe.''

Devin's hands caught Maryssa's in a desperate, crushing grip. ''Please . . . You have to—have to find a way . . . any means necessary to keep him from casting his life away in a quest that is hopeless.''

Maryssa gave a sick laugh. "Dev, I would bind him hand and foot if I had the strength, but he—"

"Nay, it must be something more subtle than that." Devin buried his face in his hands for several long seconds, and when at last he raised it, the expression on his gentle features filled Maryssa with dread. "There is a woman far on the west side of town by the name of Mab Hallighan. You know her, Dee. Tell her . . . tell her Father Devin has sent you. Tell her you need something to make a man sleep."

"Sleep?" Maryssa gasped, her stomach pitching.

"Aye. She brews a potion out of the sweet juices of poppy."

"Poppy . . . You can't mean to drug him!"

"I'd keep him insensible for a fortnight, if need be, to keep him from hurling his life away. Just pour the potion into his ale, and—"

"D-Devin, I can't. He . . . he'll hate me." The words struck Maryssa's heart like a stone.

Devin's gaze faltered. He swallowed. "He'll be alive."

She tore her gaze from Devin's, the horror of shattering Tade's trust by drugging him overwhelming her. Her gaze flashed to Deirdre's ashen face, then back to Devin's. "I can't destroy him like that . . ." Her hands fluttered to her abdomen as though to protect her child from Tade's hatred.

Devin's gaze flicked down to where she cradled her flat stomach, and the expression of understanding and raw anguish that streaked across his features brought a sob from Maryssa's throat.

"You have to save him from this insanity, Maryssa," Devin pleaded. "For yourself. For the babe you will bear him." Devin grasped her arms, bruising them beneath his fingers. "*Think*, Maryssa! They'll hang him until his throat is nigh crushed, cut him down while he yet lives and then take the knife and slash his stomach open."

"Nay, don't!" Maryssa choked out.

"They'll tie him to horses, Maryssa, four of them, and—"

"Nay!" she screamed the word, clamping her hands over her ears, wishing desperately she could blot out the vivid images Devin's words had spawned within her mind. "Don't," she whimpered, "please . . ."

"I *have* to, don't you see?" Devin's fists knotted in the curls at her temples, and she saw the tears streaming down his battered face. "Maryssa, you're the only one I can turn to, the only chance I have of saving my brother. I can't face the horrors that await me if I know Tade is condemned to endure them as well. 'Tis impossible to save me. Give me at least this one gift—peace."

Maryssa raised tortured eyes to Devin's face, the solemn, beloved planes raking deep into her heart, the sound of Deirdre's sobbing tearing at her soul. She shut her eyes against the pain, then descended into hell.

Nineteen

MARYSSA CLUTCHED THE tiny homespun pouch beneath her petticoats, the blown-glass vials inside it searing her fingers with guilt as she hesitated outside the inn's battered door. The Hangman's Fool, the broad sign proclaimed, its garish reds and oranges depicting a sly-faced harlequin ensnared in a noose. And from the raucous sounds of the patrons within, it seemed to Maryssa that half of those who reveled behind the scarred portal would most like one day share the painted jester's fate.

Yet of all those who dawdled there with their ale and their doxies, she knew of one man who stood closer to the blade of death's scythe than the others—an emerald-eyed rake with the face of a Gaelic king.

"Maryssa . . ."

She turned to find Deirdre peering up at her, her countenance so drawn from the ordeal of seeing Devin that her features seemed carved of snow. "I—I could go in to Tade and give him the potion if you—"

"Nay, Dee." Maryssa touched the child's cold cheek in reassurance. "He'd take but one look at you and go bolting out to Rookescommon if the very devil barred his way. What we saw today—the guards, Devin's face—'tis all painted in your eyes, and Tade would force the truth from you in a moment's time. 'Twill be best if I go in.'' Maryssa let her fingertips fall away from Deirdre's face, then turned away from her.

"But the babe," Deirdre faltered. "Devin said you were with child." She looked away, and Maryssa could hear the misery in her voice. "Maryssa, I don't—don't think Tade will ever forgive you for this."

"I'm not certain I carry Tade's child," Maryssa lied gently. "But even if I do, the love I shared with your brother, 'tis impossible. You knew that from the beginning, Deirdre. You tried to keep him from danger. Tade and I, we knew it, too. When all this is—is over if Tade hates me, 'twill hurt, aye, but my life will be in England, away from him. You'll be here, able to ease his pain, help him—help him heal. He'll need you to heal him once this is all past."

"Maryssa, I—"

Maryssa's lips curved into a trembling smile at the catch in Deirdre's voice. "Nay, Deirdre," she said, brushing back a tangled strand of fiery hair. "Let Tade at least be certain that no one in his family betrayed him." She shifted her gaze to the doorway, guilt grinding heavy in her heart. " 'Twill be task enough for you to keep Tade's men away from his chamber long enough for me to dr—'' She paused, unable to say the word. "To put him asleep," she substituted lamely. "Then we'll have to find some way to convince them that Tade realizes 'tis hopeless to attempt to free Devin. And that— that in his despair, Tade needs to be alone."

Deirdre nodded, biting at one broken fingernail. "Do you think they'll believe me?"

"They'll have to," Maryssa said, more harshly than she intended. "You know these men. You'll have to find a way to *make* them believe." Maryssa's gaze flitted back to the dull gold light filtering through the cracks in the grimy shutters. "And I'll have to find a way to make Tade believe in me." *Believe in me so I can betray him, make him despise me,* a voice jeered within her.

Her fingers fluttered up to the low-cut bodice of her gown, heat springing to her cheeks at the thought of Tade seeing her attired thus, her breasts half-bared, her dark hair caught in silken curls about her throat. What would he say when he saw her? What would he do? He had been in a black fury at the bonfire—hurt, angry, confused, his face rife with a misery that had torn at Maryssa's heart. What if he took one look at her and slammed his chamber door in her face?

Maryssa's fingers clenched, her chin jutting upward in determination. Even in the midst of his pain on that night, there had been love and passion in his eyes. If she had to slip the strings that bound her into the daring gown, let the satin fall from her shoulders and breasts, she would do so to gain entry into his room. Aye, and if she had to cudgel him into unconsciousness herself, she would keep him from flinging himself into Ascot Dallywoulde's heinous trap.

She shuddered, Devin's description of the death that would await Tade echoing in her mind—the noose crushing, the knife slicing deep into flesh, the horses straining, tearing at bound ankles and wrists until the limbs ripped free. Tears hazed her eyes, nausea gripping her as she was haunted by the knowledge that the gentle priest had been describing the execution that awaited him as well.

Yet it would be impossible to wrest Devin from his fate, while Tade was not yet in death's grasp. Her hand brushed the second small vial through the pouch, and she felt the tiniest of comforts. When she and Deirdre had found the redoubtable Mab Hallighan, the woman had been loading her meager possessions into a rickety cart—"Staertin' fer me son's in Kerry." But she had paused long enough to mix a philter for Tade and, at Maryssa's pleading, had concocted another, stronger mixture of the poppy's juices to ease Devin through his torment.

"This would've sent Christ from his cross peaceful as a babe," Mab had boasted, "with not a twinge o' discomfort t' pain him."

The remark had proved painful, and Maryssa had taken the vial, praying that the mysterious Mab had somehow boiled the juices into a dose so strong that it would allow Devin to drift gently into the arms of death long before the bloodlusting crowds gathered to see his torture.

Her gaze flicked to Deirdre, and she hated herself for wishing Devin dead. But Devin's loving God could not want so good a man to spend his last moments on earth screaming in agony while bestial men rended his body.

Maryssa straightened her shoulders, glancing back at Deirdre. "Better to have done with it," she said. " 'Tis not going to grow any easier or hurt any less if we tarry."

Deirdre gave a tiny nod, stepping to Maryssa's side and slipping one quivering hand in hers. Maryssa clung to it as she started up the rickety stairway.

The door, as she pulled it open, was heavy, as though built to contain the mayhem of scores of drunken brawls, but though the countless leather jacks weighting the rough plank tables were brimming with ale, and though the benches were crowded with huge, burly men, the room had not the stench Maryssa remembered from her visit to the Devil's Grin. Instead of reeking of rancid meat, sour ale, and unwashed bodies, this inn was filled with the warm smell of brewed barley overlaid with that of fresh-baked meat pies and ripe wine. The alewife bustled among men who were half drunk with revelry but whose threadbare clothes had of late met the washing stones of their wives or lovers. Even the women who lounged on the men's coarse-breeched knees had not the hardened, feral look of wearied prostitutes to their eyes. Rather, they exuded a kind of lusty enjoyment of the men they had chosen and wore the strangely innocent expressions of children well pleased with their new playthings.

Maryssa caught the limpid eyes of a pretty gold-haired woman perched on the lap of a handsome black-tressed rake Maryssa remembered having seen at the hurling match. Embarrassment jolted through her as she saw that the girl's hands were busy beneath the man's half-open shirt, but as she jerked her gaze away, nearly falling backward down the stairs, she felt Deirdre's hand tense in hers.

"Maryssa," the girl whispered, nodding toward the amorous couple, " 'tis Revelin Neylan over there. His cottage is about a league from ours, on the far slope of the hill. He and Tade—they've dredged up mischief together from the time they were breeched."

Maryssa had scarcely noticed the young man as Deirdre propelled her through the crowd, but now her eyes darted back to the figure slumped over his leathern jack of ale. Despite the blond woman's attentions, Revelin Neylan wore a brooding expression, as if anger simmered just beneath the surface. But the moment they drew near him, his bleary eyes locked on Deirdre's bright curls, and his mouth crooked in a weary grimace.

"By Christ's feet, Dee, 'tis pasht time shomebody got here who could talk that curshed brother o' yours outa his madness." Revelin forced himself to half-rise upon wobbly legs. " 'Twould be cleaner t' jes' take a sword t' Tade's throat 'n' have done with it!"

"A sword . . ." Deirdre echoed, her face graying. "Revelin, what—"

"Gone shtark crazed, he has," Neylan slurred. "Even for Tade."

"What . . . Where is he?" Maryssa demanded as she scanned the room's occupants, finding no crop of rich brown hair and no intense emerald eyes. Panic coiled around her, her mind conjuring a thousand images of Tade even now breaching the doors to Rookescommon, his broad shoulders being swallowed up in a sea of English soldiers.

But Revelin pulled a face, waggling one finger in the direction of the narrow staircase at the far end of the crowded room. "He's abovestairs tryin' t' find a way for six men t' besht the whole Sassenach army."

Relief that Tade was still alive and safe wilted Maryssa's terror for an instant before Neylan's next words crushed what small comfort that knowledge had been.

"Chrisht, musht be three hundred o' the red-bellied bashtards ready for us in the curshed place, an' he wants us to go chargin' int' the prison."

Maryssa felt talons of fear close tight about her throat. "Tade knows about the soldiers?"

Bloodshot eyes struggled to focus on her face, the man's lips twisting in a rueful grin. "That bloody bashtard knows everything," he said with a hollow laugh. "Knows he's going to get ush all murdered, too, but won't—won't hear reashon. Won't hear reashon, will he, Nainsi?" the man said, turning to the golden-haired woman still draped about him.

The woman cast him an indulgent smile. "So you've been tèlling me for the past hour, sweeting."

"See? Even Nainsi thinks I should break a curshed ale barrel over Kilcannon's thick skull."

Maryssa stiffened, the man's mutterings filling her with fear. She could imagine the stubborn jut of Tade's jaw, feel the desperation in him at the thought of Devin meeting such a hideous fate. But if he already knew about the soldiers, knew it was hopeless . . . if his men were battling to dissuade him from attempting a rescue . . .

Her hands knotting into fists, she looked down into Revelin's face. "Please, if you could tell us which chamber is Tade's, mayhap . . . mayhap we could persuade him to change his mind."

Neylan's bleary eyes alighted upon Maryssa's face, but his mouth curled in dismissal. "Already sent Finola up t' try t' convinsh him, an' he fair flung her from the room. If *she* can't—"

" 'Tis the door at the end of the hall," Nainsi offered, smoothing her hand over the pelt of dark hair bared by Neylan's opened shirt. "None save Revelin has left there since they arrived last evening."

"Deshided I might as well get drunk one lasht time afore flingin' myshelf on Tade's curshed pyre," Revelin muttered, sinking back onto the bench and hefting the half-empty leathern jack to take a long swallow. "Crazed bashtard. Gonna get us all bloody killed."

Maryssa spun away, led Deirdre through the maze of benches and bodies, and then hastened up the narrow stairway, every step driving dread and terror deeper into her heart. The Black Falcon's band was known throughout Ireland to laugh at death, take joy in besting incredible odds. They feared no one, nothing. Never had they run from a Sassenach challenge. But Revelin Neylan was afraid now, Maryssa knew; he was drowning himself in ale while the rest of the rebel band struggled to prevent Tade from leading them into a hopeless disaster. But Tade would never acknowledge that his quest was hopeless; he would storm the gates of Rookescommon with no weapon to shield him if he had to, knowing as he did that Devin was to die.

She paused before the heavy door to Tade's chamber, hearing beyond it the harsh rise and fall of voices given over to fury—Tade's voice, Reeve Marlow's, and others she knew not. Her fingers again brushed the vials tucked away beneath her gown, and she could almost see Devin's battered, desperate features as he had pleaded with her to keep Tade from courting certain death.

Her hand tightened about the tiny pouch, her gaze flashing to Deirdre's waxen features and wide anguished eyes. Maryssa would do whatever was necessary to save Tade for those who needed his strength so desperately. She would save Tade for Deirdre, for the little Kilcannons who worshiped him, for the gentle priest barred within Rookescommon and for the embattled people of the glen. Her teeth clenched against the torment that welled up in white-hot waves within her. She would save Tade for her unborn babe and, in so doing, make him hate her for all time.

The walls of the inn chamber seemed to crush Tade in a fist tempered by stark desperation. The familiar faces turning to him in varying degrees of sympathy, understanding, and stubborn refusal sent blind fury storming through his veins. He glared at them, his fingers crushing the crumpled edges of a crudely drawn map, his other hand wielding a sharpened, charred stick as though he would slash it across the face of the next man who dared speak. A dozen paths had been drawn on the map with the burned stick and then rubbed out in frustration with the heel of his hand. The floor plan of Rookescommon with its maze of lines seemed to jeer at him now in mute agreement with what the other men had been saying during the endless hours past.

"Tade, 'tis hopeless."

He spun at the sound of Reeve Marlow's strained voice, his teeth bared with rage, his lip curled in an ugly sneer, as he battled the urge to snatch up his pistol and dash the platter of food and ale to the floor. "And what would you know of it, Reeve?" he bit out. "You who've done naught but hide away in your cursed manor house while the rest of us have been dodging musket balls? We can free Dev, I know we—"

"Damn it, Tade, I may not have ridden beside you, but I've blasted well been there for the lot of you whenever you've dashed off on one of your crazed schemes! 'Tis that 'cursed manor house' that stables your horses, and it is this *coward*"—Reeve jabbed a thumb at his own chest—"who has helped you map out more raids than I can count. Never once have I doubted you could carry one out, but his time . . ." Reeve took a step toward him, his jaw thrust out belligerently at the level of Tade's shoulder. "This time 'tis hopeless, and you damn well know it!"

"Damn you, Marlow!" Tade's fist crushed the map and raised it to strike as frustration and fear overwhelmed him, but the answering torment in Reeve's eyes held him, making him drive his fist into the scarred oaken table instead of into his friend's jaw. The pistol skittered dangerously across the surface and stopped.

"Don't listen to him," Tade flared, his gaze sweeping the other implacable faces. "Mayhap he *has* helped us plan before, but he's ne'er been bloodied. You all know me. You've seen me fight. We can strike just before dawn. I can lead you to—"

"To a cursed massacre?" Gilvarry Beagan bit out. "Blast it, Tade, our man inside the jail claims there are three hundred soldiers within Rookescommon's walls—that they stand poised there to snare the Black Falcon. Somehow the Sassenachs have learned of the link between you and Dev."

"Aye, the link between me and Dev," Tade raged. "He's my brother, damn it, and the bloody bastards are going to rip his body to pieces, for Christ's sake!"

Tade saw Reeve rake a hand back through his wild hair, his mouth twisting as if he felt sickened by what he had heard. "Damn it, Tade, we love Devin, too, and we know what will befall him. The best we can do is to plant one man amid the crowd and have him bury a bullet in Dev's chest before the hoodsman starts working his horrors. I'll fire the shot myself, and I promise you I'll make it clean and quick."

"He's not going to die!" The cry was full of anguish, tearing at Tade's very soul. "Damn it, I'll not let him die!"

"Tade, the devil himself couldn't tear Devin out of the midst of three hundred soldiers and get him out of Rookescommon." Beagan reached out and gripped Tade's arm, but Tade yanked free.

"I'll sell my cursed soul to the devil if I have to, but I'm wresting Dev from that blasted prison *alive!*"

The knock on the door stilled the words in Tade's throat, making him suddenly horribly aware of how loud they had been shouting, how careless they had grown as the rage bolted through them. He glimpsed the other men reaching for the butts of hidden pistols and the hilts of knives as they glanced toward the shuttered window that would prove their one escape route if they had been betrayed to the soldiers.

The knock sounded again, but it was soft and tentative, not the crashing of fist upon wood that would precede a rush of battle-ready Sassenachs. "Leave us be, whoever you are," Tade barked. "We've no time for—"

"Tade?" the voice was muffled, but he recognized it immediately.

With a blistering oath he yanked the bar from the locked door and flung it wide. "Deirdre, god damn it, what are you doing—" The words froze on his tongue as his rage-glinting gaze caught a glow of rich sable hair and changeable blue-gold eyes beyond Deirdre's shoulder. "Sweet Christ!" he hissed, but the sight of Maryssa's face—so pale, so full of his own horrible torment—struck through him like a Saracen blade. The crumpled map fell from his numb fingers, and it was all he could do not to yank the trembling Maryssa into his arms and bury his hopelessness and desperation in her sweet warmth.

"Maura . . ." He croaked her name, scarce believing his own eyes, thinking that the madness that had been threatening to overcome him since the morning in Christ's Wound had gotten him at last in its grip.

He heard Reeve mutter a prayer of thanks, heard his men fall silent, and felt suspicion all around him as they regarded the English heiress.

Then Reeve pushed past him, drawing both Maryssa and Deirdre through the open door. "Thank God you've come. Maryssa, you've got to talk to him."

Fury surged anew into Tade's limbs, mingled with a sudden wariness, as his memory of the last time he had seen Maryssa rose within him. But he turned his anger on Reeve, scowling. "Curse it, Reeve, don't drag Maura into this."

"She's obviously been dragged into this blasted mess already, Tade! I doubt Bainbridge Wylder escorted her here in his carriage."

"Reeve, nay. Please," Maryssa begged, her gaze flashing uncertainly from Reeve's freckled countenance to Tade's furious one. "I came—came because I overheard my father and

Sir Ascot Dallywoulde plotting at Nightwylde. I thought to
warn Tade . . . all of you—''

"Warn us?" Gilvarry Beagan scoffed. "An English
Wylder—"

"Gil—" Deirdre's quavery objection was cut off by Tade's
command.

"Hold your tongue, Beagan." Tade's voice was low and
dangerous as he battled the hurt that tore at him from Maryssa's vulnerable eyes.

He heard her suck in a deep breath as her hand drifted,
feather-light, to the taut muscles beneath his sleeve and she
turned her pleading gaze to his own hard emerald one. "If I
could just—just have a moment alone with you to—to tell you
something."

The feel of her small fingers on his arm seemed to sear
through Tade's very soul. His eyes swept away from hers, the
pallor and fear in her delicate face piercing him. "Get out,"
he ordered the men about him. "Drag Neylan up and douse
him in a water barrel to rouse him from his stupor. Then go
and make your pistols and sabers ready. We'll ride in an
hour's time."

He saw Deirdre's stricken face, her thin shoulders cradled
in Reeve's capable arm. Almost as an afterthought, Tade
reached out, attempting to lighten the fear he sensed in his
sister by cuffing her gently on the chin. "Don't fear, Dee,"
he said with a mockery of his usual smile. "Once all this is
past, Devin and I'll take turns whacking your backside with
a willow switch for haring off to Derry in the dead of night,
and you'll wish us both in the bottom of Rookescommon."

He could see Deirdre struggle to bring a smile to her lips,
but the trembling of that still childish mouth made the effort
all the more pathetic and painful as Reeve led her and the
others from the room.

Tade turned and paced across the small chamber to where
the shutters stood closed against the night. Tiny cold blue
stars pierced the blackness visible through the cracks in the
battered wood. Tade leaned on the ledge and shoved one
shutter wide as the room, filled with the scent and sweetness
of Maryssa, threatened to crush his chest.

He heard the door close softly behind the last of the men,
heard Maryssa quietly shove the bolt home. His head fell

forward, his brow resting against the rough wood, as a strange sense of shyness and uncertainty filtered through his desperation. It was as if, in resisting that first impulse to catch Maryssa in his arms and hold her, he had lost the chance forever. He could feel those changeable eyes on him, pleading silently, so beautiful, but he didn't know what to say to her now, didn't know what to do.

There was a rumpling sound of paper being lifted, then a silence that seemed to stretch into eternity, drawing at Tade's wire-taut nerves until he felt he would snap. He turned his head to look at her. The map he had drawn hung limply from her fingers. Her rich hair spilled over the smudged parchment, the lustrous sable strands dripping in a silken stream over a bodice cut so low it tempted a man to taste of the treasures swelling above the narrow lace. It was a gown such as he'd never seen on Maryssa before, a gown designed to turn a man's loins to flame. But though he wanted her, needed her warmth with a desperation that terrified him, he stood frozen, one hand on the splintered window ledge.

"Tade . . ."

He had heard her speak his name a thousand times before, but the pain and terror infused in it as she lifted her gaze from the map twisted his belly into a coil of anguish and longing. And when his eyes caught the tear-dewed blue-gold of hers, saw the quivering of her sweet, innocent lips, Tade uttered a cry, lunged across the space that divided them, and caught her in a crushing, hopeless embrace.

He heard a sob catch in her throat, felt her hands delving deep into his hair, her lips upon his jaw and eyelids, her face against his, moist with tears.

And he wanted to bury this nightmare of loss and pain in the wonder of this one woman's loving.

"Christ, Maura, you came . . . I need you so damn badly." His voice cracked as he felt a wetness on his cheeks and was unashamed as it dampened her warm lips. "They've captured Dev."

"I know, love."

"They're going to kill him, and I don't—don't know how to stop it." His shoulders shuddered, and he felt her hands tighten about him, fierce and loving. "Maura, I have to do something, and—"

"Whist, now, whist." Her hand was trembling as it smoothed his brow and cheek, her fingers tugging him to the small bed that stood along the wall of the chamber. He felt her palms on his chest, pushing him gently backward until he sagged down upon the straw tick, the bed ropes creaking beneath him.

His arm tightened about her waist, pulling her with him, the slight weight of her body warming him. Cold . . . He hadn't know he was so cursed cold . . . He swallowed convulsively, opening his burning eyes to gaze into her face. "I was such a bastard the night of the fires," he choked out. "Didn't listen, didn't want to. It hurt so to hear you say we could ne'er be together. 'Twas as if someone had ripped the heart out of me, and I couldn't . . . couldn't stop bleeding. And when I thought 'twas because you were a coward . . ."

He saw her flinch as though he had struck her, her eyes turning to liquid opal. "Nay, Maura," he said, his fingers skimming the delicate curves of her face to assure himself she was truly there beside him, not some vision, some phantom that would melt away in his arms. "No woman who will dare the highroads at night to ride to her man when he faces trouble can be said to lack courage. 'Twas not until that morning, at mass before Dev was taken, that I understood . . . understood that to leave them without having given them another leader to shield them would have been to betray myself."

Her gaze skittered away, her mouth trembling. "It matters not," she murmured soothingly, her hands cool and gentle on his fevered cheek.

"Aye, it does matter." Tade pressed his fingertips against his pounding head. "When we learned about the soldiers, I thought I'd be dead before I could tell you how sorry I am. That I love—"

"Tade—" The name was a choked plea upon her lips, the anguish in her eyes stirring confusion and hurt in his belly, but her eyes were so tormented that they struck through to his very soul.

He felt her drawing away from him and tightened his grip, needing desperately to ease whatever tore at her, to comfort

her, drink in of comfort himself. "In all the years I rode as
the Falcon I ne'er feared death until this night. I didn't want
to die without touching you once more, without making love
to you, hearing you cry out in my arms . . . feeling your
hands . . ." His throat knotted, and he pulled his gaze away
from hers, letting his eyelids droop shut. "Christ, such gentle
hands," he rasped, gripping her fingers, pulling them to his
lips. "Such gentle, loving hands in a world full of hate and
lies."

He felt her body shudder, then stiffen. Trembling, he raised
his face, cupping her tear-streaked cheeks in his palms. "Put
your hands on me, Maura," he breathed just as he had in the
dream-kissed tree castle an eternity ago. "Please. I need . . .
need you to touch me."

Tears spilled from her lashes, a groan of anguish rose in
her throat, and in her eyes Tade could sense that she was
being torn in two. But she cried out, burying herself against
his chest, her lips seeking him with a fierce desperation, her
hands plunging beneath his half-open shirt. "Aye, Tade,"
she sobbed against his skin. "I'll love you . . ."

His lips crushed hers, tasting the salt of tears, not knowing
or caring whether it was the wetness of his own sorrow or
hers upon his tongue. He felt a bittersweet hopelessness, because in his heart he knew this would be the last time he
would ever know the beauty of this woman's love.

" 'Ryssa," he groaned, his fingers battling with the fastenings of her gown, the skirts, the petticoats. Her breasts
spilled into his hands, and he took one rosy crest between
his lips, teething it to pebble hardness, suckling it until he
heard her groan with pleasure. Yet his awareness of her re-
sponse was hazed by the sensations her soft hands and mouth
were wringing from his own body. Her nails raked at his
shirt, tearing the thin lawn from his shoulders, her tongue
wetting the hard bronzed curves she had bared.

He shivered as the garment fell away, reveling in the feel
of her hands on his skin, losing himself in the heat of her
nakedness as he brushed the last of her undergarments from
between them. Her flesh was infinitely sweet, scented of
wildflowers and midnight and love, and he wanted to trace
with his lips and tongue every curve and hollow, every deli-

cate blush of rose, so he might carry the memory with him when he danced this night with death.

He trailed hot kisses down the swell of breasts that were fuller than he remembered, skimming his teeth and tongue across the delicate lengths of her ribs. But as he neared the sweet down nestled between her thighs, he felt Maryssa's hands forcing him upward, urging him onto his back. He started to protest, but her voice drifted to him, penetrating the silken webs of passion engulfing him.

"Nay, Tade . . . let me . . ."

He rolled onto his back, the coarse sheets abrading his passion-fevered skin. Her hair spilled in waves of warm mahogany across his chest; her fingers were gentle, maddening, as they unfastened his breeches. His shaft throbbed, straining against the binding cloth, burning for the brush of those soft, slender fingers. Then she freed him, working the breeches down, raining kisses upon the hardened, hair-roughened flesh of his thighs.

Tade groaned, catching at the tangled tresses pooled upon his skin, wanting to drag her up into his arms, bury himself inside her, but she pulled away. She raised her gaze to his and held his eyes for an instant that seemed to stretch into eternity.

"This one time," she whispered, "let me . . . let me give you . . ."

The words drifted to silence, but Tade gritted his teeth, every muscle in his body snapping wire-taut as she lowered her luminous eyes to his turgid, hardened flesh. Slowly, so slowly, she bent down, her lips breath-soft on his taut belly. "Tade . . ." His name was a sob on the lips that were hurling him toward insanity. "I love you. Believe me . . . You have to believe that I do."

The first touch of her tongue on his white-hot shaft sent a jolt of raw pleasure into Tade's very soul, and as she loved him, pleasured him, something deep within his heart burst. It was a gift, wondrous and whirling, yet with every movement of her tongue, hands, and mouth he sensed in her a desperation and hopelessness. He arched his head back, the rage she had loosed in his loins drowning the confusion that had assailed him.

With a groan he grasped her arms, drawing her up his

body. "Maura . . . ," he choked. "I need to . . . to bury myself inside you . . ." He swept her beneath him, felt her soft thighs open to cradle his hips. She was crying, he knew, as he probed the wet heat that beckoned him, crying, not in passion, but as if she had lost . . . lost something precious. But they *were* losing something precious, both of them. They were losing a love so sweet it defied the very angels, losing a life they might one day have built together, losing the children that might have been conceived of their loving.

And in that instant, Tade knew a need so fierce, primal, and savage that it stunned him, a need to plant his seed within her body, heedless of the consequences, a need to leave her with some tangible proof of his love for her.

His fists knotted in her tumbled curls, his mouth pressing down on hers in a wild, desperate kiss as he drove himself deep. She cried out against his mouth, arching her hips to meet his thrusts, her fingers digging deep into the steely curves of his buttocks as he set himself against her.

In all the times they had made love, she had never felt so fragile and vulnerable beneath him, she had never been so fierce in her passion. He was burning and she was the flame. Her hands were all over him, her mouth hot, agonizingly sweet as he plunged again and again into her body. He could hear her whimpers, feel her writhing beneath him like a wild thing. She screamed his name in fulfillment, and her cry hurtled Tade past reason, into a madness so consuming he never wanted to leave it. He buried his lips against hers, a cry tearing from his own throat as he drove deep, spilling his love, his pain, inside her. He collapsed against her breasts, his sweat-sheened skin bonded to hers, his face buried in the delicate curve of her throat. Never had he given so much of himself to a woman, never had he felt a woman pour into his body the very essence of her soul. Maryssa had given herself totally to him in this loving. He knew it with a certainty that wrenched his heart. And yet even now, with the tremors of passion still coursing through his body, he could sense her pulling away from him.

She moved beneath him, as if his weight were crushing her, her breathing suddenly shallow and quiet, too quiet. Was she thinking of the gray stones of Rookescommon even now? And the fate that awaited him?

" 'Ryssa." He shifted to one side, starting to draw her close against his chest, wanting only to hold her until the time came for him to ride, but already she was slipping from his arms. The hands that had driven him to madness were now trembling as she pulled on her tangled garments.

Tade swallowed, a horrible emptiness seeming to yawn within him, the pain crashing over him more brutal even than the anguish he had felt before he first touched her. "Maura, don't," he said. "I want to hold you . . ."

"Until your men come barging in here?" Her voice was oddly discordant, infused with a forced brightness that unsettled him. "You bade them be ready within an hour, and nigh half that time has already passed."

"It will take us but a moment to don our clothes, and this may be the last time we . . ." He saw her flinch, reached out to her. " 'Ryssa, I have to go. You know that, don't you? If I let Dev die, I'd never forgive myself . . ."

He saw her face twist in pain as she spun away from him. Her shoulders squared. "I know."

It was as if in that moment the gulf that had always separated them—the gap between poverty and wealth, English and Irish, Catholic and Protestant—yawned between them, unbreachable, hopeless. Tade had known loss and grief before, but never had he tasted so bitterly of defeat. His numb fingers closed upon his breeches and shirt, and he donned them, scarce feeling their fastenings beneath his hands.

He saw her walk to the table with a shaky stride. Beyond the blue of her sleeve, he caught the steely gleam of his pistol barrel. "Don't jar the gun," he cautioned. " 'Tis loaded to blast the life out of some cursed Sassenach soldier."

She gave a quavery nod, avoiding the weapon as though it were a serpent. Her fingers closed instead on an empty leathern jack, and he saw her pull it close to the folds of her petticoats, shielding it there as she raised the brimming pitcher to pour out a draft. "Lie back, Tade, and rest," she urged. It was a dismissal. He sensed it, yet he scarce had the will to fight it anymore.

He saw Maryssa shiver; then he heard an odd clink, as though something hard had touched glass. But he sank down again into the smothering softness of the tick, the raging headache now throbbing between his temples making his eyes drift shut.

Still, even despite the pounding in his brain, he fought to find some reason, some explanation, for the walls he sensed she was hurling up between them. He was riding in but a little time; the odds were heavy that he would die in Rookes-common tonight. That knowledge should have drawn her closer, made her cling to him; he longed to lose himself in her embrace these last treasured minutes. Why, then, did she stand there, so still and hurt? He grimaced, cursing himself for a fool. In her silence the anger-edged accusations he had flung at her that night in the glow of the bonfire seemed to hang between them, the slashes he had dealt her spirit standing out like stripes from a whip.

"Maura," he began tentatively, "I'm sorry . . . about the way I raged at you at the fires. About everything . . ."

"Don't apologize. 'Twas not your doing but mine. I refused to go with you, and—"

"And if we had ridden from Donegal that night, not only would Dev lie in chains, but Deirdre would be dead as well. When the soldiers came, she was hit. I was scarce able to carry her out of harm's way before the bastards closed in for the slaughter." His voice was raspy with emotion as he opened his eyes. "I was scared. So damned scared. And all I could think of was holding you, touching you, sharing with you all this madness and fear that's been tearing me apart."

She turned toward him, and the agony in her face stunned him. She looked so broken and fragile, the jack of ale and chunk of buttered bread seeming so heavy in her hand. He wanted to drive away the demons that beset them both, tear through the veils she had drawn about her.

"Sweet God, Maura," he gritted, "I love you. What is wrenching at you, ripping you away from me?"

He reached out to catch her slender wrist and draw her toward him, but the food in her hands was in the way, the bread crumbling where it brushed his chest, the ale sloshing perilously near the rim of the leathern jack. He wanted her in his arms, wanted her mouth on his, the feel of her beneath him banishing the horror of what was to come and the pain and emptiness left from their last loving, but he felt her strain away from him, and the look on her face deepened the confusion within him.

He opened his mouth to speak, prey again to a flooding of hurt, but before he could put his feelings into words, she set the chunk of bread on his thigh, then reached up to smooth the tangled strands of his hair.

'' 'Tis but your imaginings, love. You're my heart, Tade,'' she said, her gaze locked with his. "My soul. Whenever you need me I'll be there for you.''

"Maura—''

"But now . . . now I want you to eat this,'' she said, raising the bread to his lips. "What with Devin being taken, the killings at mass, and trying to find a way to breach Rookescommon's walls, I'd wager you've not slept at all since we parted at the bonfires, and most like haven't take so much as a bite to eat.''

Tade let his heavy lashes fall to his cheekbones and heaved a weary sigh, his body suddenly aching, as though Maryssa's words had reminded it how long it had been since he had rested, reminded him, too, of the gnawings of his empty stomach.

"Please, love. You'll scarce be any aid to Devin if you've starved yourself faint. Mayhap if you'd rest but a little, take some bread and a few sips of ale, you'll be able to face the problems more easily.''

He took up the wedge of crusty bread and sank his teeth into its yeasty softness, hardly tasting it as it slid down his throat. '' 'Twould take a miracle to make these problems easier to manage. They plan to execute Dev inside the prison grounds after letting the spectators enter through a single gate. And our contact within Rookescommon claims the jail is crawling with English soldiers.''

She pushed the leathern jack into his hand, and he tipped it up to his lips, draining a good portion of the lukewarm liquid. It burned his throat and tasted strange, slightly bitter, as though the alewife had not tended the barrel with much skill. But it was wet, and Tade was thirsty, made more so by the dryness of the bread upon his lips.

He saw Maryssa's hands bunched in white-knuckled fists on her lap, her lip caught between her teeth, her eyes wide, frightened. She seemed to shake herself, her lips parting, and after a moment she spoke. " 'Twas the soldiers I came to warn you about," she said, urging him to take another swig of the drink. "I overheard my father and Sir Ascot gloating in the study and—"

"Sir Ascot?" At the mention of the man who he now knew had brought about the successful raid on Christ's Wound, Tade's hand gripped the leathern jack so tightly that it sliced into his palm. "Sir Ascot Dallywoulde?"

"Aye." Maryssa's gaze faltered, and he saw crimson shade her cheeks.

"What in the name of hell was that bastard doing at Night-wylde?"

He saw Maryssa flinch, her eyes flashing away from his. " 'Tis—'tis not important just now," she said. "Naught is important except Devin, and keeping you and your men from being slaughtered."

The soothing, placating tone of her voice made Tade want to drive his fist into the wall, his fury at the thought of his innocent, fragile Maura near the very monster who had captured Devin goading him into draining the leathern jack in one final gulp. He flung the container onto the planked floor, his jaw working with anger.

"Oh, aye, I vow that an honored peer of the realm would be most welcome within Bainbridge Wylder's walls, welcomed along with your puling betrothed, while a Kilcannon—"

He stopped abruptly, seeing the stain on her cheeks, the hurt beneath her thick, curling lashes, but instead of feeling that his words had placed the burden of guilt there, he had an odd sensation that this was but a further deepening of an emotion that had already shown upon her features.

She looked for all the world like little Katie when the child felt she had committed some unpardonable sin like nibbling on the sugar rock or playing with Deirdre's hair ribbons. And despite the pain squeezing Tade's heart at the thought of Maryssa's betrayal, in spite of the knowledge that she was pledged to another, he couldn't stay his hands from reaching out to her, pulling her down onto his lap as he had his tiny sister so many times before. "Ah, 'Ryssa," he sighed, running his fingers soothingly over the tense muscles in her arm.

"I much doubt you rode all the way to Derry to listen to me rage at you."

"You've every right to your fury. 'Twas deceitful . . . despicable of me not to—to be honest with you about the betrothal."

Tade's mouth tipped in a tired grin. "You've ne'er done anything despicable in your whole life, Maryssa Wylder. Now, I, on the other hand have made a career of deceiving people." At the stricken look crossing her face, Tade framed her cheeks in his wide palms. "Maura," he said, brushing his lips against her tear-wet skin, " 'tis all right, love. All is forgiven. God knows I was hurt, furious at first, but once I understood . . ." He struggled to find the words to soothe her, comfort her, but the weariness that had been plaguing him these past hours seemed to have fallen in a haze over his mind. He shook his head, trying to clear it, to recapture what he had been attempting to say. For a moment it seemed the haze receded, and he tried to smile, but his eyelids felt weighted with lead, his mind lost in a strange swirl of mist. " 'Twas agony to admit that you were right," he said, "but with you here, loving me through all this hell— I only want things to be the way they were . . . I want you close. Christ, I can't bear to see you cry . . ."

The tiny choked sob she gave twisted inside Tade as she tried to wrest herself away from him, but he tightened his arms about her, pulling her with him as he rolled back on the bed. One thigh curved over her leg as his lips sought hers. "Nay, Maura, don't . . . Don't cry, love."

His mouth opened over her taut lips, crushing the sobs that tore from her throat. He needed desperately to love her one more time, show her his forgiveness with his body, since the swirl of exhaustion, the bite in the ale, had addled his wits, robbed him of the power to put his love into words. She struggled like a trapped linnet beneath him, driving the heels of her hands against his chest, twisting and shoving at him with legs tangled beneath layerings of petticoats.

In some small but still rational part of his mind he knew she was fighting to be released, but that knowledge hadn't the strength to pierce through the roiling dizziness besetting him. "Please, Maura," he said into her mouth. "Don't . . . don't fight. I need to love you. Let me . . ."

His hand insinuated itself into the split that drew back her outer petticoats, his fingers clumsy as he groped for the ties that held the gown closed. Pulsing with need, he grasped at the soft tapes, but they eluded him. Frustration and hurt raked through him at Maryssa's struggles, and his hands knotted on cloth, almost tearing the narrow waistband and the pocket affixed to the inside. He paused, puzzled, as his fingertips collided not with bare skin, but with something hard and cylindrical within the thin cloth pouch.

With a cry, Maryssa shoved him away, as though suddenly possessed of gargantuan strength, but in an effort to hold her, Tade's fingers closed tight over the object he had touched a heartbeat before. There was a sound of fabric tearing, then a clatter as glass struck wood.

He heard Maryssa scream, saw her lunge toward the object that lay upon the floor and snatch it up. A flash of pain streaked across her features, driving back the odd dizziness that seemed to be clasping Tade even tighter. A scent assailed his nostrils . . . sickly sweet, familiar . . . the scent of the potion he had used months past to cast jail guards into a drugged sleep.

Sweet Christ . . . 'twas—

With a savage curse he grasped Maryssa's wrist and peeled open her clenched fingers. Blood dripped, warm and crimson, over jagged edges of shattered glass, and the smell of the poppy's narcotic juices filled his nostrils . . .

Disbelief and betrayal ripped through him, coupled with stark despair. He forced his eyes up to Maryssa's face, a cry of rage rising in his throat, but it was as though the drug had already robbed his lungs of their breath. "Bitch!" he croaked. "Lying bitch . . . You . . . you seduced me so . . . so you could drug me!"

The candlelight streaked her tears with scarlet, as though even her sorrow bled . . . as Devin would bleed . . . For one hideous instant reality snapped into Tade's drug-hazed mind, slashing him with crystal-clear images of Devin's chest being split wide beneath the executioner's knife, of the men binding his wrists and ankles to four stout horses, urging them to a run in opposite directions . . .

"Tade, 'twas . . . 'twas hopeless," the voice, that siren's

voice, whispered from the face of the devil's own angel.
"Devin begged me to keep you from—"

"Witch!" The cry was almost a sob. Tade's hand flashed
out, knocking the broken vials from her grip. Hate tore
through him as savagely as a hoodsman's blade, shattering
love, trust, all hope of preventing his brother's murder.
"You—you *drugged* me . . . drugged . . ." Her face was
rippling before his eyes, doubling, swirling. The delicate features he had loved were agonizingly beautiful even now, tortured as they were with the torment of the damned.

"Tade, I had to—to stop you from being killed. The soldiers are waiting . . . It's a trap . . ."

"Doesn't . . . doesn't matter . . . have to help Dev," he
cried, trying to force his feet to carry him to the door, wanting to get to the loyal men he knew were beyond it. But the
floor of the tiny chamber stretched out around him as endless
as the sea, and the room spun him about until he could
scarcely see, let alone move.

He staggered to his feet, feeling the room close in around
him, bury him beneath a thousand crushing stones. "Maura,"
he croaked. "Please help me . . . if you have any mercy . . .
help . . ."

"I'm trying to, Tade . . . I love you . . ."

Something dug into his shoulder, holding him, binding him
as he struggled toward the doorway. He felt his knees buckle,
his arms too weak to break his fall. The hard floor crashed
into his jaw, and he could feel something warm and wet trickle
over his skin. Desperately he tried to shove himself up, crawl
the last few feet to the iron latch. He could hear sobbing—
Maryssa's sobbing and his own—could see among the mists
of his mind the lusting faces of a crowd thirsting for blood,
Devin's blood. It was as though they were closing in around
him, smothering him, driving him down onto the rough wood
floor.

He cried Devin's name as he collapsed, the tiny chamber
shifting, wheeling, his limbs useless, leaden. Hands—cool,
soft, and wet with tears—cradled his face, the silken hair
brushed across the agonized planes of his face, and a broken,
tortured voice, murmured against his skin. A sob racked him,
helpless, hopeless, tearing into his flesh, the light from the
single candle shifting into the hideous gleam of bloodied steel

as the hoodsman raised his knife, plunging Tade into oblivion.

Maryssa stared down at the dark head pillowed in her lap, the bronzed jaw twisted with pain even the opium could not dull, the lips moving in pleas Tade could no longer utter. Even through the veil of tears that poured from her eyes, the sobs that shook her whole body, she could tell that he was struggling to speak, begging her to help him save the brother he so loved. Begging her . . . the woman he had trusted, showered with his tenderness and passion. The woman who had made love to him, taken the sweetness of his body, then betrayed him.

"I didn't . . . didn't want to, Tade . . . but I had to . . ." She pressed her lips to the clammy paleness of his brow, kissing him, hushing him as though he were a babe, whispering love-words, broken through with her own tearing agony of loss, pleading for the forgiveness she knew would never come.

She lifted one large bronzed hand and pressed it to her stomach, feeling its warmth against the womb that held their child. " 'Tis your son, Tade, or the daughter you used to spin dreams about," she whispered to the man who was still thrashing restlessly on her lap. "But you—you won't be with us when she begins to kick within me, won't be with us when she takes her first steps or smiles her first smile. I would have—have loved to lay her in your arms the first time, Tade, and to see the joy in your eyes . . ."

A tearing sob clawed at her throat as she buried her face against his tear-dampened cheek. "Oh, God, Tade, I'll miss you so much . . . But there was naught . . . naught I could do." Her fist clenched in his shirt, the cuts slashed into her palm from the broken vials burning as the fine lawn dug into them.

Both vials had been shattered, the one emptied into Tade's ale and the other, the pain-numbing potion that had been intended for Devin, now pooled upon the floor. And with old Mab halfway to Kerry, Maryssa knew there was no hope of obtaining more of the sickly sweet mixture.

She clutched Tade but the tighter, her eyes straying to the abandoned map, then to the table where Tade's pistol lay primed and at the ready.

Naught I could do . . . Her own choked words drifted back to her. No, Maryssa thought, swallowing hard, there was one thing she could still do for Tade, and for gentle, loving Devin, if she had the courage. She shuddered, fighting the nausea and the horror that welled up inside her at the thought that had reared its hideous head. Could she . . . ? God, had she the strength to . . . ?

It would be murder. Murder. And yet . . . She pressed her fingertips to her eyes, trying to drive away the images that tormented her, the images of Devin being tortured, his body broken, torn. Could she abandon the gentle priest to the cruelty that awaited him? Could she let him die screaming in agony, food for the blood lust of such a loathsome beast as Ascot Dallywoulde? She looked down into Tade's face, the beloved features anguished even beneath the haze of opium-induced sleep. His lips still pleading . . . silent.

Dawn bled crimson across the horizon when she eased a pillow beneath Tade's tossing head and brushed his chill mouth with her own one last time. Forcing her numb legs beneath her, she dragged herself to her feet, her shaking fingers closing about the butt of the loaded pistol.

Twenty

THE DONEGAL SKY pitched and rolled as though Saint Peter
stood wrestling the devil, huge storm clouds driving in from
Lough Foyle in massive waves. Maryssa turned her face into
the fearsome wind, wishing that the tempest unleashed overhead could obliterate the sinister walls of Rookescommon and
sweep away the masses who had gathered to see Devin Kilcannon die.

Some five hundred of them there were, nearly bursting the
high barrier of stone ringing the prison yard, crushing one
another toward the base of the new-hewn gallows. It had taken
half of an hour for Maryssa to weave her way through the
close-packed crowd to gain the place where she now stood,
a coach's length from the wood platform. Yet aside from a
sprinkling of the blood-lusting beasts she'd seen at Tyburn
Tree, the people who pressed close to the tools of English
justice were as dark and menacing as the clouds overhead,
their eyes seething with resentment as they fastened upon the
soldiers surrounding the gallows.

Maryssa shuddered as her eyes caught the flash of gold
rope ripping at its anchoring high upon the wooden post, the
neatly worked noose seeming to jeer at death, while beyond,
four massive horses stood at the ready, tossing their heads

high, their powerful haunches bunching, hooves pawing at the earth. She swallowed hard, Devin's description of the hideous death awaiting him clawing at her mind . . .

Desperate to quell the sick panic forcing bile into her throat, Maryssa turned her eyes to those around her. Nearby a woman knelt upon the ground, murmuring prayers in Latin, while scattered among the sea of people Maryssa could see rosary beads in chilled hands, lips moving in silent pleas to the God who seemed to have deserted his gentle servant.

Rare within this crowd was the thirst for torture Maryssa had witnessed among Sir Ascot's cronies. Most of those who waited eagerly for the spectacle to begin wore either the pointed, hungry faces of those twisted in their minds or the fanatical gleam of those whose religion allowed no tolerance of any outside of its circle.

Even the soldiers who stood guard at the raised platform seemed solemn and silent beneath the buffeting of the wind, as though they knew there was something ignoble about the duty of tending to a holy man's death.

And yet . . . Maryssa's gaze flicked again to the stout horses. The soldiers' task would be finished long before the executioner lowered the noose over Devin's pale blond head.

She slipped one shaking hand beneath the secreting folds of her cloak, her fingers brushing the butt of the gun hidden within, her stomach churning with fear and horror at what she was about to do. She was about to murder Tade's brother, fire a pistol ball deep into Devin Kilcannon's chest.

But she was glad of it . . . glad . . . if in so doing she could spare the loving Devin even an instant of agony at the hands of Sir Ascot's charges. She closed her eyes, dredging up the hideous memory of the girl child Dallywoulde had forced her to witness being burned at an English stake, making herself remember the child's agonized screams, the flames eating at her tender flesh. The winds had made the innocent's execution brutal but swift. For a man who faced the traitor's death the agony could stretch on for six hours.

Maryssa swallowed, forcing back the nausea that clawed at her stomach, forcing back the terror as her gaze flicked to the soldiers who stood at the gallows. Even though she would be damned by her father's vengeful God, she could not let good, gentle Devin meet his death that way.

The buzzings of the crowd nearest the prison's huge barred doors drew Maryssa's gaze to where a cluster of men were passing under the archway that led out of the huge stone edifice. Crowded as she was, nearly at the foot of the gallows, she could see little except the powdered wigs and resplendent uniforms of those escorting the tall form of Devin to his death.

Maryssa's eyes strained to pierce through the maze of faces and shoulders that blocked her view, only moments later catching the tousled white-gold gleam of his hair. A robe of coarse brown wool fell about his narrow shoulders, the wind seeming to breathe color into cheeks bruised and grayed with prison pallor. But as he placed his foot on the steps leading up to where the hoodsman now stood, it was his eyes that stole her breath.

Crystal blue, within battered circles of flesh, they shone, not with peace or with fear, but rather with a strength that seemed to reach invisible hands into the crowd, steeling their courage, their beliefs, their resolve to battle the crushing blows England was attempting to deal the faith the Irish still clung to.

The solemn, gentle planes of the face that had always been so unlike his brother's was now filled with the Kilcannon pride, the courage of embattled ancestors two hundred years dead who had also lost their lives and their land, but never their honor. And yet, beneath the mouth, set firm in determination, beneath the courage that squared Devin's shoulders and steeled his spine as he saw the implements that were to end his life in indescribable agony, Maryssa could see the simple, devout man who should still be bringing comfort to the dying, linking lovers in marriage, christening infants beside a burbling stream.

Aye, Maryssa thought, her eyes burning, christening her own babe when she laid it in Tade's arms. She bit her lip, trying to stem the rising anguish that threatened to shatter her into sobs, steal from her the will and alertness so necessary to releasing Devin from his tormentors.

The crowd surged, snarling and angry, as the stocky Protestant rector began intoning prayers for Devin's "fallen" soul. Then Captain Langworth puffed out his chest and read aloud the charges that had brought Devin to this pass: "Willfully returning from exile, poisoning the minds of the Irish with papist lies, celebrating the outlawed mass in a glen . . ." The enumerating of Devin's "sins and crimes" tore a hysterical laugh from Maryssa.

She gripped the cold metal of the pistol butt in numb fingers, drew the weapon from the waist band of her petticoats, and held it beneath her cloak as Devin stepped toward the man who was to deal him such a hideous death. Desperately she tried to remember those few times she had watched a man fire such a gun, her eyes straying to the soldiers with their swords drawn, weapons ready. A sudden sharp fear assailed her as her mind darted to the distinct possibility that the guards might open fire randomly into the crowd after her pistol discharged. Or perhaps they would level their weapons at the woman who had cheated them of their chance to witness Devin Kilcannon's pain.

If that happened, she would have no time to hold her English heritage before her like a shield, or to announce that she was Bainbridge Wylder's daughter and, as such, was protected from the law that crushed the poor cotters.

A hush fell over the crowd as Devin stepped to the edge of the gallows platform, his eyes sweeping over the faces turned up to him. Maryssa had seen those gentle features warm with concern, sweet with love, troubled as they bore another's inner anguish. She had seen him smile gently into the eyes of little Katie, watched his eyes snap with anger when the sanctity of mass was disrupted by men's shallow prejudices, and seen that beloved face contorted in hopeless misery as he had pleaded with her to spare Tade the death that Devin himself now faced.

His battered, rope-bound hands rose slowly, forming for the last time the sign of the cross.

"Kill the papist scum!" a voice deep in the crowd roared.

"Aye, cast him to the devil that spawned him," another cried in answer.

Maryssa gritted her teeth, expecting more cruel barbs to be flung at the gentle man standing so still upon the platform, but it was as though the seething resentment and simmering anger that lurked beneath the surface of the crowd had stopped the tongues of all but the most reckless.

The hooded executioner stepped toward Devin, grasping his arm to drag him to the noose, but in a gesture achingly like one of Tade's, Devin pulled away from the man's grasp and stepped beneath the dangling rope of his own free will.

Maryssa fumbled with the pistol lock, the metal slick beneath fingers that were trembling and damp with sweat despite the chill. Tears blurred her vision as Devin's eyes met those of the man who was to be his tormentor. Devin's voice drifted like a benediction over those who had gathered. "May God forgive you for this day's work as freely as I do."

Maryssa sank her teeth into her lower lip, tasting blood and grief. "Tade," she choked, "forgive . . ." She started to raise the pistol, but her hands froze as she suddenly caught the full light of Devin's gentle eyes upon her. There was recognition in that soft blue gaze, sorrow, love, and a faith so deep it crushed the hopelessness gripping Maryssa's heart.

"Devin . . ." She breathed his name, tears streaming down her cheeks, her whole body shaking and drained, the pistol seeming to weigh more than the earth itself as she dragged it from beneath her cloak.

She pointed the barrel toward the platform, leveling it at Devin's brown-robed chest, battling to snap back the stiff lock, then curving her finger about the trigger. Her teeth clenched and sick waves of horror crashed over her as she heard the lock snap to the ready. "Forgive me, Tade. Oh, God forgive—"

A scream was torn from her throat, icy terror sweeping through her as something hard cracked into her arm, driving it skyward with a force that nearly tore it from its socket. The pistol exploded, then flew from her hand, the report ripping shrieks from the crowd. The roar of gunpowder from Maryssa's weapon was followed by the crack of another gun on the far side of the gallows. In that one hideous instant, she glimpsed Ascot Dallywoulde's malevolent face, felt his hands crush her arm, but her terror was eclipsed by relief as a cry of shock and pain burst from Devin and his chest blossomed red. Maryssa's eyes snapped, stunned, to where Revelin Neylan's dark head was visible among the masses. She saw his fist flash skyward and heard his cry ring clear, "For God and Ireland!" A hundred guns seemed to explode. Revelin's big body jerked as countless musket balls tore into his flesh.

Hideous sounds of terror and pain erupted from the crowd,

piercing the wind's roar as the prison yard swarmed with soldiers. The men of Langworth's command poured from Rookescommon's huge doors, blocking the gate, spilling from beneath the gallows platform.

Their uniformed bodies blocked Maryssa's view of the gallows, only Captain Langworth's outraged shout telling the people what had transpired on the wooden scaffold. "They've killed the cursed bastard!" he bellowed. "Damn them, they've killed him!"

A sob of relief and sorrow clawed at Maryssa's throat, waves of dizziness threatening to claim her as her stomach roiled under the stench of gunpowder and blood. But the hands digging painfully into the flesh of her arms, shoving her back through the crowd, kept her from sinking to her knees, divesting her of the shimmering comfort of unconsciousness that lured her with its promise of surcease.

"So they've killed the papist devil," Dallywoulde snarled in her ear as he yanked her toward the gate. "Cheated God out of seeing his justice wreaked upon Satan's own. Yet we both know that, but for me, 'twould have been you who buried the ball in Kilcannon's chest, do we not, my *betrothed*?"

Maryssa fought to steady her wobbly legs, her eyes spitting defiance as she raised them to the frigid, fanatical gaze that had always filled her with terror. "Take your hands off me."

"I think not, madam." Dallywoulde's lips curled back malevolently from his teeth. "Not until you enlighten me as to why a weak-bellied coward the like of you would be lapping up the blood spilled at an execution site."

Maryssa clenched her teeth to keep from retching, her hands knotting into fists as she glared at him in defiance. "There was naught going on at Nightwylde." A hinting of Tade's silky sneer crept into her voice. "I thought to seek a bit of diversion."

"Ah, I'd wager there has been much 'going on' at Nightwylde beneath your father's nose, cousin," Dallywoulde purred, motioning for the guard to allow them to pass. "Imagine how stunned I was when Captain Langworth informed me of my betrothed's efforts in the behalf of 'justice,' when he told me that she had gained entry to Devin Kilcannon's cell and had spent time alone with the papist scum." Maryssa paled, stumbling. Dallywoulde's grip on her arm

tightened savagely as he yanked her around to face his piercing gaze. "Tell me, cousin, what would drive an Englishwoman—a Protestant—to risk death or imprisonment on some
Catholic scum's account? Could it be that our martyr, Father
Devin, forgot his vows? Mayhap he cast his chastity to the
winds and bedded you—"

Maryssa's hand flashed out, cracking with all the force she
possessed into that sneering, savage mouth, rage at this
monster's defilement of Devin's goodness dashing away all
but the need to lash out. She heard Dallywoulde's startled
grunt, took feral joy in the sight of the blood that streamed
from his nose. But in a heartbeat that joy changed to terror
stark and raw as Dallywoulde's hand knotted in her hair, pulling her head upward, jerking her face close to his own. Pain
shot through Maryssa's scalp, panic clenching about her chest
as she struggled to break free.

But Ascot held her effortlessly, as though his thin muscles
were honed of rapiers' blades. "Witch!" he hissed. "Sinful
witch, you'll suffer just punishment for that, I swear it. Aye,
and for whatever other shameful secret drove you to take up
that pistol."

"Turn me over to your guards, then," Maryssa challenged,
battling the fear that threatened to overwhelm her. "See what
punishment befalls the daughter of Bainbridge Wylder."

"Daughter, bah!" Dallywoulde spat. "You are naught but
a vehicle through which good Uncle Bainbridge will dispose
of his vast lands. Nay, madam, I'll not cast you to Langworth's dogs, though that would be little more than you deserve. Nay. I am a man of infinite patience when closing for
the kill."

He let go of her hair and dragged his sharp nails down over
the curve of her cheek. "I'll wait but a little while to wreak
my vengeance upon you . . . make you suffer all the more.
Within the week Uncle Bainbridge will send you to England
to wed me, and then . . ." The eagerness and fanaticism
burning in his eyes chilled Maryssa to her soul. "Then I vow
I'll cleanse you of your sins."

Maryssa shuddered as Ascot licked the saliva pooling at
the corners of his lips, his eyes filled with promises of torment and pain, pain that would be worse than the twisting
and tearing of the body—an agony of the spirit.

Her hand strayed down to cup the flat plane of her stomach as if to shelter Tade's child from Dallywoulde's evil eyes and horrible promises. An aching emptiness filled her.

"I'll never be your wife," she said, her gaze meeting his, defiant, strong.

But the laughter that rolled from between those thin lips pierced the horrible numbness Devin's death had wreaked within her, filled her instead with sick dread and terror for the infant she sheltered in her womb, as Ascot bent close. "Oh, aye, my sweet cousin, you'll wed me. You shall know what it means to suffer 'neath a godly man's hands. I swear it to you. Even if my beloved uncle and I are forced to drag you to the altar in chains."

Tade wheeled to face his sister, nearly losing what little balance he had gained as his eyes locked on Deirdre's face. "He's dead!" The cry tore itself from Tade's throat. "Sweet Christ, I let them torture—"

"Nay." Dee rushed to his side, her hands closing around his arm, steadying him, as tears coursed down her cheeks. "He . . . he didn't suffer. Rev—Revelin Neylan shot Dev before they could—could hurt him."

"Neylan? Where—"

"He—he was cut down by the Sassenachs, Tade. They said there were past three hundred of them waiting. If you had gone—"

"If I had gone, Rev Neylan would be alive!" Tade jerked his arm from her grasp, wanting to drive his fist into something, anything, shatter the wooden shutters, feel flesh split beneath his blade. "Sweet Savior, *I* should've taken those bullets," Tade gritted. "Dev was *my* brother! *Mine.*"

"He was my brother, too!" The anguish in Deirdre's voice yanked Tade's gaze back to her face. Her mouth was twisted with torment, her hair a tangle of fire about her waxen cheeks. "But I'm glad 'twas not you who cast away your life at Rookescommon! I couldn't . . . couldn't help Devin, but you . . . to lose you both . . ."

Her words seemed to drive spikes deep into Tade's fogged mind, jarring memories of the night before—the chamber door drawn wide, Maryssa and Deirdre framed in its opening.

"You." Tade felt a fist crush his heart. "You knew that

she was going to seduce and drug me—knew that Sassenach bitch was going to—''

"Don't call her that!" Deirdre blazed. "Don't you ever call her that! She saved your life . . . gave Devin peace before he died. He begged her to stop you, and he told us where to obtain the potion to—"

"Damn him! He had no right—"

"Aye, he did, Tade!" Deirdre shouted. "God knows he had not much when he faced those cursed soldiers, but he did have the right to die knowing that the brother he loved wouldn't fling his life to the same wolves. He had the right to believe that you would live to guard Rachel and the babes, to comfort Da. Aye, and to be father to your own child!''

Bitterness and rage ripped through Tade, his fist lashing out, knocking a platter from the scarred oaken table. "Aye, and did Dev think I'd e'er soil myself with love again? Did he think I would take another woman when I've seen that love leads to lies and betrayal? God's wounds, Maryssa Wylder duped me into abandoning my brother—"

"She saved the man who is father to her babe!"

Spikes drove deep into Tade's soul, the blood draining from his face. "Babe . . . what the hell? . . . ''

"Aye, babe!" Deirdre spat back at him. "That 'heartless bitch' who saved your life is carrying your child.''

A dozen emotions roiled inside Tade, shattering him into fragments of grief, pain, joy, hate, as his mind whirled with images of a tiny pink face, eyes innocent of lies, a mouth as delicate and fragile as the bud of a wild rose. A babe. His babe nested in Maura's womb. It was impossible, wondrous, devastating.

"Where is she?" The demand carried more anger than inquiry.

For the first time Deirdre's eyes faltered away from his face, her hands knotting in her skirts. "I—I know not. Just before dawn she—she came to me, asked me to stay with you until—until the drug's power palled. Then she left.''

"Left? When the hell is she coming back?"

"I don't—don't think she is. Ever.''

"Damn it, Dee!" Tade caught her wrist, jerking her around. "Where did she go?"

"I don't know!" Deirdre cried, her eyes pooling with tears.

"She said—said you'd hate her once you woke! That you'd ne'er forgive her for giving you the drug. I told her I would give it to you, but she wouldn't let me. She said you'd need your family to help you heal after Devin . . . Devin died. She said . . . said you'd hate her.''

"Hate her?'' Rage blazed white-hot within him. "Why the hell would I hate her? She lay with me when she was betrothed to another man, lied to me, drugged me, cheated my brother out of a chance to live, and now—now she's taken my child—*my babe*—and run away. Damn her!'' He drove his boot into the wall with a savagery that cracked the rotted wood.

"Tade!'' Deirdre's alarmed voice fed the fires of his rage. He faced her, his jaw knotting with fury.

"Nay, Dee. Maryssa Wylder stole my brother, broke my pride, but God damn her to hell, she'll not take my babe!'' He hated himself for the catching of a sob beneath his fury. "She'll not bear my babe in some cursed Sassenach mansion to live among the swine who murdered Dev!''

Grief ripped through Tade again, as if the claws of Maryssa's betrayal and Devin's death had gouged out his heart, his soul, gouged out all within him except devastation and rage. Even now, with Devin dead, with Tade's love shattered, she chained him, kept him from satisfying his searing need to bury his sword in Ascot Dallywoulde's belly. Bitterness raked Tade. He dared not wait to drag her from her sanctuary even long enough to send Dev's murderer to the devil, lest Maryssa fling herself into marriage with her cursed cousin. The son or daughter of the heir Kilcannon would not be raised by some Sassenach bastard who was even now most like ensconced in his perfumed London salon, dipping snuff from a jeweled box.

Battling desperately to steady his wobbly legs, Tade stalked to where his cloak lay draped across a squat-legged stool.

"Tade, where—where are you going?'' Deirdre asked tremulously.

"To hell,'' he grated. "But I full intend to drag Maryssa Wylder with me.''

It was past midnight of the second day when he reined Curran to a halt in front of Nightwylde and flung himself from his saddle to crash wide the doors. But the ornate entryway beyond lay dark as a vacant tomb, the single candle borne in the quaking footman's hand casting a haunting glow over the carved ceilings.

"Where is she?" Tade bit out, glaring until the gangly youth nearly dropped his taper.

"Wh-where is who, sir?"

"Miss Wylder. Curse it, I—"

"She and the master, aye, and their guest departed for England but a day past. They—"

"Where were they bound for? What estate?"

"I—I know not. They left in such haste that Master Wylder didn't say. He owns lands sprinkled over half of England."

Tade spat a vicious oath. So Maura had turned coward yet again and had fled to her gilded Sassenach tower. His mouth was set, grim. Nay, if she barred herself in the king's own treasure house she'd not escape him. He'd drag her out of her hiding, secure the safety of his babe, and after . . . after . . . Dallywoulde's face rose in his mind. Tade's mouth slashed into a feral snarl as he spun, almost trampling upon a wee gray puff staring up at him with intrepid blue eyes.

Odysseus.

A shaft of pain and bitterness slashed through him at the memory of the night he had given Maryssa the little beast, and the secret of the Falcon as well. He clenched his teeth. Nay, there would be no more trinkets for Miss Wylder, no more tenderness from a besotted fool. Instead, she would taste of his own pain and rage.

Tade bolted down the stone steps and hurled himself back into his stallion's saddle.

England . . . He pressed his heels into Curran's sides. He'd reach those cursed shores before the week passed, and then . . . then he'd find Maryssa Wylder, find his unborn babe, and crush the blood-hungry beast who had taken Devin's life.

Twenty-One

MARYSSA DUG THROUGH the tiny mound of trinkets on the dressing table, the waning January sun glinting through the window of her chamber at Carradown casting sparkles of crimson, emerald, and blue diamond fire across the walls. The only three jewels her meager store of ornaments had to offer lay piled upon a square of gray cloth that held, as well, her silver-backed brush and one bent shilling.

One shilling, Maryssa thought grimly. 'Twas blessed little to keep her and her unborn babe from starvation until she could find a way to sell her few treasures to the moneylenders and book passage to somewhere, anywhere, far away from the grasp of Ascot Dallywoulde's cruel hands. But the shilling would be enough to support her until she sold the jewels. It would have to be enough.

She clenched her teeth against the pain that shot up her finger as the pin upon an onyx mourning brooch dug deep. One of Tade's curses rose to her lips, and she shut her eyes, but the tears that had once flowed so easily had dried up during the eternity of hours, days, and weeks that she had spent as a prisoner in this hateful room.

A prisoner of her supposed future husband. A prisoner of her father.

She placed the chunk of onyx on the cloth, gathered the frayed fabric into a little bundle, and knotted the ends. They had managed to hold her the six weeks since they had dragged her off of the ship at Liverpool and kept her trapped between them during the jouncing coach ride through the countryside. And from the moment they had breached Carradown's door, they had held her in this gilded cell with naught but the coarsest of food to eat and naught but the dull winter moors to stare at three stories below.

Maryssa's lips twisted bitterly at the memory of that last evening at Nightwylde and of the expression on her father's face when Dallywoulde had dragged her into the chill study. She had vowed then that she would never wed Sir Ascot, never take to husband a man who thirsted only for the sufferings of the innocent, but her father had seemed scarce to hear her, his jowls swelling with indignation, anger, and a stunned surprise. Yet none of the emotions flashing across Bainbridge Wylder's face shocked Maryssa as greatly as the incongruous wisp of pain that had been in her father's dull eyes before he wheeled, turning his gaze away from her, to glare out the window.

"You'll buckle to your duty, damn you," he had spat through stiff lips. "Take as your husband the man I command you to. I'll not bear a cursed woman's defiance yet again, even if I needs must starve you into submission."

Maryssa's mouth compressed into a white line. They had all but starved her, driven her mad, locked alone in this room. Once a day her father had unbolted the door, his broad body blocking the opening, his mouth hard as stone as he demanded to know whether she would bow to his wishes. And after each refusal, the plate slipped in under Dallywoulde's watchful guard bore an even more meager portion of coarse bread, a tinier portion of water. She had endured it as long as she could, until she had begun to fear for the new life she cherished inside her.

Then the morass of grief and listlessness, which had gripped her since the horrible storm-tortured dawn when she had bidden good-bye to Tade Kilcannon, had shifted, giving way to anger and fierce resolve. Her fingers knotted in the white lawn of her chemise as she cast a fulminating glance at the heavy carved door. That evening when her father had entered the chamber, demanding she marry Sir Ascot, she had turned to him, seemingly broken, claiming that she would do whatever he wished if he would but give her something to eat and let her out of this solitary room.

It had been all she could do not to scream when confronted with the grim triumph that creased her father's features, all she could do not to fly into his face, scratching and clawing like an enraged hawk. Yet she had steeled every muscle in her body, hating him as he strode from the room, barring the door behind him.

He had dispatched to her a huge platter of beefsteak, green almond tarts, and pastries dripping with honey. And the next day he had hauled her to the dressmaker to be fitted out with a wedding gown and a costume for the masquerade ball that would serve to announce to all London society that the recalcitrant Miss Wylder had at last agreed to take the godly Sir Ascot in marriage.

Maryssa fought the urge to rend the delicate blue lace from the swan costume that hung now upon the cherrywood door of the armoire. Most likely even now her "caring" father was sitting below, observing the last preparations for the night's soiree, sloshing his finest brandywine into crystal goblets as he toasted the weak will of women with a gloating Sir Ascot. No doubt the two men were reveling in their triumph, Ascot drooling eagerly over the prospect of at last gaining total power over the vast Wylder wealth, and the woman who had humiliated and defied him, and who loathed him as well.

Maryssa shuddered. It had nigh driven her insane . . . his silence over the prison affair, his eyes piercing her, his mouth so cursed smug, so eager, as he quelled her father's wrath at her disappearance on Allhallows night. He had told Bainbridge that as her future husband, he should have the right to crush her unruliness—aye, and he would take great pleasure in doing so when the time came.

Maryssa had felt the menace beneath his words, had felt the cold appraisal of his eyes, aye, and the waiting. It was as if he were savoring the prospect of tearing her secrets from her, anticipating an unholy glee at the chance to wring from her restitution for her "sins." Waiting . . . waiting until she lay completely in his power, his wife, to chasten as he chose.

She lifted her chin defiantly. Let Dallywoulde and her father glory in their coming triumph, let them spin their plans of combining estates, investing their wealth, and wresting her soul from her body. For before this night was past, both would hold naught but castles built of air.

Maryssa picked up the tiny bundle and walked to the tall, carved armoire; her fingers reached out, touching the magnificent garment she was to wear this night. Glistening white satin overskirts parted as gracefully as any gentle wave to reveal a lake-blue silk underskirt caught here and there with rosettes of snowy lace, while upon a wide shelf sat a headdress so cunningly wrought it would have delighted a princess royal. Ice-white feathers swept back in downy wings from the arched neck of a graceful swan mask, eyes of black jet glittering against the white as though they truly held life. 'Twas the most beautiful costume Maryssa had ever owned, 'but, as she hastily stuffed the little pouch into the hem, which she had slit with her scissors earlier that day, she could think of naught except the relief she would feel when the costume lay at the bottom of some distant gutter. For then the ordeal that faced her this night—eluding her ever-alert watchdogs, melting from the crowd of revelers into the darkness—would be over.

She turned, her gaze straying out the mullioned window, her spirits lifting as the nearby rooftops turned rose with the tint of sunset. She let the wispy skirts of her masquerade gown fall back into graceful folds, a fierce resolve and gladness singing in her veins as she thought of the other dress Sir Ascot and her father had commissioned—the wedding gown with its stifling lace and heavy embroidery, which would never leave the shop of the seamstress who even now stitched upon it. By the time the sun rose on the morrow she would be far from Carradown's wintry gloom, far from Sir Ascot and the father who loathed her. Free.

Her fingertips smoothed over the soft swell of her stomach, the slight fluttering of life within infinitely precious, infinitely painful. Free? Nay, never free of the hauntings of tormented emerald eyes, broken pleas that still turned her dreams to nightmares.

"Tade." She formed his name lovingly with her lips, the memory of gasping it through laughter, crooning it in tenderness, crying it out in the fierce grip of passion filling her with aching emptiness. Even here in her silk-lined prison, far away from Donegal's hills, she had heard the tales of the Black Falcon's exploits. It was vengeance, the peaked-faced maids claimed, that drove the blackguard rebel to slash himself and his band of men in a fiery swath of fury across the emerald hills. Vengeance for the death of a common priest, fury against a woman who had betrayed the rebel rogue. And it could only be Satan himself who shielded the brigand in raids that should have left any mortal man dead.

Maryssa clasped her arms against her tender breasts, a tightness gripping her chest. Tade . . . lightsome, loving Tade . . . robbed of Devin's steadying hand, robbed of faith, of trust, left only with the searing imprint of her own betrayal to scar him. In her endless days at Carradown not an hour had passed in which Maryssa had not closed her eyes to clutch the memory of Tade's face when he had first made love to her, or to cherish the image of his laughter the night he had stood naked, hauling her from the lake.

Her hands had ached with wanting to touch him, her mouth with wanting to kiss him, her body turning traitor as well, tormenting her with dreams of their joinings, only to jeer at her and snatch him away or whirl her again into the prison yard at Rookescommon, Devin's pale face shifting until it was Tade who stood so gallantly beneath the hangman's noose.

But no matter how she fared once she escaped her father's grasp, she could never go to Tade, find him, hold him. She had lost him forever in that instant when she had emptied Mab Hallighan's potion into his leathern jack of ale.

Her heart twisted, the pain that never fully left her cutting blade-sharp, but she straightened her spine, her hand splaying again over the place where her babe lay safe. Nay, she had more of their loving to cling to than Tade did, and she would dare any danger, confront any nemesis to guard this tangible symbol of the glory they had shared.

A trickle of icy foreboding slid down her spine as Sir Ascot's skeletal face rose to haunt her. If ever the sinister knight suspected that she was carrying a child . . . if ever her father discovered that she sheltered Tade Kilcannon's bastard within her womb . . . She shuddered. The babe within her was lusty, strong, swelling its gentle world until soon even raising the waistlines of her skirts would not conceal it from those who would crush it if they knew it lived inside her.

Maryssa's eyes roved to the window, the parcel of clothes, two treasured books, and a faded blue ribbon that had decked a tree castle an eternity ago, catching her eye. 'Twas nigh time for the maid to come to aid her in dressing. She would have to trust the deepening shadows of sunset to hide the bundle of clothes from suspicious eyes until she could retrieve it.

Hastening to where the parcel lay upon the floor, she picked it up and went to the window. The icy latch was stiff as she shoved it upward and flung the sash wide. How many times had she opened that window during the days she had been held captive, staring down to the freedom of the street below. It had beckoned her, tempted her with memories of Tade's reckless scalings of Nighwylde's walls, the shallow grooves cut into Carradown's stone seeming to mock her, threatening her with a fall that would crush her spine or drive the babe from her womb if she were to dare it. She had never had much courage, and the life within her was too precious to risk.

The winter wind swept in, so cold it burned her cheeks and her breasts through the thin chemise as she held the bundle over the ledge and let it drop the three floors to the ground. It had scarce struck the mounds of snow below when Maryssa stiffened at the sound of quick, light footsteps approaching down the hall.

Hastily, quietly she pulled the window shut and darted over to sit upon the dainty chair beside the dressing table. She heard the bolt being slid to the side, heard the door latch click open, beckoning her to freedom.

Like carved marionettes trapped on the strings of a sinister puppeteer, the figures moved across the ballroom floor, their bodies cloaked in dominoes, faces obscured by velvet masks, as though something hideous lay beneath, something that lurked about brittle smiles tainted with cunning, or the cynical curl of cruel lips. It was as though in the mystery of the masking every feral instinct within the guests at Carradown had risen to the surface, leaving all, from the most elegant powered dandy to the dowdiest spinster, hungry to feed upon secrets and weaknesses, to stalk like savage wolves anything that smacked of intrigue.

Maryssa's gaze swept surreptitiously about the crowded floor, her nerves knotting, tangled through with foreboding. Aye, the guests Sir Ascot had invited to celebrate his betrothal had more the look of circling beasts than of peers deep in revelry. And the focus of their attention—for good or ill— was the notorious woman who had left England in disgrace and had now returned to wed the notable Sir Ascot Dallywoulde.

Even the supposed anonymity of the masquerade had failed to shield Maryssa, the whisperings as to the swan's identity having begun the moment she entered the room. And from the instant she had first heard the murmurings, felt the weight of hundreds of eyes upon her, Maryssa had sensed who had penetrated her disguise and revealed her identity. The cunning Sir Ascot had no doubt known that by exposing her thus she would be constantly watched by a guard more thorough even than the bolt upon her bedchamber door. Even now, the loathsome knight was openly gloating over the success of his plan.

She hazarded a glance to where Ascot hovered near her, dressed as an eerie winged moth, his hair powdered pale as a corpse's face, three black patches affixed in a sinister pattern beneath the edge of his crimson mask. Though Bainbridge Wylder had been lulled by Maryssa's sudden capitulation, Ascot Dallywoulde had stripped away her soul with his evil eyes, delved beneath her facade of obedience, to see the hopes she still harbored of escaping his grasp.

Aye, and through it all—the endless whirling about the floor in minuet and quadrille, the uncounted cups of ratafia, the tiny cakes, even the sly threats couched in flattery that made her cheeks flush, her palms sweat—she could feel Ascot Dallywoulde laughing inside, sneering at her desperation with the sadistic glee of a cruel boy watching a nestling squirm upon a spike.

"Do you remember, cousin, the last time you attended a ball at my side?" Ascot's breath ghosting across her neck sent a shudder down Maryssa's spine. "The night you dared inform Lord Newley that anyone who lusted after the suffering of a child—even, as I recall, a child accused of witchcraft—was more a monster than anything that could be spawned of hell itself?''

Maryssa's gaze leaped to his face, her mouth set in challenge. ''Nay, Sir Ascot, your memory serves you not well,'' she observed with acid sweetness. ''I told Lord Newley that *he* was a monster for wagering on how long 'twould take the flames to devour a child. It was you I accused of being a beast more vicious than any that could be spawned of the devil.''

Dallywoulde's sneer cracked into an ugly scowl, his eyes narrowing to slits. ''Tell me, madam, opposed as you are to the pleasures of the stake and the block, what was it that lured you to that yard in Rookescommon prison before we left that accursed island?''

Maryssa flinched, her gaze snapping up to meet his, the hungry, vengeful expression on his spectral features making her shield her silk-veiled stomach with her hand.

''Milady?'' his voice was thin, sharp, rife with veiled menace.

''I . . . 'tis none of your concern.''

''None of my concern why my betrothed was wielding a pistol aimed at a papist's black heart?'' He bent close, his cold hand bruising her wrist. ''Certainly even *you* could not be fool enough to think I'd forgotten your trespasses? Aye, or''—his lips curled into an ugly smirk—''forgiven them. I assure you that once we're wed—''

''Surely milady could wring forgiveness out of a stone if she had need to.'' The voice was deep, lilting, yet harshened with a chill cynicism that catapulted Maryssa's heart to her toes. She spun away from Sir Ascot's masked features, a giant fist clenching about her lungs as her gaze locked on a black silken hood, the glow from the chandeliers overhead glinting silver upon the embroidered outline of a falcon's sharp talons.

''Ta—'' She strangled the cry that rose in her throat, terror driving deep into her breast, coupled with a devastating joy as eyes pierced her through slits in the hood, burning eyes as green as a Donegal glen, yet hard, so hard they tore at her soul. *Tade*, her heart screamed, pulses thundered. *Oh, God, Tade.* But she could scarcely breathe, scarcely think, held as she was by their fierce emerald light.

A harsh laugh grated from Sir Ascot's fleshless lips, the

sound cutting through Maryssa's shock, sending dread rushing through her veins. "Well carried out, Sir Falcon," Ascot sneered, his fingers plucking at the folds of Tade's mantle. "All you need to complete the costume is a noose about your neck."

She saw the corner of Tade's mouth crook in a mockery of his once-lightsome grin. "The rope has not been woven that will set the Black Falcon of Donegal to dangling 'neath a gibbet. What think *you*, milady?"

Maryssa felt the blood drain from her face, her fingers instinctively reaching out, catching Tade's gauntleted hand. "I—I heard tell of the brigand when I was in Ireland," she struggled to keep the tremor out of her voice. "I can but say I am most glad he is across the sea in Ireland."

"I'll wager you are." There was menace in Tade's voice, silken danger, but Maryssa knew she'd accept whatever his fury would deal her if she could but draw him away from Sir Ascot's cunning gaze.

Her eyes slanted a hasty glance at Ascot, her fingers trembling upon Tade's hand as she saw the calculating light that had entered Dallywoulde's soulless eyes.

"You are acquainted, sir, with my betrothed?" Dallywoulde said.

She saw Tade's cloaked shoulders stiffen, his mouth twist, bitter beneath the edge of his hood. "We met once, sir, but I know her not at all." The words were a small, sharp dagger in Maryssa's heart, and as that implacable green gaze tore away from hers, regarding the masked Sir Ascot, raw horror bolted through her, fear that Tade had not come seeking her at all, but rather to wreak his vengeance upon the man who had murdered his brother. If Tade knew who her betrothed was, if he knew the man whose betrothal was being celebrated here this night . . .

Desperately she raked through her memories, clinging to the knowledge that with Tade she had never named Dallywoulde as the man who was to wed her, had only spoken of some nebulous cousin to whom she had been promised. But the banns had been announced, and the journals had proclaimed the match. Tade had but to ask a few questions of the guests to discover the full horror of her betrayal. Yet the hatred within his green eyes seemed fixed solely upon her, while another emotion—anger, mayhap—was evident in his regard of Dallywoulde's crimson-masked face.

"P-please, Sir Rogue," she said, turning to Tade, frantic to draw him away from the danger she saw brewing. "I know you not in your masquerade guise, but 'twould . . . 'twould be passing diverting to attempt to discover it in the midst of a minuet."

"Diverting?" The bitterness in Tade's voice dragged tears into her throat. "Naught would please me more than to *divert* you, milady."

"Are you not too weary to expend yourself upon the dance floor, beloved?" Sir Ascot's eye glinted warning. "I vow, your eyes seem a trifle glazed, and your hands . . . do they not tremble?"

Maryssa stilled her fingers where they lay upon Tade's and battled to force a smile to her stiff lips. " 'Tis—'tis the mystery of the masking," she said. "And, mayhap, I confess, a cup too many of ratafia. 'Twill do me much good, I think, to take a turn about the floor, if . . . if Monsieur Black Falcon is willing . . ."

"When, pray tell, did my willingness e'er come before your desires, milady?"

Her fingers gouged deep into Tade's leather-veiled wrist in warning, and she felt an urge to slap him for his reckless words as she saw Dallywoulde's chill eyes go frigid, his lips whitening.

"Go then, cousin, against my wishes," Sir Ascot said, fingering the hilt of the dress sword that hung at his side. " 'Twill not be long before the ring upon your finger will compel you to be wise."

A dangerous glint sparked emerald in Tade's eyes; the muscles beneath Maryssa's fingers were tense, straining. "One could hardly accuse Miss Wylder of being wise," Tade said, shooting Sir Ascot a derisive glance. Maryssa's heart caught in her throat as the two men's gazes clashed, fire to ice. In desperation, she tugged at Tade's cloak-draped arm, fighting to draw him away from what, she sensed in an instant, would flare into a war past reason.

"Please," she begged under her breath. "They—the music is about to begin. Please."

For long seconds fraught with insolence and daring, Tade

held the Englishman's gaze until the first strains of the violin moved him to turn to Maryssa and sweep her a mocking bow. "Your pardon, sir," he flung out to Dallywoulde with an arrogant sneer. " 'Twould be unforgivable to disappoint such a lovely partner."

Maryssa was nearly sick with relief as his hand curved beneath her elbow, propelling her out into the midst of the dancers. The eyes that had been turned upon her with curiosity before now gaped through the hundreds of masks with varying degrees of intrigue, envy, and approval, all the women in the room appraising the magnificent spread of Tade's shoulders beneath his cloak, the unmistakable animal grace in a walk that was purely masculine, sensual.

But the simpering belles were not close enough to the dashing "highwayman" to see the emotions that seethed in his eyes. Aye, Maryssa thought, panic fluttering in her breast, if they had been able to espy the tempest roiling beneath the slits in that black hood, even the most man-hungering among them would have fled the ballroom.

She stumbled to a halt, only Tade's hand on her arm saving her from smashing into the back of a stout matron in a purple domino as they entered the line of dancers. The strains of the minuet drifted across the floor, and the guests began to float about the wide expanse of marble to the dulcet melody. Maryssa's feet felt wooden, all sensation centered at the point where Tade Kilcannon's hand held hers. His touch was achingly familiar, his fingers warm even through the black leather gauntlet. But the way his hand held hers was devastatingly impersonal, stiff, as though he could barely stomach being forced to touch her. The fleeting joy she had felt when she first saw him—the tiny stirring of hope that he had softened, that he now understood why she had been compelled to slip the potion into his ale—had vanished, leaving a slow-burning anger at the suspicion that he might well have stormed all the way from Donegal to do naught but rail at her. Aye, and in his eagerness to lambaste her he had thrown himself into greater peril than he could ever imagine.

"Tade, are you crazed?" she snapped beneath the tones of the music. "Coming here like this, dressed as the Falcon? 'Tis insanity!"

"Nay, milady, insanity is what I was in the grips of the night I let you bed me at the Hangman's Fool."

Shame and guilt fired her cheeks as visions of the last time they had made love flashed across her memory—Tade's hands frantic upon her while her mouth rained kisses on his naked flesh. Her gaze flashed up to where his mouth slashed in an unyielding line beneath the shadow of his three-cornered hat, his eyes giving her no quarter as he forced her into the patterns of the dance.

The laugh that grated across his lips was harsh, hard. "Come now, Maura, no need to play the blushing innocent. 'Twas quite an admirable seduction for one so lacking in experience. And we both know I've been party to enough *affaires de coeur* to judge."

Pain jolted through Maryssa soul-deep. "Tade, I—," she started to explain, then stopped, knowing that naught she could say would drive the scorn from those eyes. Yet she had done the right thing—would do it again if fate allowed her to play the scene over. Her chin tilted up in shaky defiance.

"Very wise, my love, to keep your lies to yourself," Tade said. " 'Twould be a waste of breath, now that the veils of love have been ripped from my eyes. Of course, considering the myriad betrayals you wreaked, I had thought that you might feel some anguish over Devin's death. But"—his gaze swept the marble moldings, the chandeliers dripping with hundreds of candles, the richness of her gown—" 'tis evident you've not been wasting away with either grief or guilt."

Maryssa clenched her teeth, hurt and indignation welling up inside her. "I've grieved for Devin," she said. "Aye, and I've mourned . . . mourned what I lost that night when I—I eased you into sleep."

The grating, acid laugh that fell from Tade's lips seared her, making her snatch up her fragile defenses, drawing them about the raw pain that clung to her heart.

"God's feet, milady, you've learned to speak most prettily. 'Eased me to sleep,' did you, like a mother loving her babe? Only 'twas no lullaby you spun for me, was it? Nay, 'twas a drug slipped into my drink, then urged upon me with the wiles of a body dressed in harlot's garb. Christ, when I think now of the joy I felt when first I saw you in that doorway

. . . When I think of how I made love to you, flung myself into the jaws of your trap, it turns my cursed stomach."

The tears Maryssa thought had dried up forever stung at the back of her lids, her throat constricting, but she turned her gaze back up to Tade's, struggling to keep the strains of anguish from her voice. "You put yourself to a deal of trouble to inform me how reprehensible you think me. Now that I can carry that wonderful gift through the rest of my life, 'twould be well, I think, for you to leave."

"Leave?" Tade snorted derisively. "You'd like that, would you not? To have me just vanish from your gilded palace, vanish from your life like some infernal hero in a book you've had done with? But you'll not be quit of me so easily, Miss Wylder, now that you've taken my brother and tried to rob me of my—"

Tade stopped, his hard eyes catching the eager light in a nearby dandy's face as the spindle-shanked man nigh fell over his portly dance partner in an effort to discern what was said.

Maryssa could see the effort it required of Tade to crush whatever words he had been about to rake her with, and the stark emotion and fury that twisted his mouth terrified her. A gale was stirring within those emerald eyes, a storm past wisdom and reason. Enraged as he was, it would be but a heartbeat before the listenings of the whole ballroom would not be able to keep his fury from breaking free.

Maryssa's gaze jumped to where Ascot stood engaged in conversation with the hateful Lord Newley. If she could but maneuver Tade off of the floor, mayhap to the terrace doors on either side of the room, she could get him to the relative safety of the chill winter night beyond. There, away from quizzing glasses and ears sharp with curiosity, she could let him spend his fury, then storm out of her life, satisfied by the knowledge that he had exacted whatever hurt and pain he seemed to think he owed her.

The patterns of the dance brought them close to a beckoning doorway, and Maryssa's hand tightened upon Tade's. "No doubt you have much you'd like to say to me," she said, trying to keep the hurt from edging her voice. "And after—after you've gone to such trouble to come and—and rage at me, I'd not want to deprive you of the satisfaction."

"The king's whole army couldn't deprive me of this satisfaction, milady."

The silken threat made Maryssa's knees quiver, but she jutted her chin out belligerently. "Fine. Does your pride demand that you publicly humiliate me, or would you deign to seek privacy upon the terrace?"

His gaze flicked to where her costume swept low over bared shoulders, and she saw his mouth open, as if to object, but in an instant he gritted his teeth. "Milady's pleasure is my own." Sketching her a bow, he led her from the line of dancers to the doorway beyond.

Hazarding a glance back at Dallywoulde's powdered head, Maryssa skittered behind the shield of dancers and darted out the doorway.

The chill air nipped at her shoulders, the tops of her breasts, but the terrace, sheltered as it was in the lee of Carradown's walls, bordered by a row of pillars tangled with vines, protected any who walked there from the full force of winter's kiss.

She heard the terrace door click shut behind her and stood silent, her back toward Tade as she waited for his rage to be unloosed. But he said naught, only the weight of his gaze pressing down upon her.

She clenched her teeth to keep them from chattering, vowing she'd not be the first to break the suffocating silence or reveal how deeply the chill cut her, but a betraying shiver shook her shoulders. A curse tore itself from Tade's mouth, and in an instant she felt something flow about her exposed shoulders. Tears stung at her eyes as Tade's cloak enfolded her. The garment was still warm from his own body, and the fabric that had draped his broad shoulders was scented of wind and recklessness and despair.

"Tade . . ." She wheeled to face him, hoping, praying, that mayhap the flicker of emotion hinted at in his gesture to warm her might also whisper of deeper feelings—hidden, yet still there. But when her eyes caught his, questioning, achingly hopeful, the wild fluttering in her heart died.

"Nay, Maura," he sneered. "I'm not prey any longer to that cursed vulnerability you're able to call to your face. I'd not give a damn if you froze to death, milady, excepting one small difficulty. Even we Irish brigands have an aversion to watching the mothers of our babes court death of the grippe.''

Maryssa's breath caught, her hands flashing to where the slight swell of her stomach lay hidden beneath her gown. The unholy light gleaming in Tade's eyes made her take a step backward. ''Babe . . . Tade, I—''

''Nay, milady, save your confessions for the parson once I drag you down to the Fleet Street dens. I've been tearing across half of England as if hell were at my heels in an effort to find you, and I have precious little stomach for more of your lies. Six of your thieving father's estates I had to scour before I arrived here. And I might even still be on my way to Yorkshire, had I not had the good fortune to run afoul of some farmer who was carrying his late-harvested apples to Carradown's kitchen for the fete tonight.''

''Tade—''

''This much I swear to you, *Maura-love,*'' he fair spat the endearment, threaded through with scorn. ''The child of the heir Kilcannon will be bred up in no Sassenach's lair, a bastard born with naught but a lying mother and some weakling English fop to play sire to it.'' Tade's fingers caught her chin, yanking her face up until the full fury of his green gaze seared her. ''Nay, my son or my daughter will be born with a sword in its hand, weaned on tales of Devin's death and Sassenach treachery. Aye, this child will grow strong and brave—''

''And full of the hatred that burns now in you? I remember when you despised the hate your father felt for all things, all people, English, and I remember when your dearest friend was of Sassenach blood,'' Maryssa cried, fierce protectiveness raging like a tigress within her. ''I would have given my babe into your care then without fear, rejoicing—rejoicing that it would have you as father. But now . . . Nay, Tade, I'll not sacrifice my babe to your hate.''

''Hate? You dare accuse *me* of hate? You who know naught of what love is? Real love. A love that dares sacrifice all—even life, if need be—to shelter the one who has captured your heart?''

''Oh, nay, Tade.'' Her voice was soft, so soft. ''I know naught of a love that would cast all to the wind to save the one who has captured your heart.''

She saw his gaze falter for but an instant, his hand flashing up to rake at his hood-covered hair. The tricornered hat tumbled off. He cursed.

Damn her, his mind railed. Damn her for standing there, so pale, so beautiful, aye, and so cursed proud, with her eyes battling tears, and the mouth that had lied to him, cheated him of his honor, trembling with sorrow. Tade glared at her, hating himself for the sudden need he felt to reach out, draw her into his arms, cradle the babe that nested within her in the broad palm of his hand. In his mind he could hear once again Deirdre's pleas and explanations as she begged him to understand, weaving a picture of Maryssa's selflessness, love, and respect for Devin's last wishes in the place where Tade's heart had seen only lying, treachery, betrayal. Nay, his heart cried, Maura *had* betrayed him, through her plot to keep him away from Dev, but even more through her plan to steal the babe that he, Tade, had conceived in her.

He spun around and slammed his fist into a pillar twined with vines as lifeless as his faith, his trust. He turned his head to glower over one shoulder at Maryssa who stood like a tortured Madonna in the wintry moonlight. "You're coming back to Ireland with me," he bit out, "as my wife."

"Your wife?"

"Aye. Until the babe is born you'll stay with Rachel and Da, and then"—he looked away, unable to bear the suffering in her face—"then, if you want to crawl back to your puling English cousin, I'll do naught to stop you."

"But my child—"

"Nay, Maryssa, *my* child. *My* child will stay in the mountains your thrice-damned Sassenach father stole from him."

"Damn you, Tade Kilcannon!" Anger tore at Maryssa's voice, and he wheeled to see that vulnerable, delicate mouth contorted in pain and fury. "If you think for an instant I'll condemn my babe to live with a father who despises the woman who bore it, you're mad! I spent my life paying for my mother's supposed sins. My father was scarce able to bear the sight of me. My babe—"

"Stay in Ireland, then!" Tade, despising himself for the stirring of hope that raked his heart, steeled himself against it. "Raise the babe beside me to make certain I don't abuse it, as the saintly Bainbridge Wylder abused you!" The words were venom. " 'Tis none of my concern what you do with your precious life, milady. But the babe will know itself to be my son or daughter. Will know that the blood of Irish kings runs in its veins. Aye, and will know that it has as well the love of the man who rides as the Black Falcon."

"Damn you, Tade—"

"Don't waste your blasted curse. I've been damned since the moment I met you," he grated. "But you will not have to endure my company overlong. Since neither of us can stand the sight of the other and seeing as you and Dev, in your infinite wisdom, believe me capable of naught but riding the highroads, I'll take to the night with a vengeance. Mayhap you'll be lucky, and I'll be snared by some Sassenach bullet."

"Nay, milord Falcon, 'twill not be so quick and painless for you."

Tade heard Maryssa cry warning, wheeled at the first purred syllable behind him. His primal instinct was to hurl himself at the speaker, but in the fleeting instant of a heartbeat, his muscles tensed and only his lightning reflexes saved him from impaling himself upon the sharp-honed point of a sword.

Impotent rage seared through him, his gaze leaping to the six men who had trapped him within the crook of the terrace walls, pistols in hand, faces savage. And Tade cursed himself for the folly that had robbed him of instincts sharpened in scores of skirmishes and a hundred night raids, raging inwardly that he had heard naught, known naught, but the need to scourge Maryssa. Icy, evil, the eyes of the man who wielded the sword locked upon Tade through the crimson mask that had veiled the face of Maryssa's cousin.

The sword jabbed toward him, piercing the flesh on Tade's chest. A stinging pain cut him, but it was naught compared to the anguish on Maryssa's delicate face.

"Nay!" She screamed fiercely, stumbling forward in an attempt to dodge between him and the point of the blade, but a shadow-veiled hand flashed out, yanking her away.

Tade's furious gaze slashed to the man who held her, and he was sickened when he saw Bainbridge Wylder's rage-bloated face.

But before he could lunge for the hated Englishman, rough hands clamped over Tade's arms from behind, dragging him back, holding him captive. He struggled but an instant and stopped, glaring into the face of Maryssa's cursed father.

"Let her go, Wylder." Tade's voice was velvet soft, menacing.

"The trollop is my daughter. I'll do with her what I—"

"Nay, Uncle Bainbridge. 'Tis I who will have the privilege of dealing with my beloved cousin—and I shall take the greatest of pleasure in breaking her."

Raw rage and helplessness tore through Tade as those cold eyes raked Maryssa, then shifted to Tade's own concealed face.

"But first"—evil lips curled into a sneer—" 'tis time the world learned what lowling murderer cowers beneath this Falcon's hood."

Tade's head snapped back as a blunt hand closed upon the black silken mask, ripping it from his head. He glared defiance at the men who now gaped at him, the wintry wind stinging his cheeks.

"Kilcannon," Wylder choked, paling as though a specter had risen to haunt him. "A cursed Kilcannon."

Chill blue eyes narrowed, and 'twas as though Tade could see some eerie candle flame flicker in the swordsman's mind. "Kilcannon," he sneered. "Kilcannon was the name of the devil-priest at Rookescommon." Tade saw the cunning eyes flick to Maryssa. "You were trying to save your lover's kin from pain with the pistol you wielded!"

The purring, triumphant voice pierced Tade's heart. "Pistol . . . ," Tade echoed, a sick dread and certainty twisting in his gut.

"Aye." Thin lips curled, and in his gloating smirk Tade could feel the pull of hell. "Imagine my shock at finding my weak-bellied betrothed among the crowd that had gathered to gloat over the cursed priest's torture. And then to see her bring a pistol to bear at the condemned's chest . . ."

"Who are you, damn it?"

" 'Tis only fair that you should know." The man smirked again, shade-pale fingers catching the string of the crimson mask. "Though my face should be seared upon your papist soul."

The velvet-edged mask of blood red loosened in the man's pale fingers, and the rage Tade had felt before burst into hate and fury so overwhelming he nigh threw himself upon the sword to reach the throat of the man who held it. He caught a glimpse of Maryssa tearing away from her father, lunging toward Tade as the mask fell away. Features, pale as a vision from hell, seared into Tade's soul, tearing at him with the memory of Devin's gentle face.

Dallywoulde.

"You," Tade snarled. "Sweet Christ, you murdering bastard!" With a bellow of rage, Tade broke free of the arms that restrained him, his whole body roiling, half-crazed at the sight of Devin's killer.

He hurled himself at Dallywoulde as Maryssa yanked at the sword, preventing the blade from slashing Tade's side. The silvery edge bit flesh, but he scarce felt the pain; he felt naught but the need to crush the leering Dallywoulde's throat.

His hands closed over that thin neck, squeezing, crushing, but before he could wreak his vengeance, something hard cracked down, glancing off of the base of his skull. Blinded by rage and blood, he staggered, then fell, glimpsing the heavy toe of a boot arching toward him. The blow slammed into his ribs and sent him sprawling on the terrace stones, driving all breath from his lungs.

"Nay! Tade!" He heard Maryssa's agonized cry, felt her hands catch him, hold him, as he struggled to right himself.

He caught a glimmer of steel aimed at his heart, saw Dallywoulde's cold serpent's eyes narrow, gauging the kill, but the arms that curved around Tade tightened fiercely, the voice he heard but inches from his ringing ears penetrating even the blinding pain that threatened to overwhelm him.

"Kill him and I'll announce to all here that I am carrying Tade Kilcannon's child." Maryssa's words were whisper soft, yet hard as the point of the sword that gouged the flesh of Tade's chest. "Aye, Father, I will."

Tade jerked his gaze into focus, seeing the strained, puffy face of Bainbridge Wylder beside Dallywoulde's evil one. Wylder's face was as gray as old clay, his eyes burning with rage and a kind of sick horror.

"With child!" Wylder choked out. "Dear God, nay . . ."

Tade struggled to his feet, pain driving fiery spikes into his ribs, rage at the Englishman and self-loathing roiling inside him. But the point of the sword scribed deeper, biting

into the sheath of muscle beneath his lawn shirt as the loathsome knight's minions closed in on him. "Damn you," he
grated. "I swear I'll see you dead!"

"Nay, milord Falcon. You'll see me gloating as you dangle
from a hangman's noose. Aye, and whilst you go to meet
Satan, you'll know full well that your whore and your bastard
lie beneath my boot heel to be crushed as I see fit."

"Touch Maura or my child and I vow I'll kill you if I have
to fight my way out of the grave."

"Is that so, Black Falcon?" Dallywoulde chuckled. "Even
here in England I have heard the legends your ignorant Irish
barbarians weave about you. The tales of the cloak that melts
you into night, and of the sorcerer's spell that changes each
bullet that strikes you into a measure of greater strength. But
those legends will die when you swing from a gallows."

"Nay, Dallywoulde. For each priest you murder, for each
schoolmaster you hang in Donegal's hills, a hundred more
the like of me will rise up to fight you. And I will be at their
head. I swear it by God's own blood."

"Think you the God of might and justice would allow one
like you to defeat his servant? Nay, Kilcannon. You'll burn
in hell after you suffer the death I intended for that cursed
priest. And your harlot will spend her life paying for the sins
she committed in your bed." He jerked his head toward the
men circled around them. "Take him to Newgate," Dallywoulde said, "to await the traitor's death."

"Nay, Ascot, Father, for the love of God!" Maryssa's cry
ripped at Tade's heart and her hands clutched him as Dallywoulde's minions closed about him, their eyes lusting for
blood.

"Maura, 'tis all right. 'Twill be all right, love," he tried
to soothe her as the burly arms ripped him from her grasp.
His eyes clung to hers as someone bound his hands, and he
prayed she could see even half the emotions that still warred
within him. "Maura-love." His voice rasped from his throat.
"Sorry . . . I'm so—"

"Tade!" She struggled desperately against her father's
crushing grasp as Dallywoulde shoved Tade through the
breach in the pillars. One final flash of grief-laden emerald
eyes caught her, held her, as Tade stumbled forward. Then

the night seemed to consume him, engulf all except the echoes of savage, hungry taunts.

She pressed her fingers to her lips, stifling a sob as rage-driven hands closed about her, dragging her relentlessly off the terrace to a secluded door. She fought against her father's bruising grip, terror and horror clawing inside her, the dark, drafty stairway and the hall above it filled with images of Tade beneath Ascot's cruel hands, helpless in the twisted knight's power. Her eyes fastened on a doorway, carved gold with candlelight against the dimness, and the terror that had filled her exploded into a desperation fiercer than any she'd ever known.

"Father, don't . . . don't lock me in," she pleaded, as Bainbridge Wylder stalked into the chamber that had been her prison. "Tade . . . I have to go to him . . . help him. If you love me at all, if you ever loved me, don't—don't let Tade die."

"Die?" Bainbridge roared, flinging her into the chamber, cracking her hard into the carved post of the bed. "Would I had murdered the bastard when he was half-breeched before—before he could make a whore out of you. A whore . . . Damn you, girl, how could you lie with Kilcannon scum?"

"I love him!"

"Love him? The spawn of some cursed cotter with naught but a mud shack to dwell in?"

"The son of the rightful earl of Nightwylde." Maryssa saw her father flinch as she spun to face him, the terror that had crushed her in its grip bursting into fury and hate as feral as that of a wild thing defending its mate. "Aye, Father, I know the truth. You stole Tade's birthright, tried to crush his father, a man you once called friend. And if I lived with Tade in naught but one tiny room, I'd be richer far than I've e'er been weighed down with the wealth you stole."

"Close your mouth, girl!" Bainbridge roared, advancing on her in white-fisted fury. "Close it or, before God, I'll beat you until—"

"Do it! Beat me!" Maryssa challenged, eyes flashing, jaw clenched. " 'Twould be the first honest emotion you've e'er shown me! You've hated me from the time I was a babe, loathed me, locked me out of your life, your heart. But Tade

gave me all that he was. He made me feel for the first time
in my life that I was more than just some gawky, shy burden
to be borne by those around me.''

Even through her blinding anger and fear, she could see a
long-buried pain streak across her father's stunned features,
the flicker of an emotion she couldn't name. But the words
he spat out were harsh, laced with hate. ''He planted a bastard in your belly.''

''Aye! And I thank God for it with every breath I draw!''

Even in the gray shadows she saw her father's hand flash
up and arc toward her, but she flinched not at all, glaring at
him, defiant and strong as his palm cracked into her cheek.

''I'll shelter no bastard bred of a Kilcannon!'' Bainbridge
raged. ''I'll cast it to the poorhouse! I'll—''

''If you dare so much as touch my babe, I'll drive a knife
into your heart.'' Maryssa met his gaze, her voice more
promise than threat. ''Ne'er in all my life have you purported
to love me. Not once when I was a child—when I needed
you, reached out to you—were you there. I always thought
'twas I who was lacking, that you saw something horrible
within me, that I was ugly, bad, awkward. But I'm not a
terrified child anymore, Father. Now I know 'tis you who are
twisted, not I. And finally I can admit that I hate you for the
years I spent aching for your love. I hate you now, and I
always will.''

Her father's face washed gray, and despite the raw fury
slashed across his mouth, she could see the barest shade of
uncertainty in his dull eyes before he hardened them again
into loathing. ''Well, now you'll have good reason to despise
me, girl!'' he said. ''You'll stay in this room until your peasant lover lies dead. Then, if he'll have you, you'll wed Ascot.''

''I'll follow Tade to the gallows first.''

She struggled to keep the horror and helplessness from
engulfing her, fought to keep the memory of Dallywoulde's
eager face at bay, but it seemed to jeer at her from every
corner, drooling for Tade's blood.

Her father stalked to the door, one beefy white hand
clenching upon the latch. ''Nay, daughter, you'll not follow
Kilcannon to the gallows, but you may well wish you had.
You'll do as I bid you or I'll make the weeks you were barred

in here seem like heaven. I want naught but to be rid of you—
never to suffer looking at your face again, Mary.''

Maryssa started at the sound of her mother's name, and
her chin rose, defiant and proud, braced by the courage and
kindness Tade's memories had brought to the image of the
mother she'd never known. ''You can't terrorize me any more
than you could my mother.''

''Terrorize her? Sweet God, I loved her and she betrayed
me—took the side of a cursed Kilcannon against me. Damn
you, wench, you'll not scream at me from Mary's face.'' He
took a step toward her, fists clenched, teeth bared. He
stopped. ''Nay, you'll be gone from my sight soon enough.
Gone. Ascot will see to that. He vowed . . . vowed he'd take
you away.''

''You can't lock me in your cursed prison any longer, Father. Tade freed me—''

''Your Kilcannon scum will do naught to free you once
he's in his grave. And if the cursed bastard is right in what
he claims, if a thousand like him rise from Donegal's dust,
not one will be able to reach you here.''

The door crashed shut, the sound echoing despair through
Maryssa's heart as she heard the bolt slam home.

She felt tears burn at her eyelids, felt desperation ripping
away the strength that had stayed her. But she forced the
ragings of fear down, her jaw clenching. She would not crumble; she would not wilt into wailings and mournings while
Dallywoulde and her father murdered Tade and, mayhap later,
her child. This time she would fight for her own, find a way
to rob death of its due. If she could but find some way to
escape, to wrest Tade from the cells of Newgate.

The moonlight streamed through the closed window, its
silvery rays ribboning a path into the night. Maryssa's hands
clenched in the white satin of her skirts, a wild hope bur-
geoning within her. *Even here in England I have heard the
legends your ignorant Irish barbarians weave about you*, Dallywoulde had jeered. Sorcerers' tales, Maryssa thought, her
hands shaking, tales of magic that might well fill a simple of
mind with witless fears.

She turned to her armoire, ripped it open, riffled through
the garmets until she found a black silk mourning gown.
Aye, she thought with a wellspring of hope as she rushed

to her sewing basket. There might be a chance, one chance to spare Tade the horror Dallywoulde had in store for him, if she possessed the courage and the wit.

A hundred more the like of me will rise up to fight you . . . She could still hear Tade's words. *Nay*, she thought, resolve surging within her. *One. Only one.* Pray God, it is enough.

Twenty-Two

THE SNOW BEASTS were warring, their icy claws slashing at the midnight sky, wailing, shrieking in outrage as they snarled about the streets of London. Maryssa struggled to warm her numbed fingers beneath the black cape. The rough breeches and muslin shirt chafed her skin as she peered at the imposing gray hulk of Newgate jail through slits in the hood she had fashioned five days before at Carradown.

It had all seemed so simple then as she had stitched silver talons into the silk, constructing the guise she prayed would fool the dull turnkeys within Newgate's walls. Aye, even when she had risked all, lowering herself the perilous distance to the ground below her window, breathing prayers to whichever of Devin's saints she could remember, then ridden the endless, frigid miles to the city, she had nigh felt as though she wore, in truth, the magical cloak the plain folk claimed the Falcon possessed.

But now, confronted with the stark danger of Newgate, she could scarce believe she had been fool enough to think this escapade offered any chance of success. And with each chiming of the distant bells ringing the hour, she grew more certain that somewhere on the road from Carradown a rider thundered in pursuit of her, a rider with fanatical eyes set deep in the face of a specter.

She shivered, glancing into the empty darkness behind her. The hours it had taken her to prepare for this raid, to secure the things she needed so desperately to make it work, had snatched away precious time; her escape from her prison room had surely been discovered by now, and the devious Dallywoulde would need little thought to discern where she had gone.

But the time spent in the planning had been vital, and now, confronted with the huge stone jail, she wished she had taken longer to put her plan into motion. Nervous fingers trailed to the brace of pistols she had secured at her side, the memory of the dingy ship in which she had bartered her jewels for these disreputable weapons intruding upon her. The money-lender had regarded her with such ferret-eyed suspicion that she had dared not ask him to school her in using the weapons. Then the intrusion of a bandy-legged sergeant into the shop had made Maryssa flee with all haste.

She worried her lower lip, her eyes skimming the barred windows that glared down from the stark walls. Aye, now she regretted right fully the stirrings of fear that had catapulted her from the moneylender's side, wishing she had braved the soldier's curiosity in the hope of learning how to load and fire the pistols. But 'twas late . . . too late.

She compressed her lips, rubbing her clammy palms on the ragged breeches she had purchased with her bent shilling. All England had been buzzing about the capture of the Black Falcon, taking delight in spinning ever more fantastical tales about bargains with the Dark One and deeds that Satan himself would have been hard pressed to match. If she could but cling to the mystique that surrounded the Black Falcon, if she could play upon the fears of the guards in the night's eerie grasp, she would not need to prove her menace by firing the pistols.

Dredging up her courage, she drew the weapon, clutching it in one sweating hand. Her observation of the jailer's routine told her that the guard would change in a few hours. Those whiling away the hours in darkness within the eerie corridors, beset by the tortured cries of those incarcerated within, would be weary by now of their watch and could be lulled, Maryssa prayed, into growing lax in their vigil.

If she could but stun those guards, terrify them, by rising before them like one of the devil's own . . .

Quickly, stealthily, her heart a lump of terror in her throat, Maryssa hastened to the debtors' door, playing over and over in her mind the ruse she had devised to gain her entry to the prison.

With the distinctive pounding she had heard during her vigil outside Newgate the night before, she cracked the toe of one boot into the doorway, mimicking the impatience of the burly watchman who had dragged a pickpocket to the gates last evening. She listened, seconds stretching to infinity, pulse thundering, knees quaking, as she waited for some sign that a guard had heard her. She had just raised her foot to crack it again into the heavy panel when she heard a muffled grousing within, followed by a thud, as if someone had collided with the door.

Drawing farther into the shadows, Maryssa kicked the panel yet again, harder, more insistently.

"Weepin' Jesus, be that ye, Guildford?" A bleary voice rose above the scraping of the latch.

Maryssa dared not reply for fear of alerting the fractious guard, so in answer she drew back her foot and kicked the door with all the force she possessed.

"Hellfire and damnation, Guildford, I vow ye got less patience than Tupper a-whorin'! Gi' me a cursed chance t' get the blasted door open. That right nice brigand, Kilcannon, been treatin' us all t' barrels o' port an' me hands be shaky as a doxy's at payin' time."

Maryssa caught her lips between her teeth, struck by the absurdity of the guard's prattle, praying that in a few hours' time she would be caught in Tade's arms, laughing over the turnkey's antics. But whatever vague stirring of amusement she had felt vanished as she heard the latch scrape free. Catching her breath, she squared her shoulders, praying that the padding she had sewn into the cape would dupe the guard into thinking her own slender form was that of a daunting, broad-chested highwayman.

The door crashed wide to reveal a spindly grasshopper of a man garbed in a waistcoat she recognized as Tade's. The

brass buttons stretched past the guard's knobby knees, and
the rich garment looked absurd against his coarse gray homespun jerkin as he raised a candle aloft, blinking owlishly into
the night.

"Guildford?" he bellowed, staggering a few steps from
the door. "Guildford, Gor plague ye," the turnkey swore,
stalking a score of paces away from the door, his eyes sweeping the night.

Maryssa wasted not a second listening to the guard's black
curses. Heart in her throat, she slipped soundlessly behind
him and hurried to secrete herself in the dark corridor beyond. She drew back into the shadows, the plan she had
forged the night before, of taking a hostage to lead her to
Tade, shifting in her mind, changing as she watched the
straggle-haired turnkey stagger around, then stomp back in
through the open door. If she could but disappear into the
inky darkness . . . keep the guard from seeing her.

"Cursed brats," the guard muttered, grasping at the latch.
"Thinkin' they can make fool o' Hezekiah Blount! Take 'em
o'er me knee, I will. Thrash 'em wi' a hick'ry stick if I get
me hands on their backsides."

Maryssa held her breath, not daring to blink as Hezekiah
fastened the door. The wavering light from his candle writhed
drunkenly across the walls, the circling glow dripping down
upon the hem of Maryssa's cape. But the disgruntled Hezekiah seemed in no mood to waste time searching the quiet
halls. He puffed out his skinny chest, spit into one grimy
palm, and raked his stubby fingers through the tangled mass
of his hair as if to smooth it.

"Most like Prunelley herself is what's sendin' 'em,
checkin' t' see if I'm of a truth at me labors. Blast the wench,
she should know that, wi' a right-fine catch th' like o' the
Black Falcon wi'in the walls, I'd not be wastin' me night a-
dallyin'. I got more 'portant 'fairs t' tend t' than the way
Merdyce Runneymead be fillin' out 'er garters."

Maryssa held her breath as Hezekiah wobbled, then reached
out to steady himself, one hand but an arm's length from
where she stood.

"Nay," the guard continued, "Hezekiah Blount got 'portant matters t' tend t'. Got fin' out how that devil Kilcannon
be colorin' 'is cards."

The turnkey lurched forward, winding his way down the corridor, the pathetic moans of those attempting sleep within the debtors' ward a stark contrast to the jaunty little guard's grumblings. Cautiously Maryssa clung to the darkness outside the ring of light from his candle, watching his every footfall in an effort to keep from tripping over aught that lay upon the floor, or making some noise that would bestir Hezekiah from his mutterings.

As the turnkey made his way deeper into Newgate's walls, Maryssa battled the sensation that she was being swallowed in the darkness, terror that at any moment another guard would rise out of the shadows making her scarce able to draw breath.

But aside from the groans of prisoners half-asleep and the scratchings and scurryings of rats along the walls, Maryssa heard naught, saw naught, until Hezekiah stumbled up the stone steps that led away from the wretchedness of the debtors' jail and into the cleaner quarters that housed prisoners with coin enough to buy a few comforts. The Master Side, this was called, and as Maryssa crept through the corridor behind Hezekiah, she breathed a prayer of thanks that Tade had been confined here rather than in the vermin-infested hell below.

She started, nearly tripping over the hem of her cloak as a ripple of masculine laughter spilled out into the quiet hallway, the sound strained, aye, but recognizable as the rakehell, reckless amusement of Tade Kilcannon.

A spate of good-natured curses erupted from behind an iron-bound door, the laughter swelling as Hezekiah pulled on the iron handle. Maryssa caught her breath, stunned at her good fortune as the portal swung wide, unhampered by lock or bolt.

"Gor's blood, the scurvy bastard did it again, 'Zekiah!" A blurred voice rumbled from the slice of room visible beyond the door. "Beggin' yer pardon, Tade, lad, but it be a good thing yer t' dangle this week, 'er I vow I'd be payin' off this night's wagers fer the rest o' me days!"

"Blast it," Hezekiah grumbled, rubbing his hand on the elegant waistcoat. "The Falcon's won every stick an' pot I own. I'd wager Prunelly an' the young ones if 'e'd take 'em, but even a man at the gallows' gate'd not wax *that* foolish."

The spindly guard elbowed his way through the throng of turnkeys who ringed the rough-hewn table in the center of the spotless cell.

"You left the door ajar, 'Zekiah. Aren't you afraid I'll escape?" The familiar deep voice flooded Maryssa with fierce relief, coupled with an urge to jam her cape into Tade's mouth. Fear that his careless words would move the grizzled Blount to slam the cell door rushed through her.

But Hezekiah merely snorted in disgruntled amusement. "If ye can fly from the midst o' half the guards in Newgate, ye deserve yer freedom, Kilcannon," he said, plopping himself down upon a three-legged stool. "Now deal the cursed cards, ye Irish blackguard."

Shaking with relief as the guards' attention returned to the game, Maryssa eased closer to the portal, her gaze searching the cell beyond. Her throat constricted with relief and love, as she peered past the engrossed turnkeys, grimy playing cards clasped in their hands, to where Tade lounged in a chair at the head of the table.

The unruly rosewood-colored waves of his hair were bound back with a leather thong, the rich, dark locks a stark contrast to the planes of his face. Pale, he was so pale, lines carved deep in the features that had once been as smooth and untroubled as a babe's. Despite the crook of a smile that played about his lips, the emerald of his eyes held no sparkle and reflected naught but a weariness, a lurking desperation, and guilt that made Maryssa's throat ache. His fingers curved about a goblet nigh emptied of port, the dozen bottles stacked on the floor by his feet attesting to the amount of revelry with which he had endowed the bluff turnkeys.

"Come, Falcon," a brawny Scotsman burred. "At least gi' a man a chance t' gain back 'is horse. Th' saddle ye can keep, the cinchin' is well nigh worn through, but I got a soft spot in me heart for ol' Torwaddle."

Tade raised his eyes to the florid guard, teeth flashing in a shadow of his accustomed bedeviling grin. "Nay, Campbell. Enough. If I cheat the hangman yet again, I'll need a sturdy mount to hie me to Ireland."

"Blast it, lad, I—"

"Peace, for glory's sake. We've been playing since dusk,

and even the lot of you reprobates would not begrudge me one final night's dreams of my lady, would you?''

The men guffawed, throwing down their cards, but in spite of the jesting in Tade's voice, Maryssa detected a shade of sadness and longing within the tones. Tade's bloodshot eyes were fixed on the square of night framed in the barred window, his emerald gaze seeming to envision there something he alone could see.

Her fingers tightened on the pistol, the other hand drawing out the second weapon as the turnkeys started to push themselves up from their seats. She clenched her teeth, knowing it was now or never.

"Hold." She fought to keep her voice gruff, menacing, as she stepped into the doorway, thrusting the brace of pistols from beneath the folds of her cloak. As though all had been yanked by the same thread, a dozen pairs of eyes flashed to the doorway, six mouths gaping open in astonishment as the guards' port-blurred gazes locked upon the black-cloaked figure filling the open doorway.

"What the—'' Tade bolted from his chair, eyes wide with the dazed confusion of one confronted by a phantom. Had Maryssa not been so terrified, she would have laughed aloud. But she caught a glimpse of one guard reaching for a pistol at his waist, saw his hand freeze in midair as she shifted her own weapon so that it was aimed at his chest.

'' 'Twould be most unwise,'' she rasped out, the sound scraping her throat. "The Black Falcon is not well noted for patience.''

Hezekiah's eyes nigh popped out of his skull. "Falcon . . . the Falcon? . . . Who in blazes? . . . Gor damn . . . Sweet Mary . . .'' He gaped at Tade. "If that—this is you, then who—''

Her gaze flashed back to Tade, seeing that in the moments she had glanced away at the guard, Tade's mouth had widened into a grin. "Must be the devil, 'Zekiah,'' he said as he snatched a ring of keys from the thong at Campbell's thick waist. "Haven't you heard? I bartered my soul off years ago.''

"Kilcannon, ye can't—can't just—''

"Saunter out of my cell 'neath your noses?'' Tade's laugh rang out as he snatched a stubby candle from the table.

"Watch me, 'Zekiah. Just watch me! But, as a fellow gambler, I'd advise you not to try any heroics. I am personally acquainted with the Falcon's aim, and I assure you 'tis deadly." Flashing a grin at the gap-mouthed faces of his captors, Tade darted between them, then banged the iron-bound door shut and locked the shock-numbed guards within.

"Damn, Reeve!" Tade exclaimed, bolting down the shadowy hall. "I knew you'd come, but I scarce smuggled out the message, and—"

The words had barely left Tade's mouth when the Falcon's hand caught his arm, spinning him around. He reeled in shock as the black-garbed figure hurled itself at his chest with a cry that was far from masculine. Pistol butts cracked into his back as the "highwayman" flung trembling arms around him, and the shoulders that had looked so broad beneath the cape shifted to an impossible angle. The hooded face was pressed against his chest, soaking his shirt with tears. "Tade! Thank God, oh, thank—"

"Blazes! What the—" His heart slammed down to his boot soles, terror, joy, and disbelief warring within him as his hand shot out and ripped free the satin mask. "Maura!" He choked out the name when her delicate pale features, eyes blue, gold, green, glistening with love and tears were revealed. But the joy he took in the sight of her, far from the clutches of the cursed Dallywoulde, warmed Tade for a moment before the walls of Newgate, which had, moments past, seemed as breachable as crumbling clay, suddenly closed in about him, gripping him with panic.

A string of savage curses burst from his lips, his hand shooting out to crush her slender wrists and wrench her arms free of his waist. "Curse you, Maura, I should wring your blasted neck!" He yanked her toward the darkened staircase. "Coming here, and you with child, I—damn!" The candlelight caught the glint of the pistols, so ludicrous in her tiny hands, and Tade paused long enough to snatch them from her fingers, jam them into the waistband of his breeches. "Hell and damnation, you could have blown your blasted foot off with these things!" He railed as he grasped her arm again, dragging her forward. The staircase spilled them down into the debtors' ward, Tade rushing toward the door as though the devil himself pursued them.

"I—I could scarce march in here and demand they release you . . . without some weapon to convince them." Her breathless defense, filled with a new strength and confidence, only served to stoke the fires of Tade's anger. "They were going to kill you!"

"Kill me?" Tade blustered, flinging open the huge door that led to freedom. The wintry wind whooshed into him, chilling him through the thin fabric of his shirt. But he scarce felt it as his gaze darted about the deserted midnight streets. "I still damn well might hang for murder once I get you safe!"

She stumbled and, with an oath, he caught her, curving his arm about her waist. But as he bent toward her, urging her ever onward toward the safety of the streets beyond, his eyes glimpsed her face—elated, courageous, and excruciatingly beautiful—in the faint moonlight that struggled through the roiling clouds.

"Who was it who told me once that life is scarce worth the trouble unless you're willing to take risks?" The saucy impudence in her wind-stung lips, the sparkle in her eyes, made him want to rail at her, shake her, kiss her, until she couldn't breathe.

He opened his mouth, mayhap to do all three, but suddenly the words died upon his lips, buried beneath the ominous sound of hoofbeats thundering toward Newgate.

Swearing, Tade flung away the stub of candle, his arm tightening about Maryssa to aid her to run, but before they could dart into one of the twisted, narrow streets that offered safety, a flash of ghost-white horse caught his eyes, the beast's rider crouched low over its massive flanks, his cape whipping wildly in the wind.

"Dallywoulde."

Tade heard Maryssa's choked gasp, for the first time detecting fear in the voice that an instant ago had dared tease him.

Feral rage tore through him, fierce protectiveness toward Maryssa and the babe she carried crushing even his thirst for the blood of Devin's murderer. Tade's hand flashed down, yanking the pistol from his breeches, bringing the barrel up to bear on the approaching rider. He cursed under his breath, gauging the distance to the thundering horse and the man astride it. In that fleeting instant, Tade knew if he fired too soon, before Dallywoulde drew close, the pistol ball would miss the Englishman. And if his aim wasn't true . . .

"No, Tade!" Vaguely, he heard Maryssa's frantic cry, but he shut it out as the hammer clicked back, his finger tightening on the trigger.

He held his breath but an instant as he squeezed off the shot, then waited an eternity for the roar of gunpowder, the flash of orange from the long barrel. But as the flint cracked down upon the pan, the weapon emitted naught but a metallic click, and Tade's heart froze.

"Tade, I didn't—didn't know how to—"

"Load it? Christ, you didn't load it!" His eyes flashed from the useless gun to Dallywoulde. The planes of the man's evil face were now visible as he raced toward them. Tade sensed those chill eyes locking upon them, could see the loathsome knight's lips contort in a triumphant jeer. At that instant an explosion did split the night, the flare of orange spitting lead from a pistol aimed over the head of Dallywoulde's mount. Tade felt the bullet tear into the flesh of his thigh, but he paused not an instant to cry out in pain. Raw panic seized him as he caught a glimpse of Maryssa's stricken fear-glazed eyes. All thought of vengeance, aye and of honor, fled. Nothing mattered to him now except ensuring this woman's safety. He hurled the useless pistol to the ground, caught her arm, and bolted with her toward the shadowed alleyways that offered the only sanctuary.

"Run, Maura," he urged, half dragging, half carrying her over the uneven stones. "Have to—have to find a place where the bastard can't—cut us down—"

"Tade, I—"

"Run!"

A second pistol spat death into the night, but this time the ball slammed well over their heads, striking a sign swinging over the shop of a cooper.

The splintered wood rained down upon them, one shard slicing Tade's cheek. He felt Maryssa's foot catch on a stone, felt her start to fall, but with a jerk of his arm he righted her, then guided her through the narrow passage between two buildings and on into the next twisted street.

Desperately his eyes swept the shadowed fronts of shops

and houses. If he could get Maura inside one of them and force Dallywoulde to dismount and give chase, the odds would be a bit more even, and they might have a chance of besting the armed knight. But the crashing of hooves into the street behind them warned Tade what little time they still had was nigh gone. His eyes flashed over the building fronts yet again, locking on a humble arched doorway and rising to the church spire outlined above it in the moonlight.

Hazarding a glance over his shoulder, Tade saw the mist white of Dallywoulde's horse, heard the flapping of his cape, felt the icy eyes boring into him, menacing, glazed with lust for the kill. But already Tade was bolting forward, dragging Maryssa beside him.

"Hasten," he urged between clenched teeth. "The church—try the—" But as though she, too, realized the hopelessness of battling the vicious knight afoot without weapons, Maryssa charged up the few steps leading to the arched oak door, reaching the portal before him. Grasping the iron ring that served as handle, Tade yanked the door wide with a force that slammed it against the outer wall.

He could feel Maura flinch as her gaze darted back toward Dallywoulde who now raced toward the tiny building. A grimness descended upon Tade as he propelled her through the door, a primal need to crush anyone who dared threaten his mate, his child. He rushed into the dark sanctuary, his eyes struggling to pierce the inky shadows, to spy somewhere to secrete Maryssa in safety before he turned to confront the man he hated more than the dark angel himself.

A brace of candles flickered upon the plain wood altar, as though to welcome any weary traveler who might seek peace within this humble dwelling of God. Tade raced up, grasped one waxen taper, and held it aloft as his eyes searched the small room. A narrow, rickety stairway spiraled upward in one corner, the wooden steps twisting, perilous. Aye, and mayhap leading to the one place where Maryssa might have a chance of defending herself against Dallywoulde if Tade should die.

"It must lead somewhere . . . the roof, mayhap, the belfry," Maryssa gasped.

"Wherever it leads 'twill be passing safer than where we stand now," he said. Thrusting the candle up into the heavy darkness, Tade grasped the fabric at Maryssa's waist in an effort to help her to keep her balance as she stumbled up the flight of stairs. Twice she nearly fell, and once his own knee cracked into the sharp edge of a step, but they finally gained the last wooden step, their boot heels cracking with a hollow sound on a platform the size of a dray.

The candlelight picked out the shadowy zigzags of beams across the ceiling, narrowing into the spire they had seen from outside. Coils of new rope spilled nigh Tade's boots, the cord twined with aged lengths of hemp between the bell's top and the rail that guarded the gaping opening in the platform above which the mammoth bell dangled. A dusty, broken stool stood beside the rail as though the sexton had stood upon it to replace the bell rope.

Tade peered down at the humble altar; the simple carvings that flanked it were partly shadowed by the fluted sides of the huge brass bell high above.

Pray God when next it rang 'twould not prove their death knell. "Maura, I'll need your cape. Mayhap I can use it to deflect Dallywoulde's sword long enough to—" Tade spun, his fingers stilling as he reached for the flowing garment, the sound of thudding footsteps echoing up from below. Muttering an oath under his breath, Tade ripped the mantle free and hastily wrapped it around his left forearm. But the hope he had held of sheltering Maryssa, whatever the outcome of the battle between him and the evil Dallywoulde, melted as he heard a low, triumphant chuckle.

Through the slats in the wood, he saw Dallywoulde, candle in hand, bend down and reach out with gloved fingers to touch something upon the floor. The sinister knight pressed his fingertips to his lips as if tasting something, feeling it, and even so high above that pale head, Tade could feel the waves of twisted pleasure that welled from Dallywoulde's burning eyes.

Tade's gaze flicked down to the weathered golden boards, catching sight of a wet, dark glimmer of crimson on the old wood. Blood.

"Damn!" He had paid no heed to the pistol ball that had torn through his flesh, scarce aware of the burning wound in his need to get Maryssa to safety. He yanked free his neckcloth and jammed the fabric inside the hole torn in his breeches in an effort to staunch the bleeding.

"Tade . . ." Maryssa's voice was choked with fear. "Sweet God, your leg . . ."

"Hush, love. 'Tis naught. I've lived through five like it in the years I've ridden the highroads." He wanted to soothe her, comfort her, but he dared not even catch her eyes lest she see the unease in his face. 'Twas no serious wound, he knew, yet with each minute that passed, with each drop of the lifeblood that soaked into the wad of cloth, some portion of his strength drained away as well. To battle a demon like Dallywoulde, weakened by a wound, with no weapon and only a cursed cloak to meet the swine's cold steel . . .

He forced a bracing smile to his lips, but the sound of weight bearing down on one creaking step cut off the words he had wanted to say to her, his gaze finding and holding the terrified blue-gold lights of hers.

"Tade, I . . . I'm sorry . . . about Dev . . . the babe . . ."

"Stay back, love, away from the fight," he said, suppressing the terror he felt for her. "If I should—if aught should happen to me, ring the bells. 'Twill bring half of London running, and the bastard won't dare harm you."

"Nay, naught—naught will befall you. You can't—" The desperation in her face tore at him.

"I love you, Maura." Simple, the words were so simple, the love he felt for this woman driving back the bitter poison that had been twisting him in the days since Dev had died. A hundred vows of love and a hundred pleas for forgiveness rose in his throat, but there was only time enough to brush her lips for one infinitely sweet instant before he spun to where Dallywoulde's shadow lengthened upon the belfry wall.

Candlelight caught the cold blue glimmer of unsheathed steel, the razor-honed length of sword lancing the darkness. But more threatening, by far, was the icy hate gleaming in Dallywoulde's eyes. Spectral evil, Dallywoulde's visage gleamed in the candlelight—death's face—the shadowed sockets empty caverns, the sparse hair clinging as if to a withered skull, the fleshless lips drawn back, eager from jagged teeth.

'Twas as though the Falcon at last faced the demon the

tales claimed him kin to, but this battle would be for something Tade Kilcannon treasured far more deeply than his own soul.

"Coward!" Dallywoulde's voice issued the challenge, taunting, baiting, like a serpent waiting to strike. "What fear you, Black Falcon? The blade of a holy man's sword? 'Twas child's play to cut down your puling Irish papists in the glen that day—child's play to send your thrice-damned brother to hell."

Rage surged through Tade, white-hot and searing, but he checked it, holding his body taut, waiting, watching. "Aye, it took great courage to murder women and babes, Dallywoulde."

"Kits grow into foxes and all need to be poisoned."

Tade's teeth clenched at the jeering voice, his stomach wrenching as the shadows on the wall shifted into images of blood-soaked bodies of children clutched in their dead mothers' arms, eyes that had watched with wonder last summer's butterflies now glazed with horror and death.

"Bastard!" Tade snarled. "You God damn—"

Tade heard Maryssa make a tiny sound of horror, saw Dallywoulde's cold eyes flick to where she stood pressed against the outer wall. In that second Tade lunged, slamming his shielded arm into the side of Dallywoulde's head, grappling desperately for the hilt of the glistening sword.

But before his hand could close upon the gold-wrought hand guard, the knight dived beneath his grasp, not toppling, as Tade had hoped, down the treacherous stairway, but rather skidding across the floor of the small platform, perilously close to where Maryssa stood.

With pantherlike agility, Dallywoulde rolled across the platform and sprang to his feet, weapon ready. But before the knight could gain solid footing, Tade lunged toward him, swinging his bound arm high as the blade of the sword swept in a savage arc at his head. Tade slammed into Ascot's side, and both men fell to the floor as the blade whacked into the fabric that guarded Tade's arm.

The force of the blow nigh shattered the bone sheathed beneath, the momentum slamming Tade's shoulder into the rail guarding the opening in the floor.

Tade felt pain shoot into his ribs and slice deep in his wrist as he fought to force himself to his feet and shove himself away from the gaping maw that threatened certain death. But 'twas as if the sword still clutched in Dallywoulde's skeletal fingers had taken on a life of its own. Tade leaped to one side, feeling the tip of the blade rend his breeches and rip into one narrow hip.

Greedy lips pulled back from Dallywoulde's teeth, and for the first time Tade fully understood the raw terror the man had struck into Maryssa, an unholy fear, beyond reason, beyond sanity, a fear of the knight's cruelty and of an evil mind fueled by the twisted belief that he was doing God's work.

"Aye, Kilcannon," Dallywoulde hissed. "You're bleeding now, with but a taste of my blade. One more blow and you'll dance with the devil."

"Only if I drag you there beside me." Gritting his teeth against the pain that pounded in his arm, leg, and side, Tade steeled himself for Dallywoulde's charge, summoning every last ounce of strength to meet the bastard's sword.

Ice cold and triumphant, Dallywoulde's eyes were fixed upon him, both hands clasping the hilt of the sword.

Out of the corner of his eye, Tade caught a flash of movement, then heard Maryssa cry out as she lunged toward something at the far end of the platform. The sound of wood splintering and steel slashing split the air as Dallywoulde lunged toward him, both hands clutching the blood-tipped sword.

Tade's gut clenched as he awaited the agony of steel splitting his flesh, praying for the strength to evade the blow but one last time, hurl both himself and Dallywoulde down to their deaths. Yet in that instant 'twas as if the earth spun off its axis.

A scream, fierce, savage, and furious, cut through the haze of pain, and he caught a glimpse of wide eyes, tangled mahogany tresses, as something heavy and wooden crashed down on Dallywoulde's skull. Tade saw those soulless eyes snap wide with shock as Maryssa's hands drove the heavy stool into the Englishman's head. The coils of rope on the floor jerked beneath Tade as Dallywoulde's boot tangled in the twisted lengths of hemp.

The knight pitched forward, and the bell rope snarled into

a perilous web about him as he thrashed at the entrapping coils. A hideous scream split the night. The railing shattered as Dallywoulde collapsed against it. Tade felt the blade of the sword whisk past his ear, then heard it clatter into the gaping hole as the man who had held it a heartbeat before catapulted into the abyss.

A shriek was torn from the knight's throat, the sickening sound wrenched to silence as the rope jerked taut, the belfry echoing with the gut-racking crack of his neck snapping, followed by the deafening peal of the bell.

Tade staggered to his feet, one hand clutching what was left of the broken rail, his eyes locking on the horrible sight limned by the light of the candle.

The lifeless form of Ascot Dallywoulde dangled there in the flickering shadows, his eyes bulging from their sockets, glazing with death, his neck, caught among the hempen coils, twisted at an angle that turned Tade's stomach.

Dead . . . dead . . .

He heard Maryssa run the few steps to where he stood, saw her waver on the edge of the precipice, felt her hands clutch at his shoulder. But despite the burning of his wounds, the sickness clenching in his belly, Tade turned to catch her in arms that trembled.

"Tade . . . I—oh, thank God he didn't . . ." Her words were broken, threaded through with terror, aye, and love. And he wanted to kiss her, hold her, as he saw those fragile features struggle against the sobs that he sensed were clawing at her chest. But there was no time for aught except to flee the church with its pealing bell, flee the London streets, which in minutes would be crawling with watchmen and guards searching for the escaped Tade Kilcannon.

He reached out, curved his arms beneath Maryssa's knees and shoulders, scooped her up against him, and hastened down the stairway with her quivering form caught against his chest.

But already the sound of scurrying feet drifted up from the streets, distant shouts echoing through the night.

He kicked open the heavy door, rushing out into the street, relief washing through him as he saw Dallywoulde's ghost-white mount pawing restlessly with its hooves. Tade caught a glimpse of shadowy figures bursting from the darkness, heard voices, cries, as he flung Maryssa up into the saddle and swung up behind her.

He clutched her tight in his arms as the watch rattles clamored alarm. Muttering an oath that was half curse, half prayer, he pressed his heels into the gelding's barrel, urging the beast into a dead run.

Twenty-Three

THE ROSE-DRAPED COTTAGE nestled in wreaths of mist, its
windowpanes spilling fire-glow out into the shadows of twilight. Tade shifted in Curran's saddle, straining his gaze over
Maryssa's slumped, tousled head to where a single taper shone
gold in the window—the candle placed as always on the
weathered wood sill to beckon him home.

A dull ache swelled in him with each thud of the stallion's
hooves, tightening his throat with tears he could not shed.

'Twas unjust, aye, unjust, he thought numbly, leaning his
jaw against Maryssa's sleep-softened cheek. Unjust that now,
with Devin dead, it should all look the same.

Yet the crowded cottage rooms would never again be
blessed with the joy of Devin's laughter, and the tiny Kilcannons playing on the rugs would not feel those gentle, steadying hands caress them or hear that solemn voice spinning
tales of Erin's long-dead heroes. Little Katie and Ryan would
remember only shadings of their oldest brother, and even
those vague memories would fade at last into nothing.

But the greatest sorrow, mayhap greater even than Tade's
own at Devin's death, would be that of Kane Kilcannon, who
had treasured the son who had inherited the sweet face and
gentle solemnity of the lady-wife he had buried a lifetime

ago. And when the only other son born in the majestic halls of Nightwylde turned traitor by taking to wife the daughter of Kane Kilcannon's most hated enemy . . . Tade's jaw was set and hard. Aye, 'twould nigh destroy the father who had always held his heart despite the rages that had e'er beset them.

But there was naught else he could think to do, nowhere else to go . . . Tade moved his numb arms, settling the sleeping Maryssa more securely against him, the sound of her weary sigh tugging deep in his heart. His teeth clenched as his gaze swept over her pale features, taut with exhaustion, and the dark circles beneath her eyes.

In the weeks it had taken them to reach England's coast and secure passage on a ship bound for Dublin, the babe Maryssa carried seemed to have doubled in size, thrusting out against her stomach until Tade had had to slit the waist of the ragged breeches she still wore to ease the tightness that had crushed her. And as their babe had grown larger and stronger, Maryssa's own strength had seemed to ebb, the endless journeying in the wind and winter rain washing all color from the cheeks that had ever seemed too pale.

She had never complained, always urging him to rush onward in their flight. Even when she had been limp with exhaustion, quaking with cold, he had fairly had to force her to lie among the feather quilts of some hospitable farm wife.

He winced, stung deep by the memory of the times he had called her a coward, judged her naught but a weak, fragile babe, cringing from the shadows. Nay, never had he known anyone who possessed such courage and strength . . . a strength far deeper than any he could lay claim to. He loved her, this woman who had shed her chrysalis of fear and shyness and blossomed into the most beautiful of brave, bright angels. Loved her with every fiber of his being, every breath he drew, aye, loved her more even than the Donegal hills that had been his mistress for so long.

And yet, the nearer they had drawn to his home, the more deeply these feelings of unease had cut him, for despite the certainty that his love for Maura, and hers for him, now grew strong, one truth yet remained. No matter where they tried to carve out a life together, be it here in Ireland or in England's huge manors, the hatred and prejudice that had threatened to rend them apart for so long would tear at them, leaving one or the other loathed, outcast by those around them. Tade's jaw clenched. He could endure whatever fate could deal him and be content as long as he had Maryssa at his side. But to condemn his sweet, fragile Maura and their babes to the life of shadows, clinging always to the edges of love and joy . . .

Tade's eyes swept the oaken cottage door, closed against the encroaching night, and reined Curran to a halt. Nay, there had to be a place—some place free of the loathing that caused men of faith to murder, kill, and hate in the name of a gentle God. During the nights he had tipped ale with the rest of his rebel band in scores of different inns all across Ireland, he had heard tales of the colonies that lay an ocean away—raw, wild lands, rich with the promise of wealth to any man with the courage to wrest a fortune from those fertile fields.

True, those colonies were under English rule, but the people were a mingling of displaced noblemen, tradesmen, and adventurers seeking to devise their own laws and struggling to throw off the chains of the old ones—a nation of men well used to battling for what was theirs. As soon as Maura was well, as soon as the babe thrived sturdy and strong, he would take them away from the despair that was his Ireland. He would hew out a life for them in the distant Carolinas or the tobacco fields of Virginia. But until then he would seek to shield her here, within the walls of the cottage in which he had grown to manhood.

Careful to jar her as little as possible, he eased from the saddle, cradling her in his arms. A tendril of mahogany hair wisped across her parted lips, and he nudged it aside with his chin. "Tade?" His name was slurred upon her tongue, blurred with sleep, as she nuzzled against his chest, her lashes scarce stirring upon the pale curve of her cheeks.

"Shh, sweeting, 'tis all right," he breathed gently. "Sleep, just—"

His crooned, soothing words were lost in the sudden thud of the oaken door as a whirl of rose-colored skirts hurtled from the opening. The freckles bespattering the impudent little nose were the same, as was the gladsome cry Deirdre uttered, but Tade felt a tug of sadness that aside from those two features, his sister seemed much changed. She hastened toward him, catching his arm in a quick, loving squeeze, her eyes filling with tears of happiness. But the wild red curls he had always loved were no longer tangled in disarray about her shoulders; the unruly tresses were now plaited in a crown of woman's braids.

"Dee." His voice sounded rough on his tongue as he stared at her, sensing—in the new consideration that made her pause instead of flinging herself upon him and shrieking—a maturity that wrung his heart.

"Tade, did you— Is Maryssa—" Dee reached out to touch Maryssa's pale cheek. "Dear God, she's not—"

Fragile eyelids fluttered open, a tired smile tugging at the corner of Maryssa's mouth as her gaze flickered to Deirdre. Tade's heart twisted.

"Nay, Dee, I'm not an invalid yet, though your brother battles passing hard to make one of me." Maryssa wrapped her arms about his neck and struggled to get him to ease her to the ground.

He saw her legs wobble, scarce able to support her, and his arm curved tight about her waist. "She's half dead with weariness," he said. "We've been fleeing the blasted Sassenachs since she broke me free of Newgate, and—"

" 'Twas *Maryssa* who wrested you from Newgate? Reeve Marlow had scarce gotten word that the Falcon—that you had been taken when we heard all of London was agog over your escape. Reeve was half crazed with worry, what with Christa scaring him out of his wits in childbed and—"

"Christa?" Maryssa cut in, and Tade could feel her alarm. "Is aught amiss with—"

"Nay. She's the proud new mother of twins, I fear. Rebecca and Alicia Rose. 'Twas quite an event hereabouts," Deirdre said with a wink. "But I'd wager the gossip will shift from Reeve's little fillies the instant the biddies get wind of how you wrested Tade from a Sassenach prison! Maryssa, how did you ever—" Deirdre stopped with a laugh. "Nay, you can regale us all with your tale later, once you've had a bit of rest. 'Tis a wonder you have the strength to stand, the way you've been forced to flee. But you needn't fear the chase any longer, either of you."

Tade caught a hint of the old sparkle in her eyes and saw

her nose crinkle in amusement. "Dee, what the devil do you mean?"

"It seems that in the time you were in England, the Falcon's nestlings have been fledged."

"Nestlings?"

"Aye. While you were in Newgate, there were three different Falcons raiding here in Ireland. I'd not swear who they are, but the one I saw upon the road bore a decided likeness to Gilvarry Beagan."

"Beagan? Raiding?"

"Aye, with Phelan Fitzpatrick at his side. But the wonderful thing is that, between their raidings and the tales of the Black Falcon who freed you from Newgate, the Sassenachs are in total confusion. Phelan read in an English newspaper something about the men who guarded you swearing under oath that Tade Kilcannon could not possibly be the devil Falcon, that the one who rescued you melted through the walls like mist."

Tade laughed, remembering Hezekiah, imagining the wizened guard spinning out excuses to his superiors.

Deirdre's gaze flashed to Tade's, and he could see the warmth and relief there as her eyes searched his features. 'Twas as though his sister saw in him something that pleased her, comforted her. A hint of her old saucy smile played about her lips as she arched one brow at Maryssa. "So 'twas you who melted through the walls, then," Deirdre said. "The way this great dunderhead was acting when last I saw him, I'm astonished you didn't lock him *in* Newgate, instead of freeing the undeserving wretch!"

"We had discussed matters at my father's estate earlier," Maryssa said, slanting Tade a glance tinged with mischief, "and your brother had proposed marriage so prettily . . ."

Tade had the grace to feel his cheeks burn, but before he could whip out a rejoinder, he caught the tremble in Maryssa's smile, saw in the glow from the window the blue circles staining her fragile eyelids. His mouth tautened, and he railed at himself inwardly for allowing her to stand out here in the chill while the three of them bantered like beaux at a garden party. Best to get her inside, snuggled warm in a feather bed. But first, Tade thought with a grimness settling about his mouth, 'twas needful to know the temper of the lion within. "Is Da about?"

Deirdre's brow furrowed in distress at his abrupt question, and Tade saw her hands knot in her apron. "Aye. Ma and the little ones went off Tuesday last to visit at her sister's in Kerry, but Da stayed behind. His—his shoulder still pains him too much to wander far, though he nigh got out the donkey cart to follow the babes when Sheena—" Deirdre's eyes darted to Tade's, and she nibbled at her lip.

"Sheena?" He cursed, and he felt Maryssa stiffen against him.

"Aye. Sheena—she's clung to our hearth nigh every eve since her father and Dev died. Nigh drives Da crazed, the way she sits, staring into the fire, but Ma won't forbid her to come. Says Sheena most like misses her da. Greenan O'Toole—he doted on her so."

Tade grimaced. "Aye and he showed it by turning her into a spoiled, spiteful little—" He stopped, his memory filled with the image of Greenan's body twisted and bloodied upon the soil of Christ's Wound, the irritation—nay, anger—he had felt at Sheena's intrusion this night softening.

"Get her out of here as soon as you can, Dee," he said. " 'Twould be better far if Da and I were alone when first I see him. And the last cursed thing Maura needs is to endure Sheena's snipings."

" 'Tis all right, Tade," Maryssa said. He could see her attempt to force a reassuring smile to her lips, but the effect was full ruined by the troubled light in her eyes. "Sheena has lost her father, and if your fireside gives her some comfort, I'll not drive her from it."

"Drive me *from* the fires?" The raspy, terror-filled voice made all three spin to face the still open door. "You've come to drag me deeper inside them."

Tade's gaze fastened upon the figure framed by the wooden jamb, his eyes locking but an instant upon features he scarce recognized as those of Sheena O'Toole. The look of the preening, well-tended cat had wasted away till she now looked more like a starveling, all flesh shrunken from her face until her bones thrust at the meager flesh that remained, threatening to pierce the skin. The tawny masses of hair that had been her pride now hung matted and snarled beyond the power of any comb in Christendom, while her eyes, once seductive and inviting, burned with a haunted light that bordered on insanity.

Unconsciously, Tade's grip tightened about Maryssa, every nerve in his body snapping with wariness and challenge as he met Sheena's gaze. "Get out of the way, Sheena," he commanded, starting toward the door. "I need to get Maryssa inside."

"*Maryssa,*" Sheena shrilled. "Let her rot out here—freeze. You'll not bring that murderess into this house! Not bring my da's killer and Devin's betrayer to the very hearth where—"

Tade took a step toward her, anger flooding his veins. "Damn it, Sheena, stop, or by God I'll—"

"Nay, Tade," Maryssa's voice cut in, strong, firm, despite the weariness in its tones. " 'Tis obvious Sheena is tired, overset—"

"Overset? *Overset*? Don't you dare to play my defender, witch . . . Sassenach witch!"

Tade stepped in front of Maryssa, the light of madness and hate in Sheena's amber eyes setting every nerve in his body on edge. "Sheena!"

"Nay! She is a witch! Aye! And she's dragging me . . . dragging me to the Dark One! I saw her in the flames . . . knew she would come. And you—" Those white-ringed eyes rolled wildly to Tade. "She used you—used you to entrap your own brother. Aye, and to tangle me in her evil web."

Only Maryssa's hand tightening in a silent plea on his arm stayed Tade from flinging the distraught girl out of the doorway bodily. His jaw clenched, hard as granite, and thrice as unyielding as he shouldered the girl aside, easing Maryssa and Dee into the softly lit room. "Sheena," he said, forcing a reasonable tone, "I know that you are grieving. You loved your da greatly, as deeply as we loved Devin. But I'll not stand here and let you batter Maryssa with your ravings. She had naught to do with your father's death or with Devin's."

"She did, fool! Witling fool! Has she so bewitched you that you can't see the evil in her eyes? Can't see that she—she forced me. . . ?"

"Forced you to what, damn it?"

"The night—the night of Samain . . . She forced me into the fires . . . hell . . . forced me . . ."

Tade caught a glimpse of Maryssa's stricken face, and fury drove deep within him. Gritting his teeth against waves of rage, he grasped the shrieking Sheena by the arm and shook her. "Enough of your railing! Maura did naught to you, and the devil himself couldn't force you to turn one hair upon your head if you had not the desire to. Now get out!"

" 'Twas the devil! Aye, that night! Pits . . . pits for eyes, filled with fire—blue fire, and his face . . . *She* made me go to him—talk to him, else I ne'er—ne'er would have betrayed my own da."

The thin shoulders shook in a racking sob, and a sick suspicion plunged like a stone into Tade's belly. His hands crushed Sheena's arms, his eyes boring into her glazed ones, his whole body seething with foreboding.

"Betray your own da?" Tade scarce recognized his own voice, torn as it was with sick, roiling horror. "Sheena, what by Bridget's cross did you do?"

Firelight stroked hellish orange and gold down the tear-stained hollows of Sheena's cheeks as her lips curled back from the barred teeth. " 'Twas *she*—your Sassenach slut! She made me do it! She tricked me with her bewitchings. I didn't mean for anyone to die! Didn't mean for—for anyone to . . . I was coming . . . coming to warn you . . . to save everyone from the devil."

Tade clawed through his memory desperately, catching the image he had seen that morning at Christ's Wound mere seconds before Ascot Dallywoulde's horde of raiders had descended upon the defenseless worshipers cupped in the valley. He had seen Sheena riding toward them astride a gray horse, but there had been something odd in the direction from whence she had come, aye, and in her absence when mass had begun.

"Why the hell would you betray your own people? Sweet God, you knew Dallywoulde would slaughter them!"

"Nay! I was going to warn you! You would have—would have been grateful, made me your wife. Belonged—you belonged to me, not to that Sassenach witch. But I couldn't find you until 'twas too—too late!"

"Couldn't find me?" Tade spat. "You betrayed Devin and

the children, aye, even your own cursed father to the Sassenachs in some scheme to dig your blasted claws into my hide?
To drag me into marriage? God's blood, I should—''

''Tade!'' He barely felt Maryssa's hand clutch at his arm,
barely heard Deirdre's pleas, the need to shake Sheena
O'Toole until her neck snapped raging through him. A hundred hideous images of the massacre at Christ's Wound tormented him, the corpses of children, women, the bodies of
his own men rearing in his mind.

''Bitch! You God-cursed bitch! You murdered my brother,
aye, and a score of other innocents to satisfy your cursed
pride!''

He felt Maryssa trying to tear him away from the girl, saw
Deirdre tugging at Sheena's filthy sleeve, but in that instant
his fury was eclipsed by a feeling of raw pain and sick torment as his gaze caught the open door to his father's chamber
and his eyes fixed upon the death-gray face of Kane Kilcannon.

'Twas as if, in the weeks since Tade had ridden from Donegal, a mask of age had settled over the warring-king features, slashing lines of anger, grief, and despair deep into the
weathered cheekbones, lines of defeat into carving the arrogant brow and stubborn jutting chin. Never had Tade seen
the old earl's shoulders aught but squared, as if for battle, but
now they sagged beneath the weight of his anguish, aye, and
beneath the horror of what he had just overheard. Yet his
presence, the aura of command and nobility that had always
surrounded him, crushed the rage within the small room. The
gaze Kane had fastened upon Sheena's ravaged face was as
cold as the kiss of the grave.

Tade saw the girl quake in her filthy garb, her eyes wild,
terrified as she staggered back a step beneath the fierce light
of those piercing emerald eyes.

''Get out.'' The words rang like the knell of death from
Kane Kilcannon's lips. And despite Tade's rage over his
brother's senseless death, Sheena's perfidy and betrayal, he
felt a wrenching in his chest as his father reached out to
steady his tall form against the table.

''Nay!'' Sheena spun to Deirdre, clutching at her skirts,
glaring from behind the girl like a crazed, cornered animal.

Dee's face went white, and Tade could see her shrink away from Sheena.

"Nay! You have to listen!" Sheena cried." 'Twas the Wylder bitch! Kill her, make her leave!"

"Get out, or I'll murder you where you stand!" Kane's eyes were cold, so cold.

Tade started toward Sheena, intending to drag her out of the cottage, out of his sight, his father's, and his sister's, out of the reach of his own black fury. But the instant Sheena saw him pacing toward her she shrieked, the terror of the damned reflected in her face. With a crazed sob, she turned, snatching up her soiled skirts, and ran from the room as if possessed by ghosts she alone could see.

'Twas as though all within the silent cottage were held by the sounds of the girl's terror as her screams faded into the twilight, her ravaged form vanishing into the sinister shadows.

Never did Tade know how long they all stood frozen, struck dumb by the pain Sheena's confession had loosed in them. But at last he sagged down onto a bench, burying his face in one hand. "Sweet Christ," he whispered, his voice jagged-edged. "It *was* my fault—Devin's death, aye, and all the others. She betrayed them in some cursed attempt to entrap me."

He heard Maryssa hastening toward him, sinking to kneel at his feet, but before she could utter the comforting words he knew lay upon her tongue, another hand, huge and brawny, thick with calluses, clamped hard upon his shoulder.

"Nay, lad." His father's voice was rough with grief, anger, and despair, but the gruff tones were bracing, aye, and more loving than he had e'er heard them. "If 'twas anyone's doing, 'twas mine—shoving the girl at you, making it known throughout Donegal that O'Toole's daughter was my choice for you. The wench was sick, aye, warped in her heart, thinking of naught but her own grasping hands. But she'll never show her face again among the people she betrayed. She'll be outcast—nay, worse than that, despised—for as long as she lives." There was a grim resolve in Kane's face when he spoke again to his son. "Tade, what happened at Christ's Wound, to Devin"—the earl's voice broke—"and to the others, 'twas none of your doing."

Tade's hand knotted into a fist as the gentle warmth of

Maryssa's arms linked about his legs, the sight of Deirdre's loving face, and the sound of his father's voice ripped free the sob that threatened to burst open his chest. With an oath he slammed his fist into his thigh, the tears searing his cheeks, branding his soul. *"Damn* her. I should have—should have seen—known that she was desperate. That she would go to any lengths to—"

"And when, pray tell, were you to see her twisted plot? When you were battling to keep Devin hidden away, or when you were riding the highroads, protecting the very people the O'Toole witch willfully sent to their death."

Tade's eyes flashed up to his father's, and he was stunned to see the earl's craggy face streaked with tears, the warrior's eyes glinting with a fierce pride, aye, and regret.

Tade felt Maryssa's fingers curl around his hand, and his own closed around hers. "Da, you—you know?"

"That my son—the heir Kilcannon—is the most feared rebel in all Ireland? The man who has crushed the Sassenachs' death grip on a hundred different innocents and wrung from the conquerors' lying throats a measure of the lifeblood King George's soldiers have been draining from us for so long? Aye. I know it now, Tade, though—stubborn fool that I was—I was too blind to see it before."

"I would have—would have told you when first I rode, but I feared to endanger you, or Rachel and the babes. I thought it was better—"

"To allow your thick-skulled father to batter you with his pride? When Deirdre returned from Derry and told Rachel and me all that had happened, I had just clawed my way from the fever that had set in my wound. I tried to drag myself to a horse, ride to find you, aid you. But I fainted like some God-cursed court belle before I could gain the blasted beast's saddle."

"He didn't awake for another week," Deirdre said gently, leaning her tear-damp cheek against her father's shoulder. "And after that, we nigh had to bind him to the bed to keep him from riding after you."

"I was afraid, Tade," Kane Kilcannon gritted. "So damned afraid that you'd die before I was able to see you, lad. Tell you—"

Tade raised his face up to his father's hard features, felt the hot splash of one of the earl's tears upon his own skin.

"Before God, I love you, lad," Kane said. "And I—I take more pride in you than any sire that lives in Eire."

"Da . . ." Tade pushed himself up from the bench, scarcely gaining his feet before Kane Kilcannon's brawny arms reached out, and caught him in a crushing embrace. Tade shut his eyes, the pain of a thousand rages and bitter, wounding words melting in the wake of his father's choked declaration. God, it had been so long—so long since they had done aught but tear at each other, so long since Tade had felt in the earl anything but contempt and disappointment.

He caught a glimpse of Deirdre's freckled face, her nose red with weeping, as she snuffled into her sleeve, saw the old earl draw her into the encompassing warmth of his embrace. But despite the renewal of the security and family love that had always shielded Tate, that had been his strength through a thousand different trials and fears, even now he felt an aching emptiness in his arms, in his heart.

His gaze swept to where Maryssa sat curled up before the glowing fire, her knees drawn up against the swell of their child, her eyes filled with such longing and loneliness that his throat constricted with the pain of it. Always she had watched the love showered upon others, as if she were separated from life by some cruel enchanted window, unable to reach in and touch the security, feel its warmth around her.

But no more, Tade vowed in his heart. No more. Even the newfound understanding and acceptance of his father was not worth so much as a tear from those luminous blue-gold eyes.

Easing out of the earl's embrace, Tade turned to her, saw her mouth curve into a smile so vulnerable it tore at his heart.

He reached out his hand and clasped hers, willing the warmth of his love, the strength of it, to banish her sorrows as he drew her gently to her feet. "Da," he said, wrapping one arm about her thickening waist. "I've brought Maryssa home to regain her strength and to rest here at the cottage until our babe is born and grows strong enough to journey someplace where we can carve out a new life."

The lines about Kane Kilcannon's mouth deepened, and

Tade could feel Maryssa tense against him, saw her chin lift in a wrenching childlike defiance.

The earl's gaze drifted down to Maryssa's protruding stomach, his voice rough, yet tempered with gentleness. "So, girl," he said. "You are to bear the next heir Kilcannon."

"Aye." Maryssa was stunned by the fierce pride she took in that knowledge, a wellspring of strength deep within her banishing all traces of the weariness that had ground at her during the endless weeks of travel.

"Da"—Deirdre turned her face up to her father's, her voice pleading—" 'twas Maryssa who freed Tade from Newgate and saved him from falling into the trap at Rookescommon."

Kane raked his hand through his hair, his lips twisting in a wry grimace. "You've regaled me with tales of the girl's courage since the day you rode in from Derry." Kane's hand fell to his side, his voice gentling. " 'Tis not the first time I have owed a Wylder woman a life debt."

Confusion stirred in Maryssa and she felt it in Tade as well. "A life debt?"

The earl reached out to catch Maryssa's chin in his fingers, his eyes searching her face. "Aye, girl. You have the look of Mary Wylder about you. I saw it that first night when you turned Rath's wolves aside. 'Tis the same delicate face, so fragile, so sweet, it scarce seems strong enough to bear the curses of life. But the eyes . . . " He gave a mirthless chuckle and let his hand fall away.

"You—you knew my mother?"

"Aye. When last I saw her, she was flinging an ink pot at Bainbridge Wylder's head. Lady Deirdre, Tade's mother, had died but days before, and you—you were but a babe in Mary's arms. Your father was no longer willing to hold Nightwylde in trust for me and my sons. He wanted it for himself, and the legal title to it was already his. He had ordered his servants to pack the clothes and other items that my lads and I would need, and he called in a score of Sassenach soldiers to *convince* me, should I or any of my loyal kerns prove troublesome. He full intended to drive us from Nightwylde and give Mary and you the wealth the lands would bring. But your mother would have none of it."

Raw emotion streaked across Kane's features. "She loved my lady wife, and Devin and Tade as well, and she vowed that she'd not live in a castle stolen from motherless babes. When your father refused to listen to her pleas and cast my sons and me out, Mary wrapped you in a blanket and ran away from Bainbridge, heading, I'd wager, for Derry.''

Drawn by the tale of the mother she could not remember, Maryssa dared to take a step toward the daunting earl of Nightwylde. ''But what—what happened?''

''They found her two days later, dead, at the foot of a crag. The horse had fallen, and Mary had broken her neck. But you''—Kane turned his eyes to Maryssa—''by some miracle you had tumbled into a bed of wild azaleas soft enough to save you from much harm.''

''Then that is why my father has always looked upon me with naught but loathing? Because I live while my mother—''

''You're the image of Mary, girl. And, most like, whenever he looked at you, 'twas her face he saw, pleading with him, begging him to listen to her on that last awful night.''

Maryssa felt her throat tighten, the earl's words giving her the first true image of the mother who had always been elusive, as if woven of mist in her dreams. She loosed herself from Tade's grasp, holding her breath as she stepped toward the broad-shouldered form of Tade's father. ''Thank you,'' she said quietly, her fingers drifting, breeze-soft, to the earl's burly arm.

Kane's thick brows swept low over keen eyes, but Maryssa did not draw back. ''For what, girl?''

''For giving me a mother—a mother to hold, love, even if it is only within my heart. My father never . . . .'' The words trailed off as her bittersweet joy was eclipsed by haunting images of Bainbridge Wylder's face on the evening of the masquerade, spewing forth the hatred and guilt that had all but destroyed her life. Had it not been for an emerald-eyed rogue . . .

''And so Bainbridge robbed you, too, did he, child?'' Kane Kilcannon's callused finger traced a path down her cheek. ''If your father but knew, in all his stealing and grasping, how much—how cursed much—he himself has lost.''

The lawn folds of Deirdre's nightgown fell about Maryssa's freshly scrubbed body in babe-soft waves, the pristine white fabric carrying the scent of wild sweet herbs dried in the summer sun. Maryssa reveled in its warmth, the waves of her still-damp hair drying silken against her back. Despite her weariness, the travel grime had chafed her skin until she had fairly leaped into the steaming bath Deirdre had prepared for her. And the hour she had spent half dozing in the tin tub had soothed her. Deirdre's shyly whispered confidences about her Phelan as she gently worked soap through Maryssa's mahogany curls had seemed to sponge away the horror of the flight from London, the horror of Dallywoulde's death, along with the mud and grit.

Maryssa leaned her elbows on the windowsill of the tiny loft room and gazed out through the sparkling glass pane at the cottage yard. Rain had begun to fall . . . that soft, sweet rain she had only witnessed here in Ireland, the tiny droplets blessing the ground below. 'Twas as though the sky wept, not tears of sorrow, but rather tears of love, as if the heavens felt the pain and grief of those below and sought gently to give comfort.

Aye, and she could feel that comfort stealing over her like some tangible thing, like the delicate fingers of a mother's caress. A sense of peace wove itself about the wooden bedstead tucked beneath the slanting roof and curled around the scarred applewood chest.

The creak of the loft ladder made her turn, her gaze fastening upon the cherry-bright curtain that divided the loft into two rooms. But before the calico parted, she knew well who it would be. Her lips parted in a smile as Tade entered, his face scraped free of its stubble of beard, his half-open shirt clinging to skin still damp from his own bath. But the peace she had felt only moments before had eluded him; the bronzed planes of his face were still marked by the ravages of soul-deep sorrow.

"I wanted to see that you were settled," he said, moving to the bed with a stride achingly devoid of his usual cocksure aura. "I know 'tis far from what you are used to." His hand smoothed the worn quilt, the pillows fat with goose down.

"Aye. 'Tis far from what I'm used to, and I refuse to endure it." Maryssa came up behind him, her arms encircling his taut waist. "I've spent the past weeks curled up in your embrace, my head cuddled against your shoulder.

'Twould be passing cruel to expect me to make common goose down and quilts suffice.''

He turned, but instead of the hint of a smile she had hoped to coax to his lips, his face was somber, torn with sadness and a stark uncertainty that made a lump swell in her throat.

"Maura," he said, his voice so soft she scarcely heard him, "do you know, love, that I've ne'er even told you how—how much joy I take in the knowledge that you carry my babe? I want to give both of you everything—a house dripping with comforts, a thousand silken gowns, gold-wheeled carriages. But even after we leave here and sail to America, I know not whether I'll be able to give you more than you see here.'' His mouth twisted, one hand knotting against his thigh.

"You'll be giving me a home built by your own hands, Tade, and that will be the greatest gift you could e'er offer me besides the babe I carry.''

"The babe I threatened to take from you?'' His voice cracked, his eyes drifting shut. "Sweet God, when I think of what I did . . . said . . .''

" 'Tis forgotten, Tade, and I thought in the weeks that we rode for Ireland you had forgotten it, too.'' Maryssa reached up to soothe away the lines of self-loathing carved deep in his face. "You were half crazed with grief over Devin. You trusted me, and I—''

"Nay, Maura. There is naught on God's earth that can excuse what I said to you—what I meant to do. But when Deirdre told me about you, about the babe, rage was like a flame inside me. I cared not whom I struck out at, whom my fury consumed as long as I felt some sort of power over my own fate again.'' He raked his hand through his hair, turning to face her. "When Devin died and you left me, 'twas as if—as if I'd lost my soul, or cast it to the devil. I didn't want to hear aught but my own fury, didn't want to feel aught but betrayal, because to face the truth, that Dev—Dev was beyond my power to save, shattered all the beliefs and certainties I had always clung to about myself. Sometimes I think I was fool enough to start believing the tales the people wove about the Falcon. I almost believed that I could spin magic.

"But I can't, 'Ryssa. I can't sweep away all the hateful

things I said to you, can't banish the grief, the guilt, I feel over Devin's fate.''

"Devin didn't expect magic from you, Tade, or miracles. He wanted you to live, be happy, not torture yourself over things that are beyond your power. His last words to Deirdre and me were laced with his love for you.'' Maryssa stroked back an unruly wave of hair that tumbled over Tade's pale brow, smoothing her hand down one side of his face, willing the force of her love to ease from him pain and guilt.

"He always—always loved me,'' Tade said. "He loved everyone above himself. I used to bait him mercilessly, calling him a coward, without e'er truly saying it. But 'twas easier far for me to ride across the countryside with my pistols roaring than it was for him to wait in silence for his death, not stooping to violence like lesser men even when his own life lay in peril.''

"He died bravely,'' Maryssa said, tears threatening to choke her. "He was so gallant. You would have—would have been so proud. Even when they . . . led him to the gallows he was gentle, loving. He saw me there, Tade, and he smiled.''

Tade nodded, his voice raspy with sorrow. " 'Tis glad I am that you were there for him, Maura. That he didn't—didn't die in that hideous crowd, alone.'' She saw tears well over Tade's thick lashes, dampening his face, and she reached out, her fingers tangling in his dark hair.

"Nay, Tade,'' she said with a fierce certainty that stunned her. "Even after the bullet struck him, Devin was not alone.''

Tade swallowed as her words and the bright strength shining in her eyes swept in to warm the chill agony that still grasped his heart. The beauty of her face, turned so trustingly to his, filled him with love and a savage, healing pain. 'Twas as though, in her eyes, he could see the gold hair of his brother, see the solemn blue eyes, untouched by a brutal world, sheltered in the haven of a faith beyond all reason.

Tade's fingers drifted up over Maryssa's features, his heart filling with a love so deep it shattered something deep inside him, freeing him from the agony of self-doubt, the chains of grief that had bound him since Devin's death.

"Maura,'' he whispered in a choked voice. "Maura, I love you.''

She breathed a wordless reply, rife with love and joy, as she strained to capture his lips with hers, but Tade's hands closed gently about her arms, holding her but a whisper away from his own body.

"Twice before I've asked you to wed me," he said, his gaze searching her face. "Once with the wild recklessness of a boy, once with the bitterness of a man wearied of living." He fought to steady his quivering voice, drowning in the wonder of her loving gaze. "Now I ask you again. I beg you with all that I am to be my wife. Let me be father to our child. Husband to you. Let me cherish you, protect you, fill your nights with splendor, your days with laughter. Let me, Maura."

"I love you, Tade . . . love you." The cry that burst from her was brimming with wonder and promise as she broke free of his grasp and hurled herself against his chest. Her arms twined about his neck, and he could taste the salt of her tears. "Aye, I'll marry you, my tender rogue." She kissed him, her lips hungering, sweet upon his mouth, then pulled away, laughing. "But we'd best make haste, milord Black Falcon," she teased, "lest your son be trailing after us to the altar."

No merriment curved Tade's lips, his brows suddenly lowering in concern. "Damn," he muttered. "I had forgot."

"Forgot? Your own son? I can't imagine how, since he's kicked you full in the stomach three times during our kiss."

"Nay, Maura. The altar. Church. Whatever. I want to make you my wife. Now. Before the sun sets again, but no priest would dare wed us, what with the law . . ." His gaze flicked away; the pain of Devin's murder still fresh.

"Nay, Tade. I'll not have a strange priest join us, nor a vicar of my own church. I want none of their hatred to sully our joy—and their laws . . . they bind my heart no more than they bound my rogue Falcon." Her cheeks tinted delicate rose, her face tipping away as though she were suddenly shy. "The closest I've e'er felt to God was in a sun-drenched Donegal glen with you at my side."

Love so fierce it seemed to pierce his very soul lanced through Tade, and his hands swept up to frame her face.

"I'll take you there at dawn, love," he rasped, battling the tears that seared his eyes. "Pledge—"

"Love, Tade," Maryssa choked out, pressing her lips to

his damp cheeks. ''Pledge only your love. 'Tis all I've e'er wanted.''

The sun poured down over the deserted glen at Christ's Wound like melting honey, whispering of spring as it turned the last mists of dawn into gossamer wings of gold. Maryssa raised her cheeks to the March wind's kiss, cradling the bouquet Tade had given her in her arms. He had fashioned it himself while she had lain deep in slumber, weaving a nosegay of dried flowers from the summer before—from the sweet, remembered days when first she had been captured in the spell of rakish laughter and the glint of emerald eyes.

Tade . . . Maryssa raised her eyes to his face. The beloved features were soul-wrenchingly solemn, agonizingly handsome, set against the magnificence of his clothes. Velvet, the shade of emeralds, clung to his broad shoulders; breeches of snow white encased his lean-muscled thighs. A froth of lace tumbled like sea foam from beneath that stubborn Kilcannon jaw, accenting the aristocratic chin and patrician nose while his mouth—that mouth that cursed her, kissed her, swept her from despair to wonder—murmured words to her, love-words sweet and tender, that reached inside Maryssa's very soul, binding her to Tade forever.

She fought the memories of sorrow that still hovered about them, wanting Tade to see in her face this dawn only joy. Always joy. But when he took her hand in his with a tenderness that struck through to her heart, 'twas as if the warmth of his love enfolded her, banishing even those few whispered sorrows, while his voice and the tremor in his strong hand filled her with a reverence such as she'd ne'er experienced.

She felt something smooth and cool slip over the tip of her finger, and realized that it was a ring. But her puzzlement as to when and how he had obtained the gold band melted to naught but wonder as Tade's eyes caught hers. ''I, Tade Kilcannon, take thee, my Maura, to be my wife, to weave with me a life of loving and laughter, to hold, cherish, shield thee from any pain I can spare thee until my death, aye, and after.''

The ring slid into place, and she felt it in the depths of her heart. She raised her gaze to Tade's, her eyes clinging to his, her voice trembling. ''I, Maura, take thee, Tade, to treasure and love through aught that befalls us, knowing . . . knowing that in my love for you and yours for me we will find the strength and power to heal any pain, any trouble, the world can offer. I promise to hold you, cherish you, comfort you, and love you with all that is within me, to my death, aye, and after.''

She tipped her face up, feeling some unseen blessing drift down upon them, as though borne on doves' wings, an unearthly sense of serenity enfolding her spirit. Her lips parted, the words to describe what she felt eluding her, but she saw the splendor of it blushed upon Tade's sun-kissed features, felt it in his lips as he drew her gently into his arms, his lips melting into hers in the tenderest of kisses.

''Maura. My wife,'' he said, his voice husky with emotion. ''Mine . . .'' With a suddenness that startled her, he arched his head back and let his laughter ring through the air as his arms caught her up, sweeping her high. He whirled with her in a circle, the glen spinning in a glorious blend of gold, blue, and the first sprouts of green. Maryssa relaxed in his arms, feeling the wind whisk through her loose curls, dart about the delicate curve of her throat.

''Aye, milord rogue,'' she cried. ''Yours. Always yours.''

''I never thought this day would come,'' he said, whirling with her to the shelter of a grassy knoll. ''That I would see you, with your face shining, your hair sweet satin about your face as we wed. 'Twas so—so hard, loving you, holding you, yet thinking I could ne'er truly have you. And now . . . now you are my wife. And before the spring wanes, our babe . . .''

His voice trailed off, as if his joy was too great to give voice to, and he eased her down onto the soft grass. Maryssa's hand swept up to caress his lips, but a bright gold glint caught her eyes as the sunlight kissed the circlet about her finger. A tiny cry of astonishment breached her lips as she stared in amazement at the delicately wrought ring. A stone the hue of her own eyes gleamed in opalescent beauty, curled within the graceful wings of a golden swan.

''Tade!'' she gasped, her throat constricting. ''How—where did you ever . . . ? When—''

''I bought it in London just after my ship anchored,'' he said, a flush staining his cheeks. ''I was intending to chain you to me as my bride, so . . . I—er—knew I'd have need of a ring.''

''A ring, milord Falcon?'' Merriment bubbled up within her as she watched Tade shift restlessly upon his glossy booted feet. ''And how long did it take you to *find* this ring in London?''

The flush deepened farther still, but she pressed forward, grasping his hand and tugging him down until he sat beside her.

''I didn't exactly *find* it,'' he admitted, looking for all the world like a guilty school lad caught at some mischief. ''I—er—had it made. There was a shop that displayed in its window a score of gems, and when I rode by . . .'' He glared at her. ''Well, blast it, the cursed thing held all the colors in your eyes, and—''

''And so you bought it for the woman you supposedly loathed, so you could drag her into the hideous torture of being your bride?''

''I bought it because it glowed with the green, gold, and blue light of the eyes I'd not been able to drive from my mind and my heart since that first night I saw you at the Devil's Grin. I bought it because, despite all that had torn at us, I loved you more than life, more than pride.'' He turned his gaze away, fixing it upon the rising sun. ''Mayhap . . . mayhap I wanted it to show you that despite my fierce words, I loved you. The babe, aye, I wanted the child we created together, but 'twas not for that alone that I rode across half of England. 'Twas you I wanted, Maura, you I needed, with your gentleness and your courage.''

''Courage?'' Maryssa laughed, peering up at him with a love that understood all, forgave all.

''Aye. The courage that made you heed Devin's last wish, cast your own chance at happiness to the winds in order to spare my life. The courage that made you dare to face your father and that bastard Dallywoulde when they would have crushed you, aye, and the courage to rid yourself of a man who had spat naught but cruelty and hatred at you, vowing to wrench from your arms the babe that you carried in your womb.'' He turned back to her, his gaze finding hers, holding hers. ''It takes no great courage to charge a line of soldiers, knowing that, if the worst befalls you and a bullet ends your life, 'twill be over in a matter of seconds. But to face years . . . a lifetime . . . alone, casting aside happiness in the name of love . . . that is rare courage indeed.''

She felt his fingers curve beneath her chin, and the worshipful light of his eyes made her cheeks burn with pleasure and pride.

''I know not what the future holds, Maura, or to what shores 'twill carry us. But I do know this. Wherever we sail to carve out a new life, 'twill be joy for me, a joy such as was ne'er present within Nightwylde's dread walls.''

Maryssa's gaze turned toward the distant horizon, her heart filling with the memory of the castle's daunting towers, the cold walls and vast chambers filled with naught but her father's hate. ''As long as you stand beside me, milord Falcon, I vow I shall possess the courage to ride any highroad you might name.''

Her heart was bursting with infinite love as she flung her arms about her dashing rogue, banishing the dream haze of Nightwylde's shrouded turrets as she turned her gaze to the wondrous future.